Roger McDonald was born at Young, NSW, in 1941, and attended The Scots College and the University of Sydney. He worked as a teacher, an educational radio and television producer, and in publishing before turning to full-time writing a decade ago.

His novel *1915* was the Age Book of the Year in 1979, and he is author of a second novel, *Slipstream*. He wrote the original screenplay, 'Melba', for Oliver Sullivan Productions.

Melba

ROGER MCDONALD

COLLINS
AUSTRALIA

Cover painting:
Rupert Bunny 1864-1947 Australian
Dame Nellie Melba c.1902
Oil on canvas
245.3 x 153.0 cm
Purchased by The Art Foundation of Victoria
with the assistance of Dinah and Henry Krongold,
C.B.E., Founder Benefactors, 1980.

This work is reproduced by permission of the National
Gallery of Victoria.

COLLINS AUSTRALIA

© Roger McDonald, 1988

First published in 1988 by William Collins Pty Ltd,
55 Clarence Street, Sydney NSW 2000.

Typeset by Midland Typesetters, Victoria
Printed and bound by The Book Printer, Victoria

National Library of Australia
Cataloguing-in-Publication Data

McDonald, Roger, 1941-
  Melba, the novel.

  ISBN 0 7322 2401 2

  1. Melba, Dame Nellie, 1861-1931 — Fiction.
  I. Title.

A823'.3

All rights reserved. No part of this publication
may be reproduced, stored in a retrieval system,
or transmitted, in any form, or by any means,
electronic, mechanical, photocopying, recording
or otherwise, without the prior permission of the
publishers.

This book is sold subject to the conditions that it
shall not, by way of trade or otherwise, be lent,
resold, hired out or otherwise circulated without
the publisher's prior consent in any form of
binding or cover other than that in which it is
published and without a similar condition
including this condition being imposed on the
subsequent purchaser.

Contents

PART ONE
Colonial Life

1	Doonside	3
2	Shells of the Ocean	13
3	Happy Land, Far Away	30
4	Mackay Scots	38
5	The Planting Life	50
6	Determination	67
7	Love in a Cottage	87
8	The Bohemian Girl	105
9	Limits of Pride	125
10	Gold	136
11	Goodbye, Kangaroo Charlie	149

PART TWO
Europe

12	A Truth about London	161
13	The Diamond Comb	177
14	Husband and Wife	191
15	Capitulation?	204
16	Madame Melba	219
17	'Caro Nome'	233
18	Star Ascendant	249
19	Bohemia in Tiaras	262
20	Le Premier Conscrit de France	278
21	George goes to School	291
22	Secret Love	304
23	Eat, or be Eaten	315

24 We have our Proof	328
25 The Spinning Chorus	344
26 Pawns in a Game	358
27 La Traviata	370

PART THREE
The Twentieth Century

28 Legal Custody	383
29 Progress by Rail	396
30 Daddy	411
31 I am Chosen	423
32 Je suis Georges	437
33 Jolly Nice People	451
34 No Misunderstandings	466
35 Victory	476
Epilogue	487
Author's Note	489

PART ONE

Colonial Life

1

Doonside

A note of singing died in the air leaving an impression of something perfect against the ear, a sound or memory of sound as light as ash.

The man at the piano, a teacher, turned and looked at the girl singer with amazement. She waited for him to speak.

He was a foreigner, an Italian, as old as her father. He seemed to know something about her at that moment that was hidden from herself, and she wanted so desperately to please him, whereas on other days she had not cared so much.

She had done well. She had excelled herself, really, yet she wanted to say, 'It wasn't me . . . it was . . .'

Someone else? That wasn't what she meant at all.

She stood with her hands clasped in front of her and her lips slightly parted; so dutiful she felt she might burst. She might run from the room if he turned again and challenged her so oddly with his eyes and voice.

'You would die for love,' he said with smooth practicality, talking about parts of a song, though there were undercurrents. '*Amore*,' he repeated.

'*Amore*,' she echoed, giving it a careful emphasis.

'No, *noh*,' he smacked his palms together. Abruptly they were back in the lesson again and the moment of breathless fascination passed. She saw that he was ridiculous, really, as he sketched the proper stress in the air with his fingertips, sang it *falsetto*, his voice resonating away to nothing:

'*Adagio, per favore.*'

Signor Cecchi's trim black moustache, curled at the ends, glistened. When he bent to the piano there was a low creak. His corsets? He was vain, and laced himself into shape before each day's lessons. Now he nodded his signal and in she came again, singing particular variations as required. It was merely an exercise, but all the same something impersonal, unbidden, unrolled without effort. It was how it was with her always. When she sang it made no claim on her existence and she could step aside from the uncertainty of her eighteen years. In this paradox was her entire life.

'Please sit down my girl.'

He liked this moment best.

'But Miss Dawson . . .'

'Miss Dawson she wait.'

Nellie arranged the folds of her dress and smiled prettily as if it were the most natural thing in the world to have a respected teacher loom over her like a satyr. She heard the rattle of cups and saucers from the next room where Miss Dawson was preparing the afternoon tea.

She also heard, coming from her own throat, light words going against the rush of her inner thoughts.

'Very well, as you wish, *Maestro.*'

With the laziness of a tiger Signor Cecchi picked up her hand. He turned it this way and that. He pressed lightly on her knuckles. His strong white fingertips touched the clear hardness of her nails. He turned the palm upwards and almost kissed it, almost brushed it with his lips, and smiled at her with a faint, hesitant hope in his eyes. The doorknob rattled.

'*Signore*,' she said, 'I think Miss Dawson is ready.'

Signor Cecchi gathered himself together and stood. As he rose, such a big heavy man with his weight falsely distributed, he unbalanced. Nellie reached for his arm, and found herself shooting across the carpet as she tried to help him.

'Really, oof!'

DOONSIDE

As they swayed together in an involuntary embrace she noted how it felt: the man had a stiff panicky grip, like someone ill. That was all.

That was all it took.

Miss Dawson opened the door.

'Coffee and cakes on the table, *Maestro*,' said Miss Dawson with a thin smile.

She managed to convey in a quick glance that what she saw was no more than she expected from Nellie Mitchell. There was no evidence for this. Miss Dawson was inflexible in her snobberies, her gaze went clanging about a room when it contained a Mitchell.

There were many in this city like Miss Dawson, people moved by envy at the sight of Nellie and her family going about their lives in the way they chose. People who could not bear the sight of self-containment and reasonable pride, who said of the Mitchells, in the way of the envious the world over, that they led 'a charmed life', but who wanted to see misery in the place of happiness, and who felt themselves cursed by the gift of cleverness when it showed above the ordinary level.

The Mitchells lived in a large house named Doonside, in the suburb of Richmond, close by the city of Melbourne.

Doonside had an attic, a tower, a cellar containing wine from David Mitchell's Gooramadda vineyards, a good set of stables with country-bred ponies, and a groom named Syd; there was also a greenhouse, a gardening shed, and a Chinese gardener named Ah Choy. The house had been built by Mitchell himself in the year 1857, its name carved by its owner on a piece of stone now lying in the garden grassed around like an ancient monument, a source of wonder and legend for the younger children.

David Mitchell was a builder by profession. Aged in his early fifties, he was a man of splendid achievements. From the tower could be seen his greater handiwork barely a mile away, the banks, the insurance offices, the churches. And away to the north the fabulous dome of the Exhibition Building.

There was an interesting difference between Doonside and

other grand houses in Melbourne. When you looked down from the tower into the neighbouring blocks of land you did not see other mansions. You saw on one side a dusty cement works, on the other a noisy brickyard, and in between a carpentry workshop employing dozens of men where fittings for doors, windows and stairways were made under the sharp eye of the owner.

You saw work.

On work-days it was necessary to close the windows of Doonside, otherwise grit covered everything.

It was mid-morning on an autumn Saturday. Along the upstairs landing, the Mitchell daughters dashed from bedrooms, stood dissatisfied before the hall mirror, then spun around and bumped into each other.

'I'm all wrong.'

'Look at this, Mother, did you see what she did?'

'I saw nothing, now make way please . . . How is this?'

'Beautiful, Mother, but hats are being worn differently now, will you never catch up?'

A pair of strong, youthful hands made an adjustment.

'Don't tease me now . . .'

'Mother, my bow please?' It was Belle, stalking backwards, with Dora the five year old clinging to her skirts. 'Will somebody please take Dora?'

Isabella Mitchell, a light-complexioned woman in her early forties, re-tied Belle's bow with an expert flourish, and as she moved, Annie came up behind and tucked in a strand of hair.

'Mother, can't you ever keep still?'

'I'm sorry, my darling.'

They loved Isabella's soft Scottish accent. She had come to Victoria as a young girl but had never lost the gentle burr of Forfarshire. It made her seem a loving visitor in their lives.

A door banged downstairs, and Nellie leant over the bannisters.

'Daddy's home.'

They had taken over an hour to dress but the time had passed too quickly.

DOONSIDE

Nellie stood back from the bannisters and had the mirror all to herself for a second. Black-haired, clear-browed, with shining intelligent eyes, there was not a ribbon out of place. But she seemed not to think so as she angled herself critically.

'What is the matter?' her mother asked.

'What?' Nellie seemed to come awake suddenly.

She had been thinking that no matter how hard she tried, she was not truly herself.

Annie kissed Nellie solemnly and said, 'You're lovely'.

'London has Rotten Row,' the citizens of Melbourne liked to tell themselves, 'Paris has the Bois de Boulogne, but we have "The Block".' It was a quarter-mile of hard flagstones on the north side of Collins Street.

The older Mitchell daughters with their mother between them made a smooth passage along. The girls were very pretty but something in their character attracted extra attention. They were not flirtatious. Young men who would boldly walk up to other girls held themselves back from the Mitchells: these three had a spirited reputation, and were likely to answer back to some gentle banter with a bit of hard chaffing of their own.

Syd Meredith, the Doonside groom and stablehand, leaned on the wheel of the family carriage with his hands in his pockets and a straw between his teeth, maintaining an air of exclusiveness. It was not unusual for an employee to fall in love with the daughter of his employer, some made damned fools of themselves this way, and ended up in court: but Syd's secret he kept absolutely to himself; while his eyes followed Nellie right up to the next corner and around and back again. He felt immensely protective towards these girls, they filled an absence in his life. His early bush years had been loveless and hard.

'The Block' made Isabella nervous, though no-one would think so to see her strolling along. She disliked the marriage-market atmosphere, with its peacock displays for both sexes, and detested the larrikin element that pranced down the centre of the roadway aping and mocking. 'The Block' did not seem quite proper to her, although everyone from ministers of the kirk down to bankrupts and serving maids thought it very swell. The predatory, the pleasure-loving, the class-contemptuous were here in abundance. Isabella was a woman who felt haunted by lack of time for the things that really mattered: yet she made herself join them, navigating her way through the throng with a pleasant smile on her face and a sweet greeting ready for her acquaintances. She was the wife of a good man, David Mitchell, and as a foundation and a cornerstone of the city, he was the reason she was here. So she made a painful memorial for herself in this fashion, as she did in other parts of her life in this year.

'Once more around?' she asked.

'If you like, Mother,' her daughters replied. 'Why not?'

'Lord, there's Freddy Pascoe,' muttered Belle.

'Blow Freddy Pascoe,' said Nellie.

'He is quite handsome,' murmured Isabella.

'I think so,' said Belle.

'You don't count.'

'I wonder if the Boxes are here?' said Isabella.

'Stop it Mother,' said Annie. 'Who cares?' Though of course in Annie's view the whole morning would be wasted if they did not meet the Boxes.

'No-one is here today,' said Nellie, while her eyes scanned a sea of faces for a glimpse of Signor Pietro Cecchi. Meanwhile, she mocked and outstared a dozen young men in passing.

'There is Mr MacTeal.'

'Why, so it is,' said Isabella.

They stopped for a while and talked with Angus MacTeal. He had come to Australia with David Mitchell on the *Anna*. But whereas the two had started as young stonemasons together, MacTeal had not thrived in the same way as his old friend. He was a widower now and came to do 'The Block' in the hope of finding another and younger wife. MacTeal was one of those Scotsmen who denied everything about his own desires with a censorious frown. Nellie had a special dislike for him, which came from his habit of implying that she, especially, was unappreciative of the qualities of her mother. When he looked at her, he seemed to strip her down to a second skin with his small-mindedness.

'How dare he,' she thought.

'Well, good-day to you all,' he said, lifting his hat. 'Be sure to look after your mother for me.'

'Oh, yes, Mr MacTeal, of course we shall.'

Then they came upon Signor Cecchi himself.

He removed his hat, sweeping it low for Isabella's benefit. She blushed delightedly, being glad her husband was not here to see her, for he detested the Italian.

'*Fortunatissimo!*' cried Cecchi.

They tried to make conversation, but it was very hard. People kept staring at them, bumping into them because they had stopped dead and were not surging along with the crowd's flow. Having looked forward to a few lively exchanges with her singing master, Nellie found there was little to be said, strangely, considering the intensity of her life in Signor Cecchi's rooms. It was as if anything that happened in privacy could not be translated to the outdoors; as if the intensity, the pressure of things dissipated in the wide open air of an Australian city.

There was an annoying shyness, too, on Nellie's part, which Signor Cecchi shared.

He struck his head as if remembering something.

'*Che ora è?*' he said dramatically.

Annie and Belle looked at each other and pulled small faces. Isabella looked politely mystified.

'*E l'una,*' said Nellie quickly, naturally.

'Then I must go. *Arrivederla!*'

He bowed himself off, bumping people in his self-importance.

'Well,' said Isabella, taking Nellie's arm with pride 'Wasn't that nice?'

It cost good money for David Mitchell to run a family of growing female children with their fine wardrobes, their Young Ladies' Colleges, and their diversions of foreign languages, music lessons, and singing classes. He did not begrudge the money, of course. It was a great reward to see his daughters returning home to Doonside after their many outings. This was where they belonged, within the small happy world that women made for themselves so enviably. But sometimes Mitchell suffered disquiet. He was a man, after all, who broke and built for his living in a hard way. He was restless for new horizons.

So he began to think seriously about accepting an offer that had been sounded out to him by a fellow Scot, Mr John Ewen Davidson of Mackay, Queensland: which was to go north to the tropical parts of Australia and share in the sugar boom of the plantations. There was much work to be done up there on the fringes of civilisation, great mills to be built with acres of galvanised iron roofing and vaulting rafters. Mitchell was tempted to share in the excitement of it. The change.

But he said nothing to Isabella or the children about this idea. And there was too much simple pleasure and self-indulgence in the thought for a true Scot to grab it with both hands. He made a decision: he would keep the idea of tropical Queensland to himself until the right moment came.

One night Annie crept into Nellie's bedroom to agonise over Signor Cecchi. Word had reached her that Miss Dawson thought Nellie overfamiliar with her teacher.

'Nonsense,' laughed Nellie.

Annie fidgeted with the folds of her nightdress. Her face was pitiably intense, it made her look pinched and unattractive. All her focus appeared to be on the difficulty of twisting together two bits of ribbon on her nightdress.

'I know it's nonsense, but people will talk.'

'Darling, I'm begging you,' said Nellie. 'Don't do this to yourself.'

There was a look of such anxious defensive trust on Annie's face. At sixteen she loved Nellie of course, and would follow her anywhere, but now she held herself in, not showing the pride she felt in having an older sister who was, as she saw it, all certainty.

Nellie closed her eyes and leaned back on her pillows. People expected the best and worst of her always.

'Believe me, nothing happened,' she said. 'As for "talk", it's best to weather the storm. Show people you're better than they are.'

'I know, I know,' Annie castigated herself. 'I'm sorry.'

'It's all right, darling.'

'Sorry for criticising you as if I'm perfect in every way. Because Lord knows, I'm not.' She paused. 'I didn't think there was anything with Mr Cecchi.'

Nellie smoothed out the bedcover with her fingertips, comparing its touch with the satiny green cover of the novel she was reading, Scott's *Waverley*.

'How could there be?' she said.

They smiled at each other.

'Yes, how could there be,' agreed Annie. Anxiety fell away from her.

She took one of Nellie's pillows, propped it against the end of the bed, and wrapped her knees in her arms.

'I'm suddenly wide awake,' she said.

'Don't mind me,' yawned Nellie.

'When a man speaks to you,' said Annie with a look of blissful speculation on her face, 'What do you say?'

'Always wear that expression,' Nellie wanted to exclaim. Instead she said:

'Whatever comes into your head.'

'But if nothing comes?'

'Smile at him. Dazzle him, like you are now. That's lovely, really lovely.'

'Don't . . .'

Then Annie said: 'Yes, but what if it's all too much. Like men can be . . .'

'It's only a game. You mustn't take everything seriously.'

'You mean, don't you, it's a just game till you . . . fall in love?'

'Well,' said Nellie after a long pause. 'Yes. Till then.'

Down in the hall, the clock struck midnight. The stairs creaked as David Mitchell made his way up. There were rules about bedtimes still, and Nellie leaned quickly over and blew out her bedside lamp. The girls lay still and quiet, watching a sweep of light expand across the ceiling of the room, then swallow itself as their father passed along the corridor carrying a lamp. They heard a door quietly open and shut: then came the murmur of their parents' voices talking into the night. The girls went to sleep with that sound; first Annie, on Nellie's narrow bed, then Nellie herself, who gained an impression from her parents' voices of something secure and eternal, like the sound of the sea rustling and enfolding her in conversing tides and currents in the dark.

Family life would go on for ever, it seemed.

2

Shells of the Ocean

A gunshot echoed in the early morning.

Isabella, who believed she had not slept all night, jolted awake. There was nothing to be alarmed about; they were at their farm, she realised, at Cave Hill, and it was just the farm-hands scaring up cockatoos from the fruit trees and grape vines.

Isabella sank back into her pillows. She stretched an arm across to David's side of the bed: empty. He had gone without her realising, leaving just this sense of himself in his neatly made-up bedclothes. A capable man who could fend for himself, not like some husbands.

Of them all, she had fewest fears for David.

She fought off a spell of black dizziness.

Isabella was ill, but wanted no-one to know, not her dear scatterbrained sister Lizzie nor David himself, just yet, God bless him, nor any one of her eight children: so she kept clear of doctors, and hoarded her strength as best she could. But she knew that something would soon give. She just didn't have the heart to make the first move, to let the cat out of the bag.

Every few moments she heard a thin snapping sound, followed by a mild crashing rush, ending with a whoosh as branchlets slid down the shingles of the homestead roof. It was the white cockatoos in the old gum tree over the house.

She could just see them through the window. They stretched their wings, slipping from branch to branch, making quick emblematic impressions. They conversed quietly between themselves, their little blunt tongues working over dipthongs and consonants. They nipped the fresh gum-tips ceaselessly.

But nothing would stop her mind from working, from worrying away at a certain stark fact.

What a burden love could be, she thought. Her illness was like a secret shame — it would mean deserting her family in the fullness of their life, how could she dare to leave them? She came to the very edge of her piety and asked how God could permit such a thing, before her mind retreated into praise.

Isabella had always loved these fresh March mornings at Cave Hill, days with their promise of heat and massive stillness. If only she could take it all in, get the durability of the farmland into her blood; the way, in a drought year, the clear river water ran on beneath the stones, and the gums and she-oaks along the banks put their roots down and flourished in adversity. But she was weak, she thought, and nothing about her would last.

Isabella felt suddenly hot, fought off more giddiness, and pushed her bedclothes back. She closed her eyes and calmly breathed.

As she did so, Vere came into the room, trailing a flannel comforter and clutching an enamel mug containing the yellowish remainder of last night's milk. Vere sipped a mouthful, then dribbled some out with a satisfied air. She stared at her mother's flushed cheeks and dank hair on the pillow.

'Mamma sleep,' she said finally.

Isabella sprang up.

'Good morning darling. Come here for a kiss.'

Vere submitted while Isabella fussed over her. She was such a joy, this last child, so sturdy and true. Isabella had wide-ranging dreams for the older girls, but for Vere could think of nothing better than a farm kitchen somewhere, with Vere grown-up, rosy-cheeked and jolly, with a whole gaggle of dear ones of her own.

Others were coming awake through the house. Margaret and Aunt Lizzie in the kitchen pleasantly arguing, as always; Belle, such a good willing girl, dumping an armload of wood in the woodbox; Charlie and Ernie running round the verandahs calling out for Frank.

In the depths of the house, Nellie was singing somewhere.

Isabella got up from bed, put Vere in her place while she dressed, then to prove what she could do, carried the thumb-sucking child in her arms through to the kitchen.

As she entered the kitchen Lizzie exclaimed how well she looked this morning; Lizzie with her own suspicions too; and Isabella smilingly said:

'That's because I feel so well, my dears.'

The week was almost over when Nellie and her father went on a long-promised ride together.

Syd was up at dawn to get the horses in. He brushed them down, fitted blankets and saddles, and then with time to spare, boiled a billy around the back of the stables. He was just taking a good pull of tea when Mitchell rounded the corner to catch him sprawling.

Mitchell cleared his throat.

Syd leapt to his feet.

Nellie was already leading her horse through the sliprails.

'Ready to go?' Mitchell hurried Syd mercilessly along.

Syd led out Pagan. Mitchell clambered on, scrabbling for the reins in a great hurry to bring his gaze back on to Syd as he offered Nellie a leg up. The fate of any young man around Nellie, when her father was present, was to be sharply watched. It was as if the man knew how Syd treasured the quick pressure of Nellie's hand on his shoulder, the weight of her elbow in his grip.

'Thanks so much, Syd,' murmured Nellie.

'It ain't nothin'.'

Syd watched them go; Nellie, a natural rider, undulating swiftly up the long grassy ridge above the yards, and Mitchell overtaking her with mad competitiveness. He sat stiff upright in the saddle, a man whose idea of pleasure was to make a point, the point here being, that his daughter had better not think she could outpace a man of his years, that he still had something to show her.

Syd cleaned his pipe and rammed it full of tobacco. The riders lobbed over one ridge, then appeared to crawl across another. Minutes passed and they were seen on a third. The billy was cold now. Syd tossed the slops away and debated whether to start another. It would be just his luck if Mitchell reappeared early, with Pagan in a lather of foam and trembling in the forelegs. Syd believed that Mitchell asked too much of the horse, just as he did of people. Pagan was too good for the man if only he knew. Mitchell would soon give Pagan a hard mouth, the way he sawed the reins, spurred the animal along, and leaned tautly back in the saddle as if the animal was a hobby-horse with no feelings.

'Old bloody coot,' Syd muttered.

It was inconceivable to the Mitchell family that someone in their midst might feel anything but worship for David Mitchell. If they laughed at him themselves it was delightedly, if they felt his anger it was unquestioned. The only thing they asked was, how could they correct themselves and be more in his image?

Out on their ride Nellie and her father reached a long grassy flat where the horses could be given their heads.

'Catch me if you can,' challenged Mitchell, his brown beard twisted back by the wind.

Meanwhile, where the children played on another part of Cave Hill, a snake stole up a creek bank and made its way through the edge of a stand of wattles.

'Kill it,' said Frank, biting his lower lip.

The snake held the children mesmerised. It raised its head and kept very still.

At last Syd with his stockwhip appeared. He clapped a hand

SHELL OF THE OCEAN

on Frank's shoulder while the other children scampered to a safe vantage point.

'You too, Frank,' said Syd as he readied his whip. 'Get out of me way.'

'I ain't scared,' said Frank defiantly.

'Like fun you ain't. Now step back.'

Frank was close to tears.

'Step back, Frank, or you'll get your eye took out,' said Syd in a kindlier tone.

Syd lined up his whip. A swish of air, a sharp snap, and the snake twisted and writhed. It seemed to be tying itself in knots. The children cheered. Syd went forward and jammed his heel on the snake's neck. He took a knife from his belt and pierced the snake through the head, then picked it up by the tail and asked the children if it wasn't just the handsomest specimen they'd ever seen.

Suddenly, with a careless laugh Syd hurled the snake at Frank. It would have whipped round Frank's legs if he hadn't leapt backwards. The boy's face was white, his legs shook. But he held his ground.

'Not game,' taunted Syd.

'Nah,' echoed Charlie.

'Garn yer stinkin' baby,' yelled Frank.

Frank reached down to pick up the snake and hurl it at Syd. He wished there was another snake to get Charlie, a third to stifle Belle's giggles, to show them all.

There was a sudden crackle in the shrubbery and a horse appeared.

'Syd!' barked David Mitchell. Frank let the snake go.

Mitchell loomed over them like a police officer. He'd seen everything.

'Dang,' said Syd under his breath.

Nellie reined-up behind her father. 'Double dang,' muttered Syd.

'Back to your work,' commanded Mitchell. 'Now.'

Nellie averted her eyes. Syd was a whipped cur. He trudged past his employer and more words peppered down.

'Aye, boys' games are about your style, Syd Meredith.'

Back at the stables, a rough bush construction of wattle, mud and slabs, the humiliation continued:

'I'll thank you to leave off baiting my children when I'm out of your sight.'

There was more: 'I fear your uncle Dan would be ashamed to hear of you. If it weren't for Dan you'd be out on your ear, lad, be warned.'

Then came salt in the wound: 'Be sure to give the horses a proper rub down, don't skimp and idle it through.'

These last words hurt more than all the rest. Syd knew his horses. He would have exploded violently except for a glance from Nellie. Her dark eyes seemed to understand. For her sake he would have crawled across burning deserts and fought off all the snakes of the world.

'I'll do my best, sir,' he said, leading Pagan aside.

While Nellie and her father walked towards the house, Mitchell said:

'You didn't like what you heard just now.'

'I don't know,' said Nellie evasively.

She took her father's arm.

'You hear me harping on this and that,' he said, 'in relation to the servants. You think I'm dead set against Syd, for example.'

He was, of course. Nellie smiled and tightened her grip on his arm.

'I'm only trying to show something to each and every one of you,' Mitchell continued. 'Australia is a grand place for a man to get ahead in life. I myself started with my masonry chest and one gold sovereign, a gift from my Uncle Jimmy of Aberlemno. What a man has, he must hold and defend. Then make grow like the talents in the scriptures.'

Mitchell scrutinised Nellie.

'Are you listening, my girl?'

She was listening.

'Lads like Syd must never forget their position, nor who put them where they are. Otherwise out they go on their own and

SHELL OF THE OCEAN

good luck to them, maybe they'll rise in their own way, as a man may do, if he's canny. And that's that.'

At dusk on the last day at the farm, the children filed out to the verandah and sat along the edge of the boards, munching on apples and kicking their heels.

David Mitchell appeared, gazed around his rolling acres for a moment, then took up position in a squatter's chair. Aunt Lizzie fussed about like a sparrow, going to one chair, then trying another.

'Sit still in one place Lizzie, why can't you?' mocked David Mitchell.

Aunt Lizzie craned her neck, waiting for Isabella.

Isabella, at this moment, was still inside the house. She leant close to her bedroom mirror and pinched colour into her cheeks.

'I will show them something,' she resolved.

Taking a deep breath, she emerged at the end of the verandah. David raised his eyebrows in greeting. Nellie's face showed delight. The younger children were stilled. Lizzie darted nervous glances around, to see if anyone suspected what she suspected.

Isabella's song began, the sweet sound of the unaccompanied voice stealing across the quiet paddocks as the first stars came out and the sky darkened. Isabella took care to hide the effort involved. Even David was not to know what it cost her. After 'Shells of the Ocean' she turned to him, and hardly pausing sang 'Comin' Thro' the Rye', the song he loved so well. Isabella's gaze drifted across the tousled heads of her children and met Nellie's eyes. All the divisions and triumphs of family life were sealed in a single emotion, a love rich and satisfying, breathed carelessly as air, which came to them in a song.

Over at the stables Syd's lonely lantern blinked out.

The next morning Nellie passed the stables with a pannikin of blackberries. Syd was readying the carriage for the return drive to Melbourne and he called out to her.

'Oy.'

Nellie came and stood next to Syd where he worked.

'Thanks,' said Syd.

Nellie was puzzled. 'For what?'

Syd's manner with Nellie when they were alone was rather different. She encouraged an easiness in his style. He reached for a handful of blackberries but she held the pail away from him.

'What are you talking about?'

The horses stamped and waited, their harness dangling.

'Aw, you know, when your pa went after me.'

'He did no such thing.'

Syd lunged for a taste of the blackberries and found himself very close to Nellie.

'Just a kiss,' he heard himself saying.

Nellie spluttered with laughter. She pushed against his shoulders. The look in Syd's eyes, a sudden hurt, stopped her short. She angled her face.

'No.'

He kissed her. She repeated her denial but to no effect. Their lips touched, and just for a moment it seemed to Syd as if Nellie might be utterly lost in his arms. Then she broke free.

'Oh, Lord,' she gasped.

Through a chink in the slabs an eye watched them.

'The blackberries,' Nellie said awkwardly. The pannikin was half-spilt on the dirt. They bent to pick them up.

'It's no use, they're spoilt,' said Nellie.

'You can always wash them,' said Syd, feeling like the worst sort of fool, scooping up handfuls.

Nellie said in a whisper: 'Belle is watching. You must never, ever do that again.'

Belle came drifting alongside the carriage. 'Does the trace harness go through or around the mounting buckle?' she asked with feigned innocence.

Syd straightened himself.

'Through. Don't you know nothin'?'

Syd worked quickly to get everything hitched.

Belle stood holding the horses' heads.

'Ready?'

SHELL OF THE OCEAN

'Yeah. Move 'em up,' said Syd.

They emerged into the sunlight. Nellie experienced the feeling that had overcome her so often lately, that she was enclosed by contentment and happiness, but it was not enough. When singing with Signor Cecchi she had felt, somehow, that it was not her singing. Now on a dusty track in this countryside she loved so dearly, her feeling was 'not here'. Nothing that really counted for her could ever happen here. Everyone she knew had a very strong view of her, from clumsy bewildered Syd to her adored parents. She did not feel in any way complete, that was the mistake people made in Nellie's eyes. She was nothing yet.

Syd glanced back at her with a defensive, hangdog expression. He knew he had made a mistake and expected that David Mitchell would be told of it. Nellie wanted to go to Syd and say 'It's all right,' but what a confusion that would create. Instead she collected a smooth stone from the track and bowled it in his direction. It skidded across the ground and he jumped to avoid it.

'Gawd, watch out,' Syd bellowed.

'You're mad,' Belle taunted back at her, with a laugh.

It was the end of another lesson in Pietro Cecchi's darkly cushioned music room. The last exercise ended and Nellie gathered breath, looking across at her teacher.

'Enough,' he nodded.

The *Signore* was slightly breathless: nothing specially remarkable had happened today, but he was flushed with admiration. He touched his fingertips together indicating his readiness for a little conversation. Miss Dawson made her warning clatter next door.

'Better and better, you have no idea . . .'

He told her that her voice was an instrument, it could be taken up, directed, tuned to the limit; talking on, he was in a state of professional agitation, his eyes glazed, seeing past her apparently, and with none of his exaggerated silliness, his hand-holding and breathy closeness.

'So. You will do great things . . . Perhaps.'

MELBA

It was the 'perhaps' that set Nellie off, suddenly.

She found herself talking.

'Oh, Signor Cecchi. When I was a little girl of ten or eleven, at a school picnic, I wandered up a track with two of my friends. We came to a shack. A weird young woman was standing in the doorway.'

'Weird?'

Nellie waited before continuing. The door of the music room opened with a bang and Miss Dawson entered with a plate of cakes. She had baked them herself, for the special delectation of her admired *maestro*, and when Cecchi impatiently gestured for her to leave the room Miss Dawson eyed Nellie warningly.

'The woman had very blue eyes,' Nellie continued, 'like glass marbles. She offered us a drink of milk. Then she asked to tell our fortunes. We said "yes". She said, "Very well, then, show me your hands".'

Nellie turned her hands palm-upward and Cecchi gazed at them.

'Nothing very exciting was predicted for my friends,' said Nellie. 'But when my turn came my scalp crawled. She said I would always be the centre of attraction. All eyes would be turned in my direction.'

'Well,' said Cecchi, leaning back to finish a butterfly cake, and licking his fingers. 'That is good, no?'

'Perhaps,' said Nellie. 'But *Signore*, she said I would never know true happiness. Isn't that ridiculous? I'm happy nearly all the time.'

'She was a mean old woman,' frowned Cecchi, 'but a clever one.'

'How is that?'

'She knows you are artistic, in your bones . . .'

Nellie sensed a withdrawal in Cecchi's manner, a wish to change the subject. She knew he was rather superstitious.

'Fetch me the book over there,' he said, indicating a heavy volume of engravings.

Nellie set the book down on the low table between them. Miss Dawson's cakes were thrust aside — but not before Cecchi took another one.

22

SHELL OF THE OCEAN

'I don't understand,' said Nellie, 'how being very good at something, if I am, or could be, would make me unhappy. It's what my mother always wants for me. What I want for myself.'

'Yes, maybe not. It is a queer country, Australia, where we are,' said Cecchi evasively. 'Old rules change, perhaps. And anyway, to be good, she is not the same as *artistica*, so let us not worry too much about the meaning of words, dear Nellie, it make my head ache too much.'

He pursed his lips and opened the book to an engraving of the canals of Venice.

'Ah, here it is, a city built on the water. Very nice, too.'

Signor Cecchi was still evading a point.

'I insist on an answer,' said Nellie.

Cecchi turned another page. Here was the Bay of Naples with Vesuvius smoking in the background.

'Napoli,' he breathed. 'In Napoli I sing Edguardo.'

'You've sung everywhere, in all these wonderful places,' said Nellie. 'And you always tell me how happy you were. But now you won't look me in the eye. *Signore* please, what is it?'

She touched his hand.

'So. Very well. I will tell you what I mean. I am not so good. I am in the middle. *Mediocrità*. The true artist he find glory, but not me. There is a price to pay. That is what the lady see in your hand. The scars. But listen, no more, I already say too much. Here,' he went on in a rush, jabbing the page of the book with his fingertip, 'here in Napoli I sing *Lucia*.'

Cecchi staggered up from the couch. His Italian spirit was recovered. He threw open the door to the adjoing room and called Miss Dawson through. He then acted out a particular performance of *Lucia di Lammermoor*, given in Naples many years ago. *Edguardo: Pietro Cecchi*. Cecchi went through the major parts, including the female roles which he sang *falsetto*. Miss Dawson tittered now and again, Nellie did not, for this was a serious display. Signor Cecchi moved around the room singing snatches, filling-in plot lines, at once grandiose, ridiculous only because a proper setting was lacking, and absolutely convincing. At the end he died as Lucia herself, spattered with blood, you would almost think.

'Bravo,' said Nellie.

Cecchi bowed, and spread his arms.

'Lucia,' he announced, 'the same as sung by Adelina Patti . . . *Una prima donna della grada prima.*'

Miss Dawson turned to Nellie and smugly translated: 'The *Maestro* refers to Miss Patti, a great singer of the first rank, who made her debut at Covent Garden in *Lucia di Lammermoor* at the age of eighteen.'

'My age,' mused Nellie.

After Nellie had gone, Miss Dawson said to Cecchi:

'I know a story or two myself, Signor Cecchi. Not concerning childhood fancies, either.'

'Hmm?' Cecchi sipped a glass of dark red wine.

'It concerns an old man who despairs of solving the mysteries of nature. His name is Faust. There is nothing much to live for and he is about to take poison when the sound of music strangely stays his hand. All of a sudden Mephistopheles, the evil one, appears to him. He shows him a picture of a lovely girl and promises to make Faust young and give him this girl if he will sign away his soul. Faust is eager to experience love again, so he signs the agreement.'

'Miss Dawson *cara mia*,' said Signor Cecchi, 'what are you talking about?'

At Doonside the boys were playing cricket with Syd in the side garden. Syd was bowling. Frank blocked a delivery that was chased by Charlie and Ernie, who started fighting over the ball. No-one minded much until during the diversion Nellie arrived home, and pushing up her sleeves, joined the game. Then it was serious again.

David Mitchell watched guardedly from an upstairs window.

'See her play,' said Mitchell in an aside to Isabella, who was sitting in a chair farther back in the room, sewing. 'Take a look, lass,' he insisted.

'I don't need to. I really don't, my darling.'

Mitchell shook his head and clicked his tongue.

SHELL OF THE OCEAN

'You're not tired, Isabella?'

'Well, yes I am, of course I am tired, David.'

'But you're well?'

'Aye, poor silly man.'

David looked at her for a long moment. He smiled. It was amazing what he was blind to, she thought; her tiredness at the beginning of the day, not just at its end. The damp forehead, the trembling hand. When would it ever end? David turned his attention back to the garden.

Nellie was batting, and after much threatening preparation, Syd bowled. Nellie drove the ball away through a gap in the fence and the boys declared it a four.

It rather pleased David Mitchell to see his stablehand being belted all around the place, but at the same time he was distressed by an idea of what young ladies should be doing at this hour.

'Where are Annie and Belle?'

'Out walking.'

'Where, I wonder?' He came and sat beside his wife. 'Daughters are a grand headache, Isabella. What is the point, I ask? It's nothing but lessons in the piano, lessons in oil painting and what have you. We send Nellie to Mr Checky because people say he's the best. Though, by the way, I hear stories to the contrary.'

'Ignore them,' advised Isabella. 'Please?'

'Anyway here is the net result,' Mitchell threw up his hands. 'She is the very devil at cricket. She encourages young men, but when they come calling she draws attention to their shortcomings.'

Mitchell turned his head aside with slight awkwardness. He was the most transparent of men; he wanted reassurance on those matters he affected to be strongest about.

'I'd like to see her married,' he said.

'Make me a promise, David,' said Isabella with sudden strength in her voice.

'Aye?'

He turned and saw her as if for the first time in many months. In the silvery-luminous evening light the bones of her face showed. There were hollows under her eyes. A sheen of perspiration lay on her fine skin and David Mitchell experienced a jolt of panic.

'My dear,' he took her hands.

'Whatever happens, Nellie is to be allowed her chance. She is very clever.'

'They're all of them clever.'

'But she is remarkable, and you know it, David. You fight against it.'

'She has a will of iron.'

'That comes from where?' smiled Isabella.

'I'm not so hard.'

'Oh, I know that,' said Isabella tenderly. 'But when the time comes you must not block her. You watch her every move like a hawk. You don't have such a tight concern for the other girls, Annie for example.'

'Annie is steadier.'

'Annie has no gift.'

'You talk of gifts? I'm not sure I believe in gifts. Hard work is the key.'

'Well, then, David, if it's hard work you want, she will give it to you.'

'But where,' he said sardonically. 'On the stage?'

Isabella paused a moment, then said: 'If it should come to that, yes.'

Mitchell straightened himself.

'I once saw Madame Di Murska walking a dog in Little Bourke Street. The woman was unspeakable. The dog had ribbons in its tail. Years later the woman died alone, penniless, in New York.'

There was no arguing with the man, thought Isabella.

'For once I really don't care what you think, David,' she said. 'I just want the promise.'

'A blind promise?' said Mitchell.

'As you value my love,' said Isabella.

David stared at her for a long time, and at the end of that time, he nodded.

'I promise.'

SHELL OF THE OCEAN

So it was, that amid the routine family happiness, Isabella mended possibilities for the future, while at the same time her heart was breaking.

In the garden again, another day, Nellie and Annie were playing with Vere, while Belle sat off to one side reading a book. The boys were building a cubby-house on the brickworks side of the yard, deep in a dusty thicket of thorn bushes. Isabella and Aunt Lizzie were down in the vegetable patch picking out the best of the late tomatoes with Ah Choy working along behind them.

Annie played a game with her fingers and recited a nursery rhyme:

Dance, Thumbkin, dance,
Dance ye merrymen every one
For Thumbkin he can dance alone
Thumbkin he can dance alone . . .

But Vere kept grabbing at Annie's fingers and she had to start from the beginning again.

'You take her,' Annie sighed.

'Come to me,' beckoned Nellie.

Nellie was better at the game than Annie, and Vere settled down, sucking her thumb and nestling into the folds of Nellie's dress.

Dance, Ringman, dance,
Dance ye merrymen every one
For Ringman he can dance alone
Ringman he can dance alone . . .

Vere grabbed Nellie's third finger.

'No ring,' she complained.

'That's because I'm not married, dear,' said Nellie.

Feeling Annie's eyes upon her Nellie added, 'The men I know can't even say boo.'

Belle looked up sharply from her book.

'Not even Syd?'

'Syd?' said Annie. 'Our Syd?'

Annie saw a certain look pass between Nellie and Belle.

Isabella came past with a laden basket. Vere leapt up and clung to her leg.

'My Mama, my Mama,' she growled, and happily tried to bite her.

'What did you marry for, Mother,' asked Belle quickly: 'Position, or for love?'

'Why simply for love, my dears,' said Isabella, shifting the weight of the basket from one arm to the other, and disentangling herself from Vere. 'Your father hadn't a shilling.'

Nellie hauled Vere back into her lap.

When Isabella was gone, Belle poked out her tongue at Annie. 'See, there,' she said impertinently.

Annie gave Nellie a quick scorching look. It said, 'I will never understand you.'

Isabella returned with an empty basket and sang as she worked. It was her favourite song of the moment, 'Shells of the Ocean'. Aunt Lizzie followed her along the row attempting her own merry but tuneless version.

Isabella stopped and sighed with exasperation.

'Lizzie if you must get it wrong, do it where I can't hear you.'

'Well I am sorry,' said Aunt Lizzie. It was so unlike Isabella to scold; tears sprang immediately to Aunt Lizzie's eyes. She started moving away, but Isabella touched her elbow.

'Lord, what's come over me?'

She placed the back of her hand on her forehead, and then it started. She swayed dizzily. She saw the whole background of the garden darken, and heard a strange metallic humming in her ears. She found herself looking straight into the eyes of Ah Choy who was down on his knees planting onion seedlings a few yards away.

'Velly warm,' said Ah Choy sociably. 'Velly warm day.'

Then Isabella crashed to the ground in a dead faint. Aunt Lizzie screamed. Ah Choy waved his arms across to the girls.

'Come click, come click,' he shouted.

By the time the sisters reached Isabella she had blinked back into consciousness. They helped her up. 'It's the sun,' said Annie.

'Yes, darling, just the sun,' said Isabella.

3

Happy Land, Far Away

Wind in the treetops, dust blowing across the bare earth. David Mitchell clutching a hat with black mourning crape attached, the girls all in black and the boys fitted out uncomfortably in their best clothes. Vere with a runny nose, not understanding anything except the disturbances in the air, the preoccupation of adults as each held to something so private they refused to share it with her. And then the box.

The coffin being lowered into dry earth, its wood fresh from the plane and a thin coat of lacquer barely dry.

The minister intoning 'Ashes to ashes', the words snatched away by an unpleasant wind.

Scraps of paper wheeling-in from nearby streets.

Passers-by removing their hats, strangers, and Nellie wanting to rush over to them, to explain that a mistake had been made, that they should understand how this burial, this nailing down of hope, this sinking of all colour and variety of love into the meagre, grim earth was an error, a freak of chance, a mistake towards which the power of all their prayers should be bent to correct.

Other things:

The knock of a sledge hammer on metal at a nearby foundry, across the smoky roofs of Carlton.

HAPPY LAND, FAR AWAY

Delivery carts disappearing into side streets at an unassuming pace.

Ordinary actions already asserting their precedence.

A small boy running along the cemetery wall calling to his mates, not noticing a funeral in progress, that someone's mother was being locked away in the ground, and then the sight of Frank's bright quick eyes darting away from the ceremony to see what these larrikins were up to, his life and curiosity going on, an anxiety to be with them, to be someone else, to forget.

And, as they walked away from the graveside, the sight of David Mitchell's grieving face. Pale, etched clear, as if a cut had been made coldly and deliberately. No tears, and a strong concern for the feelings of those around him. Resolution visible as he took out his watch and tapped its glass face. A will, a craving, a desperation to get back to his work as soon as he was able, to bury himself in detail, to tire himself in labour.

To forget.

At Doonside nothing was the same, and the process of rebuilding their lives around an absence sorely felt, as the minister told them they must do, was difficult, fragmenting. Daily they confronted the impossiblity. There was something Nellie felt particularly; she had always had rich expectations, a secret understanding with Isabella. The curve of her life had been ahead of her like a road, but the way was now broken. Dutiful to his wife's dying wishes, David Mitchell took Nellie's hand and urged her to return to her lessons, to take up the threads again with Signor Cecchi: she must do it, he wished it for her. But she had no will for continuing; to sing, to practise, was to feel pain and although Aunt Lizzie told her there would come a time when she would gladly remember what her mother had wanted, and be driven on by this, Nellie refused to believe her. She busied herself for week after week in household tasks and in watching and guarding over Vere, who ever since the funeral had been unwell, as if her small frame was in mourning though uncannily her mother's name was the one word that never once escaped her babyish lips.

MELBA

David Mitchell went to Mr MacTeal's marble yard and selected a monument for his wife's grave, a stone angel with delicate folded-back wings that had rested for several years at the side of a shed. Weather had stained the stone grey and yellow in parts, but this lent richness to the conventional lines of the marble. A master mason was instructed to carve a biblical verse and the names of the children down the face of a slab, but when the man began Mitchell himself happened to be there, and he humbly took over, tapping and chipping until, under his hand, were revealed the words: 'Isabella Ann Mitchell, 1833-1881.'

Now a month had gone by since the funeral. Nellie sat on a garden seat and stared into the bare tops of the trees. The voices of the children intruded on her solitude.

'Push me higher,' called Dora from the swing, as Belle pushed, 'higher, higher!'

Belle put everything into it, and Dora screamed. Vere staggered around on the grass trying to lift a heavy ball the boys had left there. The boys were nowhere seen, suspiciously. Nellie stood and shaded her eyes.

'Frank! Charlie! Ernie!' she called.

Aunt Lizzie was beating a carpet nearby.

The boys at that moment were crawling through the shrubbery towards the stables. Frank went first, and when Syd came into view Frank pulled a shanghai from his pocket.

'Gawd, Frank, you're cracked in the head,' gasped Charlie.

'He's a goner,' said Frank.

They watched as Syd went into the feed shed and reappeared with an armload of hay. Frank drew back and let fly with a small fast-flying stone. It landed with a smack on Syd's tail.

'This is it,' Syd bellowed.

'Run!' shouted Frank.

The boys leapt up and fled through the garden with arms flailing. They went around the corner and disappeared past Nellie. When Syd came along, the presence of Nellie diverted him. He removed his hat and drew breath.

'Struth,' he said, 'those boys need a beltin'.'

HAPPY LAND, FAR AWAY

Nellie gathered Vere onto her lap.

'They broke into the toolshed,' Syd continued, 'that little Ernie set fire to the straw, and lucky I was there is all I can say. They got behind the horses and hit 'em with a shanghai, I can't count the things they've done, and if they want a boltin' horse, well one day they'll get one, and gawd pity the consequences.'

'I'll speak to father,' said Nellie.

'I'd appreciate that,' said Syd.

He stood by awkwardly.

'Anyway, look. I'm goin'. Well, as soon as things properly settle down around here I am. I was goin' before, but then your mother and things . . .'

'It's all right. I understand, Syd.'

'And I'm real sorry,' he continued.

Nellie angled her head politely. She thought this was another expression of grief. Her attention was already wandering.

'I am truly sorry,' Syd blundered on, 'about kissin' you that time.'

Only then did Syd realise that Nellie wasn't even listening. That her thoughts, which once had playfully included his unlikely self, were elsewhere; that whatever chance connection Syd had had with this lovely, implausible girl, was broken: for Syd, and for all of them, there was much that was finished around here.

'Well, I'll be off, then,' said Syd, tugging the brim of his hat politely.

One day there was a knock at the door and Pietro Cecchi stood there.

Margaret led him through to the parlour, and Aunt Lizzie fussed over his comfort.

'This is a pleasant surprise.'

She went off searching for Nellie.

Cecchi was nervous, but determined. In all his years in Melbourne this was the first time he had stood within the house of one of his pupils. Quite simply, he was regarded as a tradesman supplying a service . . . yes, even here, among these

MELBA

gifted humble-born Scots. Miss Dawson had said he mustn't come, that he was lowering himself. She said it was a form of canvassing beneath the dignity of a man such as he, to go knocking on pupils' doors. He could easily find others who paid as well.

The trouble was that Miss Dawson did not understand very much.

He looked around and Nellie stood in the doorway.

'Signor Cecchi,' she said. The man bowed slightly.

'My consolations, and those of Miss Dawson,' he said.

Cecchi went forward and kissed Nellie's hand.

She was very pale, he observed, very lovely in her mourning clothes. She sat away from him on the couch.

'I wanted to come to the funeral, because I like her so much. But Miss Dawson say no, she is not your family, *Signore*, and she is not your daughter.'

'My mother always spoke of you with the greatest admiration and respect, right to the end, Signor Cecchi.'

'I come for you to start your lessons all over,' said Cecchi.

Nellie dropped her eyes.

'Everything is different now. When Mother was alive we just drifted along. It was like a dream.'

Cecchi chuckled. 'I do not think you drift, Nellie. Everything you do is . . .' and he clapped his hands once, smack, decisively, as he liked to do during their classes.

The action brought colour to Nellie's cheeks. She thought, what a good man, so bearlike, so intense, so ridiculous and clumsy. He might ask me to do anything.

There was a distant banging of doors and David Mitchell entered the room bringing a gust of cool wind, and a suggestion of grit in the air.

'You'll have to excuse my rough appearance, Mr Checky. I've been up scaffolding and down into sewers. It's how I make my living. Filthy work.'

'You are very successful,' said Cecchi ingratiatingly.

They repositioned themselves on chairs and Margaret brought a tray of tea and scones. Their talk went on through various niceties for a while, with Mitchell doing his best to

HAPPY LAND, FAR AWAY

hide an instinctive disdain for the Italian.

At last Mitchell said:

'I am willing for the lessons to continue, on the terms and conditions as before.'

Cecchi gushed:

'So. It is my honour to have such a pupil.'

'Aye, but not so fast, Mr Cecchi. What does Miss Mitchell think?'

He turned to Nellie.

'If it would please you, father.'

Mitchell considered for a moment. He remembered his promise to Isabella. He must never sway from that memory.

'It would please me,' he said.

But before the lessons could properly begin again, something happened to Vere. She ran a fever at night, then was better again. The doctor came whenever they called him but there was little he could do, he said, and nothing to worry themselves about really. The child was run down, distraught, and missed the mothering that Isabella had given her, but was unable to express her lack of it, and he supposed fretted in the recesses of her mind.

Nellie felt deeply that there was something she ought to be doing, that her mother would have done, that would make Vere right. She had been told, after all: 'Always be a mother to little Vere'. Now the words rang in her mind, upset her concentration.

One evening Nellie sat at her dressing room table while Aunt Lizzie brushed her hair. It was a nightly ritual and Nellie looked forward to it.

Vere watched from her cot in the corner, her eyes bright, feverish, always staring.

'You take on too much,' said Aunt Lizzie gently. 'You think the world will stop turning if you don't do everything yourself. Leave things more to me and Margaret. We're the ones made for it. Do best what you must do, and if it means things get left undone, then so be it my darling girl.'

Vere called from her corner.

'Ne-llee.'

'Coming,' said Nellie.

'Dearie-me, now,' said Aunt Lizzie, kissing her good night. She watched for a few moments from the door, shaking her head as Nellie drew up her chair close to the bars of Vere's cot and began to read to her.

It was very late as Aunt Lizzie poured hot milk for them in the kitchen. The children were sitting around in their nightclothes, listening for the creak of the stairs. The boys were quiet for once. Nellie and Annie faced each other across the table.

'She's such a poor innocent sweet darling,' said Belle, not listening to any of this. 'Why Vere?'

Their faces were dazed and sleepy, disbelieving another illness to be faced so soon after the last one. They rested their heads on their arms, and took their hot milk from Aunt Lizzie with silent gratitude.

The stairs creaked, and their father appeared in the doorway.

'The doctor is with her,' he said. 'He says it's brain fever, and he's treated the pain, but she'll not likely last till morning.'

The faces of his children stared back at him, unable to comprehend.

Here was a baby-sized coffin on a chair, with the family gathered in a close circle; here, in the parlour of Doonside, was Nellie at the piano, and the minister making his sad prayer for the death of a child; here too were the familiar possessions of Doonside making their farewell: the gold clock with its spinning, glass-enclosed counterweights, the great murky painting of the stag at bay, the tassels on the curtain cords that Vere used to put in her mouth all the time.

After this, things could only become better, because nothing worse could happen. So much had been taken from them . . . It was the Lord's will, of course, they did not doubt it: the minister told them as much and they believed him with devotion and desperate need. Yet when all things were said, the prayer done and the picture given of dear grubby-faced

HAPPY LAND, FAR AWAY

Vere as an angel in heaven, an awful numbness remained. They would not ask each other how they were managing. They would never talk about it again. They had gloried in life and had done no wrong, they had praised and celebrated their talents and when one of them, Nellie, was told that she shone above the rest and only needed guidance and time before achieving something wonderful, she had not allowed the vanity of the idea to drive her. No. Even when the pride she had felt had come bursting through at times she had sat calmly with her mother and discussed how she might improve herself even more, and achieve that indistinct future that Isabella had seen more clearly for her than she herself had been able to.

Nellie played, and they sang:

There is a happy land
Far, far away,
Where saints in glory stand,
Bright, bright as day.
O how they sweetly sing,
'Worthy is our Saviour King!'
Loud let his praises ring,
Praise, praise for aye.

David Mitchell thought of Queensland.

4

Mackay Scots

The bow of a steam launch cut through muddy river water, and a deep, glittering tropical light lay over everything. It was July, midwinter north of Capricorn. The air was warmer than springtime in Melbourne.

On the narrow deck of the launch stood David Mitchell, Nellie, and Annie. They had left behind them a strange, flat-topped island where their coastal passenger steamer had berthed earlier that morning, and now were being ferried across to the town of Port Mackay, which was quite a distance away, impossible to say where. All around was a sea of muddy brown, with occasional logs and clumps of vegetation floating by. There were said to be crocodiles here.

'Beautiful . . .' breathed Nellie.

'Oh, yes,' replied Annie. 'Lovely.'

Annie tried to keep up an appearance of enthusiasm, but could not see or understand what Nellie was talking about. Annie was nervous. She wished she hadn't come. She hated the process of meeting new people and going to new places. She was always terrified of creating the wrong impression, never a problem at home, she now believed. But home was two thousand miles to the south.

Far ahead, where the mouth of the river dissolved into land, columns of smoke stood on a narrow plain, and in the far distance could be seen hills, mauve and darkly shadowed in the clarifying light.

'Wonderful hills,' breathed Nellie. 'I mean to explore them with you, Daddy.'

'Time for everything,' said Mitchell in a pleased voice, as he took his daughter's arm and gave it a squeeze.

'They are probably native fires,' said Annie, trying to sound lively and interested. 'I should ask about them first.'

'Well, of course,' laughed Nellie.

Annie wanted to complain: 'But neither of you have the least idea of what you're talking about, we've come all this way and all we really know is what we've been told, which is, that Port Mackay is the most primitive, raw outpost, and the white men are outnumbered by the most gigantic South Sea Islanders, who we've seen, and they grinned at us, and anyway Daddy won't have a minute to himself because he'll be working all the time. So will you both please come to your senses!'

Annie showed her inner agitation by groaning a little as she gripped the rail.

'Are you all right?' Nellie asked.

'No, I think I'm sick again.'

'Oh, you poor thing.'

'Don't mind me. I'll sit down.'

There was nowhere to sit, except on the sacks of provisions piled on the deck.

'You'll crush your dress,' warned Nellie.

'What does it matter?' said Annie unhappily.

A fellow-passenger handed David Mitchell a telescope. He saw thick stands of a green, waving crop, and it excited him.

He handed the glass to Nellie.

'There it is. Sugar.'

David Mitchell gripped the ship's rail and lifted his face to the air. He smiled at Annie, quite unconscious of her mood.

'It will be good for us here, lassie.'

When Nellie had finished she handed the telescope to her father again. He was like a boy in his excitement.

'Did you see it?' He gave the glass to Annie.

MELBA

When Annie looked, everything was blurred and swaying.

At last they approached the town wharf. A cluster of cargo lighters was moored at the end, being loaded by teams of black men. They wore a tattered collection of European cast-offs: sailors' jackets and trousers, with bare feet, and gentlemen's felt hats much the worse for wear. They were big men, healthy and cheerful. They waved as the launch plugged its way along to its mooring post, and they laughed with delight when the launchmaster was unable to bring her alongside at the first try.

Annie bit her knuckles in disbelief, while Nellie waved and the black men waved and grinned back at her.

Before the launch was properly moored a tall, dark-haired young European leapt across the gap of water and thudded onto the deck.

'Hello, Mr Mitchell? I'm Tom Chataway.'

'Well, hello Mr Chataway,' said Mitchell, stepping back a little. 'These are my daughters, Miss Nellie and Miss Annie.'

Tom Chataway gravely bowed. With more leisure than was seemly, he gave each of the girls an assessing stare.

'Mr Chataway is Mr Davidson's off-sider.'

'Welcome to Mackay,' Chataway drawled. 'You'll love it here, believe me.' It was not an Australian drawl, but English, at ease with itself: the suntanned voice of the colonial expert. Tom Chataway was in his late twenties. He made the girls feel immediately that Mackay was a much more interesting place than they had expected. Annie brightened. She would take his word for anything.

While Tom Chataway guided them up a dusty lane to the roadway he fired off orders to a ruffian crowd of loafers, and requisitioned men who were soon hefting the Mitchells' heavy trunks on to a wagonette before anyone else's were off the launch. A small dogcart stood by, and into that he put the Mitchell hand luggage.

'Up we go,' he said.

They all squeezed in together.

Tom Chataway gave the pony's rump a flick of the whip and away they went. The main street was broad, at least the width of two normal roads, and was a sea of dust. The shops had wide awnings, verandah poles, and uneven board walkways.

'Mackay is cut off by swamps on either side,' said Tom Chataway. 'So we're out of touch with the world. We've created our own little world here.' He seemed amused at the contrast between his enthusiasm and the reality they saw.

'A swamp would be welcome,' said Nellie, 'it's so dry.'

'I don't think it's too bad,' said Annie, being positive, a sure sign that she was appalled.

'Wait for the "Wet",' said Chataway.

The shops had nothing to attract the Melbourne shopper: hatchets, bolts of coarse material, hurricane lamps, walking sticks. There were also jars of multicoloured glass marbles, overlarge boots, spats, mirrors, and ready-made suits of clothes. It was peculiar.

'Trade goods, mostly,' said Tom Chataway.

The dust rose in a pall. They turned a corner past a hotel where a drunken brawl was in progress. 'It's certainly different, as you say,' commented David Mitchell, craning his neck in the direction of the hotel, amazed to see a stoutly built man emerge from the doors, throw a bucket of water over the brawlers, and then, when this had no effect, hurl the bucket at them.

Chataway chuckled his way along.

Away from the centre of the town they passed through streets consisting entirely of houses on stilts.

'Who lives in these houses?' asked Annie.

'All sorts. Everyone,' said Chataway airily.

'The Davidsons?' asked Nellie.

'No, not the Davidsons,' said Tom Chataway.

Many of the houses were so newly built that their yards still had the stumps of trees where once there had been a forest. Some were attractive, with wide verandahs for coolness and shade, but most were little more than one or two rooms on legs, square windowless places like tea chests.

'You'll like the Davidson place,' promised Chataway.

Now they began to pass carts headed for the canefields, each one driven by a kanaka, as the islanders were called. They saw a small congregation of kanaka women under a tree, singing a Christian hymn. They passed paddocks of felled trees, with clearing-fires ceaselessly burning: these were the 'native fires' that had so alarmed Annie. Soon they found themselves in pleasanter surrounds, with a forest on one side, showing vines and dusty recesses, and on the other a continuous wall of cane, rustling and mysterious.

' "Kanaka" is the Polynesian word for "man",' said Chataway.

The dogcart jolted along and the little pony went forward at a rhythmic trot. They were moving deeper and deeper into the mysterious plain they had seen from the mouth of the river.

In a patch of greenery ahead, the dull gleam of a corrugated iron roof appeared. They were approaching the Davidson house at last.

John Ewen Davidson and his wife Amy were to be the Mitchells' hosts during their stay in Mackay. In recent months David Mitchell had maintained a busy correspondence with Davidson over the building of a new sugar crushing mill. The dining table at Doonside had been a display area for blueprints and cost estimates. There had been much excited speculation about life in the booming tropics. Davidson, a Scot, had contracted with Mitchell on favourable terms. When the papers were signed, Mitchell had asked Nellie and Annie to accompany him north: he was anxious for a change of scene, but could not face the loneliness of a far place without them there.

The dogcart turned through a pair of sturdy gates and the Mitchells found themselves in a different world. A wide garden, enclosed by a forest, reached ahead of them. The pony stepped along a neatly gravelled drive. Kanaka gardeners were at work, tending each growing thing, chipping away at borders, moving along rows, sweeping from side to side with watering cans. Exotic birds screeched in the trees. A small wallaby-like creature nibbled its paws and watched them pass.

The house was now revealed before them. It was wide, low-set, with considerable verandahs surrounding it. The Union Jack flew from a pole. A woman stood at the top of the steps waiting to greet them. It was Mrs Davidson.

'Allow me to present the Mitchells,' said Tom Chataway.

'Welcome to Mackay,' Mrs Davidson said in a soft Scottish accent. It was as if this were Mackay, and not that other place with its alarming scruffiness.

Tom Chataway performed the introductions. It was curious to note that he blushed when Mrs Davidson said:

'Two lovely girls for Mr Chataway, how lucky you are, Tom.'

Mrs Davidson went on to apologize for the absence of her husband, and explained, as Tom Chataway had done, that Mr Davidson would be joining them later. Her manners were exquisite. She took to Nellie and Annie as lovingly as any mother: held them at arm's length, praised their prettiness and said something tender and understanding about all the grief they had been through lately. Well, that was over now, she said, they were to make their home here for a while. She took one on each arm and ordered the kanaka footman, Medetoo, and a kanaka maid, Cissie, to follow with their things. The atmosphere of the Davidson house was Old South, no doubt about it. The servants were expected to take a great hand in the household functions, though perhaps they did not understand them fully. Partway along the verandah, near a passage leading off into the house, the manservant stopped, looking puzzled.

'Well, Medetoo, you know where to take Mr Mitchell don't you?'

The big, cheerful man had a portmanteau under either arm. 'Oh, yes, Missus, you want 'im in house.'

'That way,' said Mrs Davidson with restraint. 'The room I showed you earlier.'

Mitchell was led off. The girls were taken a little farther along the verandah, and shuttered doors were flung wide.

'Here we are.'

Annie said, 'It's a lovely room. Beautifully cool.'

'Oh, I like it,' said Nellie. The room was large, with a rush mat on bare floorboards, and furnished to suit the needs of the girls with beds, two writing desks, two dressing tables, and a small library-shelf of books. Through a screen of latticework the garden was visible, and they saw Tom Chataway striding purposefully past carrying a riding crop.

Mrs Davidson reached up and showed them how to unhook the mosquito nets, then indicated a hand-bell on a stand.

'Cissie will come at the bell, won't you Cissie.'

'Yes, Missus,' grinned Cissie.

'That's about all, then,' said Mrs Davidson.

'Thank you so much,' said Nellie.

'Oh, one more thing,' said Mrs Davidson, before leaving them to their unpacking. 'We have a local custom, drinks, at about five o'clock on the shady end of the verandah. Lovely chance to meet everyone.'

'Five,' the girls echoed.

'Now I'll leave you to your rest.'

When she had gone, Nellie said, 'It's rather grand, isn't it.'

'Not at all what I expected,' said Annie, feeling immensely relieved to have navigated some two thousand miles and come to rest intact, in such gracious surroundings. But immediately she looked worried again. 'At five, what shall we wear?'

'Well,' Nellie grasped the hand-bell, 'let's ask the maid to lay out the clothes.'

'Dare we?' Annie stifled a laugh.

As the sun went down the manservant Medetoo moved along the sides of the verandah lighting smudge-pots against mosquitoes.

Nellie and Annie watched him through the latticework from their room. They were dressed ready, but were reluctant to make a premature entry at the far end of the verandah. Annie turned back inside, craving for a beginning to it all, and arranged her letter case on her desk, smoothing open a fresh piece of notepaper. Nellie remained looking out into the garden. They were beginning to understand now what had been meant by their father's business friend Jenkin Collier, who had said, in relation to the sugar planting society of Mackay, that the place was alive with English lords and the better type of upper class Scot. They were to ignore everything they heard about the vile frontier habits of the town. The district life was what counted. It was not like any other part of Australia, it was a veritable enclave of sugar barons whose fortunes had been made in Jamaica, in Demerara, in Java, who now were putting their money on Queensland. There was hardly a man there unconnected to the aristocracy. They were hard workers, and led simple, practical lives in houses suited to the climate rather than to their station.

The sisters were in one of these houses now, and it was like being in another world. Standing looking out into the purplish evening light, Nellie breathed deeply and seemed to shake from her whole existence the heavy weight of despondency that had settled on her since the death of her mother and Vere. Flying foxes flew low overhead, the most remarkable things. They dropped into the Davidsons' shrubbery, where they made harsh squealing noises. One slashed clumsily across the open grass at waist height. Medetoo waved his arms in good-natured hostility, tearing around in circles, till the clear patient tones of Mrs Davidson called him back to his job. Then there was a commotion down near the gates, and guests started arriving.

Light carriages came spinning up the drive followed by men on horseback. Kanaka grooms took the animals away, but Nellie, with Annie nervously peering over her shoulder, was unable to catch a glimpse of anyone properly. She only got an impression of neatly-pressed trousers and open-necked shirts, of jovial deep voices, and of ladies' skirts a little less fashionable than their own. The only man they glimpsed clearly was Tom Chataway, calling out cheerfully to sundry persons. But Nellie had no curiosity about Tom Chataway, unlike Annie, who whispered happily into her ear, 'Oh, good, there's Tom. If he's here then I'll feel I know someone and won't be so jittery.'

Soon a dozen or so sugar planters and their wives milled around at the far end of the verandah.

The men were dressed in similar fashion, as if in uniform. They wore moleskin trousers and blue Oxford shirts with red or white silk neckerchiefs. Their boots were high and polished, though dusty from the ride over to the Davidsons'. It was the habit of the men, on dismounting, to flick the corners of their pocket handkerchiefs across the toecaps of their boots, giving them a careless, anything-goes air. They clumped up the sturdy wooden steps to the verandah with a loud, confident clatter. Drinks were served from a rattan table, and with glasses in hand, the men and women separated themselves into distinct groups for conversation. The great drink of the district was called the Mackay Swizzle, a concoction of rum, lemon juice and sugar. But at the Davidsons' there was none of that. The ladies clutched gin and limes, the men favoured a good brand of Scotch whisky, or drank an excellently distilled overproof rum, the production of which was supervised by John Ewen Davidson himself.

Davidson was a tall Scot of about fifty, with sandy thinning hair, a long patrician face and the gentle air of a man used to being obeyed. He accepted a drink from a servant resembling in all respects of dress and deportment the barman of a London club, except that he was black as night. Davidson turned and spoke to a younger man at his elbow.

'Mitchell is a good man, Armstrong. I've had the devil's own job getting him up here so smooth his way, there's a good lad, make things easy for him till he grows used to our ways.'

'I won't say boo, sir.'

Charles Armstrong was English, in his late twenties, and with his friend Tom Chataway had come to Mackay in the hope of making a fortune in the sugar boom. While waiting for good land to become available, they worked for Davidson.

Amy Davidson brushed past and whispered to Charles: 'Tom already has eyes for the Mitchell girls. But which one in particular I wonder?'

Charles leant back in his chair and said with a laugh, 'Stop it now, Mrs Davidson. You're making him blush.'

'Well,' said Tom when Mrs Davidson went off to fetch the Mitchell daughters, 'wait until you see them Charlie. They're jolly nice.'

David Mitchell came round the corner wearing his jacket and waistcoat among all these cool-looking gentlemen, and had his elbow taken by Davidson.

'We're all Scots together here,' said Davidson warmly, as

he introduced Hume Black, a somewhat bluff, legalistic man, and Alfred Hewitt of Plaistowe, a more dour type, with a pockmarked, jaundiced complexion. Mrs Davidson introduced the men's wives.

Then all heads turned and the men stood as Nellie and Annie emerged to meet the company. Charles Armstrong immediately saw what Tom Chataway meant; the darker-haired of the two was quite lovely, and the other, the more nervous one, had fine character he could see.

'Nellie on the left, Annie on the right,' whispered Tom Chataway.

While Davidson took Mitchell around, and called on the manservant to put a glass of Highland malt in his hand, Mrs Davidson introduced the girls.

'Miss Nellie Mitchell and Miss Annie Mitchell . . . Mrs Hewitt, Mrs Black . . .'

'What pretty dresses.'

'My goodness, yes, you will have all the young ladies in Mackay copying your fashions.'

'Thank you so much . . .'

'They are only what everyone is wearing in Melbourne now.'

'We have a lovely fruit punch for you both.'

'Oh, yes, please.'

Annie widened her eyes suddenly. Gin, she saw. The ladies were drinking gin. She looked amazedly at the table. She had never in her life seen it drunk before. Even her revered Mrs Davidson had a glass in her hand.

'...You know Mr Chataway very well already,' the introductions were continuing. 'And this is Mr Armstrong, my husband's engineer.'

Charles Armstrong bowed laconically.

Nellie smiled at him, said a bright and sociable 'Hello', as she passed along from one set of introductions to the next.

Meanwhile Annie was left to splutter a couple of desperate words: 'Mr Armstrong, you're not from Melbourne are you? We have lots of Armstrongs there.'

'I'm afraid not. The family's Anglo-Irish, for my sins,' said Charles Armstrong through her blushing confusion.

MELBA

The introductions moved on to the older men, who made much of the presence of two pretty young lasses, and said aloud what younger men would be horsewhipped for saying in company, while David Mitchell looked a little frosty at the informality of the banter, couched as it was in terms that made free of his daughters.

With the greetings complete, everyone settled back into their comfortable cane chairs again, and the plantation conversation was resumed.

John Ewen Davidson said in an aside to Alfred Hewitt, 'I hear they found the old kanaka Hammangi.'

'Aye,' replied Hewitt, his voice lowered, 'dead as a doormat with his hands tied behind his back.'

Davidson appeared discomforted at the thought of a kanaka being maltreated.

He turned to Mitchell and explained why: 'It's a bad thing, Mitchell, when we lose a Tanna Island man. They're worth three of any from the other islands.'

Mitchell pursed his lips.

'Och, aye,' he said, beginning to understand the realities of the kanaka system operating in these parts.

'The Tanna men are natural gardeners. Look at the job they've done here,' Davidson swept a hand across the lawns. 'They are great workers in the canefields, let me tell you.'

Around the ladies' table the kanakas were also a favourite topic. Servants were being discussed. But when the subject of kanaka girls invariably having babies was touched upon, Mrs Hewitt looked uneasily at Nellie and Annie.

'Every time we sit around together we do nothing but talk about kanakas,' she said. 'Thank heavens we're going home eventually.'

She explained her use of the word 'home'.

'You see, my dears, none of us is properly Australian, the way you people are Australian. I mean to say, we all have places in the old country, and when our men are through with their establishment phase here on the plantatations, that's where we're bound. Even young men like Charles Armstrong and Tom Chataway have places awaiting them when they've finished here. We're transients, I suppose you could say.'

The men were warmed a little by their whiskies now and their voices were louder. Mr Davidson called on his manservant to pour David Mitchell a glass of rum. Mitchell held the glass to the light, sniffed it, then took a sip.

'Overproof,' commented Davidson, 'but smooth as butter you'll find, and distilled here on the plantation.'

'As good as the best Jamaican,' pronounced Mitchell appreciatively. 'No, better.'

Davidson was pleased. 'You'll do us well, Mitchell.'

He shifted chairs to put Mitchell next to Charles Armstrong.

'Armstrong will be your right hand man at the mill site, at least till you're broken in to harness,' he said.

The ladies stood, and Mrs Davidson called back to the men: 'We'll take a turn around the garden while there's still light.'

This appeared to be a signal that the drinks would soon be over. Annie was relieved. She'd had a vision of it going on into the night, she didn't know why. She felt like a poor relation among these people and it was most unfair. She watched as Nellie comfortably took Mrs Davidson's arm, slipping into the ways of these people so naturally, so assuredly, as if she belonged with them by right, as if she were one of them already after only a few hours' exposure to their ways.

Then Annie saw Nellie look back over her shoulder from the garden to the verandah and she saw Charles Armstrong return her glance. Their eyes met, the gaze held. It was a look that Annie had seen pass between two people before, and she knew what it signified for the future.

As did Tom Chataway, she realised, when she caught his eye watching too.

5

The Planting Life

Work began well before dawn, with the sound of laughter from the kitchens, the noise of kindling being split and the kitchen fires starting up, the thud of bare feet on verandah boards while it was still dark, and a tray of tea being carried in by Cissie just as the kookaburras began to make their loud calls in the trees.

An early breakfast followed: bread from the oven crusted with cinders, thickly sliced, and spread with a slightly rancid butter; duck eggs large and fatty, which Nellie and Annie ate ravenously, excited in the knowledge that each day was bringing new experiences. Tom Chataway was often free to show them around. Already they had been boating farther upriver, where vines and mossy tree trunks hung over pools of water the colour of strong tea. They had been taken on a guided walk through a native encampment, witnessing one of the dark people making fire with a twirling stick, and boys spearing fish in the shallows; they had come away with a gift of dilly-bags plaited from fibre. Back at the house, they had been taught to play croquet. Charles Armstrong stood behind Nellie, guiding her mallet. Tennis matches would be held in the near future. There would be riding expeditions into the forests of the hinterland, on the stocky ponies Mr Davidson

THE PLANTING LIFE

had gifted to them for the duration of their visit, and much more besides.

At night Mr Davidson told stories about his life in the West Indies, and showed them the night sky through his telescope, which, when conditions were right, was a blaze of glory. John Ewen Davidson was a clever man. He was not merely a stargazer for the thrill of it, he was something of an astronomer, and had once discovered a comet, doing all the calculations necessary to predict its path for centuries to come. He exchanged learned correspondence on botanical matters with the Royal Botanic Gardens in Kew. Such achievements were worn lightly by the man with an air that seemed to say, 'If you do something well, enjoy it for all it's worth.'

Now, after a week of pleasures, Nellie and Annie were for the first time invited to visit the site of the mill. Tom Chataway was ready early with the dogcart at the foot of the steps, and Mrs Davidson came out and kissed them goodbye. She was very particular that they should wear their hats at all times and keep their sleeves rolled down, as the brief winter had already run its course and lovely complexions were in danger. She had a matronly air of self-knowledge about her as she waved goodbye, giving a special nod to Tom. In the past few days she had implied more than once, in subtle ways, her certainty that one or other of these accomplished girls would end in marrying the very nice Mr Chataway.

They went in a direction they had not been before, across into the area of the great new plantations. The dogcart wound down a red track through semi-cleared rain forest. Fires smouldered all round, while distant figures worked in unison at their job of brush cutting. They passed a thatched shelter where a team of kanakas were sharpening the blades of their machetes and axes. They were strong savages without the comical touch of civilisation that marked the house kanakas. Their foreman, a white man named Jack Bellchambers, raised his hat to the ladies as they wheeled past.

They entered a short stretch of dark jungle, still uncleared. A mournful sound reached their ears, a bit like the vibrating hum of an ungreased cartwheel, it seemed to tremor the very air, persistently and invisibly. Annie shivered and briefly clutched Tom Chataway's arm.

'What's this?' chuckled Tom.

They emerged from the forest and came upon a file of kanakas walking in line on the roadway, singing an island song.

Nellie thought the melody very beautiful. Annie said it was lovely, but awesome. She would not like to hear it in the dark. Was it meant to put a spell on a person? Tom shrugged, he didn't know. Nellie turned and stared at the men as the dogcart spun by, and they broke their rhythm and laughed in a shy, friendly fashion.

At the mill site Charles Armstrong stood at a rough table studying blueprints with a master carpenter named Colin Logue, a man from Melbourne, a Scot by birth, brought to Queensland by David Mitchell as part of his construction contract. Logue and Charles Armstrong got on reasonably well together, though it was plain to them both that Charles couldn't tell one end of a plan from another. Charles was decent enough to consult Mr Logue whenever he went out onto the site to issue an order, and Logue helped maintain the illusion that Charles was originating the decisions. Things had gone on in this pleasant sort of way for the week or two of preparation before David Mitchell landed in the north.

Now everything was changed. Mitchell was a human dynamo, a veritable hammerhead of achievement. In Melbourne he was used to completion dates of twenty months or so for great bluestone and brick edifices, so solid they might be castles in Normandy, built for a thousand years. By comparison this spreading lout of a mill, with its rosewood floors and cedar joists, all bush-carpentered and slickered over with three acres of corrugated iron was a holiday diversion to the man. He would have it finished, he declared, well before the Wet closed in.

Charles was expecting Tom Chataway and the Mitchell daughters at any moment now. He kept looking around for them.

Logue scrolled-up the plans decisively. Mitchell had been in one place a minute ago, now he was in another. Already

THE PLANTING LIFE

today Mitchell had whipped the pace of activity along. He had explained with great clarity and patience to the leader of the bullock-teams that there was a better method he could use to bring logs down from the forests. Mitchell had devised it himself for the cartage of forest timbers down from the gullies of Gippsland, and it involved a modification to the metal dogs and release clips of the chains, which Mitchell then proceeded to have made on the spot in the blacksmith's forge, and now here he was helping the team boss to fit them.

He turned around to find Logue and Armstrong waiting at his back.

'Well, Mr Armstrong how goes it?'

'All shipshape, sir.'

'Aye,' nodded Mr Logue. 'Corner pegs foursquare.'

'Let's do a quick check,' said Mitchell. He was the very devil for scrupulous inspections. Off they went with Mitchell leading, and Charles, as the sun rose higher, hiding a yawn and thinking how good it would be on a day like this to be swinging from hammock or lighting a breakfast fire for bacon and beefsteak. Chataway, the sly dog, had drawn the short straw with John Davidson for all that.

'Pretty good, pretty damned good,' said Mitchell as he tapped stanchions and ticked off headings which he scrawled with indelible pencil in the notebook he always carried around.

Mitchell had formed a liking for Charles. He'd found him genial, intelligent, unversed in the ways of the building trade, it was true, but not afraid of hard work when the hatches were battened and the task turned foursquare to the wind. The nautical analogy was appropriate, for Charlie Armstrong, Mitchell had learned, had spent time at sea before coming to try his luck in Australia, and from all accounts had weathered the rigours of sea life with pride.

Charles looked over Mitchell's shoulder to see the dogcart approaching through the trees.

'Well, sir, if you'll . . . '

'Yes, yes, Armstrong, of course. I'm well and truly broken to harness now wouldn't you say?'

'Very good, sir. Then if you'll excuse me.'

'Fine,' said Mitchell. He had not yet seen the dogcart. 'Mr Davidson will be having my hide for occupying you the whole week. Get along with you now.'

'I'll join the young ladies,' Charles finished his sentence.

Mitchell was a bit stunned but admiring.

'Of course, yes, do.'

Charles crossed to his horse. He felt like a boy released from school at the end of term; he leapt onto the animal which pranced and reared and he urged it into a canter from a standing start.

'Get a load of "Kangaroo Charlie",' said one workman to another.

Mitchell raised an eyebrow. So that was the score. He was uncertain what the nickname implied; a kind of charming raffishness maybe. Armstrong was certainly a likeable chap, the sort of young man Mitchell had sometimes thought might be useful in his business: socially beyond reproach, able to put a persuasive case for just about anything at all, without needing to say very much. Charm. It spoke volumes . . .

But he must not let his daydreams run away with him.

'Come along, Mr Logue.'

The two men walked along a bit farther. Mitchell most uncharacteristically found himself blowing his daughters a kiss. He rather gave himself away there. Mitchell had had an ulterior motive in taking this contract, which he hardly dared admit even to himself, which was to widen the girls' social circle, and with particular reference to Nellie, maybe to find her a husband. Now to cover his confusion at the thought that Colin Logue was probably seeing straight through him he grumbled: 'Who ordered the four by twos here and the battens way over yonder?'

'The lad,' said Colin Logue. He meant Charles Armstrong, of course, Kangaroo Charlie.

'I see.'

Meanwhile Chataway in the dogcart saw Charles in pursuit and gave the pony a taste of the whip. They began to race. This was fun and Nellie squealed with delight. Annie clung to her seat with one hand, clutching her hat with the other.

THE PLANTING LIFE

They went dashing away.

The workers on the building site returned to their tasks muttering such observations as, 'The old dog has a few fleas to scratch there,' and, 'I wouldn't mind sitting in Armstrong's saddle for a while.' All out of earshot of the boss, of course.

Mitchell turned to Logue. They both felt freer now without their charming but useless Mr Armstrong, for whom Colin Logue had sometimes found it necessary to invent jobs.

'New broom, Mr Logue,' said Mitchell decisively.

Two pairs of walkers, Annie and Tom Chataway ahead, Charles Armstrong and Nellie following, picked their way sedately along a rocky shoreline facing the tame ocean. There was no surf, as there was in the south, because of the protection of coral reefs. The water merely swirled onto the sand.

The young couples seemingly had nothing to say to each other. After the excitement of their drive along narrow tracks and across grassy hillocks, with a galloping Charles giving an incessant view halloo, mere conversation was superfluous: how could it match the near hysteria of the chase? Tom had driven the dogcart dangerously, nearly causing them to tip over. They had pulled up, and tethered the horses to a couple of handy trees. Now they explored their way along the sand, shoes off, feeling more than rather self-conscious. In Melbourne there would have been chaperones for this sort of occasion.

When each of the couples did speak, it was to use remarkably similar words, but with meanings far apart.

'What a ride, Tom,' said Annie.

'Jolly exciting, yes.'

'I would like to go back soon, though.'

'All right then.'

Annie and Tom stopped walking. They had nothing to offer each other, really.

'Mrs Davidson will be expecting us.'

'Of course she will. But I say. What about tomorrow. Like to explore the creeks? They're lovely, mossy rocks and things, and a waterfall. Truly picturesque. Your sister must come, too.'

Tom looked across at the others. It was just boring the way

he preferred Nellie, thought Annie.

'Oh, yes. She hates to miss a single moment of anything,' said Annie.

Between Nellie and Charles the silence was companionable. Why should they ever need to say a single word to each other? But at last they did.

'You ride superbly, Charles.'

'Think so?'

'We should go back soon.'

'All right then.'

But they kept walking.

'Mrs Davidson will be expecting us.'

'Naturally. But tomorrow—'

'Yes?'

'Come riding with me tomorrow,' this was said with sudden urgency. 'I like to start early, when it's cool . . . '

Their eyes would not meet. Charles added:

'Your sister must come too, of course.'

'Of course,' said Nellie, her heart beating faster.

That night Nellie and Annie lay under their mosquito nets, each wide awake and listening to the night chorus of frogs and to the clatter of flying foxes and strange creaking night birds, not saying a word to each other. They listened to the murmur of voices farther along the verandah: David Mitchell sitting up with Mr Davidson, making conversation late into the night. Annie remembered how her parents had loved to do this, and knew that her father was happy again, restored to his old habits. It was easier for an older person to accommodate to sadness and change, Annie wrongly believed; there was a benefit to maturity granted by having something to do, by having an occupation laid out and paths designated to follow. She had no such way ahead, only the uncharted ways of the emotions, which one day were one thing, the next another. In Mackay, she had begun by liking Tom Chataway enormously, and within hours of arriving had been happier than she could ever remember. Now she was about as sad as it was possible to be.

THE PLANTING LIFE

Annie propped herself up on an elbow, and looked across at Nellie. But the mosquito-netting and soft darkness obscured everything. Annie threw herself back on her pillows and sighed. She would never sleep now.

'Nellie?' she whispered. 'Are you awake?'

Nellie did not answer. She heard Annie well enough. It was just that she was afraid of breaking a spell that held her fascinated. She lay staring at the ceiling, hardly believing the emotion that had taken her over so completely. What was it about Charles Armstrong? She could not put it into words, but simply allowed her mind to gaze at the wonder of a being so inevitably right in every way. His fine dark hair, which he would sometimes impatiently sweep back from his forehead; his habit of sitting with his legs pushed straight out in front of him, ankles crossed, as he listened with a deeply serious concentration to some point her father was making, and steepled his fingers under his darkly-stubbled chin, and listened, and listened; the way, when they walked along the beach, he had stopped, once, and allowed her to go ahead a couple of paces, her eyes had asked 'What is it?' And he, with his eyes alone, had answered 'You'. His laughter invited her to a conspiracy of shared enjoyment; his steady, serious gaze challenged her own dignity to new heights of self-appreciation; he was asking her, and telling her, all in a sombre question kindling to a smile, would she be his, and yes, she would be his: yet they had hardly spoken two words together in more than a week. She had no reason to believe what she knew to be true: that her whole life had changed from the moment she had come to Mackay and seen Charles Armstrong on the John Ewen Davidsons' verandah.

Tomorrow morning early he would call for her, and they would go riding together. Just the two of them.

Neither Nellie nor Charles had mentioned this arrangement again, after it was made. Yet later in the day a note had come from Tom Chataway to Annie, postponing a morning picnic to the waterfall. So Charles must have told Tom, and Nellie felt a small network of collusion spreading around the Davidson house. Still she said nothing to Annie, how could

MELBA

she tell her that she was not wanted? What was implied in Charles's words, 'Your sister must come too', Nellie knew, meant just the opposite. She would obey Charles on the point. It was implied in the note from Tom, in the very texture of the air around her as she breathed it in. Just being herself, and doing things she did as herself, had taken on a mysterious urgency. Wonderful life, she and Charles were in it together. She was unable to feel guilty about it. Anyway, when Tom's cancellation arrived Annie had breathed a sigh of relief. She announced quite happily that she would sleep in, and had given Cissie strict instructions not to wake her before eight o'clock.

In the early daylight Nellie hauled on her boots, and tied her hat down with a scarf. She sat on her bed for a moment gathering her thoughts. What had seemed a calm and beautiful idea as she had drifted off to sleep, an idea full of rightness and inevitability, now seemed fraught with danger and idiocy. But she would go through with it. She had given her word. She would walk down to the end of the drive, where Charles had said he would wait with the horses, and he would be there, and she would go with him.

She stood, making her way across the floor. A floorboard creaked loudly. She stopped, and looked back at Annie. The poor dear girl's head was deep in her pillows, she was fast asleep. Nellie went from the room.

But as she left, Annie's eyes blinked open and watched her.

As soon as Nellie saw Charles waiting at the gate all her doubts and hesitations fell away. Their eyes met, and the wildness in her blood that Nellie thought she would hardly be able to contain was gone. This was the ordinary world again, and lovelier for being that. How natural that the two of them should be in it.

'Good morning, there,' said Charles.

'Hello.'

'Your sister not coming?'

'No. Is that all right? She's still fast asleep.'

THE PLANTING LIFE

'Poor girl. Doesn't know what she's missing. Here, I'll give you a leg up.'

Then they were on their way. The horses walked side by side into the blaze of the rising sun. Nellie and Charles exchanged glances. The world was beautiful at this hour. Kanaka work gangs passed them on the roads, and as they went past a row of foremen's cottages little grubby-faced European children came out and stared at the pretty woman and the gentleman prancing past.

The gentleman quoted poetry to Nellie, written by the well-known horseman's poet of Victoria, and he did it in his very best, top-hole English accent with that entrancing aristocratic burr that Nellie loved:

Here's health to every sportsman, be he stableman or lord,
If his heart be true, I care not what his pocket may afford;
And may he ever pleasantly each gallant sport pursue,
If he takes his liquor fairly, and his fences fairly, too.

The sentiments were so glowingly expressed that Nellie thought she had never heard anything better.

'Is that your philosophy?' she asked Charles.

'As near as matters. Yes, I'd say so. Definitely,' replied Charles. ' "If his heart be true I care not what his pocket may afford." '

Then off they cantered across wide empty paddocks towards the sea. When Nellie's hat blew off, Charles cavorted back, and bending from the saddle scooped it up for her. It was a masterpiece of trick riding.

'You ride better than any Australian,' said Nellie admiringly, when he reined alongside and handed the hat back to her.

A while later they found themselves on a grassy bluff overlooking the sea. There were shade trees, calm clear water, sparkling sunshine, and the horses contentedly cropping grass in the background.

'You are a perfect rider,' mused Nellie contentedly.

'It's good to do things well,' nodded Charles.

'Now I will do something perfect,' said Nellie. 'I shall sing something. An English song, if you like.'

'Good-oh,' Charles bit a grass straw, he had no idea what was coming.

Nellie's voice wreathed up from nowhere, gently, with amazing clarity. The words conjured an English pastoral setting of milkmaids and their swains, as far from this blazing tropical setting as it was possible to be. As he listened, Charles sat upright, and Nellie sang on, listening attentively to herself, checking and attending to the matter of the music, which she was able to produce without coyness or the expectation of immediate reward of flattery, without wanting in return a man's grateful love-making. Charles had been sung to before, every young man of his time had been treated to the varied accomplishments of young ladies. But never like this.

'But that was good,' Charles managed, when she had finished.

'Really? So you liked it. A country song, they're the prettiest, I think.'

'Very pretty.'

Charles dropped his eyes. With an ache in his chest, and a quick stab of shame at his impetuousness, he had been admiring Nellie's beautifully dark drawn-back hair, the soft curve of her neck, the pale purplish colour of her lips, a most sensuous shade, and he wanted to reach across and crush her in his arms. He wanted everything, all at once with this girl. Why had he before, from the moment of common attraction as she walked round the corner of the Davidson verandah to this very instant, really, not seen it so clearly? He was in love.

Now it was she who steered the conversation, who made the running.

'I do like all things English,' she said.

'Hmm.' Charles was thinking that he would like to hold her face in his hands, one day, and discover the true shade of her eyes. 'What's that you say?'

'They say you're actually Irish.'

'Me?' he laughed. 'We have property there, so you could say we're Anglo-Irish, and the best kind.' He made a witticism.

THE PLANTING LIFE

'We don't go there very often.'

He offered his hand to help Nellie up from the grass. She took it in a very cool, practical fashion, the contact lasting all of a second and a half.

'I like the way you talk, the way you make the world seem a very small place. In Australia we can never go anywhere, our world goes off in all directions, but it only drops over the horizon.'

'I know what you mean,' said Charles. 'That's what I like about this country.'

'In Mackay,' said Nellie, 'everyone talks about going "back" eventually.'

'Everyone,' said Charles. 'You mean the Davidson crowd. Us.'

With what depth and resonance that word rang in Nellie's ears: us. It seemed to include her.

'Yes.'

'Hmm.'

'When are you going "back"?' The question had suddenly assumed huge importance for Nellie.

'One day when I've made my mark, I suppose,' shrugged Charles, speaking the words lightly and thinking of other things as he talked, watching Nellie's boots slide in and out of the folds of her skirt as she walked along, and catching a glimpse of pale stocking.

Thinking, suddenly, of the responsibility he had flung in the face of fortune by going off riding with this beautiful young woman before breakfast, and not telling anyone except for Tom Chataway. And then, in telling Tom, realising how brazenly careless he had been in announcing his intentions. He'd said, 'Prettiest of the two, bet I can get a kiss from her before you're up and about you lazy cur.' And Tom had yawned, 'The wager's on, you cad, a guinea?' And they'd shaken on it.

Now Charles said to Nellie, with a gruffness that puzzled and disappointed her: 'We'd better be hurrying back.'

It seemed to Nellie that they had only just arrived.

For Nellie, the atmosphere of the Davidson house was never

the same again after her return from the ride with Charles. Annie went round avoiding her eye but that was expected. Annie would have her say later, and it would be endless, and then it would be tears and sisterly kisses, a reconciliation.

No, it was Mrs Davidson who bothered Nellie, not because of anything she said directly, so much, but because of her attitude. Was it middle-aged jealousy? After the early ride Charles and Mrs Davidson had words in the garden, and whatever passed between them made Charles very angry indeed.

He came back to the verandah of the house, called for Nellie, and there in front of Mrs Davidson, with Annie peering apprehensively from their room, he drew her to him and kissed her.

It wasn't a passionate kiss, but simply a declaration of loyalty beyond the narrow suspicions of the onlookers. It made Nellie long to be properly kissed one day.

'I'll be back this evening and we'll take a walk,' he told her abruptly.

A white-faced Amy Davidson walked away into the house.

Annie's amazement was overwhelming. She trembled and shed tears, poor girl.

'I can't imagine what she said. But Charles would not have a bar of it, that was clear,' said Nellie.

'I can imagine,' said Annie. 'She would have said . . . '

'Don't say it,' warned Nellie.

'That he . . . '

'Don't.'

'Oh,' gasped Annie. 'Breach of trust, insult to Daddy, her house, you must have made him think, sneaky, morally thoughtless, ungentle . . . '

It all came out in a shuddering rapid-fire gush.

'Ungentlemanly . . . '

'I must have made him think what?'

There was a long pause. The great heat of mid-morning ballooned through the house. Nellie thought of the hours before she would see Charles again, the day stretching before her, an eternity.

'Made him think you wanted to creep away with him, that

THE PLANTING LIFE

it was the sort of thing you did with men, and he saw from your attitude . . . '

'Stop it,' said Nellie gently, tears filling her eyes. Annie, cowering in anticipation, expected a torrent of objections, but this came:

'Don't you know I love him?'

The silence that followed this announcement was total. It was broken only by a few exhausted sighs, as the two sisters dabbed their eyes with their handkerchiefs.

'So suddenly.'

'Yes.'

'Will you tell Daddy?'

'No. Will you?'

'Mrs Davidson will surely have words with him.'

'If she does, she will find her match. Daddy hates tale bringers. He says they're the worst sort.'

This was an oblique warning to Annie, who had no malice in her heart, but through an excess of fretfulness often managed to spill the beans.

Nellie saw Tom Chataway coming through the garden.

'We must brighten up,' she said.

Tom and Annie went for a walk in the garden. Nellie joined them for a while. Afterwards, Mrs Davidson called them all inside for an early luncheon. She'd had her mail from home, letters and packages and pieces of news unavailable in bustling old Melbourne, as Annie unaffectedly referred to it. Mrs Davidson's colour was regained and she was friendly enough, though one comment gave Nellie pause, and made her even warier of Mrs Amy Davidson thereafter.

'There's a concert coming up soon, Nellie, we must all hear you sing then.'

So Charles had boasted about her singing.

'You know,' said Annie as they went in for their afternoon rest, 'Tom tells me that Charles Armstrong is practically engaged to a girl named Adelaide Baker. I suppose because he's the son of a baronet, Anglo-Irish at that, he thinks he can do as he likes.'

'Oh, well,' said Nellie. 'I've heard talk of Miss Baker. She's

Mackay's great hope for a music scholarship but as empty headed as they come. The sort of girl who only has "ideas" about men.'

'That still doesn't make it right,' said Annie, flashing a dark look at Nellie, her older sister being someone with 'ideas' if ever there was such a person.

'Please don't think badly of Charles,' Nellie begged.

'Oh, it's not that,' said Annie. 'I just think we're having more of an effect in Mackay than we realise. You don't mind sticking out. I do.'

'I love it here the way people are always doing things,' said Nellie. 'Mr Davidson's comet, and everything.'

'I hardly know what that's all about,' said Annie.

'It's making the most of life,' said Nellie.

Annie put on her worried frown.

'I honestly think,' she said, 'that if all these people weren't connected to the aristocracy in some way you'd be finding it as dull and dreary as Melbourne on a rainy Sunday.'

That evening, as he sat on the verandah enjoying his glass of Highland malt whisky with the planters, David Mitchell felt himself tapped on the knee by Charles Armstrong.

'Mr Mitchell, I say, would you mind awfully if I asked your Nellie to come for a walk with me, now, before it's dark? I would so much like to show her a grove of orchids down by the river bank.'

'Orchids?' blinked Mitchell.

The other planters smiled.

'I'd like Annie to come too, if she wishes,' said Charles in a good clear voice.

'Well, of course, lad, of course,' said Mitchell. He leaned back and took a strong pull at his whisky. His daughter's first eligible suitor. He had often thought of this moment with terror and longing. He had never thought it would come with a tap on the knee like this, from a man called Kangaroo Charlie.

Annie and Chataway declined to come, so Charles and Nellie disappeared from the company under the frosty, impotent eye of Amy Davidson and the jovial knowingness of the rest.

THE PLANTING LIFE

The path to the river was part of the garden, now somewhat neglected. Going down there, Charles continually pushed fronds and spines and great glossy leaves and hairy stalks of undergrowth away from Nellie's face, so that she felt she was walking down to the river under his special care.

When they emerged into the open the broad movement of the river, normally so turgid and brown, was oily red in the evening light from the sinking sun. It illuminated the destroyed forest on the other side so that the trees that still had live ferns held in their branches made an eerie scene. If the lovers stayed here more than ten minutes they'd be caught in the dark.

'Mozzies,' said Charles, slapping himself. She liked the way he phrased the word in his English accent.

A fire of roots that had been burning for a year sent out a thin acrid smoke. Charles led Nellie across into its path to discourage the swarms of mosquitoes.

There was nothing here to be romantic about. The riverbank smelt muddy. Driftwood formed obstacles. There were no orchids. A viewing seat, placed here once by the Davidsons, was upside down after the most recent floods, its iron legs already tangled with weeds and vines.

Nellie and Charles were uncomfortable with each other, now that the longing to be together was satisfied. Satisfied? They hardly spoke. It was nothing like the companionable silence that had filled their intimate glances before, just the deadly nothingness of two people wondering if they had made a mistake.

They caught each other's eye, and turned away again.

Nellie thought about Charles's recital of the horseman's poem. It was a piece on every Australian rider's lips, she knew, nothing special, and certainly it showed that Charles was a man of simple tastes and uncomplicated longings. But then, what of it? She loved him for it all over again, catching sight of his handsome profile as he selected a flat stone from among the river pebbles, and sent it skimming out towards the centre of the river in distinct remarkable skips.

'Seven,' she counted aloud. 'Lucky number.'

'Superstitious, are you?'

MELBA

They knew hardly a thing about each other. It would be interesting to find out.

'Not at all, Charles,' she said, yet it was as though she'd already, through the power of Charles's name on her lips, wished on a shooting star, touched wood, and thrown salt over her shoulder.

As for Charles, he had kissed her smartly enough on the verandah, as a rebuff to Amy Davidson, but confronted again with the simple matter of his feelings he knew only one thing for sure. Her song had awed him. She had seemed beyond him all day, while they were parted. She had been such a lighthearted girl before their ride this morning; now she seemed to have withdrawn, and simultaneously enlarged in his thinking, and he wondered, would it be the devil's own job to follow her? His ideal was straightforwardness in a woman, but he was fatally drawn to complication. He sensed a strength in her he wasn't supposed to know about, that she was keeping from him; but then all women had that, he reflected, and guarded it from their lovers. He wanted boldly to walk up to her, to touch her lips and hair.

Instead, he suggested that they ought to be heading back to the verandah party.

And as simply as that she agreed.

They were almost in sight of the verandah when he brushed her elbow.

'Nellie,' he said, wanting to resolve something about the walk, the orchid neither of them had remembered, the unromantic river. She turned to answer him, and they kissed, and the kiss was everything. There were no doubts hidden in its fire. It was a whole world raging out before them and another darkening behind.

6

Determination

Nellie found herself filled with gentle pity for all who were not lovers.

'Dear Signor Cecchi,' she wrote one day. 'I suppose you will be astonished to hear from me. I want to tell you that although I am nearly two thousand miles from Melbourne I am not forgetting my singing. I manage to practise every day. I shall not be home for a month or two so could you please send me six or seven nice English songs, as the people here do not understand Italian . . . '

A 'month or two', she said to herself. She could not contemplate returning home ever.

Nellie nibbled the end of her pen and thought for a moment. If only Signor Cecchi knew the strange and wonderful life she was leading, the languorous, dreaming days that only leapt into motion when Charles appeared at the Davidsons' to fetch her for an outing. She wrote, 'I am enjoying myself so well. I go out either riding, driving or yachting every day . . . '

This was the truth, but the truth of feeling was something else, and could never be expressed on paper. Nellie thought about the previous Saturday afternoon, when she had sung at a small concert in a local hall. 'I had a great success,' she wrote. 'So much so that all the ladies up here are jealous of me. Everyone asks me who my master is, and when I say Signor Cecchi, they all say "When I go to Melbourne he shall be my master, too." '

Again, this had truly been said, but only in the way women talked about each other's dressmaker and insisted on introductions. Nellie knew she could make an impression if she chose. She had chosen against it. She had sung a duet with Annie, and had been conscious all the while of giving Annie the best chance.

Signor Cecchi had said, once, that the girl singer must really know love before singing about it. He had taken her hand and impressed the words into her with his eyes. How shameful the memory was. Such statements were an absurdity, the decaying wistfulness of an ageing man. It was the singing that had prepared her for love, not the other way around. It made her value things in a proper order. To really know love was to realise the unimportance of the rest; but she could not write that in this or any other letter, and so she finished across the bottom of the page, 'Believe me, Your affectionate pupil, Nellie Mitchell.'

Charles Armstrong and Tom Chataway, before the arrival of the Mitchells, had been in the habit of taking expeditions into the ranges beyond the coast. It was partly to remind them of their first taste of outdoor life in this country, when they had driven a mob of cattle overland from Brisbane to Mackay. It was also an exercise of the Englishman's birthright, as expounded by the admired John Ewen Davidson, which was to go where he pleased on the face of the planet, and bring back something new and untouched if possible.

Nellie had heard much about these bush rides and wanted to share in one. So a picnic was organised, and here they were, one day, on horseback, the four of them ascending a steep muddy slope with a canopy of trees overhead.

Charles kicked his sturdy pony along, and Nellie followed with enthusiasm. Charles ducked under a tree branch.

'Watch your head,' he warned, glancing back.

Nellie deftly leant forward and the branch swept over her back without touching.

DETERMINATION

'Nicely done,' said Charles. She thrived on his admiration.

They left the other pair, Annie and Tom Chataway, straggling far behind.

In a high grassy clearing Charles drove his horse over a log in a neat jump. Nellie, calling for him to stand clear, did the same. She sailed over as if gifted with wings.

Laughingly they dropped from the saddle, Charles tethered the ponies, and with his arm around Nellie's waist he led her across to the edge of the clearing. From here there was a view down into the valley.

'There they are,' said Charles.

Two figures on horseback were visible far below.

Tom Chataway pushed his horse under the same tree branch as Charles and Nellie had gone under earlier. Annie followed.

'Watch your head,' Tom called back.

'What did you say?' replied Annie.

Whump. The branch hit Annie and she toppled from the saddle.

'Oh, Lord,' muttered Tom.

He went to her. She sat on the sticky, muddy ground with leaves stuck all over her.

'Leeches,' said Tom. He meant it as a warning, as in she had better get up, there might be leeches.

Annie screamed and kicked her legs. He pulled her to her feet. She sobbed, clung to her pony, not to Tom, and cried:

'Take me back.'

'Oh, I say,' repeated Tom helplessly.

The picnic went on without them. Charles unpacked his saddlebags and spread out an array of things while Nellie looked on admiringly. Their eyes met.

There was something in the look that they both understood: that their life, shared and intimate in this clearing under the open sky, could well go on together in just this way, he providing for her, she serving at his side.

With a blow from a heavy knife Charles cracked a coconut and handed it to Nellie for a long dribbling draught. He unwrapped cold beef, boiled eggs and produced an entire pineapple and a loaf of bread.

'What a shame they're not here to share it,' said Charles, standing and looking around, munching on something.

'You've done this before,' said Nellie.

'A man learns to fend for himself. Have a boiled egg.'

Nellie cracked and peeled her egg, then brushed clear the small flecks of shell remaining.

'Adelaide Baker is a very pretty girl,' said Nellie.

'Oh, really?' said Charles off-handedly.

'The sort of girl who'd be impressed by a title, I expect.' As if Nellie wouldn't be herself. 'I heard her talking the other day about the Thirteenth Earl of Winchelsea and his brother, Harold Finch Hatton.'

'Yes, they were here,' said Charles casually, stripping the fat from a slice of beef. 'Look,' he continued, as if he were addressing the absent Adelaide Baker and other small-minded citizens of the town. 'I don't have a title. Never have and never will. Not unless the family goes west in a railway accident. I'm the youngest.'

Charles threw himself back on the grass.

Nellie watched him intently. Charles's eyes blinked open.

'All that matters to me,' said Nellie, 'is the here and now.'

Charles rolled up on his elbow. Her face looked up at him. They understood each other so well.

More than a hundred guests were gathered at the Davidsons' on a Saturday night. They crowded along the verandahs, spilled onto the lawns. A piano was trundled out and from a corner of the verandah John Ewen Davidson could be heard picking out a tune to the delight of all around him.

Adelaide Baker was getting ready to sing.

'They'll want you, later,' said Charles, speaking intently to Nellie.

'Not me. Everyone's asking for Adelaide Baker.'

They were standing on the grass, in the shadows. They were touching hands when they could, when they thought no-one was looking. Mrs Davidson sought them out.

'So that's where you are,' she said. She asked Nellie to play the accompaniment while Adelaide sang.

DETERMINATION

'I'd love to,' said Nellie.

Mrs Davidson's trim back retreated across the grass.

Nellie and Charles were alone together for another few moments.

He said: 'I want you to marry me, you know.'

'Oh, Charles.'

'I must have you.'

'My darling Charles,' said Nellie, reaching up and putting her arms round his neck. People were watching, but who cared? Their lips met, the kiss lingered.

Annie wrenched her head aside. It was unbelievable — everyone could see. By the time Adelaide got up to sing, all eyes were on Nellie.

The chosen piece was Wilhelm Ganz's 'Sing, Sweet Bird'. Nellie ran through the opening bars on the Davidsons' slightly dull piano. At first, Adelaide sang prettily, but the high notes were beyond her. This embarrassed Nellie acutely and she tried to help by suggesting, through her playing, that the song might be brought to an end prematurely. But Adelaide Baker had not the wit to see it — she frowned petulantly at Nellie, as if Nellie had made a mistake.

'I'll show her,' thought Nellie fiercely.

Where Adelaide failed, Nellie came in. She sang with all her heart. All in a moment, her voice went sailing out over the heads of the assembled guests into the night.

Adelaide was silenced.

Annie, doubly scandalised, clung to David Mitchell's arm. 'Do something,' she whispered inanely. But not a flicker of disapproval or doubt appeared on Mitchell's face. He merely raised his chin a fraction higher. What was done, was done, he appeared to be thinking. This was his daughter, she was doing something so exceptional it would surely be remembered for years.

Nellie lifted her hands from the keys. The accompaniment, the self-accompaniment, stopped. Still singing, she stepped forward to the edge of the verandah. To some onlookers it seemed she was making the move from arrogance; Adelaide, affronted, shamed, humiliated, and whatever else she must feel, stepped back. Nellie took room for what she was doing, room for herself as the notes came flying and twisting around each other, as she drove them from herself with mingled joy and amazement.

Charles stood isolated on the grass, his eyes never leaving Nellie's for a moment. Her one true friend and adored lover.

When the song ended, something amazing happened. Adelaide Baker kissed Nellie in front of everyone.

'You didn't mean it,' she said tearfully.

When Nellie returned the kiss, and they stood side by side holding hands, applause broke round them, and Mackay was astonished.

The next morning, everyone knew what would come. Even the servants, who'd been told nothing. Hardly anybody had been told anything, except the Davidsons whose house it was, but the word had spread.

David Mitchell sat in the darkened Davidson sitting room wearing his best suit of clothes and wishing it were possible for a man to call for a glass of Highland malt at ten a.m.

Tom Chataway dropped in. He brought mail for the Davidsons. He tipped his hat, and rode off without lingering for small talk. He knew, of course.

'I suppose if Charles was delayed Tom would have said so,' said Nellie.

'I'm as nervous as if it's happening to me,' confessed Annie.

'Do you wish it were?'

'No,' replied Annie. 'I don't.'

They tried to keep calm but it was impossible.

Annie looked longingly at her sister. She said: 'You're so in love.'

'Yes.'

Obviously there were other things Annie wanted to say. She looked out into the garden to gather her thoughts, but it was too late.

'Here he is now.'

Nellie emerged along the verandah to watch Charles leading his horse down the drive. He passed the reins to a waiting groom. He saw Nellie, and waved.

DETERMINATION

At the same time, Mrs Davidson descended the front steps.

'Hello, Charles.'

'Hello, Amy.'

Nellie held back while Mrs Davidson tidied Charles's collar in a motherly way.

Then she turned to Nellie.

'How simply lovely,' she said. 'I'm so excited.'

When Charles entered the room David Mitchell was sitting with his knuckles on his knees, in a wickerwork chair one or two sizes too large for him.

'Hello, there,' said Mitchell.

'Good morning, sir.'

Charles sat down opposite. The atmosphere was awkward and neither wanted to be first to speak. It seemed, though, that it was to be Charles.

'I have come to ask your daughter's hand in marriage, sir.'

There was a long pause.

'You've led an independent sort of life till now,' said Mitchell musingly.

Charles nodded. 'I went to sea for a couple of years. Then I came to Australia. Jackarooing, cattle droving with Tom Chataway. Now it's sugar planting.'

Mitchell looked up at these last words.

'You mean, you would like it to be sugar planting. You have no land of your own.'

'I have prospects. I am beginning to settle down,' said Charles with a smile. 'John intends to release me a couple of good plots after the next harvest.'

This reference to Davidson as 'John' put Mitchell distinctly at a disadvantage. He would never use Christian names himself. There was a class factor in play. Charles Armstrong seemed to be adept at the easy, subtle drawing of barriers. 'These English,' thought Mitchell with exasperation.

'The men call you "Kangaroo Charlie",' he returned with.

'There's no malice in the name,' said Charles with an easy smile.

'Perhaps not. Your "Irish" temper gets you into fights, I hear.'

Charles frowned. He had not expected things to come as

far as this. His last fight, with an American gold engineer, had been many months before the arrival of the Mitchells, and he was damned if he knew who could have talked about it. A bloody affair it had been. How to skirt this one?

Charm was the answer.

'We Armstrongs,' he expanded, 'are the least troublesome sort of Irish. We don't go there very often. We keep a couple of farms down in Sussex.'

'Hmm.'

Charm bounced off Mitchell, it seemed.

'I am a simple Scots-born man,' Mitchell continued, 'with a clever daughter. And once in a while I find myself out of my depth.'

Charles cleared his throat sympathetically. He was ready to help a man out of his depth. But then he realised that Mitchell scorned the deeps.

'What money have you?' Mitchell asked, clasping his hands together.

'Money? Very little . . . Enough.'

'You'll get none from me, lad. As a matter of principle.'

Charles had not asked for any. He buried his irritation.

'I want Nellie's hand in marriage. That is all.'

The blunt statement had its effect. Mitchell sighed, and adopted an unexpectedly confessional tone.

'There is a deal of confusion in my daughter's mind about whether she might keep on with her music. Her mother expected something along those lines, but I don't know . . . You saw her last night, it possesses her at times . . .'

'Ah, well,' said Charles. He leaned forward with great confidence. 'Marriage will put an end to such talk. Believe me.'

Mitchell gave Charles a deep stare.

'Good,' he said.

An understanding was established. Mitchell stood and uncramped himself.

'The men at the mill will be wondering where I am,' he said. The beggars will probably all know, he thought.

Charles went on with considerable lightness of spirit.

'It will be love in a cottage, sir.'

'You're both headstrong. Be careful you don't lose your

tempers on the same day.'

It seemed that the interview was at an end.

'Is that all, sir?'

'Aye,' said Mitchell, agonising over the intimacies. 'I think so.'

Charles reappeared on the verandah and Nellie went to him. 'Well?'

'We have his blessing, I think.'

'You "think", Charles, what do you mean?' Nellie laughed anxiously and clung to Charles's arm.

He kissed her. 'It's all right. Yes.'

They kissed again, Nellie clinging to him murmuring endearments. 'I love you, I want you, I must have you for ever my sweetest, and I have, haven't I, Charles?'

Charles laughed as the words danced around him, and her kisses flew to his fingers, his cheeks, his lips.

'I say, easy now.' Charles disengaged himself. 'People are watching y'know.' But no matter, he held her eyes, he lifted her by the waist, he raised her to him outrageously, and she shrieked.

They went down the steps into the garden.

Annie came onto the side verandah wanting to go to her sister with congratulations, but not daring to yet, because Nellie and Charles were in another world.

David Mitchell came out, fitting his hat on his head and blinking in the hard, bright sunlight. He angled across the grass to his waiting pony trap and drove off.

Amy Davidson watched from a window, not a happy woman, really, thinking of her life, the sacrifices she had made, the distant places she had lived while her husband accumulated land, capital, knowledge, and, yes indeed, the bitterest of all accumulations, years. She liked having handsome, energetic young men around the house. They lent colour to her dreams, they charmed and made her forget things. Charles had been a special favourite, and now Nellie Mitchell had landed him. A great secret envy consumed Amy Davidson as she watched Charles and Nellie disappear into the trees at the end of the garden.

Down in the shadows Charles and Nellie broke free of each

other after another long, unrestrained embrace. Charles ran a finger down Nellie's fine, pleasant nose. He touched his fingertips on her lips and she nipped them with her teeth.

'I said easy,' he grunted, putting his arm round her waist and drawing her roughly to his side. They walked on a bit.

Charles had come close to marriage twice before, once in Bristol, after his first sea voyage, the second time in Sussex when his family had wanted to tie him down. He'd made an escape but was not averse to tying the knot: the end of the equation for the rover being an end to roving. There was a swift inevitability about his meeting with Nellie and the rapid course of events between them. There was no coyness in her, no pretence that the forms had to be gone through; he could not imagine her writing letters to her friends, arranging sea voyages for entire wedding parties, getting crates of Royal Doulton sent out from England, and rifling entire warehouses of silks for a wedding gown that would be untouchable, uncrushable by any man's heated longing.

'Nellie, I want you, you know.'

'We both . . . want the same things,' she dared.

Passion, the glorious finality of touch. It was everything to them they knew.

'My darling, you're not like other girls.'

'I'm not? I don't know. Tell me.'

But he couldn't say. Or at least, he said it with yet another kiss, unable to leave her alone, and her understanding of his meaning was anyway complete.

She knew this: she wanted marriage and all it entailed with Charles, the intimate close life excluding others, the single-minded intensity of their kisses taken to the absolute extreme.

'We must be married soon,' she said, 'or I'll die.'

'Well, where shall you be married?' Annie turned from her writing desk.

'We haven't discussed it.'

'You haven't? When, where, and who's to come. Aren't they the most important things?'

'I suppose so.'

DETERMINATION

'You're not listening to me. The mail leaves in two hours and I don't have anything to tell, except that my sister is engaged, the wedding will be soon, but not *too* soon, that the bride and groom are not being very co-operative.'

Nellie laughed contentedly.

'We dream of the day, darling Annie.'

'Well, then, where? What do the two of you talk about, ever; you're always together, now, none of us sees anything of either of you any more. I'm just left with Tom and that silly crowd including Adelaide Baker, who, I might tell you, is not the least put out by it all, despite what people say.'

'Doonside.'

'What's that?'

'I said Doonside. I want to be married at Doonside.'

'But that's wonderful. Why didn't you say so before?'

Charles heard of a house coming vacant in an excellent position down near the river. It was at the end of a track, no-one went farther than there. It was a small house, but had a garden that had been well-kept by a kanaka gardener named Boslem who had gone to work for a cane gang but might be persuaded to return. They went one day to see it, the dogcart picking its way along ruts and through dust in this baking hot day, at the long endless height of the dry season.

'I'm to have my own gardener? Oh, Charles, you think of everything.'

'And maids, of course.'

'One maid will do. I already know which one I want. Mrs Davidson's Esther.'

'Amy won't like that.'

'Those people aren't slaves, no matter what she thinks.'

'There it is,' said Charles.

They overlooked a view of the house. It had a tin roof gleaming through the trees, wide verandahs with wooden railings, and an appealing secretiveness.

Charles brought the dogcart to a stop.

'Can't we go in?'

'It's not ours yet, Nell.'

'But it's empty, who cares? We've come this far, Charles.' She rested her hand on his knee.

'All right.'

The horse picked its way along to the front gate, where Charles tethered it. Nellie jumped down and tested the hinges of the gate.

'Solid,' she said.

Nellie had such gladness about her, he could only look at her, as she stood there waiting for him, and the house was nothing to him. 'I'm imagining I'm standing at this gate,' she said, 'waiting for you to come home, my sweet dear Charlie.'

She threw her arms around his neck as he squeezed past.

They went down the short gravelled path and up the rather elastic dozen front steps. The front door was closed and had a collection of leaves and dried grass-balls blown against it.

'It's not very grand,' said Charles apologetically.

'It's "love in a cottage",' she reminded him.

Charles put his shoulder to the door and it scraped open. He went around punching open shutters, loosening window jambs, and rather discreetly removing a long-dead, mummified bush rat from under the sofa. Nellie went about looking in cupboards, smacking mattresses with the flat of her hand, and driving the handle of the well pump, which stood at the low back steps, until a gargle of rusty water spewed out.

'I do love it,' she called to Charles. 'Everything about it is mine.'

Charles was sitting on a chair on the verandah. The chair had given, somewhat, as he sank into it. He lit a cheroot.

'Who lived here before?' Nellie's voice reached him.

'Parker, the plantation manager.'

'Where are they now?'

'Fiji.'

'Oh, how exciting.' A thought occured to her. 'Does that mean you'll be plantation manager, now, Charlie, if we have this house?'

'Yes,' said Charles. 'It does.'

'Why didn't you tell me?'

She sat on his knee. The chair gave some more.

DETERMINATION

'Careful.'

'Then why?'

'Because I want something better. Just being manager is nothing.'

'But you will have something better, I know.'

She kissed him, and went off to complete her exploration of the house.

In the sitting room she found the piano. She struck a note. Then another. To her surprise, it was perfectly in tune, unlike every other piano she'd come upon in the tropics, where if they'd survived sea water on the voyage out, or being dropped onto wharf timbers, or being manhandled along rough roads on unsprung wagons, they had never survived the rigours of climate.

'How long since the Parkers left?'

'Ages,' Charles stood in the doorway behind her. Nellie smiled over her shoulder as she ran her fingers across the keys, creating a melody from nothing.

'Then this is a magical place,' said Nellie. 'Blessed . . . It's so quiet here, hidden away from everyone. I love it better than anywhere in the world.' She played something else. 'I'm so tired of living at the Davidsons. They're wonderful, of course. But there's no privacy. Here there's no sense of time, no rules and dinner bells, or important gatherings brought to an end after strict intervals.'

Charles came up from behind and placed his arms around her waist.

'Charles,' she said. 'It's as if we're married already.'

'Yes,' he replied. 'I feel that too.' His voice was rough with desire.

The time was fast approaching when David Mitchell would hand the completed Marion mill over to John Ewen Davidson and his partners, collect his bonus for finishing six weeks ahead of schedule, and depart for Melbourne in good time for Christmas with his family. He had enjoyed himself in the north, but being among his fellow Scots had not been as rewarding as he had expected. He had no complaints about them in the way of business. He'd done well with his contract. They were excellent men; proconsular types, empire builders and the like. They were hard workers, and yet they left Mitchell, a hard worker himself, feeling the odd man out. One of their number had taken a seat in the Queensland parliament, Hume Black, but the motive wasn't the solid colonial feeling of home-rooted achievement that Mitchell liked so much in Victoria. Black took his politics to the state capital in Brisbane from sectional interest alone. The atmosphere here among the leaders of Mackay society, be it ever so discreetly veiled by manners and culture, by science and mathematics, and by the intricate chemistry of sugar-refining, was the atmosphere of the land grab. Aye, and of the kanaka system, which stank in a man's nostrils. David Mitchell did not like the kanaka system at all. He despised it out of his Presbyterianism and his innate decency, for the simple reason that if a man did a good day's work then he should expect to reap a good day's wage for his labour, whatever his skin colour. The value of a kanaka's labour accumulated in another man's pocket. It was not just.

Here in the Davidsons' garden the kanakas were at their ceaseless work of watering, planting, weeding. It was a beautiful place, but Mitchell longed for Doonside, the sheen of brick-dust on the roses, the verdant triumphs of his fig trees and his grape vines, flourishing there in the heart of metropolitan Richmond. Also he was sick of hearing of other men's cattle and pastures, and wished to see how Cave Hill was doing for a change. But Doonside called him most of all, the house his wife had loved and where his eldest child would be married.

Ahead of him in the Davidsons' garden sat Nellie, her skirts spread around her, a book in her hand. She was dreaming of the future, he supposed, as it was right for her to do.

He watched her for a while before approaching. She had her future clearly marked now. It had settled for him too, he had to admit, through the materialisation of Charles Armstrong. It was hard for a man to lose a daughter, but it had to come in the order of things. Better than the alternative

DETERMINATION

which he dreaded for reasons he could barely articulate: the stage. Charles was with him on that, thankfully. What Mitchell hated about the stage was its vaporousness. The men were loafers and the women something worse. He felt differently about music as an accomplishment: how he loved music, it was refreshment to him when he came in late from his work and was given a song by his daughters.

Nellie looked up.

'Hello, Daddy.'

He bent down and kissed her. Then he sat on the grass beside her.

'I'm so happy,' said Nellie.

'I wish your mother were here to share it,' said Mitchell. Then to abolish that thought, and the pain it might bring to them both, he went on: 'My work's about finished here. I've booked our passage through to Brisbane, then on to Melbourne, lass.'

'How soon?' Nellie asked.

'Three weeks to the day.'

'As long as that!'

'Aye,' Mitchell was puzzled at the strength of Nellie's response. 'That's right.'

'Daddy I'm not coming with you.'

'I don't understand.'

'I can't. I'm engaged to be married. I mean to be married. I won't sit around, waiting for Charles to come for me at Doonside, two thousand miles away.'

'But that was your wish, it's how we've planned things, Aunt Lizzie and the rest are forging ahead. What is it you're talking about? A rushed wedding? The idea is distasteful. We're still a family in mourning, you know.'

It pained Nellie to be reminded of this but she continued the struggle with her father. It was a matter of desperation to her to do so, Mitchell could see that, and he was somewhat frightened to know the reason.

'Not a "rushed" wedding,' said Nellie with quiet intensity. 'But a wedding. And fairly soon, yes.'

'In Mackay?'

'Yes'

'When?'

'I thought next week.'

'And Charles?'

'He wants the same, of course.'

'You would think he would come to me about it.'

'Oh, it's the women who organise these things, Daddy,' said Nellie with a somewhat forced smile.

Mitchell did not like it. He felt he was being worked upon, manipulated into a corner.

He said:

'How could we tell good people like the Davidsons there's to be a hasty wedding in Mackay. What would they think?'

Nellie dropped her eyes. Words like 'rushed' and 'hasty' brazened her. What she said next, she had to say. She looked up at him again, challenged him with the power of her personality as she had never in her life challenged him before, and hoped she would never have to again. For it hurt her to do this, when she loved him so much.

'Heavens, Father, what do you mean?'

It worked. She saw that her father was excruciatingly embarrassed. That he would have no more of this talk, or hint of this talk ever. She saw that she had him, now.

'Well, if not Mackay, why not Brisbane?' she suggested. 'It would make sense to everybody. Yes, Daddy, that's it don't you see? We must have a quiet wedding in Brisbane, and come straight back here before the onset of the Wet. Everything has to be done before the rains. There are prospects for Charles and you do have faith in sugar planting don't you? There are opportunities now. He mustn't miss them.'

'Aye, I know what you mean,' said Mitchell, unable to look her in the eye.

Nellie tried to divert the point.

'Daddy you're right to bring up Mother's memory. Don't think I haven't agonised over what I'm surrendering. Mother would say of course "what about my music" and worry that I'd be far from Signor Cecchi and my lessons.'

'She would. She would.'

DETERMINATION

'Well, then . . . '

'I have an important question. How can you be sure after so short a time?'

Nellie thought for a moment, then she said, 'Were you sure with Mother?'

'I was.' Mitchell's jaw tightened. She could really tie him up, this daughter. 'Och, I suppose that's it, then. If you love Charlie as much as I loved your mother, it will be all right.'

'So it's Brisbane.'

'Very well. Brisbane.'

Annie always remembered that Nellie had wanted to be married at Doonside, but then had come that troubling day when she'd gone off to look at the cottage by the river with Charles. On returning she'd had a rather distant look in her eye, and had not wanted to be married at Doonside after all. The change had occurred in a matter of hours. What had happened at the cottage?

A wedding in Annie's life was a pinnacle, a great moment: she had already been through that with Nellie. She knew Nellie agreed with her viewpoint, really. Annie thought it most strange that Nellie was unwilling now to show Charles around in Melbourne, the way girls did when first engaged. He was quite a catch, after all. It all went back to the cottage again.

White faced, Annie forced a confrontation.

'What happened there?' she asked Nellie.

'Charles and I talked, we decided on certain matters. But listen to me, Annie. You have absolutely no right to question me like this.'

'I think, that if I were marrying Charles,' Annie persisted, 'I would be asking myself if there wasn't just a touch of couldn't-care-less in his attitude. He is, after all, a member of the aristocracy.'

'Hardly that,' smiled Nellie.

It was impossible for Annie to say anything more about what was really on her mind: lonely cottage, two passionate, strong-headed people in love, the whole afternoon stretching before them . . . So she thought up other reasons.

MELBA

'It is how you think of him, as an aristocrat of some sort, Anglo-Irish and all. I know you really love him. But what if he was merely thinking, "I'm in Australia, she's just an Australian, a beautiful young colonial, righty-oh I want her sure enough, the way a man wants a woman, and marriage is the way to get her, and why waste time and bother my head with fancy colonial weddings in Scots Church Collins Street or this famous Doonside they're always talking about, weddings with all their falderol so boring to a man, why not get it all over with somewhere where I don't have to parade my face all over the country, get her settled back here in Mackay and resume my old life of horseriding, rum drinking, and sugar planting, if I can, with my dearest chum Tom Chataway." '

'Oh, such bitterness, Annie, what are you talking about.'

'You tell me.'

'You're disappointed, I know. But it's not your wedding my dear,' Nellie responded. 'Perhaps, though,' she continued after a moment's thought, 'you're pushing Tom Chataway's attitudes on to Charles. I think Tom's like that, if you don't mind me saying so. A snob underneath it all. I don't trust him I've decided. And you have been disappointed with Tom, so you take it out on your idea of Charles. But you couldn't be more wrong.'

'Oh, stop it, stop it, stop it,' said Annie in anguish.

They went to Brisbane.

The night before the wedding, Charles and Tom Chataway, who'd come down for the ceremony, entered a hotel and commenced drinking rum. After a short while they were unsteady on their feet.

Tom tried to sum it all up for Charles in the tradition of the best man at the eleventh hour.

'The father's as rich as Croesus.'

'Tell me something I don't know, Chataway.'

'He talks about marriage as if it's a business proposition. But of course one he won't invest in. The man has one theme, thrift. When you light a cigar, Charlie, ha, ha, I've noticed he rolls

DETERMINATION

his eyes. You'd think you were smoking money . . . his money.'

'What are you trying to say?'

'It's all so quick, old chum.'

'You're talking like a foolish virgin, Chataway. Take a pull at yourself.'

Chataway turned his head aside and brooded into his glass.

'I have to be frank with you Charlie.'

'Balderdash.'

'The sister lets out more than she knows, that one does.'

'What are you hinting at now?'

'I gather from Annie that Nellie led a high old life down there, in Melbourne, before she came up north and clapped eyes on Charlie-boy.'

'Dangerous talk, Chataway, I'm warning you.'

Chataway straightened himself and said airily:

'Teacher besotted with her, a stablehand lurking about with an eye for the main chance. Any number of wealthy young swains in the wings, but she has a taste for the dangerous boyos. If you don't mind me saying so, Charlie, she's continuing the pattern with you. You're not exactly solvent, are you.'

'God help me Chataway, I walk down the aisle tomorrow, what are you talking about, man.'

Charles clenched his fists. Chataway signalled to the barman for more rum. He wouldn't let things go.

'Well, what about the Italian fellow. He writes to her I believe.'

'Her teacher, yes. She writes to him.'

'Oh, she's mentioned him, then.'

'You, Chataway, are an ass.'

Charles stood back from the bar and rocked unsteadily on his feet. He drew back a fist as Chataway turned and faced him mockingly:

'Why, "Kangaroo Charlie" . . . '

Charles knocked his friend flying with a well-aimed crack to the jaw.

It was not even a church wedding. An entire church could not be given over to a small handful of strangers, not the fashionable Ann Street Presbyterian Church, anyway. How this made David Mitchell long for Melbourne, where he was a man of note. There was just the rather put-upon minister leading the small party through into the manse, into a book-lined study, where Charles and Nellie exchanged their vows with quiet sincerity and David Mitchell gave the bride away by merely nudging her forward with his elbow. Nothing grand or memorable at all, except the vows rang out clearly, the responses were heartfelt. Charles was freshly bathed and shaved but there was still about him an air of dishevelment from the night before, when he and Tom Chataway had gone carousing on the town. Chataway wore a plaster on his chin. Annie cried, of course, from disappointment and from a yearning love for her sister, who entered married life so proudly and lovingly, as if she knew exactly what she was doing, and Charles the same at her side.

7

Love in a Cottage

Now they were back in Mackay again and their new life had truly begun. All the talk was of the Wet, which had not yet arrived, but must soon, because the baking heat was creating dust storms, wells were drying up, and worse, people were so tetchy with each other. Even Mr and Mrs Davidson had been heard to exchange sharp words. The kanakas, normally so satisfied with their lot, were getting restless, it was said, and could be seen glowering if one caught their eye, and were drinking too much in their huts at night. There had been a riot last year on the racecourse, with several killed, and fears were that it would happen again, only worse this time.

Charles and Nellie, newlyweds enjoying their passion, felt none of this as they arrived back, saw none of it through eyes turned to each other, and anyway believed they were immune from the troubles and irritations of people not blest like themselves.

Charles went round closing shutters, dimming the hard noontime light. While they were away he'd had the house painted: it was a bright, clean, airy place and Nellie declared she loved it more than ever.

In the kitchen Nellie poured tea, the first possessive act of her married existence, while Charles stood with his hands on his hips and announced plans.

'We'll knock this wall out,' he said, 'and enlarge things properly. I'll get you the kanaka I promised for the garden, and you won't know the place. We'll have people over and live the life of Riley.'

'Yes, I'll make Mrs Davidson come, and play her something on the piano, and make her sit up.'

Playing the piano was the first thing she'd done when she entered the house; she'd sat there and played the Wedding March as Charles struggled up the front steps with a great basket of clothes in his arms. They'd not had music in Brisbane, or anything else much; nothing except their vows, and a hurried prayer at the end.

They kissed.

'Drink your tea,' murmured Nellie. Beyond them was the open door of the bedroom, the bed with its dusty, comfortable mattress. They forgot the tea and went in there.

Through the windows could be seen the delights of the garden, a paradise where fruit ripened and multi-coloured birds abounded. It was rather bedraggled now but they didn't see it that way through their eyes.

Each new day at the riverside cottage began very early in the morning, before daylight, as it had at the Davidsons' place. Only now it was just Nellie and Charles, with the maid Esther lighting the kitchen fire and making tea in the damply cool, candle-lit, pre-dawn darkness. Nellie had obtained Esther from Amy Davidson by the simple method of sending Charles over to ask for her.

Soon after daylight Nellie re-enacted the picture that so appealed to her; farewelling Charles at the gate. He bent from the saddle and kissed her on the lips. She stepped out to the track and waved as he cantered off for his day's work in the man's world of sugar planting. He flourished his hat in the air as he disappeared under the last rise, and Nellie, with a happy heart, turned back to begin her day's housekeeping.

Nellie's mother, through everything, had been a scrupulous housekeeper and Nellie was determined to be the same.

She unpacked the trunks from Melbourne and found a place

LOVE IN A COTTAGE

for everything. She laid out her books, her neat boxes of music tied with different coloured ribbons, and her pencilled scores from the years with Signor Cecchi, which she would take, at some time of every day, to the enclosed end of the verandah, and there practise what was second nature in herself, her singing, which in curious fashion her maid disliked. She would always manage to make a clatter over something when Nellie settled in for her practice.

One day Esther was scrubbing the kitchen floor with bucket and scrubbing brush. She sang Christian hymns as she worked. Nellie chimed-in for a few phrases:

The people of the Hebrews
With palms before thee went,
Our praise and prayer and anthems
Before Thee we present.

All glory, laud and honour
To Thee, Redeemer, King,
To Whom the lips of children
Made sweet Hosannas ring.

Beaming approval, wanting so much to be liked, Nellie failed to notice that Esther was working with the bucket on the wrong side of the room. When Nellie was gone, Esther, still singing, stepped back over the work she'd already done, leaving a trail of footprints. Nellie was always ready to overlook these imperfections, which the more established married ladies of Mackay regarded with horror.

The evening gatherings on the Davidsons' verandah were still very much a part of the Mackay social scene. Once, in rather a humorous way, Nellie mentioned Esther's shortcomings to Mrs Davidson. She was met with amazed laughter.

'Esther is a treasure, my dear, but you must never on any account leave her unsupervised. Didn't I pass that message along with Charles, when he came to take her away?'·

'No, I don't think so, Mrs Davidson.'

'Oh, yes but I did, Nellie,' said Amy Davidson with a

glimmer of hardness that Nellie was beginning to detect in her quite often these days.

In fact, as Nellie said to Charles one night, the charm of the Mackay Scots was beginning to wear a little thin for her. Their sophistication had a certain repetitiveness to it. If you were around long enough, and Charles had been around longer than Nellie, as she pointed out to him, you started to realise that John Ewen Davidson only ever sent the same sort of things to the Royal Botanic Gardens at Kew, and when he put his telescope out on the grass for the delight of his guests there were the same half dozen celestial features he invariably calibrated it towards.

Charles seemed very understanding about all this, and sympathised with her one hundred per cent. Except that Nellie was unaware that next time Charles saw Amy Davidson, and she asked him how Nellie was coping, he said, 'Very well, though a little tetchy like the rest of us in this damnable heat.'

Charles agreed with Mrs Davidson that the kanaka servant as a class needed very close watching. 'Go over everything word for word, bit of a bore, but it works.' Nellie put things to the test that very night. It was Charles's birthday. First she spent time showing Esther how to lay out a special dinner service. It was a wedding gift from David Mitchell's friend and business colleague Mr Jenkin Collier, who had visited them in Mackay. Things went well and Nellie was pleased.

'That's very good. Now go to the kitchen, Esther. Take the roast from the oven. Put it on the serving plate ready for carving.'

'Big serving plate, Missus Armstrong?'

'Yes, yes, ready for carving.'

As Esther headed for the kitchen she repeated to herself, 'Carving. Carving.'

Nellie lit the candles, and went out to the verandah to wait for Charles. Soon she heard the distant thud of his pony's cantering hooves, and was glad.

In the kitchen Esther silently rehearsed Nellie's instructions as she went: she took the roast from the oven, put it on the serving plate, then earnestly picked up a sharp knife. Then without hesitation she cut the beef into inch-thick slices. This done, she spun the plate around and carved it again from the other direction, the result being a heap of unappetising meaty chunks. Then she put the lid on the plate and carried it through to the dining room.

'Well, here we are,' said Charles, shooting his cuffs in a manly fashion.

'You carve, darling,' said Nellie. Charles lifted the lid of the serving dish and was confronted with the mess of meat.

'What's this?' he shot at Nellie in astonishment. 'How did you let this happen?'

'I? I didn't.'

Charles threw the carving knife and fork down with a loud clatter. Nellie was amazed.

'You left her on her own, that's what you did.'

'Only while I went to greet you, my darling.'

'Amazing,' laughed Charles, somewhat unpleasantly. 'You have all day with nothing to do except organise the kitchen, and a man comes home after one hellish sort of a day, and he finds this in front of him.'

Nellie still could not believe that Charles was carrying on seriously in this vein. She laughed at him; a mistake, apparently.

'Goodness, Charles, just look at yourself. In my family we'd call this a tantrum and send you off with a smack.'

'Oh, yes?' Charles stood, kicked back his chair, and threw down his napkin. 'How perfectly boring of you all.'

He left the room and went out onto the verandah, where he lit a cheroot and stood smoking in the dark. Nellie picked at her beef. It was actually rather tasty. Then she carried the dish through to the kitchen, where Esther was cowered against the stove attempting to stir a custard.

'That will be enough, Esther. Mr Armstrong is not hungry.'

'Boss beat me now,' said Esther.

'No, no, no,' sighed Nellie.

Then Charles appeared and glowered at the girl. He looked as if he really might beat her if he was driven another inch towards the edge. 'Provoked' was a word he used. He raised his arm for emphasis. The effect on Esther was amazing: she obviously worshipped Charles, and accepted his ranting, raving tongue-lashing as her fair due.

Nellie had never seen him like this before.

Things were now established to Charles's satisfaction: never again would Esther carve meat before bringing it to the table. That was understood. He seemed calmer, now.

But he had not finished.

'You,' said Charles, turning on Nellie as if she were just another servant in the room, instead of his wife and lover, 'If you don't try a little harder to adapt to the ways up here, I don't know what'll happen to you. I really don't.'

He was trembling. What was wrong with him? Perhaps he was ill.

Nellie went over and put her arms around him.

'Charlie what is it?' she asked.

Her tenderness appeased him.

'Oh, I'm damned tired I suppose. The weather. The worry about this interminable dry season. Cane's wilting, Davidson's getting really worried now. It looks like a proper drought. People said it couldn't happen up here. Looks like it can.'

'Oh, well,' said Nellie lightly, 'You don't need to take on his worries, Charlie. It's not as if you have any land yourself, and perhaps it's a good thing, the season being what it is.'

The look Charles gave her then made her realise she'd made another mistake, dented his pride when she'd thought him endlessly resilient; as if the charm he worked on others could work in reverse, back on himself somehow.

She wondered if she knew him at all well, or if it was just men and their ways that she was ignorant about, having been raised in the special atmosphere of the Mitchell family, which, she now told herself, Charles had better not pass slighting remarks about again, or he would find her his equal when it came to fighting back.

'Sorry about what I said about your family. Didn't mean a word of it,' said Charles. 'I think they're a fine bunch all round.'

Everything was all right then, as if the outburst had never happened.

LOVE IN A COTTAGE

Shortly afterwards, the rains began.

Here in the tropics the change of weather wasn't just a relief, it was like the visitation of another world. Along with everyone else, Nellie was overjoyed. Tremendous pinnacles of cloud grew in the sky in the space of a few short hours. It was like being transported away. The place itself changed. Vegetation dripped, instead of drooping. It shone. Nellie clung to the verandah railings watching great cloud masses build up in the west, and then come marching down, inexorably magnificent, hammering their spears of rain on the dull waiting soil and across the puny shelter of the cottage's corrugated iron roof. The thunderheads went up tens of thousands of feet. They were entire alps on the move, with majestic ice-cliffs and boiling blue rock faces to bemuse and fascinate the watching eye. After a few days the rain stopped, everything steamed, and the sunsets turned opalescent on the skyline, where distant thunderheads still wandered, lit within by lightning but coming no closer for the time being.

Everyone splashed to the Davidsons' where the mood was one of quiet hysteria. The sponginess underfoot, the steamy muddiness in the nostrils, the great spiders and beetles and snakes that came with the Wet meant one thing only in these first few glorious days, and that was money.

A croquet ball went spinning across the grass, sending back a flicker of spray. The mallets and balls had been left outside before the change of weather and now Charles and Tom Chataway were bringing them in. They played a sort of foot-polo, galloping around, bumping shoulders and driving the heavy balls along while leaving ugly dents in the carefully manicured lawn. They were as wild as young boys and the gardeners would have a week's work to get the turf rolled again, but none of that mattered now. It was the Wet.

Amy Davidson stood on the verandah and watched her young friends. Nellie was inside playing the piano while Mr Davidson turned the pages of the music for her. She played Schubert nocturnes; the notes that reached Amy Davidson on the verandah were beautifully played, quite eerie and splendid, leaving little doubt, she thought, that fate had landed a person of great gifts on them when Nellie had come to Mackay. And

MELBA

yet to Amy Davidson it seemed that the gifts had been misplaced. Nellie carried them so lightly. There was much that was typically Australian about the girl. She was pretty, she was bright. But already a reversion to type could be seen. The way she had thrown herself at Charles, handsome young devil but the black sheep of his family, showed this colonial blindness on Nellie's part. There was a curse of ordinariness on the country, with its tawdry landscapes and exhausted, ancient hills. Escape into marriage and a misplaced idea of exoticism, followed by cruel disappointment was the Australian pattern with these energetic girls of good colonial family. They had no hope, really. Gifts like Nellie's went shimmering away into the mirage of timelessness that absorbed so much from people here.

Thus Amy Davidson's thoughts ran on. And so too, with the logic of resentment, was added Nellie's gift to the store of reasons why she'd been a bad choice for Charlie Armstrong.

'Come on Charlie, come on Tom,' Amy called. 'Dry off and have a rum, you ridiculous boys.'

Other guests arrived, all mud spattered from cheerful drives along roads that were now little more than sheets of water. Rum was the drink for this weather, a 'Mackay Swizzle' for once, a squeeze of lemon and a good spoonful of brown sugar, which set heads spinning immediately.

John Ewen Davidson came out onto the verandah with Nellie on his arm. The music and the rum made him reminiscently sentimental. 'We have a house on Loch Lomond, Nellie,' he said. 'It's there we'll return when our planting days are over. A sweep of gardens and a view of the snow-capped hills.' Nellie was entranced. The Blacks, the Hewitts, and a new couple, the Frasers, persuaded Nellie to return to the piano and give them a brace of Scottish airs. When that was done there was hardly a dry eye to be seen.

Davidson touched his wife's hand. 'Aye, I pine for it all,' he said.

The two non-Scots present, Charles and Tom Chataway, were talking between themselves, not quite as caught up as were the others. Nellie resumed her seat. 'Well, what about you, Armstrong? No tears for the old country?' asked Davidson.

'I miss the polo,' said Charles dryly. 'The polo was always very good.'

Davidson roared with appreciation. He liked the boy's style. After a minute, he leaned forward confidentially and tapped Charles on the knee. 'Might have that land for you Armstrong. The hundred acres you're after.'

Charles looked pleased. Davidson finished his sentence, though: 'After the Wet. We'll see then.'

This was disappointing to Charles, but he tried not to show it.

After a few days of sparkling beauty, a series of heavy rainstorms began. The magnificent sunlit clouds were hidden, and the whole world became formless, as before creation. The river rose and plunged through the back garden; there was some fear that it might come higher, though it never had before in the history of white men here, a whole twenty years. The mosquitoes were fearsome. Mould appeared overnight on the smartly painted woodwork of the cottage, and ants bypassed the ant-caps on the house stumps, and got into everything with any sweetness in it. Esther was forever beating tree snakes, carpet snakes and legless lizards from the verandah rafters with the handle of her broom. Insects clung to curtains and tablecloths with sharp, hook-like legs. Geckoes as pale as junket scurried through bedclothes. Nellie believed that snakes ought to be killed, they had always killed snakes at Cave Hill, but here she was forced to live in proximity to the creatures as they came endlessly sliding in from the wet vegetation. Where one reptile was seen, another fifty hid waiting. Bamboo grew in front of her eyes, thrusting its way into the empty spaces of a garden that was now running wild. It was a nightmare, but when the sun came out at intervals, all too infrequently now, Nellie's depressed spirits rose at once.

For days at a time Nellie felt tired, a little ill, and at Charles's insistence the doctor came, crossing the river in a boat. He told her that she was pregnant, that she was to have a baby in October.

'October,' said Nellie, doing her maths with a smile, when the doctor had left the room. 'Annie will be so relieved.'

'I can't believe it,' said Charles. 'Wonderful news.'

Charles was excited, rather dazed, and secretly worried that when his son came into the world there would not be the means to support him. Cattle he'd bought with Chataway had recently been found to have blackleg disease. That was bad enough, but then overnight the entire herd went down with pleuropneumonia. They were found one morning dead, all fifty of them. He could not bear to tell Nellie the news, he kept putting it off. Fifty corpses rotting in the rain, half-burnt and bloated, while she, wearing a lace-collared nightgown, sat up in bed being tended by Esther, and spoilt silly by the ladies of Mackay, who prided themselves on getting around in impossible conditions (they had their kanakas carry them through pools of water). The ladies fell upon Nellie as one of their own once they heard that she, like themselves, was to share the burden of motherhood.

No, Charles was a gentleman and would not disturb his wife with unsavoury news from the outside world. So he went to the bank and signed for a loan, and with the money bought more livestock, this time without Chataway, who advised him against it. He was sure to make a killing, he thought, and even a modest profit would be worthwhile when the proceeds weren't to be split. Chataway had always been overcautious, his speech on the wedding eve had shown this.

Charles decided on a surprise for Nellie.

A team of kanakas hacked away at the brush with fearful efficiency, watched by the overseer Jack Bellchambers, and by Charles. One worker, the biggest, was going particularly hard at it.

'Call that fellow over here,' said Charles.

'Hey, Boslem,' called Bellchambers.

The kanaka glided over on his great bare, callused feet, still carrying his gleaming brush hook.

'Tanna man?'

'Yes, boss.'

Jack Bellchambers examined Boslem in approved plantation

style. 'We fella lookim teeth belonga you, Boslem,' he said.

The islander obliged. Gleaming red gums curled back.

'He's the one you want, Mr Armstrong.'

Charles addressed Boslem: 'Would you like im good job again, Mr Boslem. Make garden like before? Grow sweet potato? Carry wood for lady?'

Boslem swayed slightly on the balls of his feet, and said nothing.

'Too bloody right,' Bellchambers answered for him, ''im good job. You get up to house and do what boss tells you or I'll kick you in the behind.'

Jack Bellchambers was pleasantly aggressive about everything.

When Nellie was over the first pangs of morning sickness she became increasingly restless. More and more, the world she had entered with such an open heart, with such gladness, began to seem stretched around with boundaries. The thing people always said about Mackay, with such provincial pride, that it was cut off from the world on three sides by swamps, began to seem a condition of mind to her. She tried to push this thought away, for it was desperately unkind to Charles to let her mind wander, and very cruel to herself, for she was bent on making her life here in the north.

Increasingly she turned to her music. She sang as Esther cleared away the breakfast dishes, as she laid out the lunch table, and during the long, grey, stifling afternoons when she waited for Charles to return home from the mill where he worked now as engineer, life in the fields being almost insupportable in the Wet, except to kanakas. She sang for Charles too, sprawled as he was at night, exhausted in a chair, his face grim with worries he refused to share with her, and a glass of rum in his hand with the bottle nearby. There had been no recurrence of Charles's bad temper, not since the day of his birthday, but this was because Nellie watched her every action, careful not to provoke him. He seemed always on the edge of a volcano now. He'd said that the prospect of a family pleased him, he was the youngest of several brothers and he adored family life, though he had run away from it, Nellie remembered. But he didn't seem terribly happy about anything. Nellie watched him shielding his thoughts, lowering the level of the rum bottle hour by hour: she could not seem to get back to the innocent joy of their first months together. Nor could he.

Like everyone else, she blamed the weather. People always blamed the weather in the tropics.

Boslem arrived at the bottom of the garden and began his work as instructed. He slashed at vines and weeds with fearsome efficiency. He found a bedraggled red flower which he placed behind his ear. He bent to his work, with the rain pouring down across his shoulders, only pausing from time to time to flick a blood-engorged leech from his ankles, and singing, as he went, an island chant remembered from his life on Tanna.

As he worked, he became aware of another voice singing. He stopped and listened. He crept forward. Something about the melody drew him on, an echo, in Nellie's beautifully elaborated scales, of his own sounds, rousing homesickness in his belly and heart. Slowly he came along the side of the house and stared up through the verandah slats. He saw Boss Armstrong's woman there, swaying and entranced as she sang to herself. Boslem, intently drawn, put his machete up on the railing and hauled himself to chin level while Nellie's back was turned.

Nellie's scale was interspersed with humming as she improvised her way through boredom, and stared off the other end of the verandah oblivious to Boslem. Then she became aware of another sound melting in with hers.

It was enough to raise the hackles on the back of a person's neck, this great, heavy-fisted kanaka humming along with her. Grinning. Alive to the music.

Nellie's eyes rested on the machete, on the flower behind the man's ear, on the loneliness in those dark eyes which were lost in time. 'Oh, you poor, weird man,' she thought to herself.

She gave him a solo, catching his island song, giving it a twist of her own, and tears sprang to the man's eyes. It was so beautiful.

LOVE IN A COTTAGE

He sent her a solo in return, from his end of the verandah.

Her laughter and his rocked around under the spare, iron-topped rafters. Then they sang together again, louder this time.

The sound attracted Esther. She stood in the doorway, and muttered under her breath: 'Bloody bush kanaka.'

She rushed forward wielding a broom. Before Nellie could react she beat Boslem from the railing.

'Damn bush kanaka get away fast.'

Boslem disppeared from sight. The machete, dislodged in the action, clattered and spun on the verandah boards.

Esther swooped and picked it up with a look of triumph in her eyes.

'Him Boslem one bad fella, Missus. Tanna island boy, no love Jesus. All right?'

Nellie leant over the verandah rail and saw Boslem disappearing into the dripping undergrowth at the foot of the garden.

That night the inevitable happened. Esther went to Charles and told him about the visit from Boslem. Only she made it sound like an attack, and with few words, but much skill in the telling, described how she had beaten the man away, how he had thrown his machete at her, and how Nellie had done nothing. Too frightened, maybe, shrugged Esther.

'Are you going to listen to me, Charles, or to the tale of a simple-minded girl?' asked an astonished Nellie.

'You don't understand these people, it's plain you don't,' Charles replied. He twirled the machete in his hands. He sent Esther away. It was certainly a vicious-looking instrument. Mackay people talked about the kanakas being gentle souls but they were always afraid of them, deep down. She supposed she was herself, in general, but not face to face with Boslem's homesickness and voice.

'Charles I can't believe my ears.'

Charles stared at her: 'Nor I mine,' he responded.

So they were to have a confrontation over the matter, it seemed. Nellie tossed her head, and looked away, across at the oil-lamp that was turned low to discourage the swarms of insects that came in every night. His attitude was cold and unconciliatory. She didn't understand it. She supposed he felt he'd made a mistake in giving in to her request for a gardener, or in sending the wrong man, or in not being there when he came. Men had such complications and extensions of pride to deal with in their lives. She was beginning to see this now, with Charles. She went to him, and tried to take the machete from him.

'No,' he said.

'Charles, listen to me. He didn't throw it at anyone. He simply forgot he had it, the maid frightened him, and it fell to the floor. So don't make a fool of yourself over the word of an hysterical child . . . Please?'

'I'll think about it,' he said.

The next day Charles was more cheerful than he'd been in many weeks but Nellie did not dare suppose that the incident was forgotten.

On the Saturday, after a spell of a few days without rain, a run of dry weather now being the thing to cheer everyone up, they went to the Davidsons' again for the regular get-together, the men in one circle, the ladies in another.

'What a day I've had,' said Amy Davidson. 'My best girl Cissie poured ammonia on John's books.'

She turned to Nellie.

'How is your new gardener?'

Nellie did not know what to say. At that moment she looked across at Charles, settled in with the men, drinking their Highland malt, their rum, and whatever else it was they numbed themselves with in the hour set aside by the Davidsons for the 'chota peg', which was enough to make them reel when they stood up. She was out of earshot, but to her intense anger she saw Charles engaged in a mime show: his hands said machete, verandah, broomstick, etc. Mr Hewitt, the magistrate, leaned forward and listened very closely. And then Charles glanced across in Nellie's direction, and there was that cold, manly look again, which almost broke Nellie's heart when she realised she would have to struggle against it. *Very well, if that is the way it's to be*, she thought grimly. She felt that a conspiracy of 'talk' was circulating behind her back all the time, and a co-conspirator was her husband. She felt reduced, negated by the thought. It might be what some women would accept for themselves, this air of condescension, but not Nellie.

'How is my gardener? Oh, no trouble at all,' said Nellie brightly.

Mrs Davidson's eyes narrowed.

'That is the literal truth,' said Nellie. 'How can he be trouble, when he doesn't exist? As you very well know, Mrs Davidson.'

'Oh, really!'

'Everyone knows everything, in Mackay. If it has to do with kanakas, they know it ten times over, with a great deal of exaggeration thrown in for good measure, too.'

The women stared at her. She had finally, and completely it seemed, made a mistake that put herself outside their circle. She had mocked their affectation of solidarity. She did not care. It was like a breath of cool wind through her mind, to ride home that night under the damp, star-torn sky and be her own self for a change, instead of an idea fashioned by others. The only other time it had happened in Mackay was when she had stepped forward and sung over the top of Adelaide Baker; what a moment that had been, and they had all remembered it, and resented it; then she had got Charles, and he had come to her ablaze with admiration.

But now Charles was silent and withdrawn as he drove the pony trap through the night, peering forward and preoccupying himself with avoiding obstacles on the dark track.

'Really, Charles, it's not the end of the world you know. I only caught her out at her own game, she was practically begging for it.'

'I thought it was a rotten thing for you to do.'

'Why? Because it was so easy? She laid herself wide open.'

Nellie made light of the exchange, but suddenly her heart was heavy. Nothing but bad could come of this vein of behaviour, where two people who loved each other clawed and damaged themselves in each other's eyes.

'Don't be so damned clever,' said Charles.

'Amy Davidson has never liked me. Not since she realised you loved me, Charles. I don't know what goes on in her mind, it's not balanced.'

'The Davidsons have been everything to me here. You're well

on the road to ruining it all.'

'That is a lie, Charlie. You're just upset. Please take it back.'

Charles laughed. 'Like hell I will.'

This put Charles in a bad position with his own conscience. He hadn't told Nellie, but a few days ago there'd been an exchange with John Ewen Davidson after their drinks.

'The land you're always asking about, Armstrong,' Davidson had said. 'That portion down by the creek.'

'Yes?'

'I can't let it go, laddie, much as I'd like to. You see, there's been too much rain. Everything's waterlogged. Too much wet is as bad as a drought, in its way, and I'm caught way short in my annual plantings again.'

'Something else will turn up,' Charles had pluckily worn it.

'Of course it will, my boy.'

Now Nellie repeated: 'Will you take it back?'

'No.'

She took a sharp breath. 'Then let me tell you something. The Davidsons don't have the least intention in the world of helping you out. They make pleasant noises, and everything is overlaid with a veneer of civilisation, but they're just out here to suit themselves and no-one else. It doesn't mean a thing to them that you're a charming Britisher, Charlie. Oh they like you around, well enough, but they're not going to put themselves out one little bit financially. And really I have to ask why should they? You and Tom Chataway are both the same, such innocents when it comes to money. You expect favours, I weep for you sometimes. Tom recently lost a fortune in blackleg cattle I hear. I hear so much about the wisdom and might of the Mackay sugar planters, but my own father could eat them all up in a minute. My father could show you, Charlie. He's not a sentimental promise-maker, he's decent, he's fair. To think he built the mill, finished it under cost and ahead of time, and they thought him rather a funny old thing for his trouble. How dare they.'

'Who says they thought that,' grunted Charles.

'I do. I do,' said Nellie, tears streaming down her face.

With this, Charles could no longer be angry. He felt such

LOVE IN A COTTAGE

a fool, first for hiding what he must from her, and then for her nosing it out with only her intelligence for a guide. What sort of life was ahead of them? It made him sick to think of the possible disappointments. He only hoped that his cattle, sent up into the hills where a man had offered well-drained pastures at a fair price, would prosper and thrive, and that when the dry season came round again he would be able to astonish Nellie with his profits, and a true beginning could be made.

It was a precarious time, however.

One day Mrs Black came calling on Nellie and told her that on the way over she had seen a prison detail of kanakas, chained together, being walked along the road.

'A pitiable sight, my dear. But at least you will be reassured. The biggest and ugliest of them all was your Boslem.'

'Oh.'

'He was given thirty days.'

'Oh, no.'

'Charles didn't tell you?'

'No.'

'Husbands will protect their wives from unpleasantness,' she said in a self-satisfied fashion. 'Now, chin up. I have interesting news for you, my dear. You won't have heard yet. There's a touring opera company coming to town.'

'Oh, yes, I know,' said Nellie. She decided to sweep down on Mrs Black sitting there with her watery satisfied eyes smirking a little. 'The Montague-Turner Company. Yes, my teacher wrote quite a while ago. They've just done a season at the Bijoux, *The Bohemian Girl*, *Faust*, *Lucretia Borgia*. Now they are making their way up the coast. They've been in Bundaberg, now they're in Rockhampton. They arrive on the *Lady Amelia*.'

Mrs Black was astonished.

'Well, we must all go as a party,' she said.

'That would be wonderful,' said Nellie. 'We must. They are very, very good, you know.' She served tea to Mrs Black, and during the course of the afternoon talked of the usual things, the weather, the better sort of kanaka, and what made him, and the good work Charles was doing in the plantations, how everyone said they couldn't manage without him, and so on. Whenever Mrs Black steered the conversation back to the opera, Nellie steered it away again, as if that was something she was keeping for herself, as if it could not possibly be shared with a person of Mrs Black's make-up. This was how Mrs Black and the other ladies had treated Nellie on a thousand trivial topics, and now she was fighting back at them all, on her own terms and in her own way, until one day they'd wake up with the realisation that she'd been, after all, the cleverest and the best, and they had missed their chance with her.

Among much she did not say was this, that she had already been in correspondence with Mrs Annis Montague, and had received, in a small fat envelope stamped in gold, a friendly reply to a letter offering hospitality during the Company's stay in Mackay and district. The envelope now sat on the mantelshelf staring Mrs Black in the eye. Why should Nellie say a word? She had done nothing all year except fit in with other people's ideas of pleasure and civilised diversion. Now she would make the running on her own account. She had told Charles about Mrs Montague's reply, of course, and to her intense relief he looked forward to their coming as much as she did. His only worry, which he expressed rather heavily, was that they'd turn out to be a bunch of free-loaders. Then he added that she mustn't get too excited in her condition (she had five months to go yet). She kissed him for that, and they laughed fondly together as they did less often these days; the Wet was letting up, so perhaps the weather would improve people's outlook soon.

8

The Bohemian Girl

They all went to the first night in a party as Mrs Black had suggested, the six or seven of the couples Nellie had grown used to thinking of as 'Mackay'. The townspeople, the other Mackay, had a good look at these sugar barons and their ladies as they filed in, dressed as if for a night in London Town, and a very fine sight they made too. They got a scattering of applause for their gowns and coat-tails but the applause went up a notch when 'Kangaroo Charlie' and his lady made their entrance. He was popular in the town and she was as pretty as you could wish with her hair up, so confident and young.

The usual scoffers and mockers were there, but they were only waiting to be impressed, then they would settle down. There was an orchestra of five. Somebody ran past the outside of the hall with a stick, dragging it across the corrugated iron like Maxim gun-fire; the police soon saw to it. Silence fell. The curtain went up. It was *The Bohemian Girl*. When Annis Montague sang 'I Dreamt I Dwelt in Marble Halls' the entire audience knew they were being given the very best, and if any of them doubted it they had only to look at the young Mrs Armstrong, jumping around in her seat and showing her pleasure while her husband smiled and discreetly tried to contain her enthusiasm.

MELBA

The next day, Nellie took Annis Montague to see the sights of the district. The roads were dry, almost, the grass thick and green, the canefields dense with waving fronds as rich as money; but no matter how hard Nellie tried to convey a positive impression she was left with a feeling of disappointment.

They stopped at the mill, and as a surprise Nellie sent a man in to ask for Charles. He emerged from a side door with a smudge of soot on his cheek, clutching an unsavoury-looking wad of cotton waste. He apologised for his appearance, a pressure valve had blown and the whole morning, he said, had been spent in helping a repair gang. It was one of the few occasions when Nellie gained a clear idea of what Charles actually did during his day. He was no longer described as plantation manager, he was now engineer, a lofty-sounding title, but this is what it meant, something rather mean and unpromising. Poor Charles looked haunted, trapped. Nellie could not look him squarely in the eye, not for her own sake, but out of pity for him. It was an embarrassing, humiliating moment. She would weep for it later in seclusion. To think she had just been telling Mrs Montague that many visitors compared the life here with the ways of the Old South; one look at Charles and it didn't seem likely. He had the glaring, resentful look of a gaolbird.

'Is this the same young man we met last night?' wondered Mrs Montague in confusion.

'Yes, my husband,' said Nellie. Luckily Charles was out of earshot.

Nellie had set out to have such fun but the overriding impression of Mackay and district she was giving to Annis Montague was one of sadness. She had had her own dissatisfactions but had never quite seen it this way before. The bare earth of the mill surrounds, where a few scrawny goats were tethered, the post and rail fences leaning awry, the look in Charles's eye, that most of all. The hard-driven kanakas and the poor white farmers who were in the majority compared with the big landholders, but held the minority of land. There was a nasty smell over everything, which seemed

THE BOHEMIAN GIRL

to follow them until they went through a corridor of rainforest and emerged at a tranquil spot with a view of the sea.

'Ah,' sighed Mrs Montague. This is what she had come for. She fed the horse a peppermint and munched on one herself. Nellie unpacked the picnic basket and spread a blanket. 'I imagine you have many picnics,' said Mrs Montague.

'Not these days, the Wet, you know.' Nellie was quick to correct any wrong impressions.

Nellie poured cold tea, set out soggy beef sandwiches, and produced fruit cake squashed at an angle. The ground was damp. Ants marched from all directions, there were already some in the cake.

'Sorry,' said Nellie.

'No, no, lovely,' said Mrs Montague with a pleasant grimace, brushing them off. She was accustomed to roughing it, she said, all in the cause of her art. But she was tired of living from a trunk, in noisy hotels amid fever-ridden swamps. She was tired of Queensland.

Over the picnic they talked about Nellie's years of attending lessons with Pietro Cecchi, her piano playing, the way she'd mastered the organ in Scots' Church to the immense pride of her father, and all the encouragement given by her mother, right up to the day she died.

Neither of them said so, during this intimate, animated chatter, but there was a question hanging over the end of the discussion, and it was to do with marriage.

'Oh, your letter was so full of feeling,' said Mrs Montague, touching Nellie's hand. 'I do remember Cecchi mentioning your name, constantly mentioning it, my dear. Tell me about your life here.'

'What is there to tell? I am to have a baby in October, and then I suppose my true life will begin. I'm always saying that, to myself at least.'

'Your Signor Cecchi is such a dear.'

'Yes, we used to write, but less often now. I've disappointed him of course.'

'He is a teacher, he is used to that.'

'Signor Cecchi was going to prepare me for *Lucia*, then

everything went wrong in my life, I mean right of course.'

'You were married . . .'

'Oh, yes.' Nellie looked down at her wedding ring.

Then Mrs Montague said what Nellie had been waiting to hear.

'You must sing for me, my dear.'

'When?'

'What about tomorrow?'

Charles lay beside her, snoring. Nellie felt wide awake though it was after midnight. She could not keep track of what was happening in her mind, the feeling she'd had a while back that one door had opened and another closed, this had been her life in the past year.

'What's the matter?' muttered Charles.

'I can't get comfortable.'

His hand reached out and stroked her shoulder. This should have helped but there she lay rigid, horrified by the twists and turns of her own conscience. She had better bury these thoughts once and for all, she told herself. She rolled over and broke the contact with Charles, he didn't notice, and then she stared out the window into the dark, cooling night. The weather was becoming bearable again. There was a moon. The comforting noises of the riverside cottage, which frightened her when Charles was late coming home, extended away into infinity. These things she must hold to: the river whirling past at the bottom of the garden, the call of a nightbird, a pallid cuckoo attempting to rise through a blunted scale, but which could never quite make it, and had to start all over again each time. The rush of flying-foxes wheeling across the face of the moon as they rose from their island in the river.

Annis Montague was at the piano in the bakingly hot, dusty and empty concert hall. It was midday, the worst posible hour for anyone, but Nellie was oblivious to the heat as she finished the last bars of a song, something soft, touching, and coolly controlled in this unlikely place.

'My dear that was ravishing,' said Mrs Montague, deeply

THE BOHEMIAN GIRL

impressed. She stared at Nellie.

'You could make your name on the stage. To think you are in a place like this, with such a voice.'

Nellie smiled. But as she smiled she thought: 'Don't say it, please don't put these things in front of me where I might me tempted to grab them all up in my arms, please, please don't.'

'My dear?'

'You're too kind but my life is here in Mackay.'

She rather hurriedly gathered up her music, her sun hat, and made ready to go.

'I will keep tickets for you, every single night,' Mrs Montague called after her.

The last performance of this strange little season was *Faust*. Everyone was here again, the Hewitts, the Blacks, the Davidsons, the Frasers, and Tom Chataway who had missed *The Bohemian Girl*. Here were Mr and Mrs Baker and their daughter Adelaide, the girl patronisingly referred to as 'Nellie's friend' though they had hardly spoken a word to each other since the night of Adelaide's humiliation. And Charles and Nellie, of course. And the rest of Mackay that was not 'Mackay'.

Charles Turner appeared on the stage; he'd been a favourite on previous nights and now after a few days had become well-known around the pubs of the town: cherry-red nose, fruity voice, a tendency towards incomprehensible sarcasm, willingness to belt out a ballad in return for a glass of rum. In brief, a rousing good sport.

But now he called for quiet.

'I would remind those of you who've come to ogle and hoot,' he said, 'that this is a serious story about a vain old philosopher, Faust, who dreams of the love of a beautiful girl. If you pay attention to your programme, those of you who can read will find the story written down.'

The rabble subsided, the show began.

And all too soon the small company was taking its bows, and it was over.

Or almost.

Annis Montague stepped forward.

'Now by way of a special treat I am going to call upon your own Mrs Armstrong to sing.'

There was a murmur of interest through the hall. Amy Davidson drew back, astonished, and caught the eye of her lady-friend, Mrs Black, who gave her head a hard little shake as if to say 'incomprehensible'.

Nellie herself could hardly believe it was happening, though it had all been arranged, in a hurried consultation, beforehand. She put away her programme and said nervously to Charles, 'A surprise for you, darling.'

There was much interest to see how Charles was taking it. He was taking it well.

Nellie made her way to the stage. She sang something that Annis Montague had sung earlier, 'The Jewel Song', and sang it with sweet freshness, and great heart. Men who had not noticed Nellie much before looked at her with kindled interest, then looked at Charles, and wondered what sort of life they led together. Feeling their eyes on him, reading their thoughts easily enough, Charles got to his feet and applauded loudly. He would show them, and her, the meaning of the word gallantry. Nellie held his eye. It was a splendid moment.

But it went on too long for Charles's comfort. The applause echoed off the simple corrugated iron walls and redoubled in volume. Nellie stepped forward and made a gesture as if to say, 'All this for me? Please, enough!'

But she didn't mean it; a kind of isolated hunger took her over, and like a seasoned performer she spread her arms wide and invited them all in, the whole audience, the whole world if it cared to come. There she was tossing caution aside in a gesture that said, 'Oh, lovely, then, if that's the way you want it, give me more, more.'

Tom Chataway turned from his seat and caught Charles's eye. His expression seemed to sum it all up for Charles: 'What now, Charlie old boy?'

The momentum continued afterwards. There was a backstage celebration with Nellie the centre of everyone's attention.

THE BOHEMIAN GIRL

Charles Turner elbowed his way over to Charles, who was slightly out of it all, clutching a glass of rum, maintaining the bemused expression that was his defence against Nellie's praise tonight.

'My word, Mr Armstrong, you must be proud of her,' beamed Charles Turner.

'Yes, I am. Very,' said Charles.

He meant what he said, but not in the way a man like Turner would understand. He meant, proud that she was his, that this thing she could do, this wonderful perfect outburst, that could be given, then put away, as it had been after the night when she'd sung on the Davidsons' verandah, was nothing compared with the love they had and the life they would make together. Certain temporary difficulties would be survived. Charles had been feeling confused, earlier, angry with a sense of being used (the surprise, for *him*?) but now he was all right, his outrage had settled. There was Nellie, rather too obviously pregnant, turning to him with a smile, holding her hands out to him at the absolute height of happiness, inviting him to join and share with her the admiration of all around. This, he was pleased and proud to do. As her husband. As the father-to-be of her child.

And later, going home in the dark, it was the same. Nellie nestled against him and they counted off the months and weeks to go before the birth.

Charles and Tom Chataway were on horseback chasing a bullock down a gully. Where the gully fell steeply away, Chataway reined back apprehensively, but Charles went charging on. Sparks flew from the hooves and there was a moment when Chataway thought he'd seen the last of Charles Armstrong; horse and rider appeared to separate. This man could fly, though. They came together again somewhere underneath. There was the sound of crashing timbers and a flash of rusty bullock-hide, and Charles and his quarry pounded away from sight. A pair of blue cattle dogs went weaving along behind.

Twenty minutes later Chataway caught up with his friend.

The bullock was yarded with the rest, all fifty of the beasts accounted for, and Charles was lying spreadeagled on the grass beside the creek. Resting. The dogs licked his hand and whined for attention.

'Nice work,' said Chataway.

Charles leaned across, filled his hat with creekwater, and poured it over the dogs. They yelped around him delightedly. Chataway filled his hat and put it on his head, water streaming down his face.

'This is the life,' he declared.

'I'd say so,' said Charles.

They looked at each other and laughed aloud at the sight they made, two New Chums doing what they liked best. And doing it well. A buyer had been found for the cattle, which were in prime condition: Chataway was full of admiration.

'You've tripled your money, Charlie.'

'All it needed was isolation, no blackleg up here, I calculated.'

'Good thinking. You make me feel like a fool. Let's pool our resources again, think what we could do; more cattle, then hey presto, we could establish a run. Inland this time. A million acres.'

Charles shook his head.

'It goes back to the bank, most of it. The rest, well, I thought a trip to Melbourne after the baby arrives.'

'Melbourne,' said Chataway, a touch scathingly. '*Who* thought?'

Charles stared at him, wondering whether to pull Chataway up short. It was his wife he was talking about, after all. He decided not to. There was no-one else he could talk to, and talk was what he needed today.

'I've thought about a run plenty of times, but deal me in and you're dealing with two, soon be three. Won't know what's hit you. I hardly know it myself to be honest. Don't know why, but an extra mouth multiplies expenses fearfully.'

'It's women,' said Chataway.

'I'll be honest with you Chataway. I don't give a fig about music. Not in the way she does.'

THE BOHEMIAN GIRL

'What about your spine?'

'What do you mean?'

'Doesn't it tingle when she sings. Gad, mine did when she went on stage with the Montagues. Must say the town buzzed for weeks afterwards, but now they say . . .'

Chataway stopped short.

'They say what?' Charles demanded.

'Oh, you know what these places are like. They say you keep her locked up.'

'The bastards. Don't they know she's about to become a mother? And hasn't been well.'

'It's just talk. Come on, old man. Mackay's a small town. They're all the same.'

Charles got to his feet and wandered around for a while, looking at the cattle, wondering when the drovers would come, tossing a stick at the dogs, then gathering kindling for a camp-fire.

'Let's boil the billy.'

'Capital,' answered Chataway.

When the tea was ready Charles suddenly said: 'Chat, I wouldn't say this to another human being. But she's changed me.'

'How's that?' asked Chataway. He knew, of course, but wanted to hear it from his friend's lips.

'I feel like a moth in a candle-flame.'

Chataway frowned. 'Fate of the moth isn't a pretty one, old boy.'

Charles blundered on. 'That night when she sang I saw it clearly. She got other moths, dozens of 'em. Coarse animals. Men. I saw them watching, and they looked at me, Chataway, and wondered how I was faring. With a voice like that it puts a woman in a different game. She doesn't look to a man for the usual things. Doesn't need him in the usual way.'

'So,' said Chataway after a long pause. 'You're in a pickle, Charlie.'

When Charles told Nellie about the cattle sale her response was somewhat blank.

'Aren't you impressed?' he wondered.

'I am of course, but what does it mean? That you're a good man with cattle, but I knew that already. I've never expressed doubt on that score, Charles, you're a splendid bushman. So don't try and manoeuvre me into an argument about it. But as you've just said, it puts no money in the bank.'

'Some.'

'All right, some but hardly any. Here I am needing new clothes, I'm dependent on the Blacks' and the Hewitts' charity for a baby carriage and whatever else they condescend to throw in our direction —'

'A fair bit, I would say —'

'And,' Nellie continued, 'I have no money to pay for my sister's passage to come and help me after the birth.'

'Hell, if your father won't cover that, he's got no heart,' grunted Charles.

'I won't take that from you, and you know it.'

'It's beginning to look to me,' said Charles, 'as if half our troubles stem from your damnable pride, and the other half from your impatience. You seem to want everything at once. But you don't help a man.'

'I can hardly move,' said Nellie, smoothing her hands down her sides. 'I feel as if I'm carrying a field of pumpkins inside me.' She sat, immobile and huge, in a wicker basket chair. Charles made an impatient gesture and looked around the room for a drink.

'You know what I mean,' he said. 'Help me, support me. It's driving me crazy. You weren't like this at the beginning. You weren't wanting things all the time.' Charles was on his knees, feeling around in the back of a cupboard for a rum bottle. The empties clinked and he had no luck. His voice took on an accusing tone. 'My "position" was good enough for you then.'

'Exactly what was your position then? It was never clear.'

'Less than now.'

'Oh.'

'Anything was good enough for you then,' Charles continued. 'This cottage, Mackay, the Davidsons. Lord, you were in love with the Davidsons.'

'Charlie, stop it.'

'What?'

'Just stop it. I need peace. Leave me alone. It isn't us talking, it's our circumstances. We mustn't do this to ourselves, it's deadly, it's poisonous. I cannot allow it to take control of me, of us, not now, not ever, please, come over here, hold my hand, ah.'

'You're all right?'

'I'm all right, I think.'

'You're not all right.'

'Yes I am. Ah . . .'

'The doctor?'

'Send for Esther, she knows.'

'I won't have . . .'

'And the doctor. Get him, but give me Esther while I wait. The silly girl has had more babies than she can count. I can't wait alone, Charlie, you know nothing about this, you poor man, do something.'

'I'm off. Don't move.'

'How could I?'

He was gone.

The following morning the sun shone in the hard, motionless way of the tropics, pushing light up and out from under every dark corner and exposing the mould and the dampness of former months to the scorching furnace-breath of day. Yet it was still only eight in the morning. How beautiful it was to her, this particular day, suffused with an astonishing outpouring of familiarity and homeliness. Charles came in and out of her room in a daze. The ladies had begun their round of calls already, bringing gifts of astonishing generosity, Mrs Black with a pearl brooch that had been in her family for many long years, Mrs Davidson with a lace shawl of Ypres that she had been keeping for a baby of hers that had never come; a sense of the world's kindness flowed through Nellie and around her, and wretched Mackay, she thought, was like paradise.

She looked down at the newborn baby in her arms, this boy.

MELBA

He had come in the middle of the night. The doctor and Esther had been in attendance. Charles had paced around outside, smoking endless cheroots. The boy was beautiful, moulded exactly in every detail to accept her love: smooth flat little face and small perfect nose, black damp hair, tight protruding belly and clenched pink-white fists that only relaxed when he was fast asleep. Her love. That alone was a miracle of unexpected wonder. Nellie had forgotten absolutely that she had begged to have the burden taken from her, that she had fought against him through unimaginable, un-withstandable pain, at two in the morning.

Charles entered bearing a cup of tea and the two regarded each other with deep affection. They kissed, and while Nellie made ready to hand over the baby Charles drew up a chair beside the bed.

Nellie handed him across.

'There, a perfect Armstrong.'

Charles was tender with his tiny charge. Nellie loved him for it.

'But Nellie, my darling, he's all you. His eyes, his mouth.'

The baby suddenly let out a piping scream and began crying, taking air in frantic gulps.

'His lungs,' laughed Charles.

Nellie took the baby from him, rearranged his shawl and put him to work sucking. A look of concentrated contentment passed over her face as she closed her eyes, and Charles was happy to ponder that look for a while. What wonderful creatures women were, to move through their various phases so adeptly. What would a man do, Charles thought, if his whole body and being were invaded by another life like this. But to a woman it was cause for all-absorbing joy. That was the thing; and Charles thought to himself, as he watched, that while their difficulties were by no means at an end, their troubles were surely over. He was absolutely certain in his heart that it was the case. From now on, there was this business of motherhood, and clearly it was a discovery for Nellie, it had taken her by storm. She was set in a new direction and he was relieved.

Nellie opened her eyes and looked at him. She smiled.

THE BOHEMIAN GIRL

'Just think Charlie, isn't it queer? Only a year ago I didn't even know you existed.'

This pulled Charles up short. He wasn't sure what she meant. There was love in her eyes but the way she said 'a year' was as if, turning her comment on its head, another year could pass and she could just as easily forget him again. This was another side of women, their damned practicality right in the middle of happy and dreamlike moments.

Now Nellie went on in this practical vein.

'I'm cabling for Annie without delay,' she said, and he saw that she was exhausted, too, as well as blissful. 'I need her with me and I don't care if you have to go to the bank for the money, Charlie, we shall meet the fare.'

'But of course.' He would agree to anything, now, with those small, dark unfocused eyes of the boy staring into his soul, somehow. 'He knows who I am,' he said with a laugh.

Nellie sank back into her pillows with a sigh of relaxation. 'Annie is so practical. She will be able to help me around the house with little George.'

'George, yes,' said Charles. It was the name they'd agreed on, but he hadn't adapted to it yet: trust Nellie to be thus far ahead of him phrasing it naturally, while he still fumbled around in his mind.

'And,' Nellie continued, 'I will be able to start practising again, Charles.'

She saw the hurt in his eyes, which he quickly veiled.

'Yes, of course.'

'Oh, Charles, I must.'

'All right. All right,' he said. He sat there a while longer, allowing the discordance between them to flatten and leak away. On this day above all others they would not fight about things. That was tacitly agreed between them. But when he could, Charles got up, bent over and kissed her, kissed George, and left the room.

'Poor man, if he only knew,' thought Nellie, 'that I don't want to hurt him, I don't want to give him pain, and I would do anything in the world to prevent it if I could, anything except one thing.'

That she had fixed on this one thing, in the midst of

everything, had surprised Nellie as much as Charles today: even shocked her. But as she fell into a weary sleep with George curled beside her, it was what she thought about: how soon she would begin her music again, and what it would mean when she did.

When Annie came she was immediately sensitive to the atmosphere of the house. There had never been a hint, in Nellie's rushed but happy letters, that anything was wrong. Annie knew, everyone knew, that there was something wrong at the root of this marriage, but she'd been rather superior about it. Money? Everyone had that problem. This marriage was wrong, she thought, in the way a mathematical equation could be wrong, but the heart had a way of defying logic. They were such strong, convincing people. She thought that Nellie and Charles would battle it out the way many people did and be glad in the end. But now that she was back in Mackay, Annie saw that her thoughts on the matter had ignored the one thing she had always known about Nellie, in the context of the family: that when she decided on something she would try and reach for it, and the mystery in it all was, not would she, but how would she break through the obstacles?

When they sat down for their first evening meal together Annie remarked:

'Charles is late.'

Nellie gave her a long-suffering look. There was something that Annie was going to have to understand, it seemed. 'Poor Annie. You were a darling to come.'

'Oh,' said Annie, 'I see. He's always late.'

'Charles is not doing well,' said Nellie. 'We spend more than he earns. It can't go on much longer.'

'You will have to explain,' said Annie.

'If you don't hold land in Mackay then you're nothing. No matter who you are.'

'Yes, I am beginning to understand now. You want me here as an ally in a fight with Charles.'

'Not in the way you think. A fight to survive, not to destroy.'

'Am I to ask Daddy for money?' asked Annie, coming

straight to the point in a fashion.

'Never,' said Nellie. She knew Annie did not share her utterly principled stand on this point. But she could bend her to her will.

'All right, I won't,' said Annie.

Annie looked around. Things in the cottage were somehow in tawdry disarray. It was a house where people came and went, where Charles came and went. It was more like the house of a woman with a bachelor brother for a boarder. That was the feel of it.

'So there's nothing but fighting,' said Annie.

'I wish you wouldn't use that word, fighting,' said Nellie.

Annie raised her eyebrows and shrugged.

'What you call fighting,' Nellie continued, 'is intimacy.' Nellie thought for a while. 'You could just as easily call it love, married love.'

Annie thought for a while.

'I'm sorry, then,' she said. 'There are some things I just don't understand.'

After the euphoria of the first few weeks Charles learnt that with a new baby in the house a man not only felt every kind of fool as women drifted past him, a bundle of one sort or another in their arms, but also was a true impediment. Not a chair, not a couch did he occupy, that wasn't instantly needed for something else. If it wasn't the kanaka girl, it was Annie. The house was too small. Annie believed that the tropics were the perfect possible incubator for every disease known to man. Not that the boy ever developed anything beyond a sniffle. The women's life kept building and growing around Charles till it filled every corner of the place, every waking and sleeping moment, what sleep there was.

So Charles developed the habit of coming home late after a few drinks. It was better that way for everyone, he argued to himself. Sometimes, when he came in, they were all asleep, and he was able to poke around in a dozy, happy fashion, making himself a pot of tea and looking in on the baby, watching him for minutes on end, sometimes, with his thumb jammed in his mouth and the perfect curve of his eyelids twitching occasionally as he breathed in a jerky, contented rhythm.

Charles' drinking companions were Tom Chataway, Jack Bellchambers, and Colin Logue, who had found other work in the district after the completion of David Mitchell's work on the mill. Not the most inspiring company, perhaps, especially from Nellie's point of view, but it was good for a man after a day's work to drink with people who knew what it meant to come away from the canefields bone tired and sick of it all.

More often lately they'd ended up like this, deep in their cups. Chataway was always the first to go under. Tonight he could barely stand, his lips moved but the words seemed addressed to someone who wasn't at the bar. The barman slid another in front of him, and that's all he could do, drain off the last, begin on the next.

Charles sang 'The Yarn of the Nancy Belle', and his mates, with level brows and chins tucked into their chests, joined in after a few lines:

A cook and a carpenter bold,
And the mate of the Nancy brig,
And a bo'sun tight, and a midshipmite,
And the crew of the captain's gig . . .

Charles tossed back his last rum and tried to focus on Chataway.

'Keep an eye on him, Jack,' he said to Bellchambers.

'He'll be sweet.'

'See you tomorrow.'

'Hoo roo, boss.'

Charles bumped his way from the bar, being greeted and farewelled by perfect strangers and those who felt they knew him well after one or two g'days over the past couple of years. This was the life of the pub, it made up for much else in the lives of everyone, and was a good thing all round, if a man knew when to call it a night.

Charles found his horse and made his way off through the

thick darkness. It was steamy tonight. Lightning flickered away to the north making a deep monotonous glow beyond the horizon. The rumble of the thunder was like wind. It growled and echoed about. The Wet would be coming early this year, it was all starting again and Charles was as empty-handed as he had ever been in his life before.

His horse found its own way home and soon Charles was mounting the front steps of the cottage with his boots in his arms. A lamp glowed on the dining table, there was a dish of cold meat and potatoes kept aside for him, and he decided to reward himself with a nightcap: he found the bottle, uncorked it with his teeth, and tipped a generous measure straight down his throat. It was claimed that a good slug of rum last thing at night warded off mosquitoes and Charles was inclined to believe it.

He wandered onto the verandah to watch for the lightning again. He was leaning against the rail thinking of nothing much when a voice said, 'Hello, Charles, aren't you going to offer me any?'

Nellie sat there in the dark.

'You gave me a fright,' said Charles.

'Please?' she held out her hand.

'Rum, are you mad?' She took the bottle from his hand and drank. It rather disgusted and frightened him to see it. He could tell it burnt her throat, but she hid her reaction, and took more. 'You'd better not let Annie see you,' he added.

'Charles I'm dying from boredom.'

The words meant nothing to him for a moment except a dull shock of pain somewhere beneath the alcohol. Then he puzzled them into shape.

'What?'

'I hate the house. I hate the Wet, and it's almost on us again. God help me, Charlie, I hate Mackay.'

So she had said it at last. He stared at her.

She stared back at him. And though she had dithered and wondered in her mind if it was true, if it would always be true, now that it was out at last it was true and nothing could change it, ever.

'I must leave this place, and soon, Charlie.'

MELBA

It released her from something. She got to her feet and moved around. She did not come close to Charles.

'You used to say it suited you here,' he said.

'I won't go through all that again. No.'

'I've worked my guts out, I've done everything you wanted.'

'You said you'd knock down the wall, enlarge the room, have people over, live the life of Riley. Impossible.'

'Is that all you want?' he laughed. 'Well, then . . .'

'No,' she cut him short.

He drained the bottle and threw the empty away into the dark. Then he thumped his chest with his fist. Such a mighty self-delivered blow it was. It was as if his heart had given a great leaping lurch and he'd needed to order it down. The worst thing was that he said nothing, he just reeled, a man who'd taken a terrific blow at last, but one that would not kill him, not him.

Nellie thought: Oh, Lord, what have I done?

She said, 'We'll talk in the morning, Charlie, when you're in a proper state of mind.' She waited for him to come at her from the dark. 'Say something, Charlie,' she added, a little frightened. She had felt his temper these many months simmering away.

She wanted to go to him, to comfort him, but that would be wrong and he might easily misunderstand what she meant. He said nothing. It was terrifying. They just stood there in the dark, listening to the night-sounds in their dinning variations.

The next day they looked at each other and could hardly believe what they saw. Charles went to the bank and came back early.

He was pale, evasive, exhausted.

'Charles, admit something, please,' she said.

'They like me here. They like us,' he said. 'I am considered charming, and you are thought to be the fourth wonder of the world.'

These were words of considerable bitterness.

'Yes, but what did the bank manager say to you, your Mr Costello.'

THE BOHEMIAN GIRL

Nellie wished she did not have to force these questions on Charles. She wished that sugar-cane were grown on the moon, that money would evaporate from the earth, that such a simple thing as she had, her gift for singing, would not burn at the back of her mind as it did, and she wished it had never become mixed up in the processes of marriage. But she did not wish it had never come about, because she had a great curiosity about where it would lead her next. This was the warm fearless star in the otherwise cold space where she travelled.

'What did Mr Costello say, Charles.'

'He said that even if a decent portion of land were to come up, the banks wouldn't listen to me.'

'So much for name and position.'

'I set no store on name and position,' said Charles.

This was a rebuke to Nellie's expectations. She saw it clearly now. He had always thought her overimpressed by a title, even when remotely situated from this youngest son of a baronet, Anglo-Irish at that. There was an element of condescension in Charles's attitude to her, and she had loved him for it, at times. But now:

'Charles.'

'Yes?'

'There is something I can do.'

They stared at each other for a long time. There was no need for explanations. What did love mean at a moment like this? It meant, here, two people turning away from each other, turning and forever turning.

'You have a profession, Charles, but no means to practise it,' said Nellie. 'You are a farmer, but cannot get land. I have a profession already.'

9
Limits of Pride

When David Mitchell reached his mid fifties he made a count of the years he had left. There were not many, he thought. He considered he'd seen many wonders in his time, not the least being the wonder of his own life, for which he prayed thanks to God. He was not driven to make visits to foreign places, such as those made by his colleagues Bosisto, Alcock and Collier. They had been to the tessellated pavements and mud springs of New Zealand, had seen where Cook was speared in the Sandwich Islands, and had taken railway journeys into the snowbound high passes of the Rocky Mountains. These men did not share Mitchell's intense pleasure in the close at hand, the domestic, the plain ordinary local dirt and rock. Recently Mitchell had expanded his business interests away from construction. There was no great joy for him in building any more. He'd seen the end of an era in the trade; there was no magnificence now, just easy answers, cheapened shortcuts. Architects did not care as they used to. The proud but simple honour of the laying of the foundation stone had become an occasion of great pomp, with brass bands and assembled politicians, where the builder was just another bystander, and a rather dusty one at that. The ordinary labourer, for whom Mitchell all his life had had an honest regard, was as often as not turned away from a workplace and a scoundrel put on in his place. There was no warmth in men. So Mitchell turned to livestock, to his farms: to his wines, his cheeses, and hams. That was where he was headed now. The great limestone quarry kept going of course, but it was the simplest of enterprises and no challenge at all to his powers of organisation. Increasingly his thoughts turned to his family, their needs for the future.

Nellie's letter telling of her return to Melbourne was greeted at Doonside with great joy and excitement. It was 'written in haste to catch the mail boat, which is building up steam as I write'. She made no mention of Charles but it was assumed he would be coming too. The boys were excited and planned things they'd do with their legendary brother-in-law. They would go sailing on the bay, and get taken on kangaroo shoots in the ranges beyond Cave Hill. They could not depend on their father for induction into these activities. They loved David Mitchell of course, and he them, fiercely, but he retained a remoteness in their lives. The boys were wilder now than they used to be, they had the colonial spirit. He did not understand that completely. Kangaroo Charlie might.

In the following weeks more letters came. The picture changed rather. Nellie and Annie would be returning alone, while Charles remained in Mackay. This disappointed the boys bitterly, and led to David Mitchell wondering what it was all about. Underneath his dauntless Scottish manner there was still much uncertainty and a little apprehension where Nellie was concerned. Having her married was one thing, coping with his imagination was another. The matter was a little complicated for a man of fine conscience, and it came to bother David Mitchell in the midnight hours, when he had difficuty sleeping, when he sorely missed the kind reliable presence of Isabella. He knew in his own mind that nothing really had been resolved when Nellie married Charles Armstrong. It had rid Nellie of her idea of the stage, and that was a satisfaction. He owed Charles something for that, though it was distasteful to Mitchell to be caught putting it to himself in such terms. Charles was a charming drifter and despite his constantly renewed hopes was never going to amount to much in Mackay. It all came back to Mitchell himself, his role in a matter he'd thought himself out of, for he had little doubt that when Nellie arrived in Melbourne she would, after a few days' settling in, approach him with a particular troubled question. She would want to know if he could find a position for Charles in one of his many enterprises. She would ask if Charlie could, perhaps, be taken on as manager at his Camperdown property, where he raised fine wool merino sheep on many thousands of acres. Mitchell heard Nellie rehearsing the arguments in his mind: Charles the outdoorsman, the man who was good with men, as Mitchell himself had seen with his own eyes at the mill site in Mackay. Mitchell would have to decide, in the face of such pleas from his daughter, how he would respond. There were a number of possible answers coming readily to mind, but all of them, he was anguished to find, as he ran them over in his head, involved a refusal.

He would have no hangers-on in his household.

So it was that when Nellie and Annie at last arrived back in Melbourne, the father they saw waiting for them had a rather drawn and haunted look. It was nerves, a condition he despised and had never suffered from before. They kissed him and fussed over him, showing a very tender concern for his health. This troubled his conscience, as his health had never been better. There was no alternative but to get the matter done and over with. Yet he waited. He waited until Nellie was ready.

But Nellie was not ready for anything yet. The days passed pleasantly, and baby George took so much settling in. There would have to be a talk with her father soon, she knew it. But for the moment Nellie was just relieved to be here at Doonside, among all the old familiar reminders of her happy past. In the glittering Melbourne autumn everything seemed pared away, cut clean. This was a relief. It was so good to feel the solidity of a proper world. She could hardly believe that she had lived two years of her life in a place where so much decayed and melted away in people's lives, where the spirit decayed too. Rotted. Mackay.

LIMITS OF PRIDE

Sailing south, Nellie had reflected that she had much to recover from. She walked the decks with Annie and they talked about nothing much, just enjoyed each other's company and absorbed themselves in the care of the baby. Mackay sank below the horizon but still disturbed her. There had been the stilted and over-formal farewell at the Davidsons and another at the home of a friend Nellie had made in the last weeks, a kindly woman, Mrs Rawson. Only Mrs Rawson had offered comfort and hope. In the eyes of the rest, from the Davidsons and the Blacks down to women who hardly knew her at all, who passed her in the street with a frigid glare, she was regarded as a traitor. It was unbelievable. Nellie had not realised the effect she had on people. She thought it was only her and Charles, their struggle, their attempts to make a life together and have it come out whole, which counted, which was what everyone wanted from life surely. It seemed when a new arrival came to Mackay there was a settling in period, when the 'old hands' circled about with a touch of wonder in their eyes, and waited for a declaration of belonging, a gesture that would show that they themselves were right in resigning their lives to this particular dot on the map. Even notables like Amy Davidson had this view, deep down. Nellie had never made the gesture. When it became clear that she would be going, it was an insult. It was as if Nellie were saying to them: 'Get on with your contemptible little lives, I can't stand it myself, it's good enough for you, but Lord, look at yourselves.'

Simultaneously, she was involved in the deepest and most desperate conflict with Charles. It was hard and destructive. She had a determination that her love would survive it, but how this could be she sometimes doubted. It seemed that her determination alone would make this work, this love, this marriage; she must never let go, she must hold on to her idea of Charles, and dear God, she thought to herself at times during those last days, he could rouse such joy and tenderness in her with nothing more than his sideways, beguiling smile . . . when he smiled.

A few swift, hard-etched moments remained in her memory.

The first was the awful silence that filled the house after she'd declared that she had a profession and had the means to practise it.

In that silence, Nellie had written to Signor Cecchi. Her pen ran ahead of what had actually been agreed with Charles. 'We have both come to the conclusion,' she wrote, 'that it is no use letting my voice go to waste up here for the pianos are all so bad that it is impossible to sing to them. So you will understand that I am anxious to leave Queensland as soon as possible.'

Then she began discussing details of her plans with Charles. She was to resume training with Signor Cecchi, she said, and after a short interval he would help her find concert engagements. The money would be good, enough to keep all three of them comfortably, if necessary, and it would get better. Nellie reminded Charles of how the people in Mackay had reacted on the few occasions when she'd sung in public. Something remarkable had happened. And these were not sophisticated music lovers, they were ordinary people and there were thousands of them in this country, who would pay money for something good.

Charles was sarcastic.

'You could put me on a percentage,' he said. 'You'd need someone to beat 'em off at the stage door. Kangaroo Charlie would be just your boy.'

There was the constant accompaniment of the rum bottle being emptied and another being opened, during these intense, late-night debates, with Annie straining her ears through the single-plank walls to get an idea of what was going on.

Then Nellie grew tired of discretion. She spoke with a hard, clear voice to cut through the fumes of drink Charles had rising around himself.

'I will go first and you can follow when the arrangements are in order.'

Charles tried some hard, dirty gibes, she supposed of the sort that were circulating in the town, and even, perhaps, among the 'nice' people at the Davidsons.

Like, 'You know what they say about "singers"?'

LIMITS OF PRIDE

'I was a singer when you married me,' Nellie shot back.

His words hurt, how they hurt, for she knew that during the early days of her love for Charles the whole rest of the world had been dimmed from her vision entirely. In her grief for the death of her mother, and her anguish at the death of Vere, she had wanted to replace every particle of her old life with something brilliant and new. And Charles had supplied that need. Now she was telling him that he was needed no longer.

It wasn't as vicious as that, but the burden of what Charles felt could, she knew, be expressed in those words, and with a certain amount of justice. It made her weep.

'I won't come,' he said after a few days of brooding. 'I'll come when I'm ready . . . If I'm ready.'

This was something for him to admit. She held her tongue for once. She wondered at the way men stayed boys always, whereas women were able to go on, enlarging their way into life, into the interesting paths of adulthood, without aggressive self-involvement. It was why men sometimes said women had no shame. It was true for her, anyway. It was a little sad, too, for she in that part of herself that Charlie always appealed to wanted idleness and aimlessness and the drifting, dreaming life as much as he did . . . Where they would go riding and shooting together in some up-country paradise full of wild duck and wallabies.

'You won't be sent for?' she heard herself reply. 'I'd never stoop to sending for you.'

'And I wouldn't come.'

'Then we are equal.'

She'd written to Signor Cecchi again and the words were cool and calm with all their heat underneath:

'Now to business. My husband is quite agreeable for me to adopt music as a profession. Could you not form a small company and let us go touring through the Colonies, for of course I would like to study for the opera, but would have to be earning money at the same time . . .'

Charles had grabbed this letter from her hands and read it with his dark, disappointed eyes.

'This letter, by Christ, it's written by someone on the march.'

He hurled it back at her, she smoothed it over, she folded and sealed it away.

In another room of the house Annie had sat cradling the sleeping George in her arms and keeping her thoughts to herself.

Nellie went through to her dressing table. She started combing her hair, to calm herself. Charles entered the room.

'A man's pride has its limits,' he said.

Nellie held her head.

'Give me peace, Charlie.'

'One day . . .' said Charles intensely.

There was a murderous undertone to the words. The unspoken threat was understood: 'One day he would kill her . . .'

'I invite you to try,' she replied, arching her neck.

There was a sexual nuance in the air. Nellie did not flinch when he crossed the room and stood over her. She was half-off the stool. For a second he might really have been going to do it. They grappled silently, sinuously, like snakes. They moved across to the bed, where Nellie sank and he loomed. She ploughed her fingers up through his dark stubble. They clenched eye to eye.

'It's not goodbye, Charlie.'

The words came back to her now, as she sat alone in the parlour at Doonside waiting for her father to come in.

She could not keep still. Her thoughts raced. She had lost the old sense of being swept along by events. Now she was making things happen herself and it was a little frightening. Her mind went back over the previous couple of hours, then forward to the moment when her father would enter the room and demand to know what was happening in her life. How would she answer him?

She had just been to see Signor Cecchi, and the visit had left her feeling amazed.

Pietro Cecchi had missed her, he wanted her as a pupil again, he would do anything for her, he said. His excitement and devotion brought back all the old feelings of the past—

the joy of their lessons together, the forgetfulness that swept over her in the pursuit of his most extreme demands. She still needed lessons of course, at close intervals and increased intensity, 'Also at a higher fee,' Miss Dawson had sharply reminded him. But yes, there would be concerts, there need be no delay. The Ballarat Liedertafel would be pleased to put her on its programme, and an opening awaited her in the Kowalski concert season, not to mention other interesting prospects from as far afield as Sydney and Adelaide. Mrs Annis Montague had spoken on her behalf to various important managers . . . *eccètera, eccètera*. So there.

'It is all too wonderful, *Signore*.'

Nellie kissed her teacher on the cheek, while Miss Dawson coldly smiled.

After this outpouring of enthusiasm, there remained the appraisal of Nellie herself. The intimate moment alone in the music room where he wanted everything the way it had been in the past, and he wanted more, it seemed.

He ushered Miss Dawson from the room and closed the door.

'Sit on the couch, *cara mia*.'

'I have little time. My father is expecting me at home.'

He took her hand and said, 'Marriage has not hurt you, Mrs Armstrong.'

'Really?'

'Not at all, not at all,' he held her eye, his gaze wandering over her in a heavy, magnetic fashion. She felt uncomfortable with this side of the man as always. But it roused no panic in her as before, just discomfort; she pitied him as a man, more than anything. His lips parted in anticipation of something he would never have, he smiled and showed his uneven, discoloured teeth. He moved a little closer to her on the couch. 'And what of your husband, what is the story there?'

So that was it.

There was not a sound from the other room. Nellie pictured Miss Dawson down on her knees, watching through the keyhole, her ears straining.

'My husband is devoted to me, *Maestro*,' she said. 'And I to him.'

MELBA

Now it remained for Nellie to convey her plans to her father. She waited in the parlour, watching the clock move from four to four-thirty, and told herself that the nervousness she felt was inappropriate. What had she to fear from her own father? He loved her, it was his love she would appeal to now. She went to the piano and lifted the lid. She thought how charming it would be if he entered to find her playing, how it would soothe him. But she wanted no falsity in the interview either. So she turned from the piano and looked around the parlour, which had seen so much joy and sadness. All the same objects were here, the golden spinning clock, the dark painting of the stag at bay, the tapestry screen that the younger children always hid behind when they were wanted. All sorts of wild thoughts ran through Nellie's mind as she heard the crunch of her father's footsteps coming along the side path, things she might say: he'd always encouraged her to think highly of herself, to aim for the best, and that, in her darkest moments, she had always known she could depend on him, on his love and great hopes for her. If the worst happened, and she found herself struck dumb, she would ring for Aunt Lizzie and get her to argue on her behalf. Over the past couple of days Aunt Lizzie had been so warm and sympathetic, listening to Nellie's intimate outpourings of hope with all the intensity of the mother that Nellie missed all over again, now that she was back at Doonside with its sad reminders.

'No,' she suddenly thought. 'None of this is any good.'

She heard doors opening and his footsteps in the hall, and she panicked in her mind. She saw herself from his point of view. She was a girl who had married at her own insistence, from a love that was greater than anything she had ever known, and now, barely two years later, as a woman, as a mother, had left her husband to fend for himself, used him up, people would say, and had come south to seek her fortune. There was nothing she could think of to defend herself in the matter, to counteract this impression of calculation. The ease and assurance she had with her teacher was no good here. She was breathless with panic, and here he was.

David Mitchell entered the room and one look at his face

LIMITS OF PRIDE

told her everything. He placed a folder of blueprints on the parlour table, jammed his thumbs in his waistcoat pockets and without niceties cleared his throat and began.

'I've kept my silence, but I can no longer do so.'

'I can explain, Daddy.'

'Don't try,' he wheeled on her, grey with anger. 'I've learned from your Aunt Lizzie what it's all about, and I'm more ashamed than I thought I'd ever be in my life. You talked me into consenting to a marriage, into which you rushed without sufficient thought, on the basis that a life in Mackay was what you wanted; that you had given up any thought of music as a profession. You have gone back on your word.'

This was a terrible accusation for David Mitchell to make. There was no greater sin in his book than dishonour, and here he was, accusing his daughter with pitiless accuracy.

'To all intents and purposes,' he continued, 'you have left your husband, you have abandoned your life in the north. You expect my grandson shall be more the responsibility of your Aunt Lizzie than his own mother. I am only grateful your mother is not alive to see what you are doing to your life, to us all.'

'Mother always believed in me,' said Nellie with dread in her heart.

'Your mother never believed you should make a public spectacle of yourself.'

Blackness passed before Nellie's eyes. She gripped the arm of her chair to steady herself. She could barely stay conscious through this onslaught from the man she loved and respected so much. Every word he spoke was the truth.

'I am ashamed,' he hammered away, 'sore ashamed.'

'Daddy . . .'

He wouldn't let her speak, though she only wanted to say 'Give me air, open the window, a glass of water, please, anything, a respite to this heavy weight you are packing around me, this gravestone of morality and good sense, passion and reputation which you my own father are burying me beneath, have pity!'

'Here are the rules by which I will keep you in my house,'

he stated. 'They are simple old time rules. You'll not go out except with Aunt Lizzie as chaperone. You'll be home by dinnertime in the evening unless Cecchi gets you an engagement. In which case you'll be having no supper parties and the like. You'll not speak to men.'

'That will be impossible, Daddy.'

'You know what I mean.'

There was light coming back into Nellie's world now. It was a bleak, unhappy light, but events took on shape and the days opened up a little way ahead.

'I'll not ask,' continued Mitchell, 'where a man like Charles Armstrong fits into all this, because I well know it. He is being dangled on a string. And no money, not a penny from me, understand? Not a penny. What you spend, you must make yourself. If Cecchi wants money, he can wait. Otherwise, no lessons.'

Nellie waited for him to continue, but that was all.

'Leave me alone now,' he said.

She went. In the hall she passed Aunt Lizzie, who grabbed her hand and said imploringly: 'I had to tell him.'

'It was best,' said Nellie, and kissed her.

Upstairs Annie and Belle were looking after George.

'He's so beautiful I could eat him up,' enthused Belle.

'What happened?' asked Annie breathlessly.

Nellie took George in her arms. She told her sisters the best part of what her father had said, the permissions and the limitations. The inner turmoil she kept to herself. She was good at that now, she discovered. She thought she might cry, but no tears came — the confrontation had gone beyond tears to a dry and desert-like place where she hardly recognised herself, but still knew it was her. She had faced several extremes in herself lately and would be stronger now. Mackay had toughened her as people would say it had. From this cold dry perspective she could look back, and know she could come this far again if she had to.

She smiled at her sisters.

In the telling she placed the emphasis on Charles, on what it would mean to Charles to have her giving concerts. And

LIMITS OF PRIDE

that was the truth of it, she felt now. She then handed George back to Belle, and in the interval before the dinner gong she wrote to Charles. Bent over the notepaper she found herself pouring out her heart to him, for she missed him dreadfully and wanted him with her as soon as he could come.

Dinner that night was a muted affair. But at the end, David Mitchell went to the decanter on the sideboard and poured himself a malt whisky. He opened the cigar box and selected a good cigar. Through a cloud of smoke he then turned to Nellie and raised his eyebrows. For a moment she was puzzled as to his meaning. Then she understood.

Nellie went to the piano. Belle played while Annie turned the pages, and the lamplight circled them around as often before, as Nellie sang the gentle Scottish airs that her father loved so much.

10

Gold

One day Miss Dawson followed Nellie down the stairs after a lesson and spoke to her in the street.

'Pardon me, Mrs Armstrong but there's something I have to say. You Mitchells have always paid promptly before, but it's been weeks now, and you have not paid.'

Nellie hated the coarseness in the phrase 'you Mitchells'. It located Miss Dawson so exactly.

'I have no money, Miss Dawson,' she said. 'I am waiting for concert earnings.'

'You speak as if there is an agreement,' sniffed Miss Dawson.

'There is between artists,' said Nellie.

Miss Dawson fumed. 'What are you talking about. The *Maestro* must eat, too.'

'Ask him if you like. Come on, we'll go back.'

'No, no,' protested Miss Dawson. But Nellie grabbed her arm and went racing back up the stairs. She burst into the dining room; there was Cecchi, coat off, leaning over a mirror, working at his teeth with a toothpick.

Miss Dawson explained the matter to him.

He threw his arms wide, not caring a fig for the money. 'What was an artist, a money-grubber?'

'There,' said Nellie.

'This I cannot believe,' said Miss Dawson. Peevishly, she shuddered. She gazed at her adored Cecchi with eyes of smouldering coal. 'You know I handle the money side of things, *Maestro*.'

'And so you must,' Signor Cecchi put an arm around her thin shoulders.

Nellie stood at the door and announced grandly back into the room:

'When I make my success, I will be happy to pay three times over what I owe,' she declared.

In the chilly dressing room of a Melbourne concert hall Nellie made final adjustments to her hair while Belle worked on the hooks at the back of her dress. The light was poor and the mirror discoloured. Aunt Lizzie stood near the door, impatient to go into the hall.

'There,' said Belle when Nellie was ready. 'Don't look like that.'

'Like what? I can't see myself.'

'Dissatisfied.'

'They haven't heard me yet.'

There came the sound of applause from the body of the hall, then a tenor voice with a drowsy choral accompaniment.

'You're next,' said Belle.

'I am going now,' said Aunt Lizzie, darting off.

Nellie and Belle looked at each other. 'I think you look astonishing, beautiful. If only Charles could see you now,' said Belle.

'How I love you,' said Nellie, standing, holding herself carefully, her skirts rustling. She kissed Belle on the cheek.

There was a knock at the door, and Signor Cecchi entered. He carried a single rose. 'This is the beginning, the true beginning,' he enthused. Belle was amazed; she covered her mouth and smiled. He bowed, clicked his heels, kissed his fingertips and handed Nellie the flower.

'Dear Signor Cecchi,' said Nellie, offering her hand, which he kissed with a look of shy, devoted anxiety. Then he backed from the room.

MELBA

He'd hardly gone when another knock came.

'Back for more?' said Belle with a nervous giggle. She opened the door. A delivery boy poked his head around.

'Flowers for Mrs Nellie Armstrong,' he said.

'They aren't real,' said Belle, looking over the boy's shoulder. She drew him into the room ahead of an absurdly huge heart made from satin roses.

Nellie stifled a hope: 'Charles?'

Belle looked at the card.

'Crikey Moses,' she said. 'They're from a Mr Sydney Meredith. Syd. What's he doing wasting his money on something like this?'

An attendant came and led Nellie away.

A few minutes later her voice was soaring out into the hall with the piece she had rehearsed with Signor Cecchi, the '*Ombra Leggiera*' from Meyerbeer's *Dinorah*.

At the back of the hall stood Syd Meredith looking at the faces around him, at their intent, listening poses of concentration. He wanted to tap someone on the shoulder and say, 'I knew her once.' Then he looked back at Nellie, so still and remote and the voice piercing like an arrow straight to him, and he thought to himself, 'I still know her. She hasn't changed.'

Aunt Lizzie sat nearby on a chair that had been reserved for her late entrance. David Mitchell with Annie and the younger children were near the front of the hall. Mitchell had made it clear: he would come to her concerts when he could, for he would not be seen to disapprove of his daughter in public. This was not a lessening of his disapproval. No-one must think that. It was just that he drew the line at unacceptable behaviour in himself.

Nellie, up on the stage, had begun with the idea of singing for her father alone; there he sat with his shoulders squared and head up in the fourth row of chairs. She was bent on achieving a reconciliation of the kind only art could provide: nothing else would work, it seemed. But when the accompanist began she attended to the matter of the music wholly, and forgot the rest.

GOLD

At the end of her item a concert-goer in the last row got to his feet and applauded more noisily than the rest. David Mitchell turned and shaded his eyes to see who it was. Aunt Lizzie saw who, all right, before Syd Meredith dived to the floor and made a pretence of scrabbling around for his programme, thinking what a damned fool he was to show himself like that.

Nellie came on again after the interval to sing 'When the Heart is Young', and this same person, Syd, felt she wasn't being greeted with enough enthusiasm. 'By now they ought to be naming her outright favourite,' he declared to himself. He was about to get to his feet again and show them how, when Aunt Lizzie's eyes bored straight into him, and he glanced quickly away.

Afterwards in the dressing room Belle helped her to change.

'They loved you, Nell.'

'Yes, they seemed to well enough.'

'You know they did. You're drunk and dizzy with it all,' said Belle. She folded Nellie's gown over her arm. 'I'll wait outside with Daddy and Aunt Lizzie.'

When she was gone, Nellie tried to find herself in the discoloured mirror. She was hardly there at all, and that was how she felt. Drunk and dizzy? No. Her heart had beaten wildly as she'd come on, and she had loved the deep, rising applause as she'd stepped into the aura of the footlights. But it had been a mistake to think that some new, splendid revelation would come from the simple fact of something she might call her first 'true' concert. This was work she had embarked on now. Her name had been in rather small type on the programme. The people had come to hear others. Even while appearing to concentrate on her songs, the audience had thought of what was coming next, or who they were sitting beside, or their clothes, or footwear, or, indeed, whether they should be there at all. When everything was over people had folded their programmes, yawned and smiled, and drifted away, their lives unchanged. Nobody stamped their feet and shouted her name.

As Nellie recovered from these thoughts, someone slid into

the room behind her. It was Syd. She almost knocked over her chair in surprise.

Syd was fancifully dressed as his own rather flashy idea of a gentleman, and he grinned, holding out his hand to be shaken.

'Very pretty,' he said. 'Marriage hasn't hurt you, Nell.'

'Who let you in?' said Nellie breathlessly.

'Money buys everything, I've found,' said Syd.

'If my husband were here he'd break your skull,' declared Nellie.

'Well, he ain't, so he won't,' Syd replied, leaning on the wall and smiling at Nellie. 'He's two thousand miles to the north, growin' cane. Ain't that the story?'

He then launched himself across the room and tried to kiss her. It was so unexpected, ludicrous, and clumsy that she laughed and could hardly stop.

'Yer old self!' said Syd admiringly.

She was able to push him away easily enough. She gathered up the rest of her things and defended herself with them. She had no need to, really. Syd now sprawled in a chair and lit a cigar.

'I thought you were going shearing in the Riverina,' said Nellie, standing near the door ready to make her escape.

'I was. But I did some fossicking with a mate, up Bendigo way. I got lucky, Nell. I found a nugget as big as a melon. Here's a chip off it,' Syd concluded, reaching into a pocket and withdrawing something between his fingertips.

'*Gold*,' he breathed, holding it out to her.

But Nellie was already halfway from the room, clutching her carry-all, her sheet music, leaving the heart of flowers and the chip of gold for Syd to contemplate.

Syd thought about things for a few minutes, then he took a card from his wallet and placed it prominently among the satin flowers. It was a specially printed calling card, with curlicues of the finest edging and his address embellished upon it.

It was hard for Nellie to sleep that night. George kept her awake for a while, then the sounds of the house, so familiar, so strange, as Aunt Lizzie, and then her father made their way to bed. There was no comfort in that passage through the house any more, as there had been once. The night-sounds of Melbourne, the acrid smoke-filled air, were so strange. Nellie longed for the old comfort of the place, the blessed oblivion that had for long years been summed-up for her in the Doonside she remembered. It frightened her to think she no longer belonged here in her heart. The world was a much larger place for her now, for she had seen among the Davidsons, at least at the beginning, intimations of a different, larger life than was understood in Australia. She craved the company of Charles. She longed for his touch, his abrupt, searching kisses. How differently men looked at her now, including Signor Cecchi, and then Syd. She smiled to think of Syd. Her thoughts ran on. No wonder her father was ashamed, for she was ashamed herself when she thought of the explanations that must be being bandied about, among men, as to why this pretty young wife had come back to Melbourne alone. But there was no help for it, she would have to live through much else until her singing burst forth as it had that day in Mackay, on the Davidsons' verandah, to correct many a point of view.

David Mitchell was at the breakfast table eating his porridge when Aunt Lizzie entered.

'The morning papers, David. You'll notice they mention your daughter's name.' She placed them at the side of his plate, all turned back to the appropriate place.

'Oh, do they, indeed?' murmured Mitchell, looking critically at his porridge. He waited till Aunt Lizzie was gone completely from the room.

Then his apparent indifference changed to intense fascination. He snapped on a pair of reading glasses. He devoured the notices. His lips moved as they read, cracking each word and phrase for its vital marrow. In the notices little was said about her, beyond the niceties due to someone making a professional debut. But the name had its own resonance: Mrs Nellie Armstrong.

Then he sat back from the table. He pushed the papers aside

when he heard Lizzie's footsteps returning. 'It matters little to me what the papers say,' he told himself.

'Well, then, aren't you proud?' Lizzie asked as she bustled in.

'You know, Lizzie, I hate that word "professional" used in association with a woman.'

'You demanded that she earn her way, David. It's on your shoulders, I should say.'

'I just hate it, that's all I mean.'

'Och, well,' shrugged Aunt Lizzie as she cleared the table.

As she left the room he called her back. 'Tell her to be ready for me when I come home tonight.'

'What is it now?' said Lizzie.

'I'll give her a few tips. Business tips,' said Mitchell. There was no point in having a botch made of it, he thought. Not where his pride was concerned.

'Ooh,' smiled Aunt Lizzie.

He cleared his throat. There was more he wanted to say.

'Are you guiding her, as I wanted?' He meant watching her, spying on her, but lacked the nerve to say it.

'Don't you trust me, David?'

'That's not what I mean, and you know it,' said the man self-righteously awkward.

'Then there's no further point to this conversation,' snapped Lizzie, with rather a bad conscience over duties that required her to spy on her very own sister's child. Anyway she hardly told David anything, the man could make such a panic from nothing. What would he do if she told him about Syd, for example? He would have Syd horsewhipped, or worse, just for being sentimental.

There followed many months of train travel, coach travel, and despairing familiarity with the shortcomings of 'decent' hotels. Aunt Lizzie went everywhere with Nellie, and sometimes Annie, or Belle, came along too. She was well-liked by concert-goers, some were very favourably inclined to her, and said great things, and were there at her concerts regularly to cheer and give support. They were not many, though. A newspaper reporter named her 'The Australian Nightingale', but mostly the young Mrs Armstrong was valued, as much by the management as by concert-goers, for the novelty of her high notes and her ability to appear when required, no matter the difficulties.

She discovered in herself the gift of suspending her emotions, This came from necessity. Charles was an appalling letter writer and nothing changed in the north anyway. Men who called at her rooms, or dared even to send notes to Doonside, met with a blank response. She started thinking of Charles as a particle in suspension, the application of 'news' (this meant money) would bring him to life. She saw in her mind a kanaka servant picking up after him only half the time, and had a vision of Tom Chataway draped on a chair nearby, passing the rum bottle across, while the two of them discussed the perfidy of women.

Her father had given her an outline of an accounting system that she used to organise her money, and she was astonished after the deduction of rail-car fares, coach tickets, hotel rooms, hire of carriages and the like, that hardly a penny was left from the money she earned. A fixed percentage of course was put away for the future. She would hand that across to Charles, and only to Charles, in due course. For the rest, she became accustomed to thinking of herself as rather poor.

When she turned to her music, there was only the music. When preparing a new and difficult item she kept an idea of the composer in the back of her mind, what he wanted, and there she honoured him. It was absorbing work and she loved it. She followed the exercise regime provided by Signor Cecchi, she found herself capable of things she had once believed beyond her, and in her mind thanked Signor Cecchi for that, but often found herself engaged elsewhere at the time arranged for her lessons. Then she would scribble a note reminding him, and Miss Dawson, that she would pay for these cancelled hours of course at a later date.

Nellie repeated to Aunt Lizzie her notion of so much of it being work and nothing but work, where she must will herself from effort to effort, and so little of it art in the pure sense, as people saw it on the concert stage, and Aunt Lizzie smiled and said that if it was work as others knew it, then it must be likened to the polishing of pearls. They smiled at each other often and achieved a perfect understanding about everything.

When Nellie returned from Sydney, Ballarat, or wherever, the younger members of the family hardly existed for her; she had become a remote figure for them during her time in Mackay, and now her harried preoccupied air around the house, interrupted by an excess of sudden hugging and kissing, was accepted as part of Doonside. During this time, Dora and Ernie sometimes found themselves thinking of George as a little brother: he was always in the care of Belle, or in the arms of Margaret, the maid. They played with him a lot. Even when Nellie was at home she seemed to forget about him for hours at a time, and then he would come in for his share of suffocating hugs and kisses. When she chided herself for this, she thought of Charles, who was at the moment no sort of father at all. In her letters urging him to come south, she used George as an enticement, because she knew he loved the boy.

Sleep came easily to her now, for she was often physically exhausted. It was only in the mornings, when she woke with her mind filled with thoughts of the day ahead, that she quailed a little, wondering if this was to be her life from now on and forever. Then she would know a touch of despair.

Nellie did not know it, but Charles was close to surrender.

Mackay which had meant so much at the beginning was as empty as a hollow tin can, in which he rattled around without much enthusiasm. Nellie was right on several points — he missed baby George, he drank too much, the cottage was in a mess and he didn't care: she was blind to the idea, though, that he might be missing her more than anything. Miss her he did, except he couldn't put it into words, and if he did, if he wrote it, it would give her too much edge, too great an advantage over him. He loved her, he desired her, the idea of her drove him to distraction, but it was always the Nellie who had come to him at the first, so open-armed and delightfully his, that he thought about in his anguish. She was the one he wanted over and over. But she would not be that person ever again, so she said. He recognised this and it was part of the long-distance battle raging between them. She wrote, he failed to answer. He wrote, and her reply came after a one or two mail-boat delay. Or else letters would come in the wrong order, and then they were even more like futile shouted arguments into the nothingness of non-existent conversation, they were so chopped-off from everything that mattered.

And what mattered? That they should be together again, in each other's arms. But he would not make the move. No, he thought he would go to seed here, as so many did in the tropics, before doing that. He discovered the pride at the heart of dissolution, the stubbornness to be met in the pebbly glass at the bottom of an emptied bottle. He forgot his cares in another bout of his favourite dog-eared reading matter, *Mr Sponge's Sporting Tour*.

One day Chataway rode over to the cottage in a state of high excitement. 'The hundred acres you were after,' he called as he came in. 'Davidson's very definite about it. He's changed his mind again, very much in your favour.'

'Where'd you hear this?'

'At the solicitors. He's instructed them to draw up the papers. They'll spring it on you as a surprise. Amy's idea I suppose. They all feel so damned sorry for you, Charlie.'

'Good on them.'

'Oh, don't be like that. It's a choice plot.'

'Take it, old man. It's what you want.'

'He's doing it for you. People here don't like to see what's happening.'

'Don't they indeed. There's a bottle inside, Chataway. Be a good fellow and crack it with me, will you?'

Charles felt caught between two kinds of charity. How could this have happened to him, a man of prideful independence, who'd driven cattle overland, and rounded the Horn in the teeth of hell's own gale, and come through laughing? God's damnation on the complications of existence. Sometimes, when all else was driven from his mind, it was in him to go to her without delay, to throw himself at her feet, to be nothing to himself, to be everything to her. To give his life over in the service of another. That was when his mind went blank with lack of action.

Chataway appeared with the bottle and Charles took a long great pull at it. In a few moments he felt much better. He wiped his lips with the back of his hand.

He looked across at Chataway.

'They're calling her "The Australian Nightingale". In the past few months she's made more money than I've made in a year . . .'

'How can I say this?' mumbled Chataway. 'Get the money from her, old boy.'

'You don't understand a damned thing, do you Chataway.'

Chataway shrugged.

'Don't I? S'pose not.' He looked across at his friend.

He didn't like the look Charles wore these days, rather the lost-soul-of-the-dog sort of look, with a slight gleam of hope in the eye. All he needed now was the right sort of whistle, and he'd be off, tail wagging pitifully.

David Mitchell hid it from others, but in many ways this had been the worst year of his life.

He thought that the irregular, concert-giving life that had begun for his eldest daughter would never end. The money was fair and would get better, no doubt, but there was a circularity to it all. The same names were on the programmes and the same faces at the concerts. He could see that she was not absolutely happy in it. Little George fretted for her. The boy hardly knew what it was to have a father.

But still Mitchell held back from suggesting work for Charles on one of his farms. He would not do that to Charles Armstrong, not yet. Or to himself. He would wait a bit longer and see what it was Nellie would do to him, or 'with' him was a better choice of word, perhaps. It could only get worse.

The muddle in it all was that Mitchell knew, with a conviction that he had never felt so keenly before, that Nellie loved Charles; although he'd never understand either of them. That pained him most of all, for he was not a man accustomed to think of love as an unhappy emotion. Far from it.

Not a day passed without someone approaching Mitchell and congratulating him on the success of his daughter. But each word of praise emphasised for Mitchell a private sense of failure and the fact that no solution was in sight.

Until, one day, David Mitchell found himself nominated a Commissioner of the great Colonial Exhibition being planned. It meant he would go to London and play a part in the arranging and building of the Colony of Victoria displays. An array of builders, artists and decorators were being gathered not just from the other Australian colonies, but from New Zealand, Canada, South Africa and India. It would be a great challenge to outshine them all. The Governor sent for Mitchell and asked him if he would do the job, if he'd play his part in displaying to the people of the Mother Country what Victoria had. Mitchell fairly quaked with assent. He met the Governor in the eye. He swore that the 'Victorian Court' would be the most splendid of all.

That afternoon, immediately on arriving home at Doonside, Mitchell called for Nellie. The short carriage ride from Government House had been time enough for him to formulate his plans. They were clear-cut, simple, and unassailable by the time Nellie entered the parlour, somewhat mystified by the look of repressed excitement on her father's features.

'What is it, Daddy?'

'Sit down, lass.'

Then he began. 'As you know, I've been a member of the Colonial Exhibition Committee for quite a while now. Well, the thing is going ahead at a rapid rate and the Governor has appointed his Commissioners. I'm to be one. I'll be going to England in a month or so. You're coming with me.'

'Daddy!'

'I am taking you and my grandson with me if your husband consents, and I have little doubt that Charles will come too. There seems nothing to hold him in Mackay. It's always been a deuce of a blow to his pride to think of coming to Melbourne. His own country is a different matter. I suggest you wire him immediately. Why are you looking so pale, what is it?'

'I'm not ready.'

'Not ready for what, what are you talking about?'

Nellie thought rapidly. There would be letters to write and introductions to be made before she could think of making a start over there. But then the thought flooded her, to be able to make a start over there, and so soon. It might just be.

'What do you mean?' Mitchell insisted. 'Speak up.'

'I have more concerts to give. There's an agreement. Everything is arranged with Mr Musgrove.'

'Complete your concerts, then. And that's that. I'll not have an agreement broken on my behalf. Then we shall sail. I want Annie and Belle to come along too. It will be a great chance for them.'

'A great chance for them to find decent husbands in the old country,' Mitchell thought to himself, 'instead of the rag-tag collection of black sheep and rum-soaked aristocrats we've met with over on this side.'

11

Goodbye, Kangaroo Charlie

Not long before Charles left Mackay he went on a last ride into the forest with Tom Chataway. They came to the clearing overlooking the deep view where Charles and Nellie had picnicked.

'Here's where I spent one of the happiest days of my life,' said Charles.

'There'll be plenty more,' Chataway replied.

'It's a funny thing,' said Charles. 'A man marries to simplify things. But nothing gets simpler.'

Chataway and Armstrong stood with their hands on their hips overlooking the great blue splendour of the valley, with scimitar-blades of multi-coloured parrots dashing past, with the sound of falling water somewhere behind them in the forest, and away below, the magnificent undisturbed stillness of a wedge-tailed eagle riding the air currents.

'You won't get this in England,' said Chataway.

Charles was silent.

'You think you'll be back?' Chataway continued.

But Charles was resolved to think of only one thing at a time. That was his decision when he'd answered Nellie's cable. Then he'd gone back to the cottage, bathed and shaved, put on his best clothes and called on the Davidsons. They had been rather cool towards his decision, and only John Davidson had requested him to pass greetings on to Nellie, and that a bit grudgingly, as if it was the minimum requirement of a gentleman.

'You listening to me, Charlie?'

'Will I be back? Who knows?' he shrugged.

Nellie received Charles's answer by reply cable, but after telling her father kept the news to herself. She only whispered it to little George, as he grabbed at her thumb and tried to bite her nose. Her mind raced ahead over plans she could make only in her head as yet, because of the promise to her father. At meal-times she sometimes caught her father's eye; they had a secret between them, it was plain. The rest of the family didn't press for it, just heaved a sigh of relief over the fact that the black indefinable cloud that had hung over the house for so long seemed to have lifted. Nellie thought about England constantly, and what it meant to her.

And suddenly, England seemed to mean quite a lot.

She thought back to her naivety in the early days at Mackay, when she had pressed Charles for details of his family and had been so maddeningly, charmingly, put-off. She would be able to handle people over there, she thought, because of what she had seen at the Davidsons. She would not be cowed, as many Australians were, by English attitudes. Certain social forms held no fears for her, as they had once. She would be able to separate the true from the false, in among the polished manners of the empire builders.

A few days later, at the Studio Pietro Cecchi, Miss Dawson sat reading the *Argus* while Pietro Cecchi stood at the window dreaming of Italy.

'*Signore*, listen!' Miss Dawson suddenly exploded. She read from the paper: '"Mr David Mitchell, the well-known builder of Doonside, Burnley Street, Richmond, is going to England as Commissioner to the Indian and Colonial . . ."'

Miss Dawson broke off and gulped for breath.

'". . . Exhibition. Accompanying him will be his daughter and son-in-law Mr and Mrs Charles Armstrong, and his daughters the Misses etc, etc" . . . Well!'

Cecchi whistled. He was flabbergasted.

Miss Dawson slammed the paper down.

'If he can afford to take his whole family to England, he can afford to pay the eighty guineas she owes you for lessons.'

Cecchi's mind was on losing Nellie.

'Eighty guineas,' he said. 'As much as that?'

'Here are the accounts,' said Miss Dawson, triumphantly efficient. She pushed a book across the table.

Cecchi ignored her. He was a man in shock.

'We shall have her for this,' said Miss Dawson, quivering with rage and delight. 'I always knew the day would come. It is reprehensible.'

'Now, now, let us think what is to be done,' said Cecchi mildly enough. Then he paused a moment. His manner changed. He raised his chin, shook his head, and made a

'I will not go to her concert tonight, however.'

So. His pride was starting to work on him. Miss Dawson smiled at this; she liked it better, the way he virtually glowed when aroused, such a fine strong healthy man he was really.

'No thinking, my dear man,' said Miss Dawson. 'I shall go to the concert in your place.'

At the end of her last song, Nellie made a speech.

'My dear friends,' she said. 'You have been very kind. Now I must make a sad announcement. In a few weeks' time I will be sailing for England. You have given me confidence to seek new horizons, and perhaps new teachers.'

New horizons? Annie in the audience wondered what Charles would make of this speech if he heard it. For that matter, what David Mitchell would say, for Annie had a clear idea now of what each of them expected from the move, and their aims were as irreconcilable as ever, if only they knew it. She bunched her gloves in her fists and wished she'd been born into another family, where things went calmly along, and which had no member so capable as Nellie. New teachers? Oh, dear.

'I shall have so much to learn in the Old World,' said Nellie at the end of her speech, 'where music is taken so seriously. Thank you.'

She bowed, accepted the applause, which was warmer than ever before, and left the stage. As she walked down a corridor towards the dressing rooms her way was blocked.

'Miss Dawson!'

'Well, Mrs Armstrong, you have certainly sprung a surprise on us. You will pay Signor Cecchi the eighty guineas you owe him before you leave for London, or I will go straight to your father.'

'This has nothing to do with my father,' replied Nellie. 'You will have your money.'

'I give you three days,' said Miss Dawson. Then she turned on her heel and was gone.

Nellie went to the dressing room and closed the door behind her, shooting home the catch and sinking into a chair. How could she have let so much debt build up? She'd been a fool; she'd thought of Charles and their future, putting her teacher last, her loved, emotional, ridiculous foreign teacher. He would think she still had her earnings, close on seven hundred pounds in all.

But, after expenses, the money set aside for Charles was gone. She'd used it for new clothes, she'd paid for steamer tickets and handed across, with due pride, a fair amount to her father to use for rent for herself and her baby in his house. She had spent lavishly on gifts for everyone, including Signor Cecchi and Miss Dawson, they ought to remember. She had taken George shopping for brand new outfits, as befitting a boy to be shown around England.

A wave of desperation swept through her. What would she do?

Her eyes caught the months-old wreath of satin roses bestowed on her by Syd, which was still gathering dust here in the back of the concert hall. She remembered there'd been an address card with it. She looked through drawers, under this and that, until with a triumphant cry she found it. Syd Meredith, the place was a ten minute cab ride away, in Albert Park. She would place Aunt Lizzie in her confidence, she would go there now, tonight, without delay, and get the money, and be damned for the consequences.

Outside in the dark she spoke hurriedly to Aunt Lizzie. They walked up and down the pavement as they talked. The poor woman was already compromised over the matter of Syd, having said nothing about it to David Mitchell so many months ago. 'Lord, it had been innocent then, and it was just a shade less innocent now,' Aunt Lizzie argued to herself. Then, 'In for a penny,' she decided. She kissed Nellie and they hurried for a cab. As it sped along she hugged her cloak around her and confessed that she loved an adventure.

Syd's house was flashy and grand. A single lamp glowed in the hall, highlighting nymphs and satyrs cut into ruby-red glass. The verandah tiles appeared lacquered, they shone so in the dark. Aunt Lizzie sniffed the air disapprovingly. The cab-man waited in the street. After much ringing a surly, sleepy-eyed serving maid appeared from downstairs.

'He ain't in,' she yelled. 'He's away on business, he won't be home till tomorrer.'

Her manner changed when Nellie pressed a gold sovereign into her hand. She became intensely sympathetic, in a slow-eyed sort of way. She implied that she knew what it was all about. Her Mr Meredith was a fast one, that was the unstated understanding. The girl led Nellie into the hall, with Aunt Lizzie smartly following, and produced pen and scented notepaper. Nellie promised another gold sovereign for the safe delivery of her urgent message. The girl swore to do it.

Nellie wrote swiftly, telling her problem to Syd in its bare detail, and throwing herself on his mercy.

'I have heard your name mentioned, Mrs Armstrong,' said the girl, 'now I come to think of it. Old friend of his, ain't yer?'

'Yes,' said Nellie.

The next day, around noon, a message was brought to Doonside by confidential messenger. 'Mr Meredith,' it said, 'was awaiting Mrs Armstrong's pleasure in such-and-such a restaurant, in so-and-so street.' Nellie immediately burnt the paper in the grate in Aunt Lizzie's room, and the two of them left the house together, calling goodbye to everyone, and not

MELBA

arousing the least suspicion by their haste.

Aunt Lizzie entered the restaurant ahead of Nellie, to assess its respectability. It was very proper in surface appearance, but reeked of impropriety underneath. Aunt Lizzie held back while Nellie joined Syd. A waiter offered her a chair, but she declined, and stood near the coat rack clutching her shawl to herself and darting her eyes about everywhere.

Syd was eating a plate of oysters. After getting to his feet he very correctly slid Nellie's chair in behind her. He had the air of someone who'd been attending classes in etiquette. But then, after sitting down again, he slid another oyster in his mouth and was his old self.

He grinned at Nellie and shook his head disbelievingly. His Adam's apple descended, then he opened his mouth.

'Eighty guineas for singing lessons. What about your father?'

'I could never ask him, he doesn't believe in borrowing.'

'But you're borrowing from me now,' said Syd. 'If I lend,' he added warningly.

'It's the last time,' said Nellie defiantly.

Syd looked at her. There was a touch of coolness in the look. 'Oh, no,' thought Nellie, 'he is going to be difficult.'

'Please, Syd,' she said. 'I'll pay you back, with interest, when I make my name in England. A business arrangement.'

'I went around this morning and I took some advice. A man in my position has to take advice, Nellie, you understand that.'.

'Yes,' said Nellie anxiously.

'I'm worth fifty thousand pounds, you see,' said Syd.

'Goodness.'

'And the upshot of this advice was, that I should ask about your husband. Like as to say, what sort of a husband is he,' Syd flushed, allowing a veiled speculative longing to show on his features.

So that is what it's all about, thought Nellie. 'You must go to the gutter for your advice, Syd,' she said, and she stood, trembling.

'Crikey sit down, will you,' Syd commanded. 'Take a hold of y'self. You're jumpin' ahead too far, Nell. You always did if you don't mind me saying so. I only asked. These people

154

GOODBYE, KANGAROO CHARLIE

I deal with, lawyers and other persons, they're only a guide. They always go after my best interest, that's what I pay 'em for, but I don't have to agree with 'em, do I.'

Nellie shook her head. 'N-No,' she managed.

Something about Syd now roused in her a great flood of tenderness.

'Remember,' he soliloquised, 'that I never came back after that first time, when I bought you them flowers.'

'Satin roses,' smiled Nellie.

'Yep. The very best . . . I knew me place, I'm no fool.'

'No, you're not, Syd.'

Syd took an envelope from his pocket and slid it across the table.

'It's not business to me, Nell. It's a gift. I don't ask nothin' for it exceptin' you take it, shut up, and go on.'

Nellie reached over and grabbed Syd's head with both hands, and planted a kiss on his mouth.

'I'll never forget you,' she said.

Then she was gone, leaving Syd with his oysters, and feeling rather pleased with himself.

As Nellie and Aunt Lizzie disappeared through the door Syd winked at the waiter and called for champagne.

'That was Mrs Armstrong, of Metropolitan concerts, Angelo,' he said when the champagne was popped. 'You've undoubtedly heard of her, old boy.'

'Mrs Harmstrong? Oh, yes, very pretty.'

'Have a glass yourself. Here's a toast to the finest lady that ever walked this earth. I'll knock flat any man who says otherwise.'

Signor Cecchi's door was opened by Miss Dawson.

'Well, here you are, then,' she said frostily.

'Yes, here I am,' replied Nellie. 'Where is the *Signore*?'

Miss Dawson gestured Nellie through to the music room, where Cecchi sat on the couch looking very sulky, very put out.

'My dear *Signore*,' Nellie began. 'You appear to be upset about something.'

Cecchi said nothing.

'It is the money,' expostulated Miss Dawson in her shrill way.
'What do you say?' Nellie asked him. At last he spoke.
'Yes, it is the money,' he said sarcastically. 'You people think I live on air, huh? I eat lots of praise, don't need the nice things you have in your houses, you Mitchells and people of Melbourne. Give me the money.' He looked up at Nellie in a heavy, sour fashion. She had never seen him like this before. He looked poisoned, finally poisoned by Miss Dawson's malice and bile. 'Give it to me, *la moneta* I say.' He made a coarse, greedy, snapping action with his fingertips.

Nellie ignored Miss Dawson and began counting out the notes into Signor Cecchi's hand in an exaggerated fashion.

'Eighty guineas in full,' she said. 'I thought you knew me better than this. If I had made a success, I would have repaid you tenfold.'

Nellie stepped back.

Miss Dawson could leave nothing alone.

'Made a success? In London, you mean?' she mocked.

Nellie took a deep breath.

'Where else?'

Miss Dawson almost sniggered at the enormity of the hope. Signor Cecchi rose to his feet with a heavy groan and went to the window.

'We do have a high opinion of ourselves,' said Miss Dawson, *sotto voce*.

Nellie swung on her:

'If I do, it's because Signor Cecchi has always encouraged me to.'

She then turned on Cecchi, tears in her eyes. He had tears too.

'Is that not so, *Maestro*?'

'It is so,' he said.

All Nellie's sadness and exhaustion flooded out when she went to the wharf to meet Charles's boat. She dashed up the gangplank as soon as it was lowered, and rushed to him on the deck.

She clung to him, and wept.

GOODBYE, KANGAROO CHARLIE

'Well, I say, Nellie,' he murmured. She totally confused and delighted him as he stood holding her, the sailors he'd got to know on the trip eyeing him speculatively as they stepped past.

'Charles, my darling.'

'Nellie, my dearest.'

'These months have been awful. You've no idea.'

'They're over now,' said Charles. He stood back from her, looking into her dark, distressed eyes. She smiled, laughed and borrowed his handkerchief.

'We're together again. I can't believe it. Now and for always.'

'Well, yes,' said Charles. 'Always, my dearest.'

He could not quite believe it. He'd not known what would happen, what he'd feel, even, on arrival in Melbourne. This: he hadn't expected it. He was in love all over again, as if for the first time. The overwhelming contrition, the absolutely divine outpouring of devotion. It was so tender, so warm and intimate. She could not take her arms from around him, would not for a moment, and that is the way they descended the gangplank, where David Mitchell, Annie, Belle, Aunt Lizzie and the boys waited with baby George.

'Is this him? I don't believe it! Georgie!'

George howled and clung to Belle. He was dressed in a velvet suit with a lace collar. His hair was as long as a girl's. But that was all right, they would go riding soon, and in England too, Charles promised between the boy's wails.

'England, Charles,' breathed Nellie as they walked towards the waiting carriage.

'Oh, yes, all right, hmm, yes, you'll find out, indeed she will, won't she boys?'

He addressed Charlie, Frank, and Ernie. They nodded and gulped a bit. He was a god to them. They kept their eyes on the ground. They didn't even take an interest in the great sailing vessels lining the wharf, not in the company of the man they worshipped in their games, Kangaroo Charlie.

Days passed in delight and forgetfulness. Charles was a hero at Doonside. Nellie was at his side constantly; no concerts now, no lessons in the last week before departure. Just the blissful excitement of anticipated change.

On their last evening at home Nellie stood on the verandah and looked down into the garden where Charles was organising the children for a game. He was a touching figure there with the boys and Dora hanging on his every word.

He divided them up: 'You lot are the Dutchies. You are the English.'

'Who are you?' Frank asked him.

'I'm the Zulu king. Now off with you.'

He retreated towards the house while the children dashed away to their assigned positions.

'I'm counting,' he called.

Nellie linked arms with him on the path.

'Charles,' she smiled. 'I'll miss it all so very much.'

Charles lightly mocked. 'No turning back. No more "Australian Nightingale".'

'And no more "Kangaroo Charlie",' said Nellie.

The words were lightly said. They held each other's eyes. David Mitchell and Aunt Lizzie watched from an upstairs window. The children shouted happily from the depths of the garden. It all seemed possible again, as at the beginning, with Nellie and Charles, such a fine handsome pair, wandering lovingly through the dusk. Dreams filled their heads, filled everyone's head on this occasion, and no-one thought to remind themselves that this, too, was how it had been at the beginning.

PART TWO

Europe

12

A Truth about London

The sound of a cab passing through foggy, cobblestoned streets penetrated the damp walls of Prince's Hall. Nellie longed to be gone from London, already gone after only a few short weeks.

She had never felt so alone.

She stood at a small, barred window looking down into a laneway, awaiting her call. Soon she would go on stage and sing her chosen song, an old favourite, Wilhelm Ganz's 'Sing, Sweet Bird'. She would sing it well, she knew, with all her learned technique, and yet with desperation of soul. Only a few people had come to listen, and of these most were family and friends. She felt slightly ill from nerves, with the certain knowledge that only failure and humiliation lay ahead of her.

Since her arrival Nellie had spent her time making calls on various teachers, on famous composers, on concert managers who scanned her letters of introduction politely while she looked on with a fast-beating heart. She had felt the uniqueness of her path leading to their doors. Yet these men had only smiled and shaken their heads, had almost laughed at the pattern of familiarity made by Nellie's story. Many, many 'Mrs Armstrongs' knocked at their doors, they said. She must not think herself unique.

MELBA

At first Charles had accompanied her, criss-crossing the streets of inner London, feeding out coins to cab-men, pointing to the famous landmarks with an air of sophisticated familiarity. Then he grew tired of this and went to his Club, where he spent the day playing billiards with his brother Montagu. Then last week, rather scornfully, Charles had gone to Scotland for the salmon fishing, leaving Nellie to fend on her own.

'Charlie, I need a year. A year to prove myself,' she had said, just before he left.

'Hmm,' he replied. 'Here? In this stinking mess?' He laughed his old, scornful laugh.

He hated London. So already they were at odds with each other again. London was the cause of it, like the third party in a love triangle.

Since leaving Mackay, Charles had got it into his mind that as soon as Nellie saw what London was, she would come to her senses. It would be too big for her, he'd decided, too impressive. He knew what it was really like, he'd always known and had told her so under the scorching Queensland sun. Remember? But here she was taking it on, as only a determined colonial knew how, right down to the bitter humiliation of a charity concert in the sulphurous summer fog.

And a charity concert was all Nellie had left, this acrid summer Sunday, in a hall where the walls dripped, where the clammy lifelessness of the place made her tremble and shake. She drew her shawl closer around her shoulders. She resolved that Charles must never know how close she stood to defeat.

A stage-assistant signalled to her. It was her moment to go on. She passed across the stage, smiling at the accompanist. She looked out across the sea of empty chairs in the auditorium. Annie and Belle were there, and several of David Mitchell's colleagues from the Indian and Colonial Exhibition at Earls Court, though not David Mitchell himself, he was too busy to come today, being concerned with a consignment of Victorian dried and preserved fruits, that had just arrived at the docks, spoiled and weevily.

Nellie noticed with a jolt of surprise that an extra person

A TRUTH ABOUT LONDON

had come in. It was the composer, Mr Ganz, a self-confident middle-aged man with a trim beard and a flowered waistcoat. He sat near the front. He had arranged her appearance today, but Nellie had not expected him to attend the concert in person.

The accompanist began, and Nellie sang.

And slowly, as she sang, her gloomy thoughts about London disappeared altogether. Mr Ganz had come, London was awakening to her, it seemed.

Afterwards, Wilhelm Ganz found her backstage. The floor-timbers echoed to the businesslike tap of his bright buttoned boots.

'I like your voice, Mrs Armstrong, believe me I do,' he said with enthusiasm. 'I've rarely heard my own song better sung . . .'

'You are too kind.'

'No, not at all. Now see here,' he cleared his throat. 'Meet me at my house at eleven sharp next Wednesday. I'll bring Carl Rosa along.'

Ganz rather eccentrically pencilled the date and time on his shirt cuffs.

'Carl Rosa,' repeated Nellie wonderingly. 'Eleven sharp?'

'Never say die, Mrs Armstrong,' nodded Ganz with blithe confidence.

Annie and Belle were waiting in the vestibule. An attendant waited to bar the doors. The fog, the cab wheels, the nasty light awaited them in the street.

'What an afternoon,' said Nellie excitedly, as her sisters helped her into her coat. They thought she was merely practising her over-enthusiasm, at which she had become a specialist in recent weeks.

'We thought it went rather well,' said Annie, as if no-one else had, including Nellie herself.

'It's all right,' breathed Nellie to her sisters. 'Something has really happened at last. I have another appointment. Mr Ganz has arranged for me to meet the impresario Carl Rosa.'

Annie and Belle had never heard of Carl Rosa, but they made an effort to show delight.

'Wait until I tell Charles,' said Nellie.

MELBA

It was just as well, though, that Charles stayed in the Highlands for another week, for the following Wednesday, when a footman opened Wilhelm Ganz's door at eleven sharp, Mr Ganz was not there.

'I am Mrs Armstrong,' Nellie smiled. 'Mr Ganz is expecting me at eleven.'

'Mrs . . . ?'

'Armstrong.'

'He said nothing, Madame, but come in.'

Politeness closed around Nellie like a glove. The footman showed her into an airless sitting room, where a large clock ticked and whirred in the corner. The house was silent, except for the distant sound of servants' laughter downstairs, and the hypocritical softness of the footman as he left the room and re-entered at regular intervals to enquire after her comfort.

'No, no, it's all right, I'll wait,' Nellie assured him.

Eleven-fifteen came around, and still she had hope.

Eleven twenty-five and she met the footman's eye as he looked in again.

'Where is he?' Nellie demanded.

But the footman had no courage, he merely shrugged in a defeated fashion. Nellie could see that this happened often. She had no experience to counter such a situation. She wondered if it was Mr Ganz being typically English, or the opposite, for he was not typically English of course. Charles would know what to do, he was good with foreigners, and had total assurance in handling the queer social subtleties of the English. But Charles had not stayed to fight on behalf of his wife.

'The maid is wanting to do the rooms, Madame.'

She would not demean herself by seeking another appointment.

So at a quarter to twelve Nellie gathered up her music and stole from the room, left the faintly mocking house, and walked through the hard streets back to the house her father had taken in South Kensington. Her heels were sore and her smile strained from excessive politeness. It was over. She had come to the end of her hopes in London. A few short weeks and it was done. She was somewhat amazed.

When she saw her sisters she smiled, though.

Then, when she reached her bedroom she turned the key in the lock, and broke down into tears.

After her morning of humiliation with Ganz, Nellie felt devastated for days, but made every effort to hide it. Before members of Charles's family, who called daily to make their assessments of Charles's 'prize', she appeared as the handsome young mother from the antipodes, with a fine strong boy at her knee. A habit of small deceptions developed. At night she came in to dinner to smile at her father and hear of his work-filled days with interest and devotion. She went to the theatre with Annie and Belle. She thought she'd get through. But then at Covent Garden, where they came on a Saturday night to hear Adelina Patti, Nellie was overwhelmed with despair, and wept in reaction to the great singer: it was all too much, this longing she felt, this envy and desire of achievement. The applause rose up like a great wave, and surged away from her to crash at the feet of another.

The lights came on and Nellie's sisters stared at her.

Her nerves were in a storm. There would be no rest for her, she knew. The glories of London were in such passionate displays of gifts. All else, the choking fogs and the poverty and the sordidness of the streets were of no account.

'You are good, you know,' said Annie with feeling. They walked out into the lanes where their father's carriage waited for them. 'Just as good as her.'

There was a new note of admiration in Annie's voice. She had always acknowledged her sister's musical gifts, but it was a different thing to do it in London where the very greatest were available for comparison.

They climbed into the carriage.

'Yes, your Mr Ganz is bound to call soon,' said Belle ironically. 'I mean, after hearing you at his house, and everything.'

'Mmm,' said Nellie.

'Wouldn't it be awful, though,' persisted Annie doggedly,

while Belle gave Nellie sidelong glances, 'if Mr Ganz called to make his arrangements while we were down in Sussex with the Armstrongs. I mean, it would be a disaster. He's not the sort of man to wait around.'

'Indeed not,' said Nellie. 'He is, though, the sort of man who finds a person if he really wants them.'

This alarmed Annie. It would do Nellie no good to be haughty from the start. She muttered to herself, 'Pride comes before a fall.'

The carriage rocked along.

Belle stared at Nellie with sombre, precocious understanding. She knew very well, without having to be told, that Nellie had ceased to exist for Mr Wilhelm Ganz, except that Nellie would never admit it. She would lie, she would sell herself into slavery before admitting it.

'Doors are opening for you at last,' said Annie, while Belle thought: 'Poor Charles, he is the one who will never understand.'

Belle wondered to herself if Nellie and Charles would be coming back to Australia with the family, or if they would settle somewhere else, in Canada, as Charles had sometimes hinted, or even the Argentine. There had been plenty of time for dreaming and speculation on the boat coming over from Australia. Fanning herself on the deck, Nellie had talked about the wonderful opera in Buenos Aires while Charles had laughed delightedly, picturing himself crossing the pampas at an easy canter for days on end, working great herds of cattle.

But really everyone knew it was London at the centre of Nellie's thoughts, always London. However, as smart young Belle knew, such matters were never openly discussed between people like Nellie and Charles. Not until the last minute, and then they ranted and raved and made the very earth tremble; such juvenile gods they were.

Everything was up in the air, always, with Nellie and Charles, until one of them decided to bring the other down to earth.

Charles had entered into the sporting side of English county

A TRUTH ABOUT LONDON

life with enthusiasm. There was the fishing, the shooting, and now, as Nellie and her sisters, with little George and a nursemaid in tow, arrived down in Sussex, the horses. Charles was busy rediscovering the pleasures of a life he had affected to scorn in Australia. Nellie felt neglected.

He had promised to be at the station to meet them, but sent a groom instead. Nellie was quiet about this: quietly angry as they drove along exquisite laneways, through mossy gates and up to the house.

'Where-my-Papa?' growled George.

'Lord!' gasped Annie and Belle as the house came into view. Rows of windows reflected the deep afternoon sunlight. It was splendid.

'Where is he?' Nellie wondered, as Lady Armstrong and her eldest son, Sir Edmund, a rural dean, a widower, advanced to greet them from the top of an imposing set of steps. Nellie and Lady Armstrong had already met in London several times, and liked each other. There was something of family feeling between them all.

But no Charles.

'Such a lovely day,' said Lady Armstrong.

'Oh, indeed.'

'Never seen the old place looking better,' said Sir Edmund, putting an arm affectionately around Nellie's shoulders.

'We don't believe it,' enthused Annie.

This was the England they had waited to see. Beautiful trees with limbs weighted down with greenery, and the whole vista sweeping away into parkland. There were European limes, elms, and oaks. There was a lake, a broad drive, an air of stillness and riches. A skylark ascended. From the woods, came the call of a cuckoo. After Australia, after the sea-voyage of many months, after all the earnest striving of London, it was as if they floated several feet above the ground, buoyed-up by the realisation of an ideal.

Lady Armstrong guided them to a vantage point.

'There is your husband, my dear,' she pointed. 'Thundering around, trying to strike an undersized ball with an overlong stick, while mounted on an animal unable to keep still.'

MELBA

'Well, he always said he liked polo,' said Nellie with a slightly forced laugh. In a distant field Charles and his brother Montagu were practising, driving their ponies around in circles, apparently unaware that Nellie and her sisters had arrived.

'How seriously they take all that nonsense,' said Lady Armstrong as she led them inside.

Nellie was ready to show her anger to Charles but when they came face to face that evening in their rooms she found herself pushing it back. Her determination to 'go at it' in London, from their very first day there, had infuriated Charles. By sending a groom to meet them at the station he had said as much with scorn. There was certainly a lot she wanted to say to him now: that he must not think she was defeated, far from it, for she understood the English way of doing things a little better after several weeks at the receiving end of polite indifference. That her harder vision of the road ahead was cause for self-congratulation. That in apparent failure lay the seeds of success.

They kissed. He said how delighted he was to see her after their separation, and how comical it had been in Scotland among the knobbly-kneed ghillies and wildly ignorant beaters with their kilts and tam-o'-shanters. Charles always made the Scots into figures of fun, seemingly careless of the offence this gave to Nellie, with its implied criticism of her father.

'And what did you do?' he asked, as they readied themselves for dinner. 'Take London by storm?'

'Me? Oh, I . . .'

Charles stared at her confusion, then began talking about his brother Montagu, how Monty's eye for a good piece of livestock, for a nice portion of land, for a good hard-driven bargain, etc, was really quite astonishing. In Australia, Charles had often described Montagu mockingly as a typical English townsman who liked to play the squire: now he was to be taken seriously.

'Monty's as good as promised me a farm,' Charles revealed, as he made the finishing touches to his evening dress before a great mirror, and Nellie brushed his shoulders with a silver-backed clothes-brush.

A TRUTH ABOUT LONDON

'A farm?'

'He thinks he can make an arrangement. There's an attractive lease coming up. No promises, of course.'

'Of course.'

This sort of talk was so reminiscent of their Mackay days, when Charles had hung for months on the word of John Ewen Davidson, that Nellie felt an overwhelming pity.

'Oh, Charlie.' She hugged him. 'No.'

He held her at arm's length. 'What's that you say?' His eyes showed hurt. 'No?' She could only turn aside, allowing him to think whatever he liked, for now.

'It's time we went down for dinner,' she said.

Dinner was a noisy affair at which Nellie and her sisters were the main attraction.

Lady Armstrong surveyed them serenely from her end of the table.

'I am so glad that Charles seems to be settling down at last,' she said. 'He was something of a black sheep, we feared, for a time. Rather a quick temper, like his father before him.'

'Not so,' protested Charles good-humouredly.

'Will you sing for us?' pleaded Sir Edmund, his eyes on Nellie.

'Not tonight. But as soon as I can,' Nellie promised. She pleaded a sore throat, which she blamed on the London fog. It was the simple truth. She deeply desired this evening to show gratitude to her mother-in-law, that elderly, steady-eyed old lady who seemed to offer no hard judgements, even as she understood Nellie's inner nature in a glance.

'Nellie made quite a splash at Prince's Hall,' gushed Annie. 'London is ready for her now.'

'Not really,' frowned Nellie.

Charles said nothing, merely tackled his serving of Loch Etive salmon.

'Prince's Hall? Well, well,' said Montagu. He waited a few moments until the others weren't listening. Belle at her end of the table was giving an hilarious account of Singhalese bazaar-boats in Colombo.

Then he murmured to Nellie:

'Now what about these concerts, m'dear.'

MELBA

Nellie frowned at Montagu as if pleasantly puzzled, at the same time wishing the floor would open under him.

'I am not sure I understand you,' she said.

'Going to keep Charlie up in the air for ever?' he persisted softly. 'I mean, what if it's just itchy feet? Hmm?'

He touched her on the wrist and enjoyed her reaction of amazement. The hand just as quickly withdrew.

'Oh, yes,' Montagu said expansively. 'Typical thing with women, this never knowing their own mind. Don't like it m'self. No amount of scratching helps, once it starts. Hard on a man, you know.'

Nellie felt herself trembling with suppressed rage. She said tightly:

'You go too far, Montagu.'

'Do I?' Montagu replied, chuckling to himself. 'Yes, I suppose I do. Look here now. I've found a nice little farm for Charlie to rent. Good pasture, pretty cottage. What do you say?'

Nellie, as pleasantly as she was able, avoided saying anything.

'A matter for you and Charlie to decide, of course,' continued Montagu.

'Of course,' Nellie replied.

She thought to herself that surely no two brothers had ever been more unalike. Charles' fine dark good looks came differently arranged in Montagu, coarsening every roll of flesh and putting unpleasant pouches under his eyes. He drank rather a lot, always grasping a decanter to bolster an argument, and for all the time he spent astride a horse, he had the look of someone ill-equipped for the sporting life.

As the dinner continued Nellie sensed that Charles was slightly drunk. He kept seeking her eye in a mood of amorous forgiveness. She knew she would have to match his mood or there would be an uproar under Lady Armstrong's roof tonight.

Towards midnight Nellie was sitting at her mirror combing her hair when Charles entered the dressing room ready for bed. He stood behind her for a while, his hands on her shoulders. She reached up and touched his fingers.

'Well?' he said.

'Your mother is quite wonderful, and everything here is so perfect. I don't know why you ever left the country in the first place.'

'Just wait for your first winter,' said Charles. 'There's a chill off Siberia and the stink of decay everywhere. It's forever damp and cold. It's an abomination.'

'Oh, I won't hear of it.'

He bent and kissed her in the arch of her neck.

'I won't be long,' she said.

Charles went through to the bedroom. Nellie continued brushing her hair a while, knowing that she loved Charles for exactly what he was, and there would surely be a thousand such nights as this one ahead of her, requiring a particular givingness on her part, and a generosity of desire on his, with the glow of candlelight and the promise of uncomplicated intimacy. Surely there would be: if only they could see it through together.

Nellie had just completed the last braid of her hair when a knock came on the dressing room door and Belle entered.

'You're still up,' Nellie smiled.

Belle kissed her.

'Wasn't it good, tonight?'

'Oh, yes,' said Nellie.

'Have you told Charles?'

'Told him what, darling?'

'About London . . . your "triumph".'

Nellie pulled a face. It was too late in the night for pretence, too ridiculous to be airily dissimulating all the time, when she knew that Belle knew everything.

'Oh Belle,' Nellie confessed, 'London was a disaster.'

Suddenly they were both close to tears. Belle kissed Nellie in a rush of sisterly understanding. Nellie felt flooded with relief. How good it was to have someone with whom she could be intimately truthful. Now there need be no more sidelong glances, no more of Belle being arch and secretive while Annie went blindly on with her own simple version of events, while

Charles stomped with ill-grace around the length and breadth of the countryside. Belle would have the truth from Nellie now. The girl's absolute loyalty and love could be bought only by candour.

Nellie submitted to the untying and rebrushing of her hair.

'What about your letters of introduction?' Belle asked.

'They're all used up. I've never been so humiliated in all my life.'

'Well,' said Belle with forced cheerfulness. 'It's back to Australia, then. Or is it Argentina? I thought Charles looked rather happy tonight.'

'Charles knows nothing,' Nellie whispered, clutching Belle's hand. 'He thinks I will continue singing here, singing there, and that is how things will be for the rest of our lives. He might even become quite proud of me eventually. You know, the wife who was almost something.'

'You are desperate, then.'

'Not quite.'

'Oh?'

'Dearest, when I said all my letters were used up I meant all bar one.'

'Which?'

'You will find out,' said Nellie.

A decision had been made. She would go on from here, no matter what.

Charles of course would be first to know about the special strengthening of resolve Nellie had found inside herself. But while at the Armstrongs', Nellie's courage, upon which she prided herself, still failed her a while longer.

In the afternoon there was a polo match. Charles played magnificently. Sometimes in the midst of the game Nellie, pacing the sidelines, felt that he was doing this just for her, wheeling his horse with superb ferocity, risking all for the sake of galloping through, across the rich, spongy turf to where she could applaud him.

'How does he do it?' she wondered sociably.

'Confidence,' Montagu murmured in reply. They stood under a tree beside the field, watching Charles once more drive all opposition before him. 'Confidence is the key to everything, even, I would hazard, to your elusive musical genius m'dear Nellie. Look at Charlie there: grin on the lad like a Cheshire cat.'

Charles drove the ball again between the posts and cantered past with an easy wave of his polo mallet to show what a lord of creation he was.

They were back in London, staying in David Mitchell's house in Kensington. Mitchell was away in Scotland making farewell visits to his ageing cousins in Forfarshire. Packing cases were everywhere, sea-trunks stood open in corridors and it seemed only yesterday that the family had arrived from the London docks in a state of confusion and wonder.

'It's not fair,' Belle complained as she and Annie packed their treasures to be sent ahead in a slow cargo vessel: lace tablecloths and fine china, cut glass and other good quality souvenirs of Britain. They saw the next step in their lives inevitably laid out. It would be home to prosperous Melbourne and then, in good time, they would enter into marriages. Not for them the star-blazing enthusiasm of Nellie. Looking at their sister, they felt deprived of glory, a little bereft at the coming shrinkage in their horizons. But at the same time, they knew they were meant for something more settled.

'I will never return,' Nellie had frighteningly confided in them. 'Not until I am a success'.

The house now had a transient feel. In the streets, the chill of late autumn was in the air. Coal fires were being lit. The rich rounds of the coming concert season would go ahead without Annie and Belle. The servants developed a particular guarded insolence, now that the Mitchells were going. Nellie was remoter from her sisters' intimacy, day by day.

She had still not announced her intentions.

Charles was spending his days with Montagu, going the rounds of lawyers, seeing to the possibility of doing some farming here in England. He talked of houses, rooms, gardens and domestic peace. It was all quite out of character, as when, in Mackay, he had talked of knocking walls out and living the life of Riley. He made sure Nellie understood he was creating a setting for her, for her changeable hopes and aspirations. She would not have to return to Australia with the others, so, he seemed to say, in his manner, that she had better appreciate it. He knew by now that London had been a disaster for her. In response, he wore a rather smug expression. 'See how at ease I am in this English world you admire so much,' he implied. 'I can knock it for six and make it bounce under my hand, I can lie back and let it tickle me, if I like . . .'

The day came when Nellie at last received a reply to a letter she had written to Paris. She opened it with a fast-beating heart, read it twice in rapid succession, then put it away in a safe and secret place, just as carefully as Annie and Belle had packed the precious items of their trousseaus.

Late one night, after a dinner at the Armstrongs' London house where Nellie had hardly touched a bite of food from excitement, Charles loosened his collar, getting ready for bed. He was pleasantly tipsy from Sir Edmund's excellent port. He smiled at Nellie boyishly and tossed his cufflinks across the room, landing them neatly in his stud box. He was delighted with himself. Nellie was touched; she looked at him admiringly, thinking how handsome he'd been in his evening dress that night. But also a little fearful for him because of what she was about to reveal.

'Charlie,' Nellie touched his cheek. 'When we came to England, remember we agreed on a year. I would need one year to prove myself. To make people see . . .'

'Can't remember actually promising a damned thing.'

'I'm not talking about promises, darling. It's just that you didn't exactly contradict me.'

'No 'spose I didn't,' said Charles languidly. 'But you've certainly done the rounds darling, haven't you.'

He almost laughed.

'There is still plenty of time,' said Nellie, a touch coldly.

'Mmm.'

'Well?'

'I meant one year to get it out of your system,' Charles

reflected. 'Whatever "it" is.'

So he was challenging her. She felt a surge of anger. His manner was mocking as he twisted a shoe from his foot and let it drop to the floor.

'Well,' Nellie said, 'I still have Paris.'

Charles looked up.

'Paris?' he said flatly. 'I said nothing about Paris.'

Nellie rose to her full height.

'It's where I mean to study,' she said.

Charles stood and came over to her. Without ceremony he struck her across the face.

'Not Paris,' he repeated.

Even as she held her hands to her eyes, and wept tears of anguish, detesting him for a weakness, she was grateful to him for making it easier for her to go.

The following day Nellie told the news to her father. He was even more astonished than Charles. But he did not lash out, merely turned pale and at first was painfully reasonable. She could see he was hurt, mystified; it was terrible. More terrible than being struck on the face.

'Paris,' he sank into a chair.

'There is a great teacher in Paris,' Nellie said. 'Her name is Madame Mathilde Marchesi. I have a letter of introduction to her. It was given to me by Mrs Wiedermann-Pinschoff, the Austro-Hungarian consul's wife in Melbourne.'

'What about your letters of introduction here in London? All used up?'

'You know they are, Daddy.'

'Are you sure you're not deceiving yourself, lass?'

There were tears in Nellie's eyes. Deceiving herself, yes, she had to do that in order to get anywhere. The direction she felt herself moving in was so uncharted. Here she was in a strange land and wanting to do only what she must. It was painful for her too. What more could she say?

Her father continued:

'I won't ask what a man like Charles Armstrong thinks of all this,' he said, twisting his beard. 'Aye, to a man like Charles the city of Paris would represent the worst elements of moral decay. The thought of his wife and child alone in such a place would be torture.'

Nellie sought refuge in self-righteousness.

'I am only proposing an interview with Madame Marchesi, to find if I am suitable,' she said. 'That is all.'

Her father glared at her.

'Nay, not so, it's all you dare propose at present,' barked Mitchell, rising from his chair. 'You may deceive yourself, girl, but not me.'

'Charles agrees that I am to go there, and take my chances.'

'Of course. He has always wanted to see you fall flat on your face, and thus restore your rightful position in the marriage.'

'Daddy!'

She hated to see bitterness in him, this stern father who had never shown it before. It was like poison.

She clutched his hand and tears rolled down her cheeks.

'You were at my farewell concert in Melbourne, Daddy. The people cheered and stamped their feet.'

She wiped her eyes while her father stared at her, quite stunned.

'I don't know, I don't know,' he repeated. 'I was hoping you and Charlie might sail home with us. I dreamed, maybe, that he'd accept a managership at Camperdown, then one thing might lead to another . . .'

He smudged away a tear. His canniness rang hollow to his ears. These were things he should have done for Charles back in Australia, when he had the chance.

'Oh, Daddy,' said Nellie. 'I can't go back.'

'I blame myself,' said Mitchell quietly.

'Ever,' added Nellie.

Later, confessing it all to her sisters, she explained: 'No, never, ever go back; not until I am a success.'

13

The Diamond Comb

She was sick crossing the channel. Calais reminded her of nothing so much as the Melbourne shunting yards. These were fleeting impressions. Her thoughts went on ahead of her.

And then Paris. It should have been glorious. But on this first visit the city meant hardly more than a series of frustrating encounters with a foreign language half-remembered from school. Rain slanted through the long boulevards. Her mind raced ahead with possibilities, and seemed not to exist at all in the restrictive present moment. She passed from train to cab, from cab to a small hotel favoured by diplomatic people. Her father's agents, Dalgety and Co., had made all the arrangements smoothly. There she slept fitfully, listening to the sounds of a city that stayed out late, and began its new day early, but had no relevance to the intense weight of hope she carried inside herself.

Only one small point of location existed in her mind as she hurried through the streets the next morning. A particular house in a certain street. And at last she was there, outside the stout door of the Marchesi house in the Rue Joffroy. She clutched her letter from the great teacher herself, and reached up to bang the doorknocker, but found the door already swinging open.

MELBA

Revealed was a short, chisel-faced woman of about sixty with tightly pulled-back hair. She was plain-faced, powerful.

'I am . . .' struggled Nellie.

'*Ach*. You must be Mrs Armstrong. You are exactly on time.'

Nellie hesitated. The German accent was unexpected. Could this really be the world-famous teacher, answering her own door-pull, when the great of London hid their faces?

Inside was an atmosphere of order and riches. Nellie immediately felt a sense of belonging. She was guided through to a music room and shown where to place her things, and without any ceremony whatsoever found herself singing '*A fors' e' lui*'.

The walls were high and dark with curtains. At the far side of the room stood a small wooden platform, scuffed by years of lessons. There was a magnificent chandelier overhead but the furniture and drapes bespoke a single object: the production of voice and its acute appreciation.

Before Nellie had a proper sense of beginning, Madame Marchesi made an abrupt cutting-off gesture.

'Enough.'

Nellie held her sides and drew in a deep, measured breath.

'Madame?' she wondered. Fear and excitement raced through her.

The older woman then said: 'Why do you screech your notes? Can you not sing them *piano*?' She raised a finger and brought it down on the piano keys. 'So?'

And Nellie, realising what was required of her, sang the C as softly as possible.

Madame Marchesi bent and struck another note . . . top E.

Nellie sang it, still *pianissimo*.

Then abruptly as before, everything stopped.

'Very well, I have heard enough.'

Nellie breathed steadily, fighting off tension and uncertainty. It was all new to her. She remembered the warm flooding of delight that had so often overtaken her in the studio of Pietro Cecchi. There would be none of that here. In this singing there had been no release, but merely a tighter stretching of nerves. And yet it promised magnificence.

THE DIAMOND COMB

Madame Marchesi grabbed Nellie's hand and studied her wedding ring.

'Where is he?' she asked, breathily close.

'Madame, in England,' Nellie replied.

Madame Marchesi gave an emotionless nod.

'Mrs Armstrong, are you serious?'

'Yes.'

'Then, if you are serious, and can study with me for one year, I will make something extra-ordinary of you.'

'One year . . .' Nellie's gratitude brought her close to tears.

'It is usually much longer, but you are well prepared already. You have had a good teacher, but if you will believe in me, I will believe in you, and we shall make progress. Wait here.'

Madame Marchesi started leaving the room but at the door she turned back.

'I hope you are not thinking of having babies?'

Nellie was mute. To speak would be a lie and a betrayal: she thought of George in London, standing at a windowpane, wondering why his mother kept leaving him. She had not been a good mother, she reproached herself. The reason was her presence in this room.

'So. Please wait a moment,' the teacher said.

Madame Marchesi climbed the stairs away from Mrs Nellie Armstrong. She went as fast as her short legs would carry her. She had lately wondered if she had seen the last of these miracle pupils who came through her doors from time to time. She had not had an Australian before. South America, the Wild West, Guadaloupe, the Cape. Colonial places breeding vigour. Young roots went out into the inexhaustible minerals: art plundered the new worlds for the old. Yet it always seemed there would never be another one. Her faith would sag as she went on with her busy teaching life, with only the excellent and the unexceptionable to fill her days. And then, like a gift from God, some nervous, lovely initiate would come through her doors.

At the top of the stairs Madame Marchesi was hardly out of breath. It was a tribute to her fitness. She threw open the door of the reading room, where her husband, Salvatore Marchesi, the Cavaliere de Castrone, sat working at his studies.

He lowered his reading glasses.

'*Alors* Mathilde . . . Why aren't you teaching?'

Madame Marchesi loomed over his chair.

'Salvatore, at last I have a star.'

There was the ring of absolute conviction in his wife's voice.

'Let me see her,' he said.

Madame Marchesi brought her husband downstairs to meet Nellie. They sat in a comfortable corner and drank coffee. The Cavaliere confided to Nellie that during her time in Paris she must regard the two of them as her parents. They would guide her and help her in this new place. She must tell them all about herself.

'Tell us all about Melbourne,' said the Marchesis. 'We heard, many years ago, that the streets were paved with gold.'

'Only if one works for it,' Nellie laughed.

Nellie talked of her sisters, her brothers. She spoke of her mother, long gone, whose musical hopes for her were wonderfully strong. Nellie was still too frightened to mention George, however. She believed she would lose everything that had just been given to her if she breathed his name. So she talked about Melbourne from a musical angle, the concerts and the life there, in streets that bore the mark of her father's building hand, almost every one of them.

'Your father. He sounds interesting. I would like to meet him one day,' said the Cavaliere.

'Oh, you would like him so much,' said Nellie, already feeling she had two fathers in the world, one of them this fine, silver-haired European aristocrat, to whom she could talk on equal terms about the musical world to which she aspired, and the other impatiently awaiting her in London, mistrusting all that was beautiful and inevitable in her life.

Throughout this meeting Madame Marchesi smiled at Nellie and patted her hand.

'What shall you have for me at the end?' Nellie asked. She wanted something certain to take back to London with her. But she knew she was asking too much, too early.

THE DIAMOND COMB

'We shall work together, and then we shall see,' said Madame Marchesi.

The next day, Nellie returned to London with the determination of a soldier storming the battlements. The two men she loved must be defeated: her one tactic had always been a belief in herself. Now she had an ally.

David Mitchell's desk was cleared of all the papers and sample-folders that had cluttered it these many months past. It contained only an inkstand, a paper knife, a small sheaf of bankdraft forms, and the two reddish-chapped fists of a man who had begun life as a stonemason and who'd gone every day, rain or shine, out into the practical world of men and affairs. Facing his daughter, he wished time had taken a different turning somewhere. He thought of Melbourne in the old days, when in the evenings he'd returned to the comfort and closeness of his family. Aye, there had been many a good dinner, and later, a pleasant song. Life had for many years been all he could have wished. He should have known, he told himself, that nothing stayed still, that everything grew and pushed past what it had been before, that the world flourished on newness and change. He should have remembered that. His own wealth and position depended on such a natural law after all. But he had allowed himself to be lulled by the having of daughters. One daughter especially. He had become ignorant. Now he was paying for it with a twist of irritation that had lodged itself inside him like a persistent colicky pain. Having brought his daughter to London to solve a particular problem he now found that he had been unwittingly feeding the problem and allowing it to grow until it had reached this unthinkable proportion, which Nellie was outlining to him as she sat on the edge of a chair in front of the desk.

How she talked! The clear candid eyes that had captured Charles never left those of her father.

'If I devote myself to Madame Marchesi's method,' she said, 'and work eight hours a day on musical theory and vocal technique, she says she will make something "extraordinary" of me. After what's happened to me here in London I can hardly believe it. I feel as if a miracle has happened, as if my whole life has been aimed at this point. Even from the time I was a little girl. Everything makes sense to me, all the twists and turns. So I must try.'

'Aye, the twists and turns,' said Mitchell. 'They'll remember the twists and turns, particularly, at home. Think of what they will say, the good people of Melbourne. They'll talk of a man who went with his daughter and her husband and child to London, of how that same daughter broke away from her husband and crossed the channel, to Paris of all places, where she sought a career on the stage.'

Mitchell looked at Nellie directly. She held his gaze.

'There is a good *pension* near the Studio Marchesi, run by a decent woman. They will take me and George, and Charles may come too if he wishes.'

'Hmm.'

There was a long silence in the room.

'I must not think of what people will say,' said Nellie. 'If I do, and accept their estimate, then I am lost.'

He, David Mitchell, of all men, knew what she meant. Without warning, he broke his gaze and studied his hands. A queer emotion touched him; he was humbled by this mirror image of his own values, manifested here in his daughter.

'Oh, Nellie,' he murmured.

'Yes?'

'The woman said,' he continued, 'the word she used was "star"?'

'Yes,' nodded Nellie excitedly at this unexpected turn in her father's attitude. 'She meant the absolute pinnacle of achievement. Nothing else will satisfy me. You know that.'

'And Charles?' Mitchell changed tack. 'What does he think now?'

Nellie hesitated. She had not seen Charles yet. He was in the country with Montagu, impressing horse copers and cattle agents with his colonial know-how. What could she say to her father that would establish a truth? Nellie thought rapidly. Certain things with Charles had been half talked about, half established. Nellie clung to these shreds of uneasy agreement and used them like a clever lawyer arguing a shaky brief.

'Charles and I have worked it out together. I have a year.'

There was that stare again between them, which Mitchell broke off by reaching for a pen. He began writing on a square of paper.

'What are you doing, Daddy?'

Nellie leant forward to the desk. She could not believe what she saw.

Mitchell slid the paper across the desk.

'Here is an order on my bank,' he said, 'to cover board and lodging, in Paris, for one year.'

When he said "in Paris" his voice rose to a reedy high pitch, like a bagpipe chanter.

Nellie took the bank draft.

'I won't disappoint you,' she said.

Mitchell chose his words deliberately, with the Scottish skill of giving discomfort along with agreement:

'It may be too late already for that,' he replied.

A note came from Lady Armstrong: the Mitchells were invited to the Sussex farm for a farewell visit, just a few days before they sailed.

They went down on a slow train, the whole family; Nellie and her sisters, little George, a nursemaid, and David Mitchell. All except Charles, who met them there. He was working with a string of hunters that Montagu had bought in Hampshire.

'You feel good to me,' murmured Charles on the platform, his arms around her, the whole family looking on. It was a more auspicious start than last time. It had to be: Charles had no bargaining power over such a singleminded wife. Nellie, always feeling that Charles might do something irrationally desperate, did not see it that way. But it was true. She had struck a vein of helplessness in him. He'd tried anger in Mackay, vacillation on the sea voyage, languidness in London, and then he'd tried absence in Scotland. His weapons, like Nellie's letters of introduction, were all used up. He'd tried to turn her head with the assembled impressiveness of his very English family. No progress.

MELBA

She saw it in him. How does a woman strike a man a final blow, she thought, across the whole stretch of his life? She does something absolutely for herself, because she must: and yet at such times people must treat each other as brutally as dumb animals. It was not fair, she thought. There must be another way.

What tenderness there was, that evening, as she wandered about Charles's dressing room, touching his things: his evening clothes laid out on the bed still steamy-warm from a valet's pressing iron; his silver-backed hair brush, which he'd always carried with him, even when droving cattle with Tom Chataway, she felt its bristles against the palm of her hand; these were men's things, they came from a world she would have to put away from herself in Paris. And yet, how she longed for the simple directness of Charles's arms around her and the forgetfulness she found in their mutual embraces. She thought, 'What if he came too? There would be just enough room in the *pension*. It might work. Nothing need be final.'

And yet, when Charles entered the room holding George for his goodnight kiss, she could not bring herself to make such a suggestion. A far-back part of her mind worked ceaselessly at unravelling obligations, then using the thread on another part of her conscience, the part that reminded her she might be 'extraordinary'. If her father could see inside her head, she thought, this is where he would find the shameless woman, not in the theatre-world he despised so much, but in the price of entry to that world demanded by the conscience.

'Give Mama a kiss,' said Charles.

'Good night, Georgie dear,' said Nellie. His quick dutiful kiss over, George held his arms out to his nursemaid, and clung to her more tightly that he ever did to his parents. He was beginning to be a small English boy already, it seemed.

'Sleep well, my boy,' said Charles, a bit pompously. He had never quite adjusted to the idea of being a father. That came later with men, if it came at all.

At last Nellie and Charles were alone.

'Charles, the Marchesi school in Paris expects nothing but hard work from me.'

THE DIAMOND COMB

'You'll eat it up.'

'Charles, I can't thank you enough for letting me go.'

She touched his cheek with her hand. He trembled on the edge of tears.

'So it's Paris,' he said.

'Yes.'

By some miracle, there was avoidance of direct argument. They were creatures of extremes. It was either an avoidance or a terrible flare-up between these two, there was no middle way ever. There was a desperate need, if they were to be civilised in someone else's house, to avoid the point, to arch it over like a bridge across a raging torrent, and arrive on the other side without a misplaced footfall.

They kissed. Charles pressed against her, wanting her, right here on the bed with its array of fine clothes spread out, when the dinner-gong might sound at any minute. 'My God, Charlie,' Nellie laughed a little throatily, resisting him.

'One year,' he said drily. They separated.

'It's a year I need,' Nellie replied.

As with many matters of great moment, the words were spoken, the agreement made, but each speaker meant different things. He thought, 'One year and it will all be over.' She thought, 'One year and it will all begin.'

They kissed again; Nellie, her heart beating in surprise and gratitude, willing to surrender to Charles any gift except the one she reserved to herself, her gift; Charles amazed at all the letting-go he was doing when his mind argued with itself constantly and destructively.

Charles took a small wrapped package from his pocket.

'Something for you.'

'Oh, Charlie.'

'It's a family heirloom. You're the one to have it. Mother agrees.'

Nellie unwrapped the paper to find a diamond hair comb. The light caught on the brilliant jewels. It was like something hauled up from the sparkling depths of a fabled ocean. She would love it for ever.

'Now,' said Charles.

MELBA

The guests assembled downstairs for dinner were all familiar faces. They were 'the Armstrongs'. They had become such good friends in a brief space of time that Annie and Belle would think of them henceforth as their English family: they would talk about them endlessly back in Melbourne.

There was Lady Armstrong, the kindly, always aristocratic widow; hard to believe she was in her seventies, and quite ill, as she dedicated herself to the comfort of her guests, directing the butlers and maids to each detail.

There was Sir Edmund, the widowed rural dean, so different from the harried country ministers at home with their brisk nervy wives and broods of children. Sir Edmund, widowed from theology even, seemed to have no ecclesiastical duties whatsoever. His entire year was spent being sociable. He strolled the fields, he rewarded himself with good dinners and fine wines. He was man of God living in his English heaven. He was warm, likeable and charming.

But Montagu and his wife Florence were harder to categorise. Their every gesture was boastful of class and position, and yet, among these nicer Armstrongs, they seemed like pushy newcomers. There was something calculating about Montagu. He always had business going of one sort or another, and Florence egged him on. He was secretive and superior about his own family, whereas the family itself was an open book. Florence showed constant impatience for no apparent reason. She gave the feeling that she would sell off the old furniture if she could. She thought of nothing but money, and wondered aloud what everything had cost.

'Charlie and Nellie not down yet?' said Montagu as they took their chairs.

There was a flurry of small talk. Lady Armstrong gave directions. 'Mr Mitchell, you are to sit up here next to me.'

'Thank you kindly.'

'Annie, you are to go with Montagu . . . Belle with Edmund.'

'Ah, Belle's my girl,' smiled Sir Edmund, holding Belle's chair for her.

'Monty, please leave room for Nellie. Charles is to come over here.'

THE DIAMOND COMB

Lady Armstrong seemed to realise something.

'Where are those two?' she puzzled, sending a maid to find the cause of delay.

Montagu leant close to Annie. 'What's the latest with your sister, then?' he asked.

'She's found a very respectable *pension*,' Annie replied. 'It's near the Rue Joffroy and highly recommended by the best teachers in Paris.'

'Oh, those places in Paris charge like heathens,' shrilled Florence, 'no matter how "respectable" they are. Take my word for it, my dear.'

'Nellie will be living a very frugal life over there,' said Annie. She looked around. 'Lady Armstrong's table is a splendid surprise.'

They were to eat grouse, the thought of which was already making Annie feel slightly ill. Earlier, she had seen the carcases heaped together in a crate.

The maid came back from her errand: 'Mr Charles begs their pardon, my lady, but they are coming down in ten minutes.' (The maid had ascertained this from the other side of a locked door.)

'How like Charles,' said Lady Armstrong stiffly. 'Well, we shall start without them. Robertson, the wine.'

The butler poured, and the men took their time over savouring it. David Mitchell looked pleased about something. Montagu made several important grunting noises.

'What do you think of the claret, Monty?' asked Sir Edmund.

'Devilish tricky one,' said Montagu as he lowered his glass from his lips. 'Good, though.'

'It's a dry wine,' David Mitchell announced to the table, 'which I made myself. I call it "Gooroomadda Shiraz". Grown from my own plantings I'm proud to say, at a little place I own, it's called Cave Hill.'

'Oh, Cave Hill, Father,' said Annie nostalgically.

Montagu raised his glass. He liked to bring himself back to the centre of attention.

'Here's to a safe voyage home, Mitchell,' he said. 'And for two dear young ladies, Annie and Belle. We'll all miss you, m'dears.'

Murmurs of assent went round the table. Montagu could be rather nice, after all, they thought.

Lady Armstrong said quietly to Mitchell: 'We shall be sorry to lose your family, Mr Mitchell. But we shall have your Nellie, because Paris isn't far away.'

'Aye,' said Mitchell, controlling his sentiments.

Heads turned as Nellie and Charles entered the room.

They were arm in arm. Nellie wore her diamond-encrusted comb. She laughed and glanced around the room, while Lady Armstrong looked on admiringly.

'How beautiful she is. Oh, yes,' said Lady Armstrong. 'Lovely.'

After dinner Nellie sang 'Comin' Thro' the Rye' in the music room. The nostalgia, the heartbreak, the promise of eternal return packed into those simple words!

David Mitchell listened for the hundredth time as his daughter sang the old favourite; listened, not with tears and obvious feeling, but with a kind of hard pride, as he gripped a whisky glass and angled his jaw without moving a muscle. The song was all about coming together at the beginning of love, but here was a parting. They would all miss her so much.

Annie and Belle were openly weeping.

Later the same night Charles and Montagu stood outside smoking their cigars.

'Look at the night sky. Quite something,' said Montagu, gesturing at stars which hung low over the dark woods like blurred, swinging lanterns.

'We used to sleep in the open,' said Charles. 'With just a blanketroll on the ground.'

Montagu inhaled decisively. 'You wish you were back there, don't you,' he said.

'Oh, I don't know. I can't really say.'

Montagu went on in his authoritative fashion.

'You're in very big trouble, Charlie. She's good. Damned good. Even I can tell, and Lord knows I've a tin ear. But it's the steamroller department. Watch out when she really gets going, that's all.'

THE DIAMOND COMB

'Just me and Tom Chataway, and six hundred head of cattle,' replied Charles quietly.

At Victoria Station the soot, the crowds and the clamour left little George wide-eyed. Luggage trolleys bumped and competed. Foreigners talked in a Babel of languages. Train whistles sounded shrilly in the clammy depths of the station. George was infatuated immediately with the sweeping changes going on around him. He was no longer a baby. He noticed things, and they exerted a pull on him.

'Hurrah, hurrah!' he strained to be gone.

'One thing at a time, darling,' Nellie promised. 'We shall ride on a train down to a wharf, then go on a steamship to France.'

Between arriving in England and leaving for Paris, George had changed. Now, with a small boy's excitement, he broke from his mother and ran alongside the shunting engine as it backed into position against the carriages, under the guidance of a grimy-faced, black-neckerchiefed railwayman.

'You will have your hands full with him,' said Annie, as Nellie dragged him back. 'Don't lose him in a foreign city.'

'Or turn him into a Froggy,' warned Belle.

'Where is his father?' Nellie wondered, scanning the crowds for Charles's face. She was fearful of some last-minute crisis.

A stern David Mitchell stood by.

Nellie wiped soot from George's cheek. Belle presented her with a bunch of handpicked flowers, brought down from Lady Armstrong's garden.

'This the silliest thing you've ever done, Nell. And Lord knows you've done some silly ones,' said Belle.

'Stop it,' smiled Nellie.

David Mitchell murmured to her: 'Guard your money . . . Make it last.' He was very stern and unhappy. His kiss of farewell was quick and dry, and he did not squeeze her elbow as he so often did, to hint at reserves of feeling.

And there, suddenly, pushing his way through, was Charles. He apologised for his lateness and drew Nellie aside. They clumsily kissed, while George clung to his mother's skirts.

MELBA

There was something reserved about Charles's embrace. Now that he had agreed to Nellie's plans he was not about to break his word. She would have her year. But they were at odds here, even as they showed a good public face. Enough that he would show her the English virtues she professed to admire so much.

'I'll come over in a few weeks,' he promised, 'when this farm business is sorted out.'

He could not help it, there were tears in his eyes.

'For pity's sake, Charlie,' murmured Nellie. She would show him where her gifts would lead.

Small, domestic farewells took place; things had to be kept on an ordinary level. But she knew it was a momentous day. There had never been another so strange in her life, nor would there perhaps be another like it. Annie bundled George into her arms and Charles hoisted them both into their compartment. Belle passed up a basket of food for the journey. David Mitchell thrust a last bundle of notes into her hand, excusing it as 'Something for the boy'.

She hardly knew herself as the train jolted into motion. Paris . . . what was she doing? All this restrained farewelling, with its threat of irreparable breakages, this going away from those she knew and loved, it was as if she suffered from a malady of compulsion. She was sick with wanting something badly. And yet it frightened her. She could only face it, and all the changes to come, one small part at a time, otherwise she might collapse under the enormity of the knowledge of what she was doing.

14

Husband and Wife

In the *Pension* Nathan, close to the Rue Joffroy, Nellie found a second home. The landlady was young, tall, with a somewhat distracted air. She was shrewd in managing all the disparate departments of her life, including a husband who was lazy to the marrow of his bones. Madame Nathan adopted a protective air in relation to Nellie. They were soon friends. When she wasn't at work in the studio, or at her exercises and studies, Nellie found herself absorbed into the Nathans' world. They had a small son, Robert, who played with George. A maid was found, a girl of twenty named Marie, who came from the same northern village as Madame Nathan herself. As a foreigner, Nellie felt a new freedom, almost an invisibility. There was one task ahead of her, and she set about tackling it free from distraction. How different it would have been in London. She tried to express some of this in her first letter to Charles, but knew he would sense only the closing off, the exclusion.

Each evening Nellie recounted to Madame Nathan the achievements and frustrations of her day, and the other woman listened with an absorption that implied great hopes of her own, that she would never see realised, but which she lived-out in the lives of the young singers who came to stay under her roof.

In halting French, Nellie repeated to Madame Nathan the things that Madame Marchesi said to her, and the landlady was able to compare the statements with what had been said to previous students.

'She is so impatient with me,' complained Nellie. 'I feel dazed, as if I am a child learning my alphabet over again. Today I stumbled, going out her door. I hardly knew where I was.'

'You are doing better than you think,' said Madame Nathan, when Nellie felt particularly distressed after days of little or no progress. She touched Nellie's hand fondly. 'Wait and see.'

The waiting seemed endless. Then a few weeks after Nellie had started there was a change in the atmosphere at the Studio Marchesi. Nellie was singing a scale with Madame Marchesi urging her on with the special manner she used with her pupils, which could be frightening sometimes. 'Why screech your notes?' demanded the teacher. 'Can you not sing them *piano* . . . *piano*?' In the one sentence, she changed from a commanding general to a sweet supplicant. How grotesque and hypnotic it was. On that last word, *piano*, Madame Marchesi's voice hung like a glittering spider web. Tenderly she struck a note, and Nellie sang as softly as she could the top B.

Now Madame Marchesi struck the C.

'Higher!'

As Nellie sang, a sly flicker of triumph came into Madame Marchesi's eyes. She struck the top E, and Nellie sang it *pianissimo*.

'Good! You have been taking your chest notes always too high. That is why you force your voice. Again.'

As Nellie sang, Madame Marchesi moved away from the piano and stood in another part of the room. She swayed in time with the scales, then when Nellie was finished came and took her hands.

'Splendid.'

That night Nellie was happy. She took George from Marie

after his bath, and sang a little French song to him. Marie was delighted. Madame Nathan paused at her work to listen. Even her husband, the mournful Gilles, pursed his lips into a bemused smile as he drank a glass of brandy. The singing drifted through the *pension*.

Nellie put George into his bed, which was in a small alcove off the corner of her room, where he slept alongside the nursemaid.

'*Bonne nuit, mon petit,*' murmured Nellie.

She picked up his clothes scattered about.

'*Le pantalon . . . le bas . . .* ' She moved around the room touching things, while George repeated his lesson. '*Le . . . la chaise.*' He was already far ahead of her in his French, learning playground words at a rate that would have surprised Nellie if she knew it.

She blew out George's candle. She had never been happier than she was now.

But then the hammering demands came again. Night flooded into day. Her shoes had almost worn a groove in the cobblestones leading to the door of the Studio Marchesi.

'No! You are not getting better. You resist me!'

Nellie came close to tears as she drew a deep breath.

'I am willing, Madame.'

'Try harder. We shall do it together.'

Now and again Madame Marchesi looked pleased, but not for long. Her facial expression slid too readily into something like scorn.

'You lied to me Nellie.'

The lesson came to a sudden stop. This was something different, a bolt of lightning from the empty sky.

Nellie reeled in confusion. Was it, she wondered, part of the teaching to perplex like a torturer, making wild accusations?

'I do not understand.'

'Word has reached me that you are the mother of a little boy, whose name is *Georges*.'

Nellie dropped her eyes.

'I did not lie to you, Madame. I only thought that you hated children . . . I was afraid you would send me away.'

'I too have a child, her name is Blanche. There is no love like a mother's.'

'Oh. I am so sorry for what I said,' replied Nellie tearfully. 'For what I didn't say.' She felt an arm slide around her shoulders. Madame Marchesi kissed Nellie on the cheek. She felt twelve years old again, with her own mother scolding her.

'Just promise me one thing.'

'Anything.'

'You won't surprise me with another one.'

'No, Madame,' Nellie promised, hotly blushing.

Now the difficulties were technical, physical, hardly ever intellectual. They related to the lung, the larynx, the palate. They had nothing to do with the young Mrs Armstrong but projected an idea of her into the future, when this physical form that was hers, yet had hardly felt itself before, would draw on what it was learning here in Paris. Madame Marchesi led Nellie into something fiendishly hard, devised as a test for her best pupils.

'It's no good,' sobbed Nellie at the height of the demands. Madame Marchesi looked black with authority.

Nellie ran from the room. Her teacher found her, minutes later, in the ante-room, being served a glass of water by a footman.

'Nellie, Nellie! You know I love you,' said Madame Marchesi. 'If I bother you, it is because I know you will be great. Come back and sing as I wish.'

Back in the music room Nellie again attempted what Madame Marchesi was reaching for. She reached it with ease, surpassed it, even, as earlier difficulties fell away. A glitter in Marchesi's eye told her something new had happened between them . . . holding her fingers to the air like a religious subject in an old canvas, the Madame indicated that this was the breakthrough.

A single note of great purity wound its way through the Marchesi house.

Charles looked around the untidy room of his farm cottage, searching for shotgun shells. Papers were stacked on chairs.

HUSBAND AND WIFE

A plate of crumbs held mouse droppings. Empty claret bottles were fallen over each other on the floor. Reins and leatherwork hung from a chair, and an entire saddle was dumped in a corner. Nellie's letters were folded under an old half-brick, on the hearth: Charles hated letter-writing, and was falling weeks behind in his replies. Hers were slower in coming.

Charles scratched his head and said to himself, 'Where was I sitting last night when I emptied my pockets?' Then he saw the shells scattered under a cupboard. He felt inordinately pleased at the discovery, as if it signified something very important in his life.

That was how it was now, with Charles.

He stepped outside, into the stillness of late afternoon. With a gun cradled on his arm he felt better connected to the world. It was a relation he could force on things, by his own actions.

He walked for a long time without realising where he was going, climbed several gates, and trudged through a black, icy, ankle-deep stream of water. On a ploughed corner of pasture he sighted a loping, halting hare. He brought the gun to his shoulder and fired. A strange pleasure. One moment the animal had been creeping forward and looking around, the next it was fallen back dead. Charles savoured the smell of gunpowder in his nostrils as he went forward and collected the still-twitching carcase.

It was the pattern of other days before this one, except that now darkness came sooner every day, and shortly it would be impossible, even at four in the afternoon, to take a pot-shot at anything. There would be nothing to do at night except stare at the walls. Charles had even lost his enthusiasm for Surtees. Words mocked him from the page because they had a life, he didn't.

He trudged home again in the cold, empty dusk. Fallen leaves filled the boggy lanes. Bare elm branches scratched the first stars. Blood from the dangling hare stained Charles's trousers.

When he re-entered the house he hung the hare behind the door, lit the lamp, poured a whisky, and sprawled in the only empty chair feeling numbed by exertion. It was good. The whisky woke in him, as always, a craving for human company. He poured himself a second glass.

The door opened and his brother stared at him.

'Good God, Charlie,' Montagu exclaimed, surveying the mess. 'Does Mother know about this . . . degeneration?'

Charles brightened and gestured his brother towards the bottle. 'Help yourself. We don't stand on ceremony here. We live like a colonial.'

'I can see that.'

Montagu's visits always stirred Charles along. He liked his brother. Monty might decry the impression Charles made by sitting alone in his messy room drinking, but would never hesitate to join him.

Montagu kicked some of the mess aside.

'No clean glasses, nowhere to sit?' he grunted. He sat on the edge of the table, and smoothly tilted his head back as he drank. There was something invigorating about Montagu's 'bad egg' way of looking at the world: he had a relishing troublemaking air about him.

'Heard from Paris lately? No?'

Charles stared at the half-brick on the hearth, where Nellie's letters were kept. Monty's eyes quickly darted there, picking up clues rapidly, like a stoat.

'You're just marking time, Charlie. Seeing what she'll do next. You let her go without a fight and now you wish you hadn't. Admit it. You're just half a man and it's hateful.'

Charles said nothing. Montagu continued.

'I think you'd better go to Paris, old boy, before the rot really sets in. Put an end to this nonsense before it puts an end to you.'

Charles thought for a long time. Then he said: 'Not yet.'

Madame Marchesi's plans for Nellie Armstrong were taking shape. The Australian pupil showed herself to be very good, very early; much better, after a few months, than any other pupil in the famous teacher's experience. There had been no visits from the husband, and the child, George, was well cared for. Nellie was an assiduous pupil. Her gift for languages flowered: excellent French, good Italian. In her singing it was

HUSBAND AND WIFE

not so much the imperfections that had to be controlled now, but the dangerous possibility of too easy accomplishment. More and more, Marchesi's task was to strew difficulties in Nellie's path. It was a great effort of teaching, as much as learning, that went on in the fine, many-roomed house on the Rue Joffroy. Marchesi confessed to the white-haired Salvatore that Nellie had come to her 'naturally prepared'; but she sensed that the teaching and learning Nellie had left behind her in distant Melbourne had been more than naturally inspired, it had been passionate, too.

'Do you still write to Signor Cecchi?' she asked one day.

'Madame, I wrote from England, but he made no answer,' Nellie replied.

'It is best.'

Marchesi wondered about the two of them together, a middle-aged Italian and an energetic, lovely young girl. The pairing, save for its happy outcome, was a standard one in the repertoire of art's sordid pictures. She pursed her lips at the thought of the tasselled couches of other Cecchis she had heard about, in Buenos Aires or Santiago, in Bari or Genoa. Seduction and submission, how often that particular exchange was tangled up in art. But Nellie had come through unscathed, apparently. When she sang the pieces that Cecchi had rehearsed with her Marchesi could clearly read the other teacher's mind, and while she intensely disliked the way Cecchi had given Nellie freedom in particular practices, she also, silently, pitied him. For he was an artist and Nellie was lost to him now. Nellie rarely spoke of her former *maestro*. When she did, it was offhandedly, almost slightingly. Marchesi calculatedly encouraged this. There must be no confusion in the mind about correctness, the pupil must never straddle two ways. That was a cornerstone of her method.

Mathilde Marchesi's considerable reputation had come about not only through her gifts as a teacher. She also had an influence on her better pupils' careers. Already Marchesi had started a process of making Nellie's name known in certain important circles, and was beginning to arrange performances for her in notable salons. Marchesi enjoyed the exercise of power, and with Nellie in hand, it was a delight. 'Such freshness, such freedom from continental preconceptions . . .' she told her favoured sponsors. She believed that colonials and Americans, if they were good, had the edge on the competition. They were not crippled by German arrogance, French disdain, Italian exuberance or English reserve. So much in a national character could spoil an artist. What was it about Australians? Marchesi sometimes wondered. She introduced Nellie to many of her powerful friends. She loved this part of her work as a relief from the long hours of instruction. It was not merely the genius for meddling. There was an investment involved, for in their years of triumph, her best pupils would always come back to her, to lay tribute at her feet. And into her music room she would take these grand stars of Covent Garden and the Metropolitan, of La Scala and the Théâtre de la Monnaie, and she would put them through their paces as if they were humbled beginners again.

One evening in Paris, in a great house, Nellie found herself moving through a smartly-dressed crowd, wearing a beautiful gown selected and paid for by her teacher. The dignifed Salvatore, the Cavaliere de Castrone, steered her by the elbow. Nellie had just sung a small song of Gounod with scrupulous attention to the way she had been taught to sing it, and now she would meet the composer himself. The crowd parted to reveal an old man sitting in a chair.

Gounod barely acknowledged Nellie, but turned to the older woman:

'*Brava* . . . Madame Marchesi,' he said.

'*J'ai enfin une 'etoile,*' whispered Madame Marchesi.

'Ah!'

Gounod waved up a waiter, who handed around glasses of champagne.

With his eyes on Nellie the great composer proposed a toast in English.

'To your star, Mathilde!'

'Wait until Charlie hears this!' Nellie determined.

She had, so far, adhered to a rule of breeziness in her letters

HUSBAND AND WIFE

to Charles, describing in great detail George's latest sayings and doings, otherwise keeping things vague. Of sinful Paris she said nothing, except to emphasise that she saw little of it. She hardly ever thought of Charles, really, in the old way. No more did she experience the see-saw of emotions, the whirling confused clash of opposite impulses in herself. She was grateful for the power of complete separation, which she had not properly tasted before. Back in Melbourne after her time in Mackay she had felt very differently from this. There, she had been under constant observation, displeasing all with a delinquent view of marriage. Here, no-one disapproved of anything. Nellie walked the streets a stranger. No-one knew her as an individual. With Charles she had found herself too predictably loving and exasperated, usually in the space of a single minute, while little George crawled around the floor at their feet and they shouted each other down. They had thrown crockery at each other. They had wept. Now, disdaining the nightmares of the past, Nellie gained a new perspective.

In her letters to England, Nellie told Charles she was 'making wonderful progress, but still had much to learn'; that 'Madame was pleased with her, but always very stern'; that life in the *Pension* Nathan was 'warm and comfortable in the Parisian winter'.

But the day after the salon meeting with Gounod, she broke her rule. She wrote to Charles excitedly of her triumph among the great connoisseurs of Paris.

Montagu detected the change in Charles immediately. He rather took credit for it.

'Coming to his senses at last,' he mused, when Charles announced he was going to Paris the next day.

Montagu watched his brother drive a mob of sheep up a narrow laneway behind the cottage. The look on Charles's face, as he concentrated on the animals, was one of complete absorption. 'He's a simple soul,' thought Montagu indulgently.

'What did you pay for these, Charlie?' he asked when the sheep were penned.

'Eight shillings, on market day.'

MELBA

Montagu straddled a sheep. He made a great show of examining its mouth. He liked to manhandle the livestock: it satisfied him to wrench their necks around, to bare their discoloured, grass-eating teeth. He wiped the saliva from his hands in the wool.

'I told you to wait till I got back from Ireland. You don't know the markets here, Charlie.'

'The men said it was a good price for young ewes.'

'The men!' laughed Montagu. 'This is not Australia, my boy. Here your average Hodge tells a fellow what he wants to hear. It's usually a good price, I'll grant you . . . But not if they have cotted wool like these.'

Montagu parted the fleece to show Charles the fault.

'I thought you once ran stock with your sugar-cane. Isn't that the story?'

'No sheep in the tropics. Cattle. And half of those died of disease . . .'

Montagu put his arm around Charles's shoulder.

'I'll make you rich,' he chuckled. 'But patience, patience Kangaroo Charlie.'

Back at the cottage Montagu read Nellie's letter and whistled softly.

'At least we know where she goes at night,' he said.

'Mmm,' grunted Charles.

'So it's "off to Paris",' said Montagu, with sharp satisfaction.

Nellie was taken to an even grander reception than last time. It was in a palace, near a great park. Here were gathered people of political importance mingled with industrialists and others. Nellie rather trembled. She noticed a cardinal of the church. She saw a young man with glowering eyes and untamed hair, said to be a fearsome connoisseur of the vocal arts and a close connection of exiled royalty. She noticed his gaze with something like a chill of excitement. Locked between 'Papa Salvatore' and Madame Marchesi she passed under the admiring glances of some of the most powerful men in France. The wives and mistresses examined Nellie with interest. She entered the music chamber, and the crowd, flowing like a river of jewels, quickly surrounded her. She sang most beautifully, with Madame Marchesi providing the accompaniment. Her voice was deeply appreciated, it was savoured, but more: a value was placed on it here, for these were people of money most of all. They were men who built cities and razed them, depending on the demands of the day. They traded in gold and ivory. They owned silver mines, they shipped coal from one end of the continent to the other. They had a special liking for human perfection.

A murmur of admiration passed around the room as the notes died from Nellie's lips.

It was past midnight when Nellie returned to the friendly lodgings she now called home. Madame Nathan was waiting up, ironing her husband's shirt-collars. She moved piles of clothing from chairs, and settled Nellie in front of the stove. She gave her a cup of English tea.

'An old general was there,' said Nellie, her fingers closing around the cup. 'A hero of the siege of Paris. He told Madame I was one of the great ones of the world . . . I cannot begin to tell you about it.'

Nellie thought of the cardinal in his voluptuous silks, and the fierce young man who understood music.

'Your eyes tell it all,' said Madame Nathan. She turned her back and busied herself for a moment. There was wistfulness in her voice.

Then she faced Nellie again:

'You have entered a different world now. They have seen you and heard you. They will come after you all the time.'

The wistfulness was gone. Nellie looked quickly at her young landlady. Something was wrong, it was a harsh warning.

'It was a different world, you are right,' said Nellie.

Madame Nathan pursed her thin lips. 'And a dangerous one,' she added.

Nellie felt a quick touch of anger that her first small success should breed resentment in one whom she had so quickly come to love.

'Madame escorted me there,' she reminded the Frenchwoman. 'Papa Salvatore took my arm.'

'*Oui*, Madame is proud of you. No doubt of it. And the Cavaliere de Castrone is a good man. But be careful in those places. Please. That is all.'

'Thank you,' said Nellie after a pause. She kissed Madame Nathan on the cheek, and went to bed wondering about the limitations of young Frenchwomen, with their morality based on provincial disappointments.

Charles leapt aboard the boat-train at Victoria station just as it started moving from the platform. He stood finding his balance, then stowed his carpet bag carefully. It contained two small valuable items, purchased in Bond Street, that were the reason for his lateness. Presents, bribes of love, appeasement tribute: he had passed beyond the point of giving for the simple pleasure of it. The other passengers made a space for him. Charles settled into his seat as the train clattered over a bridge. For a moment he found himself looking back across the roofs of London, the city where Montagu took his pleasures by night, discreetly, expertly. They had gone on the town together a few weeks ago, to gaming rooms in Westminster, then on to a house in Knightsbridge, a place of incense and echoing female laughter. Charles had stepped outside leaving Montagu to his pleasures, out into the foggy streets, where he walked for hours, feeling the pain of belonging nowhere. This was the same Kangaroo Charlie who had enlivened Mackay society, and put light into Nellie Mitchell's eyes with his talk of home.

The thought of Paris filled Charles's head as the train clattered along towards Dover. What he would gain there he hardly dared hope, but at least he was moving towards something at last, after many weeks of inaction. He had been to Paris once before, in his youth. The city appeared to him in his memory as a labyrinth of strange alleyways, flaunted temptations, inverted values. English was not spoken there. The life of French people of his own class went on behind heavy closed doors. Charles had been excluded: people he had been recommended to visit by mutual friends were unknown at the address given.

HUSBAND AND WIFE

His lawful wife was behind one of those heavy, ornate Parisian doors. Charles in his fevered mind imagined he heard the sound of her laughter while he stood outside once more.

15

Capitulation?

There was something new every day at the Studio Marchesi. Today Madame Marchesi took the waltz song from *Romeo et Juliette* through its final few bars. When it was finished, Nellie waited for the analysis that always came.

'How was I, Madame?'

Madame Marchesi made a conspiratorial gesture.

'Again, please, dear child.'

Mystified, Nellie waited for her moment to begin. Then, as she sang, a young woman stepped into the room and stood by the door listening. Nellie felt herself falter. The young woman was studied in her bearing, rather haughty in manner, and quite obviously was Madame Marchesi's daughter, Blanche. No-one else would have the freedom, or the temerity, to enter the music room in the middle of a lesson. Not even Salvatore. Blanche had been away in Vienna, singing at the *Hofoper*. Hardly a day went by without a letter from her, from which Madame Marchesi would read extracts.

As Nellie sang, Blanche tapped her toe under the folds of her very expensive dress. Nellie felt wooden. She had the feeling that whatever she did, Blanche would be critical. Madame Marchesi frowned, disappointed at her new pupil; Nellie feigned a cough, then recovered, and smoothly went through

CAPITULATION?

to the end, and was a pleasure to her teacher after all.

Madame Marchesi immediately swung from the piano keys and performed the introductions.

'My daughter, Blanche, meet Nellie Armstrong. You have heard so much about each other.'

Nellie and Blanche murmured pleasantries. But when Madame Marchesi left the room, to call for coffee and cakes, Blanche changed her manner. She affected to forget she was back in France.

'*Sie beginnen sie studierten mit meinem Mutter dan?*'

Nellie felt confused. 'I have very little German,' she said.

'So,' Blanche condescendingly repeated in very good English, 'you are beginning, I said, to study with my mother?'

Nellie did not know what to say. She had not expected a remark of this kind, almost an attack. Some people could not help their manner.

She was saved from a reply by Madame Marchesi bustling back into the room.

'Not "beginning", dear Blanche,' she said, smiling at her daughter. 'She is naturally prepared. She has only to work hard, which she is doing. She pursues mastery of technique, theory and traditions . . . The coffee is coming. Let us go through to the other room.'

Madame Marchesi went ahead. Blanche said airily to Nellie:

'I have just returned from Vienna, where the critics praised me.'

'How wonderful,' Nellie replied. But Blanche scowled, as if this wasn't nearly clever enough, or generous enough.

As they drank their coffee in mute defensiveness, Madame Marchesi smiled at them.

'My daughters!' she sighed.

Nellie and Blanche feigned smiles.

That same afternoon, when Nellie repeated it all to Madame Nathan, they laughed uproariously together. Nellie gave an imitation of Blanche—she stomped, glared, and sang a few phrases of a heavy German song. She said, '*I haff yust come from Wienna!*' She was getting into full sail when there was a movement at the door, and Charles stood there.

MELBA

'Charlie!'

Nellie stifled a giggle and wiped aside a tear.

Charles looked affronted. He had heard his wife's laughter as he climbed the endless flights of stairs. He waited in the doorway stonily. A mocking tableau met his eyes, Nellie hastily rearranging her skirts, a rather slatternly young girl sitting in the corner with his boy on her knee, and a skinny woman up to her elbows in flour. At the same instant, entering through another door, was a slightly-built, dark-complexioned Latin with sneering lips, who looked like a pimp. Confirming the impression, Monsieur Nathan tried his one word of English:

"ullo.'

Charles made a strangled noise of greeting. All this lasted only a few seconds, but felt like an eternity.

'*Papa*,' said George suddenly. '*Tu viens me voir!*' He raced across the room from the grasp of his nurse. Charles plucked him up for a kiss. Then Nellie kissed Charles, and turned to introduce him to the people in the room.

During the introductions, Charles tried to be polite, but only succeeded in being disdainful. These people embarrassed him. They had the privilege of knowing his own wife better than he did. He could see the knowledge in their eyes. He was an invader in their small *pension*.

His silence did not end until he and Nellie were alone in her room. Then he turned on her.

'Now,' he said, taking Nellie by the shoulders. 'Why are you avoiding my eye?'

Nellie tried to explain her confusion.

'Charlie, you surprised me. You just walked in . . . unannounced.'

'Haven't I the right?'

Nellie lowered her eyes.

'Haven't I?' he repeated. 'I remember our marriage vows, our promises. I keep turning them over in my head, and you, you keep spitting them out.'

'Which ones?' But she knew he meant to begin with obedience. 'Don't be like this,' her tone softened.

'Then answer me.'

CAPITULATION?

'Of course you have the right, Charles. Every right in the world. It was just the suddenness. No messages, no warning, I didn't even hear your knock . . . You're so pale, you've lost weight, my darling.'

The 'darling' touched him. It wasn't much, but Charles relented. A thread snapped. He went to the window and stared out over the roofs of Paris. The last light of a wintry afternoon made things look even more leaden, more strange.

It was a view Nellie loved, but she dared not ask him to share her pleasure in it. She dared not ask him anything, she thought: he would only turn on her accusingly. Yet if she stayed silent he would only suspect her of hostility. She felt trapped.

'How is the farm?' she ventured at last.

'A lot you care about the farm.'

He banged a fist on the window jamb.

He exploded.

'If you only knew what it's like. Marking time. Waiting. The farm is all very well but the nights . . .' Suddenly Charles had no resources, no defences to pit against his wife's. She was powerful here in Paris, at the renowned Studio Marchesi. He felt his own deficiency. He was past the age of thirty, had lost the knack of living in England, and only a vast tract of land somewhere would make him happy. His only capital, though, was his yearning, which he now delivered up to her.

'Nellie I love you,' he said. 'I want you, I can't bear it. I can't stand it.'

He held nothing back.

Nellie crossed the floor.

'Oh, Charlie,' she murmured, putting her arms around him. 'You poor man.'

Her head rested on his shoulder. She felt him give, as if from exhaustion. He said nothing more. He had something from her now: her pity.

It made her frightened to think what she had done to him.

Suddenly George came bounding into the room, and Charles recovered himself.

'Georgie, my boy. Would you like a present?'

George scrambled against Charles's legs.

Nellie smiled. Charles upended his bag and withdrew a small toy horse for George. The boy loved it instantly and for ever. It had bristled horsehair in its mane and a pair of black, shining glass eyes.

As George and Charles played together, Charles's belongings became scattered over the bed. Charles plainly expected to sleep there that night. He smiled at Nellie while tossing George in the air. 'He should ask the Nathans first,' Nellie thought.

Charles's gift for Nellie was a shawl of Chinese silk, embroidered with faintly-seen pavilions. She touched it to her cheek while Charles's eyes stayed on her.

They went through to the kitchen to show the Nathans the gifts. Charles was jovial towards them this time, managing his shame, Nellie supposed, feeling pity again: an Englishman at the mercy of a woman, and foreigners, in a city he despised. The question of where he would sleep was decided, not in words, but by Charles's authoritative manner. Madame Nathan lowered her eyes and understood.

As further proof of his independence Charles insisted on taking Nellie to an important restaurant for dinner. Nellie had been there once with the Marchesis, and was delighted at the choice. It seemed to Nellie to be the best possible place for her to go with Charles. English was spoken there. There was no touch of 'gay Paree' at all. Important people were dining there, including a British government delegation. As they were shown to their table a minister stood and greeted Charles. He was an old friend of the Armstrong family. Charles's pride was assuaged. He and the minister threw their heads back and laughed over some trivial memory of Charles's childhood. Nellie looked magnificent. She wore the diamond comb that Charles had given her so touchingly, in England.

A vision came to Nellie of a possible life for herself and Charles. At its centre was this image of Charles, at ease with important men. But as soon as the few words were over, the image dissolved. It was only passing politeness, and Charles was nothing to the statesman, except as a fellow-countryman from the ruling class.

As they studied the menu Nellie's hand rested over Charles's on the starched white tablecloth. She was outwardly calm but

CAPITULATION?

her mind raced. Charles's visit to Paris, beginning so shatteringly, had to be controlled. That was her task over the next day or so. To be calm and managing. The question was how to get Charles away from Paris without his feeling empty-handed, leaving her free to pursue her goal. At the end of his visit, she must put him back on the train for England, satisfied and in one whole piece: she must not be shattered herself. It would have to be done by trick, by illusion, she had nothing else.

He wanted the impossible, though he hadn't said it yet: that she should pack a bag and return to England with him forthwith. She thought of the lesson she would miss tomorrow, and felt a quick stab of resentment that she was not back at the *pension*, even at this moment, within a circle of warm lamplight, studying her scores.

'I don't understand a damned word of it,' said Charles, cheerfully pushing the menu aside. He drained a glass of champagne, which a waiter assiduously re-filled. He would be drunk soon.

'What are these things?' he grinned.

Nellie gave a quick translation, but there was no question of Charles allowing Nellie to do the ordering.

'Shall we eat?' he asked.

He jabbed his arm in the air, just as the government table had done. The *maitre d'* came running. Charles spoke loudly, demanding to have the items named in English, so that *Oeufs en Gelée à L'Estragon* became 'eggs in jelly', and *Canard à La Serviette* was reduced to 'boiled duck'.

The food preoccupied them for a while, and Charles drank an entire bottle of Bordeaux, then called for another.

'It's a pretty farm,' he was saying. 'You'd like it. In spring we're putting in corn and barley. I'm running sheep, and of course cattle. Montagu takes an interest in things. I like it well enough, but it's tame after Queensland.'

He did not talk about the time he wasted simply staring at a wall, drinking whisky and thinking about Nellie. He was *with* her now. The farm had a reality it lacked when he was there.

Nellie replied, 'I'm learning so much here, Charles. Things

I never dreamed were possible. Madame Marchesi is like a mother to me, a guide and a friend.'

'She seems decent enough,' said Charles vaguely, making Nellie wonder if he had somehow seen her. Then he pounced.

'Come back to England with me,' he said with intensity.

'I can't,' whispered Nellie.

Charles dragged his fingers through his hair. 'I love you, you know.'

Diners at a nearby table stared.

'Oh, Charlie . . . No.'

'Lord, you must be hard-hearted.'

'I could never be that,' she repeated.

Nellie made no reply, but thought: 'Yes, that's it. I can't do what I must without making myself hard-hearted.'

'I could never be that,' she repeated.

When they returned to the *pension* Nellie smiled to discover a made-up spare bed in her room. Charles's bag was at its foot, his night things laid out ready. What a tactful and observant person Madame Nathan was.

Charles sat on the bed and rubbed his eyes. He was sleepily drunk, there was none of the dangerous hilarity that had followed his nights of grogging in Mackay with Chataway and the men. None of the sarcasm he sometimes produced, either.

It was just that his thoughts seemed to plough their way slowly to the forefront of his mind. Nellie could sense them coming. The night threatened to be endless.

'Where's little Georgie?'

'Ssh!'

Nellie pointed through to the small side room, where George slept within hearing of Marie.

Charles removed his shoes and crept through in stockinged feet. George was asleep, clutching his toy horse.

Charles looked down at his son for a while with a loving, unsteady heart. Nellie stood at his elbow.

'Yes,' he said. 'He's growing.' Suddenly Charles was filled with conviction. What did anything matter? They would, both of them, always have the boy. He was their shared miracle. Nellie's hand touched his. There, by his bedside, they kissed.

CAPITULATION?

Nellie drew Charles back to the other room, and they sat together on her bed.

'I still have my year,' she said, gently.

'What's left of it,' said Charles. 'Darned if I know what this is all about.' His old, charming smile was there in the candlelight. The flickering flame, an aid to illusion, brought it up. She touched his lips with her fingers. They kissed again.

'It's all right, Charlie,' she said. 'You think you're returning to England empty-handed. But you're not. It's only a matter of time, then we'll be together again and everything will be all right. You'll see. I promise. I promise.'

They sank into the bedclothes.

It was the next day. In a state of great excitement, Nellie hurried along the uneven pavements towards the Studio Marchesi. The time was early afternoon, and already Charles was half-way to Calais on the return boat-train.

She could hardly believe it. She was restored to herself. Her life had fallen abruptly in place again. She had eaten a light lunch. She had helped Marie to settle Georgie for his afternoon sleep. There had even been time to study her lesson. It was hard to believe. Charles had come and gone in less than twenty-four hours. She was tired, exhausted, but elated. She would not miss even a single minute of Madame Marchesi's time. Relief and a renewed vision of future possibilities flooded her thinking. She was able now to push a short way into the future. She dared to think ahead, and Charles was there, to her wonder and astonishment, in her mind, at her side, restored to his prideful bearing.

She forgot, absolutely, that this same picture had once captured her in Mackay. She could be spellbound as easily as Charles. Last night they had slept in each other's arms.

Nellie burst into the Marchesi sitting room, where she adjusted her hair before the mirror, getting her breath. She exhaled a long breath to compose herself, and noticed Blanche sitting in the corner. She was reading a book with superior concentration.

'You are late,' said Blanche.

'Madame will understand.'

'Because of your husband? I don't think so. She has a mortal dread of husbands and their sudden visits. They ruin her work.'

Nellie was amazed. What was Blanche talking about? What did she know? Then Charles's words at the restaurant returned to her, his semi-drunken allusion to having met Madame Marchesi.

'He was . . . ?'

'He was here,' nodded Blanche. 'They always come in the end, to rescue the married ones . . .'

'Here? When?'

'Early yesterday.' Blanche smiled. 'Before he went to you, I think.'

Nellie felt herself trembling. The ground seemed to shift under her feet. So Charles had been intent on rescuing her, while she had been intent on rescuing him. Their intentions had sailed past each other, and on towards the horizons, oblivious to other signals. All her wasted pity evaporated. She felt helpless, the way a victim of a conspiracy feels . . . As if deeds had been done in the dark.

Then to reinforce her isolation Madame Marchesi came to the door and said abruptly:

'Well? Have you analysed the exercise, or have you been with your husband?'

'Both, Madame,' said Nellie quietly.

Blanche took up her book again, with that look of superior understanding on her face.

Madame Marchesi was quite frank about it. It emerged that Charles had caught a cab straight to the Rue Joffroy after arriving in Paris, had rung the bell at the Studio Marchesi, and after introducing himself, demanded a tour of the premises. Madame Marchesi, in recounting this, pictured Charles as a typically eccentric Englishman. Her anger and annoyance she kept just under the surface. Clearly she would not tolerate another invasion of that kind. Whatever problems Nellie was having, they must never, ever, intrude on her teaching again.

'Your husband has ideas about the duties of wives,' she said.

CAPITULATION?

'Also, he has no wish to see his son raised in wicked Paris. This much he made clear.'

'But I am only here as a student,' said Nellie meekly.

Madame Marchesi bored her gaze into Nellie's brain.

'I felt that my existence in his eyes was that of a provider of services. "I had better be as good as people said I was." "I had better not ruin the goods in my charge." That was the implication.'

'Or what?' wondered Nellie. 'What could he threaten you with, Madame?' Charles had obviously arrived here partly demented. How dare he.

Madame Marchesi did not say, but kept to herself the thought that had occurred to her as Charles Armstrong had stalked around her house: *He was threatening me with your murder, my dear Nellie. The death of a loved voice. Not actual physical murder, of course. He would only need to take you away, to exercise his rights as a husband, and that would be an end to it. Yes, murder.*

Nellie realised that the white face Charles had presented at the Nathans had been a coming-down, not a working-up of the emotions. 'I am so sorry that you were troubled by him,' she said to her teacher.

'Nellie,' Madame Marchesi continued. 'Very soon you will have to make a choice. A final choice. It would be better if you hated him . . . Forgive me, he is a strong, handsome man, and he loves you with an obsession. But that is all to one side and must never touch the heart of what is done here.'

'I only want to do something well,' said Nellie despairingly. 'It is what I have always told him. And I will do it . . . I will make my heart hard.'

Madame Marchesi nodded abruptly.

'That is better. One must die in life in order to be utterly artistic.'

They began the lesson, and Nellie sang her exercises as never before. She made sure that Blanche would hear. And there was never a hesitation in her delivery. Her emotions were in disarray, but she found she could sing nonetheless; it was what she had learnt. Madame Marchesi had taught her such control.

MELBA

In the midst of a scale, she smiled at her teacher.

Madame Marchesi smiled in return from the piano.

Montagu could hardly wait to hear about Paris from Charles.

He rode across to the farm as soon as he could, clearing fences and gates on a mare he'd brought over from Ireland for the hunting season.

'What's the story, old boy?' he called as he reined up.

'The weather in Paris was deplorable,' said Charles.

'I'll be damned,' said Montagu. 'And it's always sunny when *I'm* there.'

They walked up to the cottage for a drink. Montagu kept shooting him quizzical glances. Charles looked contented, like a horse that had had its oats.

'So he capitulated,' Montagu thought to himself. 'He will need more help from now on.'

Nellie hoped she would not see Charles again for a while. She railed against him in her thoughts. His secret visit to the Marchesi School left her feeling embittered. How dare he try that one, she thought. He could not be trusted, he was out to trap her. All she had in mind was her music. He should have known it. The only positive result was that anger improved her application: at her work, in the eyes of her teacher, she soared higher. Madame Marchesi was intoxicated by her pupil's capacities.

Charles, as a result of his trip to France, was in a contrasting state of mind. He felt drained, chastened. He'd been rather a fool. His ideas of singing teachers were fixated at the level of Pietro Cecchi; he'd expected an air of barely restrained greed and envy, cheap dago elaborations, and some equivalent of that hungry female watchdog, Miss Dawson, always hovering around.

Instead, at the Ecole Marchesi, he'd found elaborate decorations, manifest riches, a sense of the whole history of an art being nurtured and advanced.

He'd behaved badly there, he knew. Mentally fuming, he'd gone to Nellie's lodgings, hating the narrow-roomed *pension*, the lack of privacy, the three or four pairs of froggy eyes staring

CAPITULATION?

at him. There had certainly been no scandal to uncover, only a chapped, worn economy.

In the night, though, Nellie's embraces had appeased him. The next day when he left on the train it was with unexpected feelings of relief.

But yet, it was still as if they circled each other, establishing and re-establishing their ground. One went forward, the other back. It was by no means the same old ground they had trodden in Mackay. That was Charles's discovery in Paris. 'How confoundedly boring,' he thought, 'that the Marchesi woman really thinks my wife's something special.'

To his surprise, however, Charles found himself more reconciled to life in England. On the farm he looked about with a fresh eye for what could be done. He no longer burnt himself up with whisky and wall-staring, but planned a set of horse yards, bargained over cattle at the sales, and prepared for the spring planting of crops. Montagu, always hating to see a man got-to by a woman, as he thought it, took time to work out the proper measure of his brother again.

Charles thought more about George now, too, who had in Paris become a real person to him. Instead of his girlish frocks, George wore woollen trousers, and played with a toy gun. He was no longer a baby.

As the winter drove on, Nellie hardly thought of herself except as an instrument for the production of voice as commanded by Madame Mathilde Marchesi. Each minute of every day was promised in advance: so much time for her breathing exercises, so much for her scales, her lessons, language practice, and the constant study of roles.

'I will make something extra-ordinary of you,' repeated Madame Marchesi, with the special emphasis she gave to words.

For days on end Nellie would forget where she came from, or who she was, outside her narrow round of preparation. Her letters from England sometimes stayed unopened for a week. Australia, her life there, her family there, no longer had any immediacy for her.

She was astonished, then, when the warmer weather came,

to be overwhelmed by feelings she had thought gone for ever. Abruptly, one bright, hazy morning, she felt a promise in the air that excited her. It was spring.

Everyone felt it, of course. Parisians shed their winter coats and sat about drinking glasses of white wine at outdoor tables: the air itself was like wine, they said. The boulevards exploded into masses of greenery: planes, elms, and limes. Along the River Seine, where Nellie walked with George and his nursemaid, the light was golden. The season stirred Nellie's emotions, which had been set in one direction all winter, and exhaustingly controlled. She remembered Melbourne in this season, the picnics, boat parties, outdoor parades.

And in her heart she found herself a young girl again, as if she had never loved him.

On a carriage drive with the Marchesis, she sniffed the air in the Bois de Boulogne and immediately was taken back to the family's trips to Cave Hill. Looking around, she was astonished to find wattle blossom growing in the park. Then in the evening, she experienced sadness when Madame Marchesi, in the small garden of the Ecole Marchesi, sang softly in her native tongue. It was a central European folk song of other places, other times. Nellie and Blanche picked blooms and piled them into Madame's arms. Nellie envied Blanche as she remembered her own mother, so long ago, singing 'Shells of the Ocean' and other favourites. One feeling swirled into another: spring had been the time of year when young men dawdled at the gate of Doonside, when Syd Meredith had sat in the recesses of his coachman's stables plaiting his whip, watching Nellie growing and changing.

Remembering all this, it was not homesickness that Nellie felt, but a steadying of identity. With a great surge of vanity and sentiment she resolved that when the time came for her to take a professional name, it would honour the city of her birth.

Spring hardened into summer. When Nellie thought of Charles, during this time, she put him as usual some way into the future, at the stage door. When she mooned on the past, she excluded him from the centre of her thoughts. It was as

CAPITULATION?

if the interval of Mackay had been cut out. Charles's life in England she hardly dared think about. She made constant excuses to herself, to Charles, and to Lady Armstrong, in letters, to avoid visiting them there. He made no more return visits.

All winter she had gone to the opera with the Marchesis, and sat in their privileged row like one of the family. Her letters back to Australia were full of talk of what she had seen. She now wondered about the world beyond Paris, just as, once, she had wondered about London. How would people take to her? Would they like her in Berlin, St Petersburg, New York?

She fell into her old habits of mind, longing for new beginnings. Her year at the Marchesi School had heightened her natural confidence immeasurably. Back at the *pension*, the talk was of contracts, 'What might she be offered? And when?'

One day Madame Marchesi said to Nellie:

'Your husband thinks you are disgracing him. I wonder if you understand.'

Nellie looked long at her teacher.

'I understand. I have always understood,' she said. 'But it makes no difference to what I must do.'

'Now let me look at you,' said Madame Marchesi in a changed tone of voice. 'How is your father's allowance lasting?'

Nellie was mystified. 'Well enough,' she answered.

'I want you to go to my *couturière*. She will make you a new dress. And here, take this.' Madame Marchesi opened a drawer and produced a small, black jewel case. Inside was an exquisite pearl necklace.

'No words of gratitude, please. When you are a wealthy woman you shall repay me.'

Nellie was unable to say how she felt. It was as though she were a small child again, filled with nameless emotions. She only knew that where she was guided, there she would go.

When Madame Nathan saw the necklace she read the signs:

'Madame Marchesi is lavishing gifts on you because you are

doing things her way now. You have made everything clear to your husband. You are set on a certain course. It is what she wants. She has worked for it. She is pleased. Soon, she will be ready to make the arrangements for you.'

'The arrangements,' said Nellie breathlessly.

'Yes. You know what I mean. A contract with an opera house. I hope it will be in Paris, then I will hear you sing.'

Wistfulness filled the young landlady's voice. She had found a friend and would soon lose her.

16

Madame Melba

One day a messenger-boy appeared with a note from Madame Marchesi.

Tomorrow, it said, *wear your new dress and pearls. Come late in the afternoon. At five. Be ready to give your best.*

When Nellie arrived at the Rue Joffroy, Madame Marchesi was in a state of high excitement. She ushered Nellie through to the music room as if for a normal lesson. There she made a great show of sorting through the music, delaying the start.

'What is it, Madame?' Nellie asked.

Blanche entered the room. She ignored Nellie.

'Monsieur Strakosch is here, Mama,' she said.

Madame Marchesi reacted decisively, with a glitter in her eye.

'Leave the door slightly ajar, Blanche.'

'Yes, Mama.'

'Now,' said Madame Marchesi, turning to Nellie. 'I want "*Caro Nome*".'

Slightly nonplussed, Nellie moved to her position. Madame Marchesi sat at the piano, played through the introduction, and nodded to her pupil.

In the next room Blanche gestured Maurice Strakosch towards a couch. He was a balding, stockily-built man, clasping a heavy, silver-topped cane.

'Sit beside me, *Fraulein* Blanche,' he whispered coarsely.

'Herr Strakosch!' Blanche coloured.

Nellie began singing. Blanche raised her chin in the air, affecting uninterest, and started to creep from the room. But she could not get away. Strakosch smiled to see how the voice followed her, prevented her from closing the door, held her, unwillingly, entranced . . . As it held him.

When Salvatore came downstairs Strakosch was in a state of high excitement.

'Who is that?' he gabbled. 'I must have her. He prowled about the ante-room, swinging his heavy cane.

The song ended. Salvatore said nothing, Blanche fidgeted. Strakosch flicked her an ironic glance. He had known Blanche since she was a small girl of twelve, sitting at a virginal playing sacred music with mechanical precision.

Madame Marchesi ushered Nellie through.

'Monsieur Strakosch, I would like you to meet Mrs Armstrong.'

'*Brava, Brava,*' murmured Strakosch, bowing low.

'Monsieur Strakosch is a great impresario,' said Madame Marchesi. 'He is the personal manager of Adelina Patti.'

Strakosch eyed Marchesi's find. He was gratified. The young woman was beautiful as well as talented. He would be able to do much with her.

'She is ready,' said Madame Marchesi with pride. Strakosch saw that his old fellow-campaigner in the arts, Mathilde Marchesi, had committed herself to this Mrs Armstrong, making it easier for him to get his own way.

A few days later, Nellie found herself at the centre of protracted negotiations.

'Seven hundred and fifty francs a month, to double each year as your value increases, for ten years. But you must sign now. Today.'

Madame Marchesi nodded emphatically. 'That is about thirty pounds a month,' she calculated aloud.

'Yah, yah, good money,' said Strakosch, rather coarsely.

MADAME MELBA

Madame Marchesi was strange to see, having decided on Strakosch over the other impresarios: it was almost as if she was keener than the Czech himself for a signature.

'Why must I rush?' said Nellie, looking at the man, not her teacher. She trusted her teacher, but she had an instinct for bargaining, which came from her father.

'Herr Strakosch is a busy man,' offered Blanche, who was filling an inkwell at the writing desk. 'Boatloads of young "Mrs Armstrongs" arrive in Paris every day.' Blanche wanted the thing done and Nellie Armstrong gone from her parents' house.

'Not so,' said Madame snappishly. She turned her attention to Strakosch again. 'One thousand francs a month. If Mrs Armstrong agrees. She is worth it, Maurice.'

Immediately Strakosch placed a contract on the *escritoire*. Blanche dipped the pen and proffered it to Nellie.

Nellie glanced at Blanche as if to say only a fool would sign anything before reading it.

Strakosch smiled at Madame Marchesi, who smiled back at him. The clock ticked.

As she read, Nellie's thoughts whirled and her heart beat rapidly. But she showed nothing of this. At last she accepted the pen and signed with a flourish.

Strakosch grabbed the contract from her. 'What is this name you have signed, Mrs Armstrong?'

'Melba,' said Nellie with simplicity.

Montagu rode across to the farm with the news. He found Charles in the stables.

'Hello, Monty. Good to see you,' said Charles. He was feeling cheerful. He'd just heard that more land was coming available nearby, with an excellent, charming house, and it was cheap. Montagu would help find the money. Charles had just written to Nellie, enthusing about it, and conceding that she might be able to sing, occasionally, if they lived there. The concession was so enormous, though, that the letter still sat on his mantelshelf, unposted.

'Well, what is it, Monty?'

'Mother's had a letter from Nellie,' said Montagu, climbing down from his horse. 'And guess what?'

Montagu could barely contain himself. He wore the expression of a man who has just backed a winner, at extremely favourable odds.

'Tell me,' said Charles.

'She's dropped "Armstrong" from her name. Calls herself . . . "Melba".'

Charles barely reacted. Only stared at his brother in a jewel-hard fashion.

'Rich, what?' said Montagu.

'"Melba",' said Charles. He smiled bitterly to himself.

He went back to the house and tore up the letter he had just written to Nellie, outlining his plans for the coming year. Then he went for the whisky bottle.

'So what are you going to do,' demanded Montagu, following him in, hand extended for his drink. 'Go to Paris again?'

'No.'

'Poor little George.'

Charles stood at the window. Montagu rambled on.

'Ever think of a horsewhipping? No . . . couldn't do that to someone called "Melba", could you.'

'Couldn't I,' thought Charles flatly. He poured himself another drink.

'Easy, there,' cautioned his brother.

'Go home, Monty,' said Charles.

Montagu drained his glass and left the room.

Charles knew there'd be whisky terrors tonight, but was unable to help himself. When Montagu was gone he put the bottle to his mouth, and tipped his head back. She had gone past him with this. Professional name. Living nightmare.

The smooth, poisonous liquid ran down his throat.

One day Madame Marchesi realised that she had made a mistake in relation to Nellie. The effect was shocking, for Marchesi was a woman who never made mistakes. She was invulnerable. In her teaching record she had achieved a method for transforming the gifted into professional performers. Her former students were in demand by the greatest opera houses the world over. Only a personal failing in the pupil sometimes prevented that happening. That was where mistakes happened, in other people. Occasionally they left her school in disarray. She herself, however, was indomitable in the face of such happenings.

Then came this error of judgement. After a year of intimate knowledge she had underestimated the young woman now calling herself Melba. In order to launch her as soon as possible, somewhere, anywhere, not necessarily just here in Paris, her loved city, she had urged her on to Strakosch.

He was the wrong man, and Nellie knew it. On the night of the signing, Marchesi had seen her hesitate. It had not seemed important at the time.

Then last night Nellie had sung the waltz from *Mireille* by Gounod, at the prestigious annual concert for the *Association des Artistes Musiciens*. Present in the audience were Joseph Du Pont, principal conductor of the Théâtre Royale de la Monnaie in Brussels, and Monsieur Lapissida, one of its directors.

They had listened to the voice of this woman who had been announced, for the first time, as Melba.

Afterwards, Du Pont quietly drew Madame Marchesi aside:

'We are seeking a certain voice,' he said, 'certain qualities. Despite the fact that your Madame Melba is not a native French speaker, she is the singer we are looking for.'

'She is not already signed?' asked Lapissida. 'I have heard that Strakosch is interested . . . No?'

Madame Marchesi thought rapidly.

'Come to my house tomorrow,' she said. 'At noon.'

She mentioned the arrangement to no-one else. Indeed, as the night went on, and morning came, she wondered if she had dreamed it. We live by our mistakes, Madame Marchesi told herself with a sigh.

At eleven o'clock she sent a messenger-boy around to the *pension*. Nellie was to come at once.

When Nellie arrived, out of breath, it was Madame

Marchesi herself who answered the door.

'There are people here from the Théâtre de la Monnaie,' she whispered. 'They have been in Paris for a week. They have heard everyone who speaks French. Last night they heard you.'

Nellie showed wordless alarm. What about Strakosch?

Madame Marchesi silenced her with a gesture.

Nellie could only comply . . . Perhaps, after all, she thought, things are done differently here on the Continent, and I will never learn.

She followed her teacher through to the drawing room.

Here the two gentlemen waited in their dark and shining clothing. Lapissida was a wide, spreading man, while Du Pont, silver-haired, darted forward, and clutched Nellie's hand.

'You were superb last night.'

They breathed riches, assurance, and artistic finesse. Du Pont produced a contract and explained.

'Three thousand francs a month for ten performances, exclusive of costumes, which are to be provided.'

The men were already treating Nellie as a star. *Their* star, on the fabulous stage of the Théâtre de la Monnaie in Brussels. Strakosch had not had this attitude. His eyes had seemed to say, I will make you, or break you, young woman, time will tell. Meanwhile remember that I am the personal manager of Adelina Patti, the greatest of them all.

Lapissida kissed her hand.

Du Pont handed the contract to her. The terms, as Nellie read them, made Strakosch's contract seem meagre. Madame Marchesi leaned over her shoulder.

Lapissida murmured, 'Your own *Rigoletto*.'

'Sign,' said Madame Marchesi. Her manner seemed to say, it is all right. I shall fix it with Strakosch.

Nellie took the plunge and signed.

In the *Pension* Nathan there was amazement. Madame Nathan had seen much happen with Ecole Marchesi students who came and went in her establishment. But she had never heard of this particular variation.

'Marchesi has gone mad,' she said.

That night at the dinner table Madame Marchesi told her husband and daughter what she had done. She hung her head contritely, but there was a glitter of triumph in her eye as she raised it, and looked down the length of the table.

'Maurice Strakosch is a great friend of mine. He will understand perfectly. I will arrange everything with him.'

'Oh, dear Mama, no,' reacted Blanche. 'How could you?'

'For her. For her alone. There is an end to it. I explained to Lapissida and Du Pont that the other is meaningless, and so it is.'

'Yes, they understood,' murmured Salvatore. 'But will Strakosch?'

'Why?' insisted Blanche. 'Why take such a risk? You have never done such a thing before. For no other pupil. Certainly not for me!'

'Blanche,' said Salvatore warningly. His wife's eyes met his, appealing for understanding. He smiled back at her as if to say, Oh, yes, he understood: women, at least.

Charles stepped from the farmhouse clutching a suitcase, and shaded his eyes. The light splintered into his brain. What had started as a whisky-binge had ended, days later, in a bout of fever. His legs shook under him. If he did not leave now, he knew, his mother would catch him and order him to bed, then try and do things her way. She had promised hot food, and a manservant to tidy in the cottage. She would make an invalid out of him yet.

But Charles was going to Paris, and damn them all.

A gig waited to take him to the station. He passed his bag into the arms of the waiting driver.

'Steady there, sir,' said the driver, taking his elbow.

Charles was deadly pale. For days on end the name 'Melba' had thumped in his head like a nauseating pulse-beat.

'Faster,' he said to the driver as the gig sped down the lanes, past his mother's house.

The driver cracked the whip.

At the Ecole Marchesi the sound of Nellie singing the role

of Gilda from *Rigoletto* rang through the house.

At the end, Marchesi embraced her.

'You are ready for Brussels,' she said. 'Go, and be magnificent there.'

Maurice Strakosch sat in a restaurant eating a lobster. Juice trickled down a napkin. He splashed his fingers in a bowl of water, then tackled the crustacean again. He was having a fine time.

An acquaintance came across to his table and whispered something in his ear.

The name 'Melba' shaped itself on Strakosch's lips.

He ripped off his napkin, enraged.

Nellie, dressed for travel, opened a letter from Charles. The handwriting was slanted and distorted, a sign of drunkenness, or rage, or both. The words themselves were as hard as steel. He loved her. He could take no more. He was coming to her in Paris, for the last time.

There was no tenderness or understanding.

'Bloody nuisance!' said Nellie grimly to herself.

Madame Nathan appeared with a basket of bread, sausage and wine for the train journey. She was tearful.

Her husband was downstairs with a cab-man, Nellie's cases packed aboard for the drive to the station. While Monsieur Nathan gossiped in the street a stout gentleman wielding a cane hurried past, and disappeared into the courtyard of the pension.

Monsieur Nathan lazily shrugged. A betrayed lover of Madame X, in one of the downstairs apartments, he supposed.

Footsteps thundered all the way up to the *Pension* Nathan. It was Strakosch.

Madame Nathan and Nellie came to the landing and looked down at him. They were afraid. As he advanced, they retreated into Nellie's rooms. George came runing from the arms of his nursemaid.

'Hide him,' panicked Nellie.

Strakosch staggered in the doorway, ashen and breathless.

MADAME MELBA

Madame Nathan plucked at his elbow. He thrust her aside and advanced on Nellie.

'Sir,' she quavered.

She could think of nothing except to offer him a chair.

His cane came crashing down on the chair and splintered the wood.

'I want no chairs,' he roared. 'What is the rumour, that you have signed a contract with the Théâtre de la Monnaie in Brussels. Of course, it cannot be true.'

'It is true,' said Nellie, remembering her father's adage, that truth was a defence, no matter the circumstance.

Strakosch reeled.

'Your contract with me?' he raged. 'What of it? Is it nothing?'

'You are frightening my little boy,' said Nellie.

Strakosch levelled his stick at Nellie. It was a cane of the old days, whittled and shaped as weaponry somewhere in the forests of Moravia. It had already splintered a chair, and now it wavered in the vicinity of Nellie's skull.

'You are finished,' boomed Strakosch.

Nellie was already in Brussels when Charles arrived in Paris.

Charles climbed the stairs to the *Pension* Nathan. His lungs ached and his head thudded. Once again, he found himself standing in the doorway of the kitchen. The sour-faced husband was eating soup.

''ullo,' he said, and smiled.

Madame Nathan, his wife's friend, as she so often described her, gestured generously towards the table.

'You have come. Please eat,' she said.

A wave of delirium possessed Charles. Unsteadily he went to the table and sat. It was the last thing he had expected himself to do: he was sicker than he realised. Too sick to refuse succour. Now that he was here, at his destination, his entire inner momentum slowed to a stop. He lacked the power to ask questions. One thing was clear, Nellie had gone.

Charles's aching, reddened eyes took in the things that were so intimately familiar to Nellie and George: the flame under the soup pot, the crowded order of the kitchen utensils. He felt a longing for oblivion, anything to escape his feelings. He put his face in his hands for a minute, as if giving thanks for bread.

Madame Nathan had disliked Charles on his first visit. Now she looked at him softly. He was a man susceptible to gentle handling.

Charles's head crashed to the table in a dead faint.

In Charles's pockets the Nathans found the name and address of a man at the British legation. A messenger was despatched immediately. Then the Nathans carried Charles across to Nellie's old bedroom, and made him comfortable for the night.

Telegrams sped across the Channel. Within twenty-four hours Charles was in a Parisian hospital bed, his mother and Montagu at his side.

The next day he was taken back to England.

It was mid-morning as Nellie hurried through the streets of Brussels. She had hardly slept from excitement. Today was the day set down for *Rigoletto* rehearsals to begin. She had received a message from Lady Armstrong to say that Charles was taken ill, and was returning to England in her care. She felt light-headed with relief. It was as if the walls and bars of the past few weeks had fallen away around her. She could not handle Charles now. She wanted him at her side, she told herself, but only when her position was absolutely established at the Théâtre de la Monnaie. He was exhausting himself, poor man. His mother would care for him beautifully.

The only obstacle left was Strakosch.

Here in Brussels, Nellie's fate was cast like a leaf on water. Sometimes she glanced behind her, as if fearful that the thundering bulk of the scorned manager was in pursuit. She crossed cobbled squares, stepped over cabbage-reeking gutters. The people of the gloomy city surged along, spilling in and out of factories and offices, with Nellie part of their flow. Low clouds scudded over. Fine needlepoints of rain began. She stopped to raise her parasol. A stream of men flowed around her on the pavement, bowing slightly, appraisingly. Nellie felt their regard as if from a great distance. One day, very soon she hoped, they would know her name.

For the first time in her life she was absolutely on her own. In Brussels there was no David Mitchell, Charles, or Madame Marchesi to steer and guide her. Not even a worldly, slightly defeated Parisian landlady. Only this young woman she saw reflected in a shop window, in the cool rain of early autumn. Herself, wearing the invisible armour of a new identity. Melba.

The knowledge elated her. Drove her on. Ever since Mackay she'd had to live with the hurt she'd caused Charles, the puzzlement given her father, the confused despair in the loving eyes of her sisters. She had depended on others for so much. Now there was nothing she needed from them. It was a vindication. It was her turn to give something in return.

She was glad for her responsibilities. George and Marie were back at the hotel. Arrangements had been made to inspect a small house later in the day. It was in a fashionable location, just off the Avenue Louise. The rent was high, but when things were sorted out with the Théâtre de la Monnaie money would be no problem . . . Perhaps Madame Marchesi had already sent telegrams, already smoothed things over.

She was almost there. She prayed that Lapissida and Du Pont would ask her to sing for them as soon as she arrived. This was almost a superstition with her. It would be a sign. So many of the most fearful frustrations in her twenty-six years had dissolved away to nothing when she opened her mouth and sang. (She forgot London.) She pictured herself being led out on to an empty stage, her voice soaring to the empty heights, with just a charwoman, or a stagehand, to be pierced to the heart by this remarkable new voice . . . And the directors, of course, ready to deal with whatever Strakosch had in mind to throw at them.

Nellie paused to check her whereabouts, studying a small map supplied by the hotel. She found she was standing against the side wall of the theatre.

She walked around the front, into the square. She found shelter and furled her parasol. She felt eyes watching her. She was expected. She faced the wide, low steps, and began an ascent in style. A doorman wearing gold braid squared his shoulders.

Nellie reminded herself of who she was: 'Madame Melba, Madame Melba . . .' an inner voice insisted.

Then an actual voice came at her elbow: 'Madame Melba?'

It was not the doorman who spoke, but a seedy individual with mournful eyes.

'Yes . . . I am Madame Melba.'

The man whipped out a legal document and poked it at her.

'*C'est pour vous, Madame. Pour vous.*'

The man disappeared.

Nellie opened the document and quickly scanned it. She was banned from entering the Théâtre de la Monnaie, by rule of a magistrate.

Stunned, she tried to keep on coming, only half understanding the flowery legal French. Disbelieving it, really.

But the doorman raised an arm. Shook his head.

'No.'

It was a most humiliating moment.

An attendant led Nellie to a side door, where she was admitted to M. Lapissida's office.

To her intense relief, Madame Marchesi was there.

'I came on the train, at first light,' she exclaimed, embracing Nellie.

For a second, Nellie believed that all was well. But only for a second.

Lapissida and Du Pont stood side by side, grim-faced.

'There is no hope,' they said.

'She is a star. I have made her a star,' declared Madame Marchesi. She grasped Nellie's hand.

'It is not enough,' said Lapissida.

'Do something,' Nellie stared at them.

'There is nothing to be done,' added Du Pont. 'The law is a barrier even to you, Madame Marchesi. The writ has been served. No rehearsals, no performances.'

'It is a pity,' said Lapissida, 'that what you described as a meaningless agreement with Maurice Strakosch has proved to be such an obstacle.'

MADAME MELBA

'I have known Strakosch for years,' said Madame Marchesi with a brief toss of her head. 'I cannot believe he is being so unreasonable.'

Du Pont and Lapissida stared at her. Was she temporarily insane? Their drawn smiles seemed to imply, at the very least, that her words were an example of female logic.

Nobody spoke for a while. It was two women versus these smooth Belgian musicians. Nellie listened to the rain striking the windows. Maybe she should simply refuse to get up from her chair. Then, after a while, they would relent, and show her into the rehearsal rooms. She too had her special logic.

'Well, Madame Melba,' said Du Pont, breaking the silence. 'Only seven nights remain until your debut. There will need to be a miracle.'

'She is the miracle,' said Madame Marchesi sharply. But words were no use to anyone now.

Maurice Strakosch was at a circus in the suburbs of Paris. He sat on a padded bench that had been brought specially for him. His boots stomped the sawdust floor in time with the 'oom-pah' music of the circus band. His stubby fingers searched in his waistcoat pocket for a small pill case. Opening it, he munched on something for his blood-pressure. He liked simple pleasures. The circus was but one example. He had come to see if what people said was true, if this woman, The Amazing Pepita, a trapezist, was able to hurl herself into the air and balance between the forces of nature. She was said to be able to hover, airborne, for up to five seconds, without movement in any direction, while drums rolled and lights played upon her. If she could do it, thought Strakosch, then he would sign her up. Meanwhile, watching, he thought of other things.

Even when eating, even when fracturing lobster tails, spooning up pâté, tossing down wines, Maurice Strakosch churned over in his mind his prospects and problems. A doctor had told him to rest a little more, not to dash about everywhere like a bull elephant. And not to eat as much. But the doctor was a man secure in his profession. Strakosch dealt with artists: he was in the business of plucking them back to reality when they thought they could live on fairy dust. He saved people from themselves. He saved lives. He did not wish to climb stairs, smash furniture, frighten children, or destroy the careers of lovely young sopranos before they had even begun. But necessity forced it upon him. If he once let go in any direction, once conceded the contract to Mathilde Marchesi, for example, who seemed to be in love with this new voice more than any other, then what would he be in his profession? Nothing.

So. What was it about this Melba? he thought. Strakosch had liked the voice himself. He was interested in it. True, it was good. It was very good. He would never let it go.

The Amazing Pepita left her perch and sailed up into the air. Drums rolled, lights played across the darkness with every colour of the rainbow. A great sigh rose from the audience. The trapezist is not bad, thought Strakosch, as he watched her slight, lithe body fly a little higher, and then, certainly, hesitate, perhaps even hover; it was an illusion, but a good one, the trick was in the light, he smiled. It was light that kept her suspended. Strakosch rose to his feet to applaud, but instead found himself staggering forward.

He clutched his chest. A most remarkable splintering pain was there. The Amazing Pepita, where was she?

Up in the air, suspended for an eternity.

Maurice Strakosch fell face-down on the sawdust floor. Dead.

The bandmaster seeing him there, stony-still, waved his baton frantically, and the band struck up its merriest 'oom-pah' circus music.

More than one miracle had happened. Strakosch dead, his various contracts rendered null and void.

17

'Caro Nome'

Posters announcing Madame Melba in *Rigoletto* had not been torn down yet. They met Nellie's eyes as she went about the city buying certain necessities. Yesterday she had farewelled Madame Marchesi. Today had been spent settling in to the small house off the Avenue Louise. It was not a happy time. The house was an extravagance, but it was too late to back away from the lease. Besides, Marchesi had urged her to stay put. She had returned to Paris to confront Strakosch, to remind him of the many favours she had put in his way over the years.

Scrubbing a bench elbow to elbow with her maid, Nellie paused in her work, closed her eyes tight, and wished hard for the death of Maurice Strakosch.

'What is it, Madame?' asked Marie, surprised to see Nellie smiling.

'I have just had a happy thought,' said Nellie grimly.

The landlord came to see her, waving aside any mention of advance payment. But then he announced extra charges that had not been spoken of when she agreed to take the house. The services of a footman, a second maid; fees for the upkeep of the small, beautiful garden. Oh, it was an honour to accomodate the new star of the Brussels Opera . . .

Bitter, ironic bad dream that it had all become!

233

MELBA

Then:

In the middle of the night a wild banging and convulsing of the doorbell occurred. Nellie struggled from a deep and uneasy sleep. She hardly knew where she was. Bells, foreign voices, a ship? Was she already on her way back to Australia, in her shame? Then details forced themselves on her, and she felt even more uneasy in her stomach. She was in her newly leased house, but it would not be hers for long because she was without the means to earn a living.

Wearing nightclothes, Nellie hurried down the hallway, only half-awake. She put her mouth to the door and shouted, 'Who is it?'

Marie came running down the stairs carrying a lamp, and stood behind her.

'Lapissida,' came the voice from outside.

Nellie opened the door and a wild-eyed Lapissida stepped in. He was without his usual decorum. Marie held the lamp up to his face. His collar was undone. He too had been roused from his bed.

'*Strakosch est mort*,' he declared.

Nellie covered her mouth. It was what she had wished, but never actually desired, had she caused this? It was a moment of horror. Marie led them through to the sitting room, where Lapissida accepted a glass of schnapps, and Nellie had one too.

'My dear young woman,' he murmured. '*Il est mort hier au soir, dans un cirque.*'

Nellie recovered herself. A picture entered her mind of the apoplectic overweight Czech enjoying himself: 'He died at the circus?' she said wonderingly. 'Then he died happy, Monsieur.'

'God rest his soul,' said Marie.

'I did not wish this,' said Nellie.

'No, of course not,' replied Lapissida. 'But nevertheless Strakosch is dead. He was a good man. A feeling man. But his heart was weak. And so he died, and you are free to begin, Madame Melba.'

Her voice soared to the heights of the empty theatre.

It was a few days later. Marie and George, by special

'CARO NOME'

invitation, sat in the stalls of the Théâtre de la Monnaie watching the activity on the stage during morning rehearsal. Lapissida was showing them around.

'You are witnessing a miracle, young man,' Lapissida whispered to George. The boy did not know what he meant. Or care. That was his mother on the bare, distant stage. The sounds she made had been with him all his life. They were his assurance of warmth and security, they were indistinguishable from the arms that enfolded him, in which he often wriggled as he tried to escape. Love was the air he breathed; he could not distinguish whether it came to him in the deep sadness or exquisite joy of a voice. He wriggled in his seat impatiently. Marie frowned at him, and tapped his hand in gentle reproof.

Lapissida leaned forward, entranced.

Up on the stage, Du Pont sat at a piano. Stage-hands trundled barrows across the boards. There was activity everywhere, but Nellie's voice, inhabiting the measures of Verdi's great *Rigoletto*, was oblivious to the activity going on around. Such a small figure in the empty magnificence of the theatre, thought Lapissida. So much life and tragedy distilled into a human instrument. It brought tears to his eyes. He trembled when he thought how close Brussels had come to losing her.

Marie, too, was spellbound. She was a simple girl, but the singing started all manner of thoughts racing in her head. She had begun her service by disliking Nellie, but now loved her desperately, and would die for her, if asked. It was the music, the voice, that brought her to this pitch of emotion: Verdi, as much as her beautiful young employer, if only she knew it.

George slumped back in his seat. He sucked a rainbow ball supplied by the resourceful Lapissida. He would wait until the next interruption to the singing, when he would demand to be taken into the dungeons under the theatre. It had been promised.

When the time came, Marie waited behind. The man and the boy walked through a damp stony passageway, then descended an iron ladder. They emerged under the stage, where safety lamps glowed and bearded men were at work among crossbeams and ratchet-wheels. Lapissida put a finger to his lips. From above their heads could be heard, faintly, the sound of singing. The bearded men were dressed in peajackets. Some wore earrings, like pirates. They were sailors, whispered Lapissida, retired men of the sea. The below-stage workings of the theatre resembled nothing so much as the rigging of a ship. Here were stanchions, buckles and stays. The silence was weird. Each man, as he worked, kept an alert ear for the cues in the music denoting that a wheel should be turned, a rope hauled. George wished he were one of those men. He would dream about them that night. Lapissida showed him a tombstone set into the floor, where people were buried hundreds of years ago, before there was a theatre here.

During rehearsals, Nellie was hardly aware of the effect she was having. She only knew that she had never sung as well before. The feeling of release, of doors opening, of walls flying back stayed with her. She sent flowers for the funeral of Maurice Strakosch. At night she fell into an exhausted, dreamless sleep.

Each day her voice soared to the heights. She held nothing in reserve. Her only fault, Du Pont warned her, was this one of enthusiasm. She must not ruin her voice before using it. Thus cautioned, the discipline she had learned from Marchesi kept her to the task. Not yet. Instinctively she knew that this was no time for self-reflection. She had expended all that in the days before the death of Strakosch, when it seemed that nothing was due to her. This was work in the name of art, as her teacher had insisted. She did not stop to gauge the effect. On the last day, though, at the end of rehearsal, the cast stood amazed as the notes of '*Caro Nome*' declined and died away, sinking down from the catwalks where fly-men were tying off ropes, down past flimsy flats to the bare boards of the stage. Here Nellie stood, humbled in her triumph, and the entire cast applauded her.

It was another of those times in her life when an outer personality seemed to be shed. Each occasion felt like the first

'CARO NOME'

and only time. She stood in awe of the newness in herself. Tomorrow, the theatre would be full.

She gave no thought to Charles.

On Charles's return to England he was found to have pneumonia. He became rather ill. Montagu was all for sending dire telegrams to Belgium:

'To scare her out of her wits,' he suggested. The Armstrongs knew nothing of the trouble over Strakosch. It would have been food and drink to Montagu, had he known.

'No, no, no! Leave everything to me,' shuddered Lady Armstrong. She loathed the way Montagu fed his appetite for malice so incessantly. It was not as if Charles was at death's door.

No. There would be no more disruptions if she could help it. During these weeks Lady Armstrong wrote only the most careful of notes to Nellie, and refrained from telegrams. She told Nellie that Charles was progressing as well as expected, considering his self-neglect. On the worst aspect of the case, Charles coughing blood, and raving in delirium, she said nothing. People recovered from such things. It was the marriage, really, she thought about. She projected every woman's younger idea of herself on to the idea of Nellie on the stage of the glorious Théâtre de la Monnaie. If it hadn't been for Charles she would have crossed to Brussels herself for the debut, despite her own infirmities. Her only thought was that Nellie must do what she must. What a wreck of bitterness and disappointment would lie ahead for them both if she failed to take her chance there.

None of the family knew that every day Charles hoarded a little more strength secretly to himself. When the moment came he would slip down to Dover and catch the night packet to Ostend. He was kept going by the thought. He could be in Brussels within twenty-four hours. The twenty-four hours of his choice.

One day his mother brought him a box of his old toys, found gathering dust in the attic.

'You might like to sort through these, for little George,' she said. There were lead-moulded guns, soldiers in pith helmets and turbaned tribesmen. There was an American Indian chief, in headdress.

It was the night of thirteenth October 1887, the stage of the Théâtre de la Monnaie. Nellie was singing in her debut.

She looked out at the audience and it seemed she might be standing on the edge of the earth, at evening.

The quietness, as she drew breath, was celestial . . . The steady shine of the footlights, the delicate movements of Du Pont's arms as he addressed the orchestra; the violins; the pale, anxious face of her *répétiteur* in the wings.

She sang 'Caro Nome'.

Her voice soared out. She stepped forward in the hush of her own making.

The white shirtfronts of the men, the diamonds of the women were faintly reflected, way up into the heights of the theatre, like stars.

She could not, herself, hear the perfection of what she gave to these many hundreds of people. She could not turn around and become a listener. She was held within the beauty of what she made. She was the forge and the crucible of its creation.

Her singing was as familiar to her as her own life, and as strange. It was the gift she gave.

She began to be an artist then . . .

After the aria there was tremendous applause, and she made her exit.

Trembling with nervous energy, she entered her dressing room. Her dresser attended her, whispering 'A success, Madame Melba, a success.'

Time passed so quickly.

She returned to the stage area. From the wings she watched the baritone singing '*Cortigiani, vil razza dannata*'. Then she stepped out once more, amid stupendous commotion.

Soon it was Act III. Back in her dressing room, she heard the tenor singing '*La Donna e Mobile*'. She assessed herself in the mirror. She drew breath and quelled disbelief. Was it really her? Neither Nellie Mitchell nor Mrs Armstrong stared back at her.

'CARO NOME'

She was Madame Melba . . .

Then the climax: '*Non morire . . . mio tesoro . . . pietate . . . Mia colomba,*' sang the baritone. '*. . .Non morire . . . o ch'io teco morrio.*'

'*Non piu . . . a lui . . . perdo nate . . . ,*' sang Nellie, as she indicated her death. '*Mio padre . . . Addio!*'

'*Gilda! Mia Gilda! . . . E morta . . . Ah, la maledizione!*' sang the baritone at the last.

The curtain fell. There was a sound coming from the other side, a rumble, a movement as of mountains. Nellie rose from Gilda's death and navigated the passageway through the curtains, holding her costume.

She was aware only of applause.

It rained down on her, this tempest of noise. Dazed, she gestured into the orchestra pit. Du Pont raised his arms in appreciation, then with a quick flourish gestured the applause back upon her. She could not escape it. She came forward yet another pace. She bowed low. What human could survive it, she thought. Acclamation came on her like a wild surf on a reef. It was wonderful to feel. It was better than any dream of it. After an age she retreated through the carefully held-back curtain. Her fellow cast-members urged her forward, and again forward. Several times she returned through the curtains. Attendants hurried behind her with flowers. It was all for her, everything: the adoration, the cheering. She touched her throat. Du Pont raised his arms once more. The thunder subsided, and there she was, again, singing '*Caro Nome*', her curtain call.

In the dressing room afterwards Madame Marchesi came to greet her. They embraced.

'You are the dream that comes true,' said Marchesi.

'I can never repay you,' replied Nellie.

'Not all the gold in the world can repay a teacher,' said Madame Marchesi. 'The only reward is the teacher's success.'

In the rain-pitted night the patrons of the Théâtre de la Monnaie waited for their carriages. There was a large-headed young man among them with dark eyes and a passionate,

MELBA

artistic expression. He despised the crowd for its crass and hearty salutations of the new young star. They believed they had discovered her tonight, but they understood nothing. To them, she was but a new sensation, a novelty of the moment: their admiration had an aspect of hysteria. It was redolent of the mob.

His eyes searched for the carriage he had ordered. As he pushed towards it he strove, as always, to disguise a marked lameness in his left leg. To this young man, whose name was Eugene Benoit, Madame Melba had already become an obsession. He had been present in the Paris salon when she'd first shown herself to the discerning. It was delectable to think what she had. Quite simply, he was in love with the voice and would surrender to it through any passage and variation of music. There would be delight in savouring it for many weeks to come.

He would return to the Théâtre de la Monnaie again and again, during this season.

He thought she was a very great prize.

A man named Augustus Harris came from London to Brussels especially to listen to her: he was director of the Royal Opera House, Covent Garden. He could not credit that she had sung in London before. Impossible to think that concerts and auditions had been held, and nobody attended.

Rather nervously, afraid of missing out on this prize, he arranged with Lapissida for her to come to London when she was finished in Belgium.

He made no excessive promises, because it was un-English to be extravagant. He did not use the word 'star'. But there was an anxiety about his attitude that gave Nellie assurance.

A routine was established between the small house off the Avenue Louise and the Théâtre de la Monnaie.

In the mornings, in Nellie's light and airy living room, she sat for her portrait, which was being painted by the well-known artist Emile Wauters. Madame Marchesi had sent him to her before returning to Paris: there would be no

'CARO NOME'

moment, she said, like this ever again. Afterwards, she played with George. Then mother and son ate a small luncheon together. In the afternoons she rested, and studied her scores. A prodigious effort of remembering was being demanded by Du Pont and Lapissida. All the operas she would perform in the coming weeks in Brussels she had studied with Marchesi, but she would make no mistakes. Her routine here was as close in its way as the one she had followed in Paris, except instead of each day's climax being a closing away of herself in a studio with her teacher, she arrived each evening into a splendid and glorious world of light, music, and adoration: the great and beautiful Théâtre de la Monnaie, which she loved.

Soon, posters for *La Traviata* replaced those for *Rigoletto*. The commonest sight in the foyers, above the crowd of heads, were placards announcing 'House Full'.

Another week, and the posters were saying *Lucia di Lammermoor*.

Every night, Monsieur Eugene Benoit was there, sitting in his regular seat in the stalls. He sent no flowers or cards, as others did. He kept no vigil at the stage door. His adoration had a purity and nobility of purpose.

Outside, it rained incessantly. Black sheets of water swept down the deserted avenues.

The time came when a man with an umbrella stood reading a poster announcing Madame Melba in *Lakme*. He was pale. His hands shook in the chill. After a while, he turned away and continued walking in the direction of the Avenue Louise.

It was Charles Armstrong.

Late at night Charles was shown into the living room of Nellie's rented house.

'Please sit down,' said Marie.

'Yes,' said Charles. 'Thank you.' But he remained standing, warming his hands by the fire as if they could never be warmed. There were several displays of flowers, and a collection of cards on the shelf expressing admiration of 'Melba'.

The visit was not really a surprise. Marie and Nellie had

talked of Charles's impending arrival several times: 'When Mr Armstrong comes,' Nellie had said, 'You will show him every courtesy.'

Marie asked him if he would like a drink.

'I would like a glass of whisky. A large one,' said Charles. He indicated the measure with his hands, as if Marie understood nothing.

They were hands that trembled.

He stared around at the very objects that must have fascinated Nellie when she took the place: a frieze on the marble fireplace, a gold clock, an eighteenth century Venetian painting. The room was wide and warm, its fireplace glowing with coal. But it was repellent to him.

So this was what attracted her now, he thought: gilded, useless, hired places that existed only to demonstrate recent access to money. A house for wealthy transients, for opera singers. For 'stars'.

Marie handed him his whisky.

'Madame will be back from the theatre at eleven-thirty,' she said. Charles thanked her, and Marie departed from the room.

In the window bay stood an easel and canvas. Charles adjusted a lamp to illuminate it. It was a portrait of his wife, recently finished.

She was more beautiful than ever.

He sipped his whisky and felt warmth creep through his veins. The dark creamy quality of the paint was alive. Whoever the painter was, he had put the richness of desire on with his brush. Men would want her, seeing this picture, as he wanted her himself, now, in a feeling he fought against. It was if he stood at the start with her, and had never possessed her at all. He hated the humiliations of lust.

He heard voices at the door, and drained his whisky. He put his empty glass on a shelf. He ran a hand through his hair.

Nellie entered the room.

'Charles,' she said, and without hesitation crossed the room and kissed him. Her lips were cold from the outside air. She gave out the bold, emphasised scent of the theatrical dressing

'CARO NOME'

room. Her gestures had become exaggerated, he thought.

Nellie stepped back. She sensed his sour illness, his desperation, his worn-out longing. She would not indulge her pity, however.

'How do you like my room?' she asked.

Half an hour ago she had taken her curtain calls while applause dinned in her ears, and the eyes of a thousand enthusiasts were on her. Surely it was possible for Charles to gain from that adoration. She felt, suddenly, a distant and tender emotion; as if he had struggled across a vast space to be with her, and must be rewarded.

She led him to a chair. She sat opposite him. She saw that he was terribly thin.

'Charles, how sick have you been, really? Your mother made light of things, but you've been very ill, yes?'

'How solicitous you are,' said Charles, looking down at his hands. There had been days, as he lay in his delirium, when these hands had wanted to grab hold of and terrorise the woman sitting opposite him now . . . or else, in his convalescence, had desired nothing except to hold her tenderly.

'You have a very fine house,' he said, with awkward formality.

'Oh, Charlie, don't speak to me like a stranger. I'm still your Nellie, you know.'

He looked up and met her eye.

'My God. Are you?' he said.

Her heart sank. 'Well, of course I am.' She laughed nervously. 'I know it's been a horrendous year for you Charlie, but it's all over now. We can be together.'

'The year is up,' nodded Charles.

'Oh, the year,' said Nellie in agreement. Excitement rose in her. She would tell him all about it. 'Look at me now, I am the most astonishing success, that even if I think about it, I cannot believe what is happening. I am said to be a sensation. They love my voice.'

Charles nodded. 'I've come to ask you to let it all go.'

'I don't understand.' Nellie's voice went very cold. 'We're free to travel, see places, do things. Our families will be so proud. The things I've learnt in twelve short months would amaze you!'

'That was our agreement,' Charles continued, 'that you'd have your year. To see how far you could go. Well, you've seen how far. We all have. And I've done what no other man would permit: allowed my wife to go to the limit. It's very good what you've done, mind, I'm . . . so proud of you,' said Charles with difficulty. 'Now I want it all to stop. I want you and Georgie to come back to England with me.'

Nellie stared at him. His words, as he spoke, were more and more clipped and demanding. So this was his answer: after everything, after all she'd been through, he understood nothing. She felt a wave of irritation, then contempt. She felt close to nausea.

She stared at him. She had just come from the opera, where a thousand voices had called her name. Couldn't he see?

Because Nellie said nothing, Charles became a little easier. He thought there were still gaps in her life to exploit.

'We'd live in the country, of course, on the farm. But London's not far away. There'd be nothing to stop you giving a concert now and then.'

'London. Concerts,' repeated Nellie, as if measuring the smallness of Charles's ideas. She could not hide the contempt in her voice. He seemed very provincial to her, in his tweeds. His mental certainty about matters beyond his experience was frightfully narrow. To think she had once adored him as the most careless and commanding man on earth.

Very well then. She would spell it out for him.

'Charlie,' she said, 'a whole new world has opened to me. You must see that, after what I've achieved. Next month I go to London, to Covent Garden. Don't you want to be there? It will be glorious, Charles . . . You'd like more land, I know. Very well,' she laughed, 'buy the farm outright. No more petty poverty and enforced separation. We'll be rich.'

Charles's eyes searched around the room for the whisky decanter. Without asking, he poured himself another glass. Strangely, his hands no longer shook. Her insult steadied him. She was asking him to be a paid man, a consort to an opera

'CARO NOME'

singer. She did not know what she was saying. She was mad with the success she talked about.

He drained back the whisky.

Nellie watched him, feeling a little apprehensive about what would happen next, remembering Mackay and his rum binges. He put the glass aside and fingered one of the congratulatory cards on the shelf, reading its dedication with a sour smile.

'Very nice, I must say.'

'You can see how everyone thinks of me as Madame Melba,' said Nellie lightly. 'I still have to repeat the name to myself, to believe it's true.'

'I didn't marry "Madame Melba",' Charles replied. 'I'd never heard of "Madame Melba" in Mackay.'

'I went to Mackay as a young girl in mourning for a mother I desperately missed. I found you Charlie and I fell in love. But there was always today. It was coming. My whole life has been aimed at this point.'

Charles gave a surprised, bitter laugh.

'You tore me away from one of the greatest opportunities of my life. That's what it means,' he said, draining his whisky. He looked around the room with an expression of finality. 'Ask your servant to bring my coat,' he added.

Nellie felt relieved.

'You know, of course, that you are welcome to stay here,' she said. 'And come to the theatre tomorrow night. As my special guest. Please.'

'What a foolish thing to say,' said Charles.

There was a long silence between them.

'I'm at the "Hotel Splendide",' continued Charles grimly. 'It suits me very well. I will come tomorrow to see my son.'

Nellie rang for Marie to fetch Charles's coat. When she turned her back he hurled his whisky glass into the fireplace, where it smashed into pieces.

'Damn you,' he muttered, avoiding her eye.

Early the next morning a note came from Nellie by messenger: *I beg you to think what our life could be together*, it read. Charles held the paper at arm's length, and put it to the

245

match. Smoke swirled through his narrow room. When he opened the window to let it out, scraps of ash drifted over the rooftops of this foreign city. His calmness today was really quite something to feel. What a nervous waste all his longing and anticipation had been, making him ill. Action was the tonic he needed: coming to Brussels, going to her house, seeing how she lived, smashing the glass in the fireplace. Rejecting her.

When Charles returned to the house before noon, Nellie was out at the dressmaker's. She had left a message, imploring him to wait.

Marie propelled George down the hall into his father's arms.

'Papa,' said George, awkwardly kissing him. Charles dangled him in the air. The boy was shy, but would always know his father, always love him.

'Feel in my pockets,' said Charles. They played an old game, with Charles on all fours on the floor. Objects from his pockets spilled out, all over the rug.

George murmured in wonder. There was a nest of string, a pearl-handled pocket knife, a railway ticket with punch holes in it. The most wonderful thing of all was a finely made toy artillery piece, painted bright red.

'Like it?'

'*Oui.*'

They knelt together while Charles loaded a match into the gun. The boy's face was concentrated delight. Charles drew back the spring.

'Now. It's cocked. Loaded. Ready to fire?'

'*Oui* . . . Yes.'

The match sped through the air and reached the far end of the room. George ran and fetched it, then reloaded the gun himself.

'I had this when I was a small boy,' said Charles.

George wasn't listening.

'And here,' continued Charles, reaching into another inside pocket, 'is something else.'

George glanced quickly around, then his eyes widened.

'What is it, Papa?'

In Charles's hand were four perfectly moulded lead figures. Three Indian braves on ponies, and a chieftain with a

'CARO NOME'

rainbow-coloured headdress reaching down to the ground.

When Nellie returned from her dressmaker's at noon, George was still on the floor playing with his gun and his Red Indians.

'Where is your Papa?' she asked.

'Gone,' said the boy.

She thought about her afternoon rest, her studying of scores. She wanted no more disturbances. It was not good enough for Charles simply to come and go as he pleased. It was her house, after all. She wanted an agreement between them settled as soon as possible. When that was done, she would be able to concentrate on her work.

'That is most rude of him,' said Nellie, touching a finger to her lips. She looked at Marie inquiringly.

'He will come back,' said George, lining up a target.

'What time will he be back?' Nellie asked Marie.

'No, no,' whispered Marie to Nellie, drawing her out to the privacy of the hall. 'Please understand. Monsieur Armstrong he will not be back. He is catching the train today, for England. He said to tell you goodbye.'

Marie was embarrassed to report Charles' message, and Nellie was humiliated to hear it: Charles in his fury could be so calculatingly insulting. Nothing in writing. No tender word of farewell. Just a few words left with a servant. She thought it cowardly of him simply to walk away.

'Yet it proves something,' Nellie mused to herself. 'He really meant it last night. To think I offered him a charmed life, free from financial care.'

Charles did not leave in the afternoon as planned.

Instead, he changed his ticket to the midnight train and went to the Théâtre de la Monnaie, where he obtained a standing room position for the evening's performance.

After the overture he felt a great stirring of interest in the audience. Nellie came on. Her voice filled the theatre in a way he had never heard before. It was strong, it was beautiful. Its loveliness was ethereal. He could hear people around him murmuring with astonishment as they listened. It told him everything.

She had been right. This voice would make a fortune. It

was all beginning here, as she had said, and would go on from here to greater and greater success.

He stood listening, his eyes on the small distant figure on the stage. Everything belonged wholly outside Charles now, remote from intimacy, fixed in time. He might just be able to think of her like this, hold her like this in his mind if he tried.

Before the end of Act I he turned and left the Théâtre de la Monnaie without a backward glance.

18

Star Ascendant

When Charles returned to England, Montagu found him closed up as tightly as an oyster.

'What happened?'
'Nothing much.'
'She toss you out?'
'No.'
'Put you off again? Make promises?'
'No.'
'Disarm you?'

Montagu raised his eyebrows. They were inspecting the fields. The first faint touch of green was in the weeping willows along the streams.

'What do you mean?'
'You know, women old boy . . . They have their ways,' said Montagu.
'No.'
'Hear her sing?'
'Yes. Indeed I did.'
'Good?'
'Better than good, I can't tell you.'
'Ah . . .'
'It wasn't that.'

'Well, for pity's sake, Charlie, tell your brother. I've only your best interests in mind.'

'No.'

'She threatened you, then,' said Montagu with a distinct edge of satisfaction to his voice. 'She's in a position to do that, of course.'

'How?' asked Charles.

'Through the boy,' said Montagu unfeelingly. 'He's hers till he's a bit older. Still dresses him in velveteen and ruffles, does she?'

'George is bonzer,' said Charles with a smile.

'"Bonzer"?' frowned Montagu.

'Spiffing, then.'

Charles knew what was coming next.

'Men?' asked Montagu after a pause. 'All around her, were they? Like moths to the candle flame, ha, ha.'

'Not a sign of 'em,' said Charles.

Nor had there been. He would not have been able to leave Brussels otherwise. He would have sensed it at once, if sexual betrayal had been in the air. It would have been murder for him. Men were not the point of anything in her life, any more, he could see that: indeed, as it related to him, this was the truth that hurt. It was part of the pain he bore, part of the shame and the impotence of pride . . . She who had once been so warm, so importunate in her loving, would take nothing on a man's terms now.

'So you're not going to tell me a damned thing.'

'No.'

'You will one day, Charlie. You'll need me like poison, old boy. You'll come running.'

'Look. Shut up will you, Monty? I'm just a little tired of everything,' said Charles. He turned and walked up to the cottage.

Montagu smiled and shook his head.

The next day he went to Lady Armstrong. 'I never thought I'd live to see it,' he said. 'Charlie's absolutely poleaxed. Lord knows what happened in Brussels. Everything ventured, nothing gained. Who knows? My own personal feeling is that he tried like the very devil to get her back, but she out-foxed him. Charlie is a simple soul. She's not. Dirty days for our family, Mother.'

He looked at his mother, expecting her to interrupt and defend Nellie as she usually did.

'I have no explanations,' said Lady Armstrong. 'Except what I have said before.'

Obviously, conjectured Montagu, she had heard nothing from Nellie lately. Montagu was gratified by her discomfort, and for the moment this was enough: his malevolence fed on hiatus.

All three Marchesis came to Brussels for the last night of Nellie's triumphal season, which did not end until the wintry early months of 1888. They stayed as guests in Nellie's house, where Marchesi saw how adept Nellie was at managing the new and elevated circumstances of her life. Papa Salvatore played with George, firing his toy gun with delight, a stand-in grandfather, and Nellie remembered Doonside in winter, her mother making visitors welcome: warm firelight and friendly laughter in the parlour, and the knowledge of comfortable beds waiting upstairs. The Marchesis were captivated by this well-managed air of domesticity, combined with a ready sophistication. A few well-chosen, artistically important guests came to the house for a late supper. Even Blanche was impressed, knowing she would not be equal to it herself: for secretly, Blanche had a terror of the public existence, and would rather spend her time in a quiet corner reading a book than be praised and fêted loudly. Her ideal of success was to have an article written about her in an important musical paper, by a certain Berlin professor whose mind she greatly admired, whose only blemish she would hardly admit even to herself, being that he had a wife and several children.

Despite her jealousy Blanche was humbled by the beauty of Nellie's voice, defeated by it in a part of herself that would never begrudge achievement, for Blanche had something rare among the artistically competitive, an aesthetic conscience. As Nellie sang in *Lakme*, Blanche seemed to feel a hush falling over all of Europe, and tears came to her eyes.

On the train travelling back to Paris, however, Blanche let herself go a little on the subject of Nellie's forthcoming season at Covent Garden.

'Can't you see what is happening, Mama? The English have waited their year, while you did all the hard work. You made Nellie's voice. Now they are clamouring to have her. They will take her away from you, and make her their own. That is how the English do things. They are without originality of soul.'

'All my best pupils return, year after year,' replied Madame Marchesi. 'I am satisfied.'

'Yes, but the English,' continued Blanche, 'they have merely adopted the opera as they take up other things, as an aspect of fashion. Who is the driving force behind Covent Garden now? Lady Gladys de Grey. She is a detestable snob. She uses her social position and money to dictate to Augustus Harris. She knows nothing about music but uses the opera as her social playground. It is where she finds her lovers, I am told. She will ruin your Mrs Armstrong with attention. No credit will come your way.'

'Nellie will always show her gratitude,' replied Marchesi. 'I have faith in her.'

With Brussels over, Nellie's attention became absolutely focused on developments in her professional life. Paris was now clamouring for her, but London was promised first. She wrote to Charles, telling him when she would be there, giving particular dates, and saying that George talked of him endlessly. How wonderful to think they would be seeing each other again, so soon, she wrote.

Charles made no reply. Nor did he say anything to his family.

Nellie crossed the Channel, settling into rooms in the Savoy Hotel. When still no word came from Charles, or from anyone close, she decided she had estranged the entire family, and in particular, Lady Armstrong. There was little doubt in Nellie's mind that Lady Armstrong had closed ranks with her son. Who could blame her?

STAR ASCENDANT

Nellie was determined, however, to feel guilty over nothing. She had only her singing, and her singing had only her.

London. What had it been before? The foggy streets, the indifference, the warm circle of her family against the cold glory of the Empire's capital; door after door closed in her face. All of that had happened to another person, she thought, as maids ran her bath, a footman arrived with baskets of fruit, and a lovely young nursemaid sat on the floor playing tiddlywinks with George. The only thing she had gained from her earlier humiliation in London, she thought, was the armour to return. Now Augustus Harris smoothed the way, personally coming to her hotel suite, escorting her to dinner, and attending to her every wish. She asked him to be sure that Randegger, Sullivan, and Ganz received tickets to her opening night, at her own expense.

She acquired a ready smile, the firm ability to say no, if required, and when she got her own way in something, she gave a prompt expression of gratitude.

Harris was impressed by the forceful presence of one so young, amazed at her ability to express the exactitude of her requirements, ranging from dressing room space to rehearsal time, and at the way she skimped no detail of planning, neither musically nor contractually. Her mind, he thought, was the sharpest he had encountered in a singer.

Nellie decided that if she did not sing brilliantly enough for London this time, why then, there would still be Paris and the whole of the Continent awaiting her. She developed a comforting disdain for the idea of England turning her head. England would have to do the head-turning, she thought.

After a series of rehearsals she opened in *Lucia di Lammermoor*.

Augustus Harris sat with Lady Gladys de Grey in her special box. As Nellie sang, they leant forward attentively, the middle-aged manager and his young, beautiful, aristocratic patron. The hush in the theatre was extraordinary to their ears, and Nellie's voice thrilled them with its remarkable spontaneity. They were of course disappointed that the theatre was only three parts full. But they interpreted the hush all around them as a good sign. It had a certain electrical charge, they felt, not dissimilar to great nights with other singers in the past. Harris felt doubt slip away. He was pleased at his choice of Melba. From now on, he declared to himself, his faith in Nellie would be unwavering.

'Beautiful,' whispered Lady Gladys, and Augustus Harris nodded.

But Nellie knew differently. She sensed the audience's mind as only a performer is able: the mood of the pack silently waiting, attending to every nuance of phrasing and actions, considering its collective verdict: never warming to the enthusiasm of love. She remembered Brussels and what she had tasted there for week after week. She despaired of London again.

Not that it affected her performance. She retreated in her mind, and sang in recollection of a young girl's emotions. She loved this role. *Lucia di Lammermoor* was the opera she had studied with Signor Cecchi. Her memories of the day he had introduced it to her were tinged with passion and a supremely tormenting beauty. Cecchi had sung each part in succession, including the role of Lucia. He had wept, creating the blood-spattered night-dress with his expressive hands.

'Triumphant,' murmured Augustus Harris during the Mad Scene. Nellie's voice died away. Lady de Grey nodded enthusiastically. She stood, leading the applause, which rose heartily from the body of the theatre but was, to her amazement, and to the bewilderment of Harris, not overlong.

It had faded completely by the time Nellie reached her dressing room.

The next morning, at breakfast in her London house, Lady Armstrong opened the papers.

'Good Lord!' she exclaimed to Sir Edmund.

'What is it, Mother?'

Lady Armstrong indicated an item in the *Times*.

'Nellie's in London. Charles didn't tell us.'

'Let me see . . . Well, I never.'

'She actually sang in *Lucia* last night,' continued Lady Armstrong. 'Listen: "Madame Melba availed herself of the dramatic opportunities to considerable advantage . . ."'

Sir Edmund leafed through the *Pall Mall Gazette*: 'Here we are again: "Accomplished in acting . . . Strong dramatic instinct . . ." They don't say much about her singing, do they.'

'"Truth . . . delicacy . . . intense feeling",' Lady Armstrong read in another paper. 'Well I think it's rather good. Nellie must be so proud, singing at Covent Garden.'

Charles entered the room.

'Oh, Charlie, you are a disappointment to me,' murmured Lady Armstrong as he kissed her.

'Don't suppose you were at the theatre last night?' asked Sir Edmund pointedly.

Charles buttered a piece of toast, and said nothing.

'Charles, don't be so obstinate,' said his mother, bringing it all into the open. 'Call on Nellie. Congratulate her. I should like so much to see little George again.'

Charles bit into his toast, and took a sip of tea. He wiped his lips with a napkin.

'Mother, I'm sure I can't explain what I don't understand myself. I've worn myself out.'

'You still love her, surely.'

'What does "love" mean any more? If it doesn't mean a life together, it means nothing. 'She's at the Savoy,' he continued. 'I went there this morning, while she was out. George and I went to the park. I'll bring him to see you tomorrow, Mother.'

'I should love that,' said Lady Armstrong.

'The day after that I'm going to Ireland with Montagu,' said Charles. 'For the fishing.'

'Good for you. Keep the spirits up,' said the Reverend Sir Edmund.

Augustus Harris sat rigid in his chair while newspapers crashed to the surface of his desk: the *Daily Chronicle*, the *Morning Post*, the *Standard*, the *Observer*.

'They hated me,' declared Nellie, slapping the last one down.

'Damned if I understand,' murmured Harris.

'I'll sing again next week, Mr Harris, but then I'm going. Paris wants me, and for considerably more money than you are paying me at Covent Garden.'

'Please be calm, Madame.'

'I am calm.'

'My belief in you is unflinching,' Harris declared.

'Much good it has done, then,' said Nellie cuttingly.

'I implore you,' said Harris. 'Reconsider. The English mind is like a creaky hinge, it takes some oiling.'

She gave him a hard, challenging look. It was as if she hated him. Quite disconcerting. He felt his blood pressure shoot up. It was he after all who had initiated her engagement to sing at Covent Garden, and here the young Melba was showing not a whit of appreciation.

'I shan't reconsider,' she replied. 'Not after the way they've written about me.'

Scorned in London a year ago, and in a special English way scorned again last night, she already believed herself to be a star. She was not prepared to wait for the magnanimity of English opinion to swing in her favour, as it would eventually. Well, let it be.

Harris spread his palms in a gesture of surrender. He smiled. He had found himself a true *prima donna*.

'Quite right too, Madame, quite right. Teach the critics a lesson. Damned tone deaf Fleet Street scribblers!'

'They can't stand the idea of an Australian at all,' said Nellie.

The door opened, and Lady Gladys de Grey entered the room. Nellie realised who she was, though they had never met.

'Madame Melba,' said Lady de Grey without preliminaries. 'I heard you last night. I was absolutely enchanted.'

'Thank you,' said Nellie. 'I am afraid you were in the minority.'

'That will change, believe me.'

Harris then introduced them. Nellie was amazed that the famous woman should be about her own age. When people talked of English grace and beauty, they meant women like Lady Gladys. Harris was in awe of her: she had done much, of course, to bring people of money and fashion to Covent

STAR ASCENDANT

Garden. He was constantly in her debt.

Now they had business to discuss, and Nellie, important as she was to both of them, must leave the room.

There was a look in Lady de Grey's eye that said they must meet again soon, however.

'Good day, Mr Harris. Lady de Grey,' said Nellie.

As she stepped into the corridor she heard Augustus Harris's voice:

'Colonial or no colonial, in no time the English public will clamour for Melba above all others, and, by gad, Lady Gladys, they'll have to pay for her too.'

In the evening a card came from Lady de Grey. 'Could she call on Madame Melba the next afternoon?'

So things were happening, and perhaps it was nothing like the indifference of London the first time. Suffused by calm pleasure, Nellie scribbled a reply in the affirmative.

When Charles came to see George, he read the card while he waited. It had been placed on the mantelshelf in a position of prominence. It made him smile in a relieved kind of way. 'Can't imagine myself spending a lifetime standing around,' he thought, 'greeting titled visitors like a flannelled fool, discreetly retiring while women sit on a couch and touch each other's hands . . .'

He was glad to be out of it all.

When he reached Ireland a few days later he was told by Montagu that Lady de Grey was famous for her lovers. 'Women of her sort,' said Monty, 'love to draw other women into their conspiracies.'

'I hear they're biting farther downstream,' Charles merely replied, shouldering his creel.

Nellie was hardly aware of the extraordinary self-assurance she had acquired. It seemed only natural to her, after years of searching out her abilities, of striving against misconceptions and obstacles, to believe in herself openly as she had privately for so many years. Her talent had been so triumphantly confirmed by her year in Paris, and then by the success of

Brussels. His Majesty the King of the Belgians had presented her with the gold medal of the Brussels Conservatoire. On her last night there, there had been more than sixty bouquets from friends and admirers. So her scorn for London was hardly mere defiance.

'They hated me,' she repeated to Lady de Grey, as they took tea at the Savoy Hotel. 'Therefore I hate them.'

'These London critics must be told what to think, that is all,' said Lady Gladys. 'There is a current opinion that *Lucia* is too conventional a vehicle on which to base a definite judgement.'

'Nonsense,' Nellie expostulated.

'Yes, I agree with you,' smiled Lady de Grey.

'It is passion and sentiment the whole way through,' exclaimed Nellie. 'I adore it.'

'Your Englishman hates to trust his feelings, my dear Madame Melba. But a nudge in the right direction works wonders. When you come back from the Continent again, things will be very, very different. I promise you.'

George came into the room with his nurse and was introduced with much fussing over. With her son on her knee, Nellie spoke about her past: her happy childhood, her father, her sisters. It brought a tear to her eye. How she missed them all.

'Your husband is English, is he not?' Lady de Grey gently inquired.

'Yes. I am sorry he is not here today,' said Nellie, ushering George from the room. 'He's in Ireland with his brother Montagu. They are the Armstrongs of Gallen Priory, King's County. Perfectly horse mad every one of them.'

'How very interesting.'

Lady de Grey had a particular way of speaking, a particular way of handling her tea cup, a lovely sense of fashion, and an impressive aura about her. Nellie found herself copying her manners, her mannerisms. She found herself envying the other's aquiline nose. She wished she could say, 'Call me Nellie' with the same translucent shimmer of authority Gladys showed when she said, 'Call me Gladys.' These were schoolgirlish feelings she was unable to check in herself.

'Interesting, as you say,' Nellie repeated. 'Charles has a superb eye for horse-flesh.'

'Are you fond of the outdoor life yourself, may I ask?'

'As a girl in Australia I was forever swimming and riding,' said Nellie.

'My husband, Sir Frederick, is the greatest shot in England. But speaking for myself, I abhor all outdoor sports.'

'No, I am not keen now,' said Nellie, striving for agreement.

The two women's eyes met, and at the same time they laughed.

Lady Gladys extended her hand to Nellie.

'I know we shall be friends,' she said, with a warm promise in her beautifully modulated voice.

At the door, she kissed Nellie on the cheek.

'Goodbye, Gladys,' said Nellie.

London did not seem so uninteresting after all.

But as soon as Nellie arrived back in Paris thoughts of England disappeared from her mind absolutely. She slipped into the French language with ease and naturalness. She reminded George of the simple incantation he had used at Madame Nathan's: *'Je suis Georges. J'habite à Paris avec ma mère.'*

Greeting Madame Marchesi, Nellie enthused:

'Paris. This is my true home. I don't care if I never see England again.'

She leased an apartment in the Rue de Prony, near the Parc Monceau, and soon George was happily settled there. He loved to play in the small, walled garden, where iron railings spiralled down into a leafy paradise. A rather frightening letter followed her from Ireland, suggesting that George be placed in a boarding school in England. It was written by Charles, but behind every word and every sentence Nellie sensed the looming influence of Montagu. How cruel to lock a small child away at his age. It would be a prison!

She tossed the letter into a drawer.

Then came the night of her Paris debut. The opera was Thomas' *Hamlet*.

MELBA

The theatre was packed, the doors bolted, the audience hushed. Very briefly, as Nellie began singing in the duet '*Doute de la lumière*' and then the air '*Mieux vaut mourir*', she caught a sense of the same reserved assessing mood that had lasted the whole way through in London. But by the end of the first act word came back: the audience was buzzing with talk of a triumph. By the fourth act there was a feeling of a veil being thrown aside. Nellie sang astonishingly.

Madame Marchesi felt it, as did everyone there including the mysterious Monsieur Eugene Benoit, who was in Paris at that moment by happy coincidence, just as he'd been in London for *Lucia*.

He would later enclose a critic's description in a letter to a young nobleman, his closest friend: 'When Ophélie was seen to enter in her white garments, garlanded with flowers, and her fair hair floating down over her shoulders, Madame Melba was transfigured. That which ravished us was not alone the virtuosity, the exceptional quality of that sweetly timbred voice, the facility of executing at random diatonic and chromatic scales and the trills of the nightingale; it was also that profound and touching simplicity and the justness of accent which caused a thrill to pass through the audience with those simple notes of the middle voice, "*Je suis Ophélie*". And when at length the echoes of the lake wafted to us the last high note of the poor young creature, an immense acclamation saluted in Madame Melba the most delicious Ophélie that has been heard since the days of Christine Nilsson and of Fides Devries. She was recalled three times after the fall of the curtain, and, as statisticians, we have calculated that three recalls like these in the Opera at Paris are quite equivalent to seventy-five recalls in Italy at the very least.'

She was a star in Paris from that moment on.

Nor was it only the voice that made an impression that night. The physical beauty of Madame Melba as she stepped across the stage was breathtaking. She bowed low, expressing a lovely mobility, a superb grace. In her dazzling gown she stepped back a few paces. The French were quite open in their admiration of her as a woman.

STAR ASCENDANT

At the front of the theatre attendants moved around unbolting doors. This action usually precipitated a rush of departures. But tonight no-one left. In the boxes and in the stalls everyone was on their feet. A chorus of acclamation surged forth, a chant of 'Melba!', 'Melba!', 'Melba!'

The cry had a resonance that would now be heard wherever she went.

'Melba!', 'Melba!', 'Melba!'

Even, it seemed, in England.

If Lady de Grey's letter had come from the Queen herself, Nellie could not have treasured it more. Intimately addressed to 'My Dear Nellie', it told of the Princess of Wales's enthusiasm for her singing, and how her name was often mentioned in court circles. It promised that when Nellie returned to London everything would be different. She would be under Lady de Grey's personal care and would lack neither for friends nor hospitality. The letter told of Augustus Harris's plans for *Romeo et Juliette*. A whimsical little drawing was enclosed for George. At the end it was signed with friendship, admiration, and love.

Nellie folded Gladys de Grey's letter carefully away. England, she thought. There had for long been a sense of English doors being closed against her. But now she had been given a key, and the means to turn it. After much hating of the idea of going back to face another frosty reception her ideas changed. She felt she understood England so much better now.

19

Bohemia in Tiaras

A reception was held at the Paris Opera to mark the end of Nellie's first season there.

There was applause as she entered a room crowded with admirers.

Monsieur Eugene Benoit did not rush forward to introduce himself, but allowed the magnetism of his position gradually be felt. He was known not so much for his connoisseurship (which he would have liked) but for his connections to the exiled aristocracy. He had arranged with the Director that at an appropriate moment he would have a few words alone with the *diva*.

Benoit took up a champagne glass in his hand and, after pausing a few moments, advanced bearing his tribute.

'Champagne, Madame?'

'*Merci*.'

'My name is Eugene Benoit, Madame.'

The Director and his assistants tactfully withdrew.

'What do you do, Monsieur,' Nellie asked, 'apart from bringing champagne to ladies?'

'I am the first connoisseur of your work, Madame Melba.'

Nellie sipped her champagne, looking amused.

'Then you must have been a little boy in Australia . . . But I don't think so. You are too pale.'

BOHEMIA IN TIARAS

'I heard you sing in Paris,' Benoit persisted, 'when you were still a student. I was there in Brussels, Madame, at the Théâtre Royale de la Monnaie, when you sang Gilda in *Rigoletto*. London, too, of course. And finally I was here in Paris, for your debut in *Hamlet*.'

'You were in London, when they hated me?' asked Nellie. Her curiosity was thoroughly aroused by the intense Monsieur Benoit.

'A most passionate *Lucia*,' Benoit nodded slightly. 'And I swear I shall be there the second time, too, when they shall love you more, if I know the English.'

'I am beginning to take you seriously, Monsieur Benoit,' said Nellie. 'Very seriously indeed.'

A waiter hovered with the champagne tray.

'Another glass?' Benoit attentively asked.

'No, no, I am leaving for London on the early train,' said Nellie.

'Madame, I have friends who wish to meet you,' said Benoit abruptly, in a low voice.

'Then bring them to me,' said Nellie, misunderstanding him and looking around. 'I am sure that any friends of yours would be connoisseurs of the first order.'

'Indeed they are,' Benoit replied in a hurried whisper. 'But they are not here. They are in England, and wish to make contact with you there.'

'They are English?' frowned Nellie.

'French.'

'You mystify me,' said Nellie, a touch coldly.

'There is no mystery, Madame. Of gracious artistry my friends know less than I, but that is of little account. They are most appreciative of feminine charm. You would find them . . .'

Nellie swiftly interrupted. 'It appears you have another role in life, Monsieur connoisseur.'

'Madame, you misunderstand . . . They have heard me praise your art . . . I merely wished to flatter . . . They wish to meet serious people only,' he bowed low, flustered, apologising.

When he raised himself, Nellie was gone.

Later, composing herself for sleep, Nellie thought about the encounter. The world of opera, of theatre, was regarded as a sexual hunting ground by some, but it was the first time that a man had spoken to her in the hope of procuring a mistress. She smiled, thinking of Charles and his talk of 'singers'. How little he understood her, or the pure heights of achievement that were hers. The man Benoit had been persistent in a most peculiar fashion. He was physically unfortunate, with a tendency towards profuse sweating, and a most pronounced limp that he tried to hide. But she had not really minded him, indeed had been flattered, until the moment of his fumbled frankness. His own passions were musical, she thought. He could not be faulted on dedication and knowledge. If she had more followers like him, she would have a *claque* of her own in no time. But on whose behalf was he asking?

The story would be sure to amuse her new friend, Lady Gladys de Grey.

After the years of anticipation and hope, of planning ahead, of averting obstruction and misunderstanding, the new conditions of Nellie's life remained a cause of wonderment to her. Each night for a few hours she lived in the immortal present moment of performance, radiating, as might a source of light, fantastic variation: it was the spectrum of calculated beauty that was music, that was art. To perform as she did meant unremitting hard work and sometimes physical exhaustion, yet she exulted in the very circumstances. There was no looking back, nor any of the straining forward that had been part of her for so long.

Now . . . always now . . . Now she is being dressed for *Romeo et Juliette* at Covent Garden. She kneels, and at the same time seems to glide forward. The train of her costume spreads behind her.

'Perfect!' says the wardrobe woman.

Her hands are clasped, her head lowered. For a few seconds she might be praying. She is able to gather the forces of fragmentation into herself at these times. It is instinctive meditation, a focusing of power that was never taught by any

BOHEMIA IN TIARAS

Cecchi or Marchesi. Perhaps one day it will have to be summoned by mental practice, but not yet. It is simply there, in her, burning like a cold fire. Nothing else matters except to rise and walk from here, through the backstage labyrinth and purposeful mess, to step out on those few square feet of illuminated stage, and there to sing.

As Nellie rises, Lady de Grey enters the dressing room, bearing an armful of flowers. Nellie turns and smiles, utterly sure of herself.

'The house is full,' says Lady de Grey. 'The Prince and Princess have arrived.'

Now . . . now she is on stage, a small distant figure singing the '*Waltz Ariette*'. Benoit and his friends sit motionless in a box. They are captivated. Their heads swim with visions of France as the words of the libretto reach them.

Augustus Harris is pleased, sensing the mood of his audience properly this time. The critics are there, and they will say what they like and it will make no difference. Mostly, they will glorify. The astonished audience, unconsciously instructed by the machinations of Lady de Grey, feels only the uniqueness of the night. They are privileged in their magnanimity. These people have come bearing their gift of adoration, which has somehow occurred to them all at once. To have been ignored in London for a while was only Madame Melba's due. You never give people what they ask for at once. Withhold, and the glory shall be thine, is their attitude to appetites of all kinds; they have been shown this lesson at their chilly public schools. Lady de Grey knows their minds well, for she is one of them herself: more intelligent, more original, perhaps, but now deeply satisfied to have them gathered together at the focus of her energy, the Covent Garden Opera House.

The Prince of Wales and Princess Alexandra lead the applause.

Afterwards, there is a supper party in the room behind the royal box.

'Be calm. Be natural,' advises Lady de Grey. 'The Prince will already know something about you. The Princess Alexandra is a friend, she knows her opera, she loves you already, you know.'

Nellie dressed as Juliette takes a deep breath and enters the room.

The Prince of Wales and his wife are sitting on a couch. He is a portly, pleasure-loving man. The Princess sits beautifully erect, with lovely grey eyes and a clear Scandanavian complexion.

After the introductions, the curtsies, the Princess asks:

'Did you come to England as a girl, Madame?'

'Oh, no, I came as a student, a few short years ago.'

Nellie nervously adjusts the folds of her dress, but is otherwise composed.

'London did not like me then,' Nellie admits.

The Prince speaks:

'Madame Melba's father is a highly respected building contractor in Melbourne, and that is where she gets her name: "Melba". It is a good choice . . . You are not as tall as you seem on stage.'

He eyes Nellie in a pleasant, easy way. Lady de Grey from experience can see that Nellie attracts him. But there is a certain reservation there. She is very lovely, the Prince appears to be thinking, but not the kind of woman who would respond to intimate overtures of the kind he likes. She would have no long empty afternoons in her life, to be filled by royal jollity. It is perhaps time to withdraw. Inconspicuously, the Prince nods to Lady de Grey.

'I will come and hear you as often as I can,' says Princess Alexandra. 'Your friend Lady de Grey is my friend too.'

As swiftly as she came, Nellie is taken from the room.

That night, as she brushes her hair before bed, she catches her reflection in the dressing table mirror, she stares at herself. Can this really be her?

She lies back full-stretch on the bed, her head resting on a satin pillow. Her eyes are open and she stares into the dark. She feels a wonderful sensation along her limbs, in her nerves, as if she has risen after a great struggle to the surface of a stream, and is now being borne along through a world of beauty and wonder . . . lightly . . . effortlessly . . .

BOHEMIA IN TIARAS

Nellie woke from a restful, dreamless sleep.

A voice reached her from the other side of her bedroom door. She felt abruptly disturbed.

'*All right, tiger. One. Two. Three. Jump!*'

It was Charles's voice. He had come to see George.

There was the sound of small pounding feet, and then a playful 'ooffing' from Charles. George's delighted, devoted laughter filled the air.

Nellie sat up in bed with a dry mouth and a sensation that nothing had changed in her life. But then she realised that something had much changed: a thousand things.

The voice of her lawful husband, only feet from where she lay, rang dully on her emotions.

Nellie swung from the bed and crossed the floor. She twisted the key in the lock. She leant against the door breathing sharply. She felt giddy from this act, which was a kind of betrayal.

'*Ready, Papa?*'

'*One. Two. Three. Jump!*'

'*Ssh!*' from Marie. '*Your Mama is still asleep.*'

An outer door clicked, and all was quiet.

Nellie hurriedly dressed, and went shopping. A little later, she called on Lady de Grey. A small luncheon party was held: the brothers Jean and Edouard de Reszke were there. Other guests clamoured for Nellie to sing, but Lady de Grey would not permit it.

'Your voice is your fortune,' she said to Nellie. She might also have added, 'And ours at Covent Garden too.'

Instead, the de Reszke brothers performed an exquisite rendition of 'Echo and Silence'.

When Nellie returned to the Savoy Hotel at mid-afternoon, Charles had been gone for several hours. There was no message, no attempt at communication. It was a clear separation between them now. As if by agreement, each move and counter-move was calculated. Their defences against each other had replaced the intimacies.

It was later in the season. Nellie and Lady de Grey were taking tea in Nellie's hotel suite. Nellie handed a sheet of paper over to her friend.

'I am sorry,' she said. 'I have crossed out Mr Harris's figures and replaced them with my own'.

'Are you aware that Augustus's figures are, as it were, my own figures, dear Nellie?' said Lady de Grey.

'Yes . . . But these rooms are too small,' replied Nellie. 'I will have to take a bigger suite. Then there's my house in Paris to keep up. If I don't find a second maid I shall never get anywhere on time. You said yourself that Mr Harris must be made to appreciate me: "to the limit" I think were your words . . . Gladys.'

'That is over,' smiled Lady de Grey.

'He will try even harder for sixty pounds a night,' said Nellie, not feeling quite as brave as she sounded. She could never have bargained like this without thinking of her father and his principles.

Lady de Grey began to laugh.

'What is the joke?'

'You make me smile.'

'Then . . . we are agreed?' Nellie pressed the point.

Lady de Grey conceded rather a lot. 'Of course. You are our new star. You have power over us all. If people know you are to sing, then "Melba" tickets are scarcer than gold. You are the rage, Nellie. I hear your name mentioned wherever I go. Even at Windsor.'

'Windsor?'

'The Queen asks about you.'

'Oh,' said Nellie, suddenly shaken. 'Really?'

Lady de Grey was curious to see Nellie's reaction. A moment previously, she had been pacing the room, making her amazing demands. Now she gripped the mantelshelf as if to stop a fit of giddiness. A photograph of her father was there: trim silver beard, gimlet eye. Nellie stared at the picture with almost frightening concentration.

'She wants me to, I am to, sing for the Queen?' asked Nellie.

'Yes,' nodded Lady de Grey. 'Tosti will take you to the palace. He taught singing to the royal children. He will put you at your ease.'

BOHEMIA IN TIARAS

'When?' asked Nellie.

'Next Tuesday week,' said Lady de Grey.

'So soon?' Nellie asked.

'Yes. Why ever not?'

She could not explain. It was as if she needed more time to perfect herself. Everything else had happened so slowly for her in England, she had needed to push and to persuade: but now to sing for the Queen, that was something different. The thought rushed at her as if from the dark. She had imagined such a summons coming at the end of her career, as a mark of the highest recognition.

But she quelled the fear.

'I will be ready,' she said.

Before it could happen, though, Nellie caught cold and everything was postponed. Another date was fixed some time ahead, after her return from a series of new engagements at the Paris Opera. It was a curious feeling, to reach out and affect the destiny of the most famous woman in the Empire. Today, Queen Victoria would be doing one thing instead of another, all because Madame Melba had decreed it.

Daily her thoughts leapt about like this, as she adjusted to the idea of her achievements. In her regular but rushed letters home she could not help sounding a little boastful.

When Lady Gladys de Grey spoke of small, intimate gatherings she meant no more than fifty or sixty guests. Several times each month, at her house in Bruton Street, she entertained 'with a touch of that apotheosised Bohemianism of which nobody else ever quite had the secret'. It was sometimes referred to as 'Bohemia in tiaras'.

One such occasion took place soon after Nellie's recovery from her cold. This time, Lady Gladys asked Nellie to sing, breaking her own rule. She wanted to elicit astonishment from her guests.

A footman near the door made regular announcements of arrivals:

'Monsieur Edouard de Reszke . . . Signor Paolo Tosti . . . The Duke of Cambridge . . . Lady Warwick . . . Madame Melba . . . Monsieur Jean de Reszke . . . Mr Alick Yorke . . .

The Duc d'Orléans . . . Monsieur Eugene Benoit . . . The Duc de Luyns . . .'

With some surprise, Nellie recognised the name of Monsieur Eugene Benoit from Paris. She looked around. The sallow Benoit caught her eye and bowed slightly. What was he doing here? She was mystified, and slightly annoyed, as if he had contrived to follow her, exploiting Lady de Grey's innocent connivance. She turned her head aside. He confused her, still.

Everyone was happy and laughing. The whisper had gone around that Melba was to sing.

Lady de Grey pointed out the various guests to her.

'Alick Yorke will try to monopolise you over supper. You must not mind being rude to him . . . Lady Warwick will want to know all about labour conditions in your country, for she's recently adopted the fad of socialism . . . The Duke of Cambridge hardly knows whose house he's in, poor dear . . .'

Nellie's attention was caught by a tall, thoughtful young man in conversation with Paolo Tosti.

'That is the Duc d'Orléans,' said Lady de Grey.

'Oh, yes,' said Nellie.

She had been told he would be here tonight, but had not expected one so young, or so handsome.

'His father is very ill, so Philippe came in his stead. When the Comte de Paris dies, Philippe will become pretender to the French throne. A romantic idea, is it not? But rather doomed by the obstinate republicanism of his nation, I am afraid.'

Lady de Grey, intoxicated with the success of the occasion, and from champagne, took her elbow and began steering her around.

'You must meet my husband,' she said. 'You know, if husbands and wives don't occasionally attend their own parties, they have no opportunity of meeting at all. Does your husband go with you, anywhere?'

'Well, I . . . ' managed Nellie. She had so far in their acquaintance avoided the subject of Charles.

'Ah! There is Tosti alone at last,' said Lady de Grey.

They made their way to where he stood. Tosti bowed low

BOHEMIA IN TIARAS

and kissed Nellie's hand.

'Lady de Grey tells me you are a little nervous of our coming royal occasion.'

'No, not at all.'

'You will see. I am very at home there, at Windsor Castle. I shall look after you . . . Do you know my "*Serenata*"?'

'Of course, it is one of my favourites.'

Tosti turned to Lady de Grey.

'May I have the honour of accompanying her?'

'Delightful.'

Tosti took her arm, and they walked towards the music room. Lady de Grey signalled to a footman. It was all made to seem impromptu, an impulse derived from the effervescence of the moment. But really, the plan for Nellie to sing tonight, and for Tosti to accompany her, had been organised well ahead.

Footmen went around whispering to the guests:

'The music room, if you would be so kind . . .'

The assembled guests stood expectantly about.

Nellie faced them, standing a little to one side of the piano as Paolo Tosti prepared to play his '*Serenata*'. Her pose was simple and dignified.

A silence fell. Louis Philippe Robert, the young Duc d' Orléans, thought her very lovely. Her fine profile and upswept dark hair were much to his liking. He had sometimes discovered that women who seemed beautiful on the stage were coarse and blatant in their features on closer acquaintance. Not so Madame Melba.

His older companion, the silver-haired Duc de Luyns, was rather bored. He was not musical. The company tonight was elevated socially but had none of the diplomatic *cachet* he favoured. He would have preferred a game of chess with his old friend the Comte de Paris, to this duty of escorting Philippe about.

Eugene Benoit, at Philippe's elbow, blissfully closed his eyes, awaiting the first pure notes.

And then they came.

Nellie's voice soared out over the heads of Lady de Grey's

privileged guests. It was very beautiful.

After the '*Serenata*' a second song was demanded. Then a third.

It was already midnight. From the door of a private club opposite Lady de Grey's house a group of men spilled on to the pavement. They had been drinking and gaming. They talked noisily among themselves for a few moments but then, abruptly, one of their number raised a hand for silence.

A voice reached them from a high, lighted window on the opposite side of the road.

Unmistakable whose voice it was.

They looked at each other.

One of their number, Charles Armstrong, staggered on to the road as if magnetised.

'Easy, old boy,' said Montagu, grasping his brother's elbow.

The others lit cigars and listened.

Charles thrust his hands into his pockets. He stared down at the pavement. Then, reluctantly, he lifted his eyes to the window.

'God Almighty,' he muttered under his breath. It was a curse or a prayer.

The song ended.

'Thought you didn't care any more,' said Montagu, putting an arm around Charles's shoulders. He led him down to the next corner, where a group of cab-men waited with their horses. They drove off into the night.

Lady de Grey's assembled guests applauded in gratified amazement. The very tones of Madame Melba's voice were intoxicating. Alick Yorke stamped his small feet and cried '*Brava!*' in a high-pitched voice. The Duke of Cambridge woke from an exceptionally pleasant dream.

Turning her head to acknowledge the praise, Nellie discovered the handsome Duc d' Orléans staring at her disconcertingly. Their eyes held for a few moments.

Then Tosti kissed her cheek, and Lady de Grey expressed her appreciation by graciously taking her elbow.

'You were superb,' she said. 'Quite, quite the very best, my dear.'

Footmen moved among the guests. 'Supper is served,' they murmured.

A short while later the young Duc d' Orléans, flanked by Benoit and the Duc de Luyns, spoke with Lady de Grey.

'Tell me, my Lady, when is Madame Melba to sing again?'

'She sings Juliette next week. But in Paris, I am afraid.'

'I shall be there in Paris to hear her,' said Philippe.

'Really?' exclaimed Lady de Grey. 'How extraordinary.'

Her surprise came because she knew, as everyone did, that Philippe and his father were exiles from France, under pain of imprisonment if they returned.

The Duc de Luyns frowned, disliking such open talk. A clandestine Channel-crossing was planned; it had a definite political purpose; he hated the idea of its being mixed up with any romantic adventures.

Eugene Benoit keeping his thoughts to himself, merely sought out Madame Melba with his eyes. Yes, what a great prize she was!

The Duc de Luyns took Lady de Grey aside. He spoke to her in rapid French, betraying guarded irritation. 'Philippe is a gallant youth, so intensely romantic,' he said. 'His qualities are those we French love very much. He is, perhaps . . . a little impulsive?'

Lady de Grey understood what the Duc de Luyns required of her. 'Of course, you have my word,' she replied. 'Not a whisper concerning his visit to Paris shall pass my lips.'

When Nellie returned late to the Savoy Hotel there was a steely-grey suggestion of dawn in the sky.

It had been a memorable evening. The manner in which the young Duc d'Orléans gazed at her stayed in her mind. But of course so did many other impressions of Lady de Grey's salon: the Duke of Cambridge dozing in a chair; the touch of rouge on the cheeks of Alick Yorke; the glorious style of Lady Gladys as she moved among her guests. At the de Grey house in Bruton Street she had found a blend of sophistication, social prestige, and artistic excellence that gave deep satisfaction. It was the *milieu* she had always dreamed about. Dukes, footmen, and artists. She had come from Australia for this. No exciting detail dominated over another. Tosti had kissed her hand and told her that no-one had ever, could ever sing his '*Serenata*' as she had.

As she drifted towards sleep, starlings already making a noise outside her window, she smiled to think of the compliments she received these days from composers. What a contrast it made with her first weeks in London. She had passed the houses of the great, then, with their ranks of carriages waiting outside, and had felt only the cruelty and the coldness of it all.

She found she had little sympathy left for the callow girl who had arrived so hopefully. 'One must make one's way,' she told herself. To think also: she had once gone to the London house of the Armstrongs, and been humbled by its magnificence. Now she thought of the Armstrong house, indeed of the Armstrongs themselves, rather differently. Of course she still liked Lady Armstrong enormously. With a sort of wistful guilt, she resolved to call on her on her next return to England. Why should she deny herself a friendship just because Charles was busy cutting himself out of her life?

The next morning there came an incessant banging on Nellie's bedroom door. She was wrenched from a confused dream of the night before: tantalising reflections in glass, subdued candlelight, voices murmuring in French, dawn breaking too early.

A maid announced that Mr Armstrong wished to speak to her. All the pleasure of the the night before slipped away, leaving in its place a feeling of apprehension.

'Very well. Give me ten minutes. I should like some tea. A large pot. An extra cup for Mr Armstrong.'

'Yes, ma'am.'

Hurriedly Nellie dressed and tried to calm herself. She felt dull dread where once there had been the excitement of love. Before opening her door she placed her hands on her hips, breathed deeply, and as if going on stage, recovered her nerves.

BOHEMIA IN TIARAS

Charles looked as if he hadn't slept for weeks.

'I'm sorry,' said Nellie, stifling a yawn. 'George is out walking with Marie. What *time* is it, Charles?'

'Eleven-thirty.'

'Oh,' she was surprised. 'So late? Please sit down.'

'This won't take long. It's about George.'

'Sit, Charles. I can't think without a cup of tea. I had an engagement last night. It went on until all hours . . .'

'My apologies,' muttered Charles. He sat down heavily. She feared his sarcastic expression. It always meant difficulties. 'I, of course, have all day,' he shrugged.

He punched a fist into the palm of his hand, and stared about at the decorations of Nellie's suite. Apart from the hotel items, everything else had come from a suitcase: family photographs, mostly.

'My father has gone grey. It was a shock to everyone.'

'Time passes,' said Charles. 'He was never easy on himself . . . Look, it does a boy no good, you know, living in hotels like this.'

'I have a large house in Paris. That is my home now. But please, let us wait for the tea.'

'All right. All right.'

'How is your mother?'

'Mother is well. She sends her love.' It cost Charles something to say this. She was grateful to him, though.

'Give her mine, please Charles.'

'Yes, of course.'

The tea came, and Nellie poured.

'You like it black, with two sugars,' she remembered.

He accepted a cup, but put it to one side. He gave the impression that if he drank her tea he might compromise himself somehow.

'Let's get to the point, for Christ's sake,' he said. 'I have a request to repeat to you. George must have an English education, in an English school.'

'I have always believed so myself,' said Nellie. 'You know that.'

'Then why did you ignore my letters?'

'Letter. There was only one.'

'Ah,' Charles smiled calculatingly. 'Then you received my request, and chose to ignore it. How very interesting.'

Poking from one of Charles's pockets was the corner of a buff-coloured envelope. There was a glimpse of sealing wax. Nellie sensed, with great heaviness of heart, that Charles was acting on legal advice. How shameful to both of them that he had been driven to it. Yet she must fight him on it.

'He's so young. He's still a baby,' said Nellie.

'I would remind you,' said Charles with a hard stare, 'that English boys go away to school at an early age. You are an admirer of all things English, I do recall. Some things don't change.'

'What do you suggest?'

'The new term at Priory Grange starts in six weeks. Keep him until then. I will come to you, wherever you are, and collect him from you.' Charles stood and looked down at her.

'No,' she was at a loss. 'You sound like a cruel figure in a fairy tale.'

He laughed drily. 'Deny it all you like. I am his father. I have the full weight of the law behind me.'

'Everyone says what a good mother I am.'

'I will tell you how it will look in a court of law. You are a performer on the Continental stage, living a life of wealth and frivolity, without moral restraint and normal standards.'

'Good God. I can't believe what I'm hearing. You are threatening me with lies.'

'Hardly that. I am realistically suggesting an outcome. If you continue your attitude.'

Nellie stood, and began pacing around the room. Her voice rose in volume.

'I've always noticed this about you Charles. An ability to twist circumstances to suit yourself.'

'Look who's talking.'

'I have friends in high places now. English friends. They will speak for me in any dispute.'

'Now you are threatening me in return,' Charles tiredly smiled. 'It won't help. English friends are all very well. But

BOHEMIA IN TIARAS

I am talking about English law, not your scarlet-robed Continental imitation.'

'Stop it,' said Nellie. 'Stop it and let me think.'

Charles' words had given her a wild idea. English law was all very well in England, but how far did its power reach across the Channel?

She decided to gain time.

'Very well,' she said. 'I agree. But when the time comes, I will bring him to you, Charles.'

Charles was surprised by such a rapid capitulation. He was ready for it, though. 'I must have it in writing,' he said.

'I shall write,' said Nellie, feeling quick anger.

'Now,' Charles insisted.

'Don't be so silly.' Charles pulled the envelope from his pocket and held it out to her.

'I had best make myself clear. A special constable is waiting outside with my brother Montagu. If you like, they will stay there until George returns from his walk. Then they will take him away.'

'Today?'

Charles nodded. 'Unless you sign this agreement.'

'So all along you had only one thing in mind,' said Nellie, tearfully opening the envelope. 'How coldly calculating you are, Charles. You were not like this once.'

'Well, I'm a good student,' said Charles. 'I learnt from someone who was once close to me.'

Nellie scanned the prepared agreement. It was simple enough. Cold enough. Cruel enough. And there was a copy for her. She signed, thinking: in France I will get an opinion on the weight it carries there. Charles will pay for his hardness.

'I am sorry it came to this,' said Charles, tucking the paper in his pocket.

'Leave me, please,' said Nellie. Her tears burned.

That afternoon she left with George for Paris.

20

Le Premier Conscrit de France

Her Paris engagement in *Juliette* began.

Each night, repeated cries of 'Melba!' thundered from the body of the theatre. It was one voice, ten thousand voices. The walls echoed and shook to the expression of admiration. Flowers piled high on the stage. Outside, a crowd of students and the poor accompanied her walk from stage door to awaiting carriage.

It was not work, but ecstasy. She lived in the music, pouring energy and emotion into her role. She was never absolutely satisfied, but the applause, the adoration, told her how close she came. On many nights, Mathilde Marchesi was there. Emissaries arrived from various opera houses around Europe. A series of engagements was offered for months, years ahead. Monaco, Milan, Stockholm, Berlin, St Petersburg.

The copy of the letter that Nellie had signed for Charles was studied by a highly-placed Parisian lawyer who called it an empty threat, without power to do immediate harm, although she should not have signed, he said, without consulting a lawyer of her own in London. The next stage would undoubtedly be legal proceedings from that side, should she fail to come to an arrangement over George. There were ways and means of blocking English court orders from France, but

LE PREMIER CONSCRIT DE FRANCE

they would cost a great deal of money.

'I have the money,' said Nellie.

'Well, that is good,' said her lawyer.

She went away to think about what she should do. She came to no clear decision.

One night after repeated curtain calls, which seemed, if anything, more wildly adoring than ever, Nellie arrived back at her dressing room to find it filled with orchids.

She was amazed. Small candles were lit among the creamy, seductive blooms, creating the soft, deep effect of a forest cave. She spun around. Everywhere she looked there were flowers, with wisps of flame flickering like fireflies. The rich scent of the petals was intoxicating. Everything was doubled, and redoubled, in the mirrors. She sat at her chair, her costume settling to the floor around her, wondering who could have arranged such a tribute. There was no card. She was alone. Her dresser had been bribed, she supposed.

She looked up into the mirrors, into the reflected orchids again, and there, in a reflection of the glass, the door opened. There was suddenly a face. A young man stepped into the room.

'You?' she was startled.

It was Philippe, Duc d'Orléans. For a few mysterious seconds he was in the mirror with her, drowned in flowers.

'These are your flowers?' she turned to face him.

'Oui, pour vous . . . "Juliette",' he bowed slightly. 'You were enchanting. I have never felt such emotion at the Opéra before. Never in my life.'

He took her hand and kissed it.

It was strange, exciting, and she smiled in disbelief; if he'd been an ordinary admirer she would have asked him to leave at once. But he was of exalted rank, a prince.

'Madame, I should consider it an honour if you would have supper with me. All is arranged.'

'No, it is impossible.' (Though suddenly the impossible was what she desired.) Their eyes seemed unwilling to leave each other.

MELBA

The moment was broken by a quick tap at the door. Monsieur Benoit glanced in, his eyes bright with excitement. They seemed to say, 'Look what I have brought you. Such tribute!'

Philippe snapped his fingers and Benoit disappeared.

'My friends worry too much,' he turned back to Nellie, covering a slight irritation. 'Madame, I await your answer.'

'I cannot take supper with you. I simply cannot. You must understand.'

'Tomorrow?'

Nellie shook her head.

He bowed low and left the room. She regretted her words at once.

She rose from her chair, her heart hammering with confusion. What was happening to her? She remembered the way Philippe had stared at her at Lady de Grey's. She believed she had hardly thought about him since, but now it seemed she had thought of him under every other thought. She sank down into her chair again, and started unpinning her hair.

As it fell to her shoulders the door opened and Philippe stood there.

'Madame, I beg of you.'

She threw a cape around her shoulders, and still dressed as Juliette, without a thought for the consequences, left the theatre with Philippe, Duc d'Orléans.

Much happened in a short time.

They emerged by a side door, where Nellie was recognised by a crowd of devotees making a dash along the pavement calling 'Melba!', 'Melba!' A carriage with drawn blinds waited at the kerb. Philippe helped her up, and climbed in himself, quickly securing the door. Benoit scrambled up beside the driver, and the horses began moving.

'Melba!' 'Melba!' 'Melba!'

In the muffled darkness Philippe took Nellie's hand and stroked her fingers.

'Madame, please understand me. I am not like other men. I value your art and your person above everything. Your honour I would defend with my very life.'

His murmured words came at her as if from a dream. Impetuous, passionate, they were quite out of context as far as her life was concerned. They were inconceivable. Yet they were spoken. Nellie had no way of answering such intensity.

She could only submit.

They arrived at an apartment building about ten minutes' carriage drive from the Opéra. The street was dark, but as they alighted Nellie saw enough to recognise a building in a respectable quarter, with nothing to distinguish it from others nearby. The door was held open by an older man who spoke a quick, muffled word to Philippe: 'All's well.' When the door closed behind them, Benoit turned up a lamp. The older man was introduced as Colonel Florian D'Aurelle. He was aged about sixty, and had the steely-grey hair and weathered features of an old campaigner. His eyes raked across Nellie with indifference or contempt: whichever, she disliked him.

It was then that doubts began. She felt trapped among strangers. What sort of place was she in? What was she allowing? She had put her trust in Philippe but he, born to a certain attitude, walked briskly ahead. She was being shepherded along by Colonel D'Aurelle, while Benoit shambled in the rear. They passed along a corridor decorated with hunting trophies, African spears, and watercolours of forested rivers. An ancient maid, with a face like a walnut, bowed low as they passed.

At the top of a stairway Philippe opened a side door, gesturing her into a sitting room. Benoit and D'Aurelle withdrew.

The door clicked softly shut.

Nellie stood in a spacious room with a warm fire burning in the grate and a small supper table laden with food. Philippe removed her cape and folded it on the back of a chair.

'Warm your hands by the fire, Madame.'

She was trembling. But if he noticed he kept the observation to himself. He poured two glasses of a golden wine.

'You will feel better after this.'

'Thank you.'

'I see I have surprised you,' he said. 'You expected the Palace of Versailles, at the very least.'

'No, no,' smiled Nellie, though it was true.

She sipped her wine, which was sweet and very rich. She felt much better now, though still somehow afraid. Her thoughts spun themselves out into separate components. Her fears related to herself, rather than to the praetorian D'Aurelle or the furtive connoisseur Benoit. She had no experience as a guide for the situation she found herself in, only the knowledge that while the actuality was cause for great excitement, the bare fact of it (opera singer with duke in private room) was intolerable.

Philippe led her to a chair and became suddenly serious.

'I am here in Paris incognito,' he said. 'But one morning soon I will proceed to the *mairie*, where I will express my desire, as a Frenchman, to perform my military service. They will probably arrest me, and throw me into a foul-smelling prison cell. That is how far I am from palaces, Madame.'

Nellie looked at him while he concentrated on his words. His chin rested on his hands. Reflected firelight played across his face. She realised now the full meaning of his presence in Paris, and was filled with a great tenderness at the thought of his bravery and resolution.

'But surely you were seen at the opera tonight.'

'*Pour vous . . . "Juliette"*,' he smiled. 'You may imagine what Colonel D'Aurelle thinks of music and the arts. But I say to him, I am practically a stranger in my own country.'

'If they arrest you . . . '

'It is a matter of duty and honour. And who knows? Perhaps the people will become incensed, and call for a *coup d'état*, and I will become crown prince of France.'

Nellie detected a touch of irony. She wondered whether he saw himself as merely acting things out for a lost cause, the youthful instrument of his ailing father the Comte de Paris, and of such severe unrelenting adherents of the Orléans party as Colonel Florian D'Aurelle.

'I can imagine you, a future king,' said Nellie resolutely.

Philippe met her eyes. Abruptly their conversation was

fraught with intimacy.

'I am very young,' said Philippe.

'I would obey you, if I were one of your subjects,' said Nellie.

'But Madame, you should command me,' said Philippe artfully.

There was a knock at the door and the elderly maid entered. Swiftly and silently she served the supper things, and then stood with her hands folded in front of her apron, her eyes lowered.

'*Merci, Madame Claire*,' said Philippe. When she withdrew from the room he said with great sincerity:

'I know what you are thinking, Madame Melba. That every young man must come to the theatre at a certain age, and seek out an *artiste*. That I am no different from the others.'

'No,' said Nellie earnestly. 'That has never been my experience. I am thinking no such thing.' (She had thought it earlier, but not now.)

Philippe offered her food, and poured two glasses of Bordeaux. He drank some, then leaned back in his chair, and said, somewhat ingenuously:

'Eugene Benoit led me to you. He is a very great connoisseur. When I saw you in London, I knew we could be friends.'

'The Colonel does not like me.'

'D'Aurelle? He prefers deserts and jungles to people. Do not mind him, Madame.'

The house was very silent around them now. No more footsteps, no doors opening and closing.

'Yes, we are alone,' said Philippe, sensing her thoughts. 'I have dreamed of this moment day and night.'

He leaned across the table and took her hand.

'Please,' murmured Nellie, lowering her eyes.

'While you are dressed as Juliette I feel it doesn't matter that I am so young. She was so young.'

'She must always be played by someone older,' said Nellie, bewildered by Philippe's intensity, yet wanting to match it somehow. 'How old are you?'

'Twenty-two years.'

'Your manner . . . Your confidence astounds me.'

'I am trembling, Madame . . .'

MELBA

Nellie realised that she had finished her glass of wine and was half-way through another. She continued rather hectically:

'Gounod once told me, *Juliette etait une affrontée*. It was Juliette who proposed to Romeo, not the other way around.'

'That is delightful.'

'When I was twenty-two I lived in a primitive town in the tropics, where the bamboo grew in front of my eyes and the vegetation steamed. There were snakes as long as fire hoses. Crocodiles swam in the rivers nearby . . .'

'Wonderful . . .'

'Your Colonel D'Aurelle might think so. I hated it. I was far away from everyone I loved.'

That was not entirely true. She had loved Charles there. But now, for Philippe's sake, it seemed important to picture herself alone.

'We are both exiles,' he responded. 'I was born at Twickenham, near London, during the first law of exile. I am practically English.'

'You are very different from the English I know,' said Nellie with emphasis.

'Ah,' said Philippe. He was, for the first time, slightly embarrassed. She guessed he knew she was married, knew all about her, in fact. Eugene Benoit would have told him every last detail of career and background, that she was married to an Englishman, but was apart from him because of the demands of her chosen profession. She hoped he would not ask about Charles: even to think of him in the presence of this noble young man was a further betrayal she could not contemplate.

Now their supper was almost finished, and with gracious regret, Philippe announced that it was time for her to be driven back to her house.

'You have had supper with me, and was it so terrible?' he smiled.

'No,' she said. 'No, it was not terrible at all.'

In the carriage he sat away from her a little, and smiled. Standing at the door of her house (with D'Aurelle and Benoit waiting in the carriage), he said: 'I would like to be your friend, Madame Melba.'

'I would like that too,' she replied.

Many thoughts battled for possession of Nellie's mind as she drifted towards sleep that night.

She tried to make things clear to herself. A handsome young man of impeccable background had confessed, in the most charming manner possible, a devotion that came to the very brink of passionate declaration. In the enclosed carriage his words had been like an unexpected burst of light. He'd spoken of honour and devotion: the after-image still blazed along her nerves. He had captured some part of herself, as surely as his explorer friends captured trophies in Africa. She had panicked, walking into the house, but had relinquished no decency there. She might have done so had they kissed. She did not think of herself as endangered in any way, except by excitement.

Reflecting on Philippe's use of the word friendship, she realised that her triumphs in Brussels, London, and Paris had blinded her to an emptiness in her life. She had craved for intimate contact and had not known it. She needed a friend too, perhaps even in the sense that lovers used.

They would meet again, take supper again in other circumstances, and would take up where they had left off.

She did not, of course, even consider that she might have fallen in love with Philippe, Duc d'Orléans.

She thought of it as her small secret.

The image of his fine features and youthful, gentle eyes stayed with her now: it was something she carried in her mind as other women might carry a likeness in a locket. Outwardly, nothing was changed. He did not, she believed, represent anything momentous in the way of an alteration to her life. Each evening flowers came, delivered to her dressing room by Eugene Benoit. There was no card, but a wealth of understanding in Benoit's eyes as he breathlessly thrust them into her arms. Three nights passed like this. And still, she told herself, the emotion she felt was merely excitement.

By the fourth night, which marked Nellie's opening in *Lucia*, she was anxiously scanning the boxes for a sight of him. Ridiculous to try, of course. If he was there, he would be well back. If his arrest had come the papers would be full of it. And anyway, the singing controlled her. She went on with it, never faltering . . .

The wonderful notes of '*Regnava nel Silenzio*' wafted towards the rafters . . . the intent faces of the audience were captivated . . .

Earlier that morning, unknown to Nellie, Philippe had presented himself for military service. He was now behind bars.

Now through the darkened streets of Paris hurried Eugene Benoit, carrying flowers. Nobody blocked his way, no police or special agents. There was no hint of any popular uprising.

Benoit thought with bitter amusement of the dreams of Florian D'Aurelle. The old man prided himself on realism and practicality. According to D'Aurelle, the streets of Paris should be alive by now to the sound of running feet and the reflection of burning torches. 'Reaction to the barricades' was the dream of the man. But the trusty bourgeoisie were asleep in their beds tonight, those who weren't disporting themselves at the opera . . .

The doorman was well bribed.

'A biting wind, Monsieur,' he mumbled, unbolting a door and admitting Benoit to the back corridors of the theatre.

Lucia was still playing. Benoit stood in darkness and shook his head in wonderment. Even here, among packing crates and property barrows, the pure notes of Madame Melba's voice reached out, small but undimmed. He thought of the passion and the blood in this last act, of how men like D'Aurelle, in scorning the power of art, denied the blighted humanity in themselves.

He tempted Nellie's dresser from the dressing room with a handful of gold coins, and waited impatiently for the *diva* to return. He was in a mood of strange delight. If he had staged this *Lucia* himself, and sung every role, he would not have felt more satisfaction than he felt now. He thought about the look that would come into Madame Melba's eyes when he told her his news. How, in one stroke, he would penetrate her heart, thus binding himself closer to Philippe, and at the same time establishing himself at the centre of her drama, which he did not think she understood properly at all, as yet, being a woman.

When she entered the dressing room, still wearing the bloodstained costume of her role, he thought it very operatic.

'What news?' she demanded.

'The Duc of Orléans sends his apologies, Madame, but he has been arrested and is awaiting trial for having infringed the exile law.'

Benoit handed her the flowers. She sank back into her chair and clutched them to her chest.

'Oh, my dear God.'

'Excellent,' thought Benoit.

'I heard you singing "*Regnava nel Silenzio*",' he said. 'You were magnificent, Madame. You have surpassed yourself.'

'What will they do to him?'

'Who can say? He will be tried in conformity with the law of 1886. We think he will get a sentence of at least two years.'

'An eternity,' she said. 'He spoke about . . . "the people",' she wondered.

Benoit shook his head. 'The streets are very quiet.'

'The poor boy. Prison.'

'*Oui*. But honour is satisfied. There will be some who remember, and they are the ones that count . . . Just as they will count who remember your voice, Madame . . .'

'Did he speak about me?' Nellie dared ask.

Benoit pulled a letter from his pocket and passed it across to her. Nellie ripped it open and read swiftly down to the bottom. Her lips trembled and her eyes filled with tears as she did so.

'He awaits your reply,' said Benoit.

It was the following midday. As prison cells went, this one was most comfortable. A rug lay on the floor and the sun slanted in through the branches of a plane tree in the courtyard, which was filled with a noisy chorus of birds. The cell had held, over the years, other specimens of national foolhardiness. There was no vindictiveness in the Republic in relation to the Duc d'Orléans, just forms to be followed, rituals to be obeyed. The life of the great city rumbled on in the background. Yes, it could be worse, much worse. Other prisoners had to submit to the attentions of the coarse, belligerent guards, but Philippe was looked after by the prison commandant himself.

Footsteps echoed down the long stone corridor. Philippe lay on a couch with a book propped on his chest. He did not turn his eyes when a key scratched in the lock, but when he smelt delicious cooking odours his stomach reacted.

The commandant stood to one side and gestured the visitors through. Colonel D'Aurelle came first, bearing a heavy silver tray covered with a white cloth. Benoit followed with an armload of books. The commandant wished his highness *bon appétit*, and then withdrew, leaving the door ajar.

Philippe jumped to his feet.

'I have brought you duck with peas,' said D'Aurelle.

'Have you heard from my father?' asked Philippe, hungrily eating his first mouthful.

'He is very proud.'

'That is good. So very good, Florian.'

Philippe placed his hand over the Colonel's, and squeezed it. There were tears in the eyes of the old campaigner.

'They have a nickname for you already in the streets,' said D'Aurelle. '*Le Premier Conscrit de France.*'

'I like that . . .' mused Philippe.

'There is news from our informant in the President's office.'

'Yes?'

'The President believes that after a decent interval, say two months following sentence, you should be released under special orders and escorted to the frontier. It shows a certain fear of demonstrations, if you are known to be on French soil.'

'Very interesting,' said Philippe. Then he turned to Benoit. 'How did she sing, Eugene?'

'It was indescribable. She is born to the role of "Lucia", there is no doubt. She sang with great affection in her voice. As if her heart had been captured, and she was joyous over the fact

LE PREMIER CONSCRIT DE FRANCE

... Ah, if you had been there ...'

'In manacles, a prisoner?' laughed Philippe. 'I should ask the commandant. The President! He will arrange it.'

D'Aurelle disliked this levity over serious matters. He frowned.

'She too is a prisoner, Philippe,' chuckled Benoit, pleased at his conceit.

D'Aurelle looked increasingly troubled. He placed a hand on Philippe's cheek.

'You are a good Frenchman, Philippe, a good Catholic. The French people are not truly republican, not in their hearts. One day you will make a fine marriage. You must be ready.'

'You take much upon yourself, my Colonel,' said Philippe warningly.

Philippe turned to Benoit and continued with deliberate lightness.

'What about the pretty notepaper you promised, Eugene?'

'It is here. Now which pocket?' playacted Benoit.

D'Aurelle turned his back in humiliation and disgust, and stared out through the barred window.

After a swift, concentrated reading of Nellie's letter, Philippe tucked it between the pages of a book, and continued eating. Her words surprised him a little. They were ardent and naive, the thoughts of a young girl expecting much, rather than the worldly outpourings of a twenty-eight year old opera star ... Especially one who had already enjoyed the diversions of the marriage bed, and had a lively high colour in her cheeks that showed she remembered them very well.

Nevertheless he was too far gone in his desire for her to hesitate now.

He scribbled an ardent reply.

Nor was Nellie prepared for such a frank, unguarded declaration of love as this letter of Philippe's made. The words were like a whisper against her ear, astonishing her, making her dizzy, setting her blood racing. She adored each stroke of the nib, and gazed at his name on the bottom of the page as if looking into his eyes.

Eventually she folded the notepaper away, and dismissed

the waiting Benoit. She did not know what to say yet, in response to such an escalation of fervour. Thinking hard, she went about her daily routine.

It was astonishing, this idea of him locked in prison. At night she spoke his name in her prayers. Writing home to Australia, to her father and sisters, her hand trembled at the enormity of what she withheld: the glory of his name. Her life completed its great wide shuddering turn; she was already a different person. Yet, as she kept reminding herself, no single practical circumstance had altered. She sang as usual, pouring energy and splendour into her art, while a young man languished in a prison cell.

21

George goes to School

The Paris season ended and she found herself busy with a multitude of business arrangements. Soon she was to go to England again, to sing for Queen Victoria at Windsor Castle. Meanwhile directors from the Madrid and Berlin opera houses arrived on her doorstep. Augustus Harris came, competing with the rest, and she was reminded, though she would not admit it openly to Harris, that London still represented the pinnacle to her. The money and conditions he offered, combined with proceeds from her European engagements, would make her rich.

Apart from singing for the Queen, there were other matters of personal concern that made a short visit to England imperative. For reasons that Nellie would barely admit to herself she had changed her mind about keeping George with her in France. When a letter from Charles's solicitors came, demanding a meeting on the subject of George's English preparatory school, she decided to act. One bleak and drizzly morning, she left George in the care of Madame Marchesi and caught the boat-train.

She took her own lawyer, a Mr Crisp, to the meeting at the Inns of Temple. She said little, sheltering behind his protective bluster. But her own feelings were so momentous that everyone would surely see the truth: that whatever she said or did, her thoughts were filled with the idea of another.

Montagu was there, with his calculating sneer. Charles, whose eye she could barely meet, surveyed her like a stranger. How could she hide anything from them? They were so viciously contemptuous of her, under the veneer of good manners. Yet, curiously, neither showed any specific curiosity as to why she had become so amenable about George's schooling. They so generally mistrusted her they were blind to any fault except one. Incensed that she had left George in Paris for these couple of days, they showed frank scepticism as careful arrangements were finalised for handing him over, and a clear date laid down in a document made hot with sealing wax.

'We shall see him on the day, and no tricks,' Montagu muttered as they left the legal chambers.

That night, Lady de Grey came to Nellie's hotel suite to complete arrangements for the royal concert party. She found Nellie sitting at a window, dreamily altered.

She guessed immediately the reason for the change: Louis Philippe Robert, Duc d'Orléans, that most handsome and sensually attractive young man.

'There he was, imploring me to go to supper with him, at that very moment, without delay.'

'Did you go?'

'How could I, a married woman, and so much older . . .'

'But?'

'He returned, minutes later, and I went without hesitation.'

'Oh, my dear Nellie!'

'Then came the arrest,' said Nellie.

'Word reached us here in London,' nodded Lady de Grey. 'It was a terrible risk, his going to Paris.'

'I keep wondering, if it hadn't been for me . . .'

'No, no. Don't torture yourself over it, Nellie dear. He was in France and available for military service, like any true patriot. They arrested him, of course they arrested him. But what a glorious imprisonment!'

GEORGE GOES TO SCHOOL

'Two years,' said Nellie anguishedly.

'Well,' said Lady Gladys, changing her tone, 'perhaps it is just as well.'

'Oh, Gladys, no. It is cruel.'

'Nellie, my dear Nellie. There is more involved than one charmingly romantic young man. The family is very rich and very powerful. The Comte de Paris is a sick man. He has political aims, and Philippe's life is part of them.'

'I know. I know.'

'Do you, though? I have to be brutally frank with you. When this imprisonment is over the Comte de Paris will be pressing Philippe to make a marriage. A royal marriage with another of the great houses of Europe.'

There was no answer Nellie could make to this. Her head was full of pleasant thoughts, her heart excited by emotion. Yet here was Gladys de Grey, a beautiful young woman experienced in the delights of romantic subterfuge (for she had a lover herself, somewhere) laying down the law coldly.

Lady Gladys gathered her things ready to leave.

'Oh, I say,' she changed the subject. 'Aren't you just too excited about going to Windsor Castle tomorrow?'

'I can hardly believe it. The Queen,' smiled Nellie.

'I shall look forward to hearing all about it. Good night, Nellie dear.'

They kissed, the door closed, and Nellie was alone at last.

She drove the words of Lady de Grey from her mind, drove out the talk of great families and marriages and impossibilities of all kinds. She knew already that her situation was impossible, without other reminders. The person she loved was locked away from her. He might almost be dead, she thought. She lifted a flower from the vase on the hallstand and cradled its perfume as she walked through to her bedroom. Yet he wasn't dead, not truly: he was gloriously alive. That was the promise of the letters he wrote to her, passionately, from his cell.

Morality and caution slipped away when Nellie thought about him.

MELBA

The corridors of Windsor Castle were cold and formidable as Nellie moved through them in the company of Paolo Tosti, Jean de Reszke and his brother Edouard. Tosti wore a cape and was flamboyantly 'at home'. He did little to put Nellie at his ease, as he had promised. It was Jean and Edouard who smiled at her, and helped quell her nervousness. A footman asked them to wait in a small side room.

Jean took out a cigarette, tapped it on his silver case, but put it away again when Tosti made a click of disapproval with his tongue.

A cat looked at them from a window ledge. Nellie forgot what she had expected to find here . . . a world away from the world, she supposed. It was too late now for her to be captivated by Windsor Castle. Her impressions of royal grandeur were sealed away in the smile of a certain young gentleman. This part of the castle seemed rather like a dungeon. From somewhere far away came the smells of greasy English cooking.

Tosti seemed to be reading her thoughts, making her uncomfortable.

'*Ma chère*,' he said, '*qu'est-ce que tu fais? Tu n'as pas peur, toi?*'

'No, I am not afraid,' replied Nellie.

Tosti smiled and nodded annoyingly. He did not have the least idea of what was running through her mind. Nellie found him unlikeable, suddenly. She found she looked down on many people, lately, who might have over-impressed her once; though not the de Reszke brothers, especially Jean, who had become her friend during their stage appearances together.

'Melba would not be an artist if she were not excited, eh?' Jean said to Tosti, putting him in his place.

A few minutes later they found themselves in the presence of the Queen, a tiny figure in black attended by ladies-in-waiting. Nellie was presented to her. As she curtsied, she had the impression of immense remoteness, of eyes drawn inwards with age, like an old tortoise. Otherwise it was as if a well-known portrait had moved, just a little, in its frame.

The Queen spoke:

GEORGE GOES TO SCHOOL

'You are from the colonies, Madame Melba. Which colony is it?'

'Victoria, Ma'am.'

'Thank you.'

She was dismissed.

Tosti sat straight-backed at the piano. Nellie, Jean and Edouard took their positions for the trio from the last act of *Faust*.

They sang, and the music washed over the Queen as she sat in her chair. Her small eyes remained veiled. She might not have been hearing a thing, she might be stone deaf, thought Nellie . . . except that way down in the folds of her dress, just touching the floor, the toe of a royal slipper beat time.

The next day Nellie found herself back in Paris.

Rug layers had been to her house. New curtains were hung. Light streamed through with the limpid quality it seemed to have only on this side of the Channel, only in Paris. For a moment of silent, almost religious contemplation, Nellie reminded herself that she was back under the same sky as Philippe . . . if what covered him over could be called sky. He was held near the river, where damp fogs lingered at night. 'Exquisitely comfortable,' Benoit had told her, but still without his freedom. Philippe did not wish anyone except his close associates to visit him, to witness conditions humiliating to a man of his station. Nellie of course was not invited to go there.

Benoit called daily at the Rue de Prony, his stories of Philippe's conditions becoming more and more unbearable. At first he'd said how comfortable Philippe's cell was in comparison with the rest of the prison. Now he mentioned other things: cockroaches the size of small cigars; bed-lice. He loved to watch her eyes widen.

'Oh, it can't go on!' Nellie exclaimed.

'It shall, Madame, for two years, unless the President decrees.'

'But there's been no word.'

'None. Yet.'

He loved to dangle the possibility of early release in front of her eyes, then snatch it away again.

She was short-tempered with George, cautioning him about marking walls, scratching furniture, and possibly breaking her crystalware.

'Darling, you mustn't.' She lifted his hand from a door-catch, which he loved to wiggle. Her glasses and bowls made a most satisfying tinkle, when he did so.

'Sorry, Mama.'

He stood with his hands behind his back, rather bored. He was so sweet! She would have him only for a week longer, and then his dear baby-boyhood would be taken away.

She drew him to her, though as usual he struggled a little to escape her loving embrace.

'Darling, there is something I have to tell you.'

'What?'

'Well . . . soon . . .'

'Yes?'

His eyes lit up. He expected the announcement of a treat, a ride in the woods, a visit to the fire station, a chance to view a military parade; the parades in Paris were great spectacles, with music and horses: she loved them too.

'I'll tell you later, when you go to bed.'

'Please, Mama, please!'

'Later.'

Off he went to play in the small garden he loved so much.

In the early evening, Madame Marchesi came to see the changes to the house.

George trailed them around.

'Everyone in London keeps telling me I sing like a nightingale. But Paris is still my home.'

'The French have adopted you as one of their own. What a remarkable tribute that is to a foreign singer.'

'Berlin wants me, so does Monte Carlo, Madrid, and possibly Milan. There's hardly time to draw breath. But first I'm off to London again.'

'Everything I ever predicted for you has come true. And this is only the beginning.'

'Dear Madame . . . Come and I'll show you the rest of my apartment.'

GEORGE GOES TO SCHOOL

They proceeded from room to room.

George gave a yawn, and broke off. He went through the side doors and down a set of stairs into the garden. Here he loved to play with his toy animals, particularly his horse, which his father had given him. The horse and the tiger fought against each other. When the tiger was bad, George wedged it between the bars on the stairway, which he called 'the prison'...

There was a real prison, he knew, close by in Paris, with a Duke in it: this much George had divined from the regular, and mysterious, visits of Monsieur Eugene Benoit. George was frightened of Monsieur Benoit, who had once twisted his ear while his mother was out of the room. George had a strong idea that Monsieur Benoit was the one who kept the Duke imprisoned.

At bedtime, his mother sat on his quilt while she settled him for sleep, reading one of the storybooks his aunts had sent from Australia. Closing the pages on jumping kangaroos and small boys with billycans, she said:

'Your surprise, Georgie . . .'

'Yes, Mama, yes?'

'Next week I am taking you to London, to see your father.'

'Hooray!'

'And . . .'

He waited, holding his breath, belling-out his cheeks with excitement. She could not bear to go on.

'And you will have such fun, won't you.'

'Yes, Mama, yes!'

He was satisfied with so little. Talk of school could wait, Nellie decided. She was so afraid of losing him, afraid he would love too much the idea of running about with other small boys, making friendships, playing cricket, being turned into an absolutely perfect little English boy, a small copybook Armstrong. Love the idea of it and hurt her by saying so, by giving a wild war-whoop here in his delightful nursery room, so recently decked-out with a frieze of big game animals. She was afraid of something else: that he would come to easily despise her, in an atmosphere of strict conformity.

And yet she knew it must be done. Within days.

She turned down the lamp and blew George a kiss from the doorway.

'*Bonne nuit, Mama.*'

She went downstairs and began working on her correspondence. The latest offer was from the Metropolitan in New York. Would she be free to open there in six months' time? She looked in her diary, knowing her dates were taken for two years ahead. She wrote to the people in New York, telling them in the nicest possible way that they were underestimating her status if they thought she could come so soon.

There were other letters demanding answer but Nellie's concentration slipped away. It was past ten o'clock, and Eugene Benoit had not called. He usually came earlier than this. She stared out the window, into the night.

'Philippe,' she shaped a whisper on her lips.

It was pitch dark and very still. Philippe lay motionless on his bunk. There came a distant rustle of sound, then the heavy, muffled clang of an iron door far away. Someone coughed, they were always coughing here. Another prisoner called out in his sleep. Uncertainly, the long stone corridor outside Philippe's cell echoed to the tap of footsteps. The sound swelled, enlarged. The pure darkness became washed with lamplight. Footsteps halted outside his door. A key grated in the lock. Light flooded his cell, and he blinked at the sight of his father's emissary, the Duc de Luyns, standing there with Colonel D'Aurelle, Eugene Benoit, and the prison commandant wearing his medals.

The Duc de Luyns advanced and kissed Philippe on both cheeks.

'The government has relented. You are to have an armed escort to the border, and there you will be released, under orders never to return to France.'

D'Aurelle gathered up Philippe's belongings. Benoit smiled at him, and bowed knowingly.

'Let us go,' said the Duke de Luyns.

GEORGE GOES TO SCHOOL

In the morning Nellie's parlourmaid found a finely penned letter slipped under the front door of the house in the Rue de Prony. She carried it to her mistress, who opened it with trembling hands.

It was not from Benoit as she had expected, nor from Philippe. The penmanship was impeccable, the elegant French cold and distant. The letter informed Madame Melba that Philippe was free by special dispensation of the President, and today was travelling towards the Belgian border under guard. Within the week he would be back in London, re-united with his father. The Duc d'Orléans, said the writer, had been recalled to his sense of duty by the stern experience he had undergone in his dungeon.

The note was signed, with gracious salutation, by Philippe's humble servant, the Duc de Luyns.

'How kind of him,' thought Nellie, even as she realised that the letter was fatal in intent. Benoit's intermediary role had been silenced. Philippe, at his moment of release, was being held back from her. She, a mere singer, was being stamped-upon by an elegant outrider.

At the same time, she was filled with joy.

Long before the afternoon boat-train arrived at Victoria Station, Charles and Montagu were on the platform waiting for it.

Montagu was exultant. Charles brooded, smoking a cheroot down to a hot, bitter stub, and then lighting another one. His coat-collar was turned up, he shivered.

The weather was mild enough, but Charles's blood was running thin these days. The farm was now getting along without him; a man named Benson did most of the work. Charles spent his time with horses, breaking them to the saddle with singleminded ferocity. He courted danger and death as hooves flashed around him, but when it was over there he was again, back from the brink of danger with a dull heart. All the effort of the past couple of years had exacted an irreversible toll. Part of him was dead. He craved his evening whisky as never before, and subsisted on very little food. His mother thought him a sorry case. He talked about wandering off somewhere, away from England, to America maybe where he could ride, shoot, climb mountains, cast a line and catch fish. He was back in the mood that had sent him fleeing from England years ago. Life was over before it had begun. Or else it was just another version of its primal disappointments, to be endlessly repeated.

Nellie? He'd been cheated and used. He no longer wanted her in the way he had once. There was a certain relief in that. She'd become remote, unreal; she was less to him than she was to thousands of strangers. At least to them she offered hope . . .

The girl he'd courted, though, sometimes entered his dreams, pretty and teasing and touching his hand with her cool fingers, leaving him shaken with desire.

But she was not this woman coming towards London with his son, this Madame Melba, whose return to London had been announced in the morning's *Times*.

He thought, deep down, that Madame Melba was rather a joke. He saw through her as no-one else did, except perhaps Montagu. He had once struggled to equate the woman he loved with 'Melba's' image of herself, and then to match himself to her, but had given up the try. One look into her world had been enough . . . That was when he had gone to Brussels, when the effort had almost killed him.

'Couldn't see you as "Mr Melba",' Montagu had chuckled. Charles had come to rely on Montagu more than ever. Montagu was a fighter.

Now, on the platform, Montagu looked at Charles huddled into himself, and found it intolerable. Something important in Charlie had been dimmed: that was what Montagu fought to retain. And blast the woman for it, he thought.

A whistle was heard. Far down the rails an engine appeared.

'When the moment comes, don't take any nonsense,' said Montagu urgently. 'If necessary, grab the boy and I'll block your escape.'

'Don't be so bloody silly, Monty.'

George's head showed from a window all the way along as the carriages bumped into the platform. His arms flailed with excitement.

GEORGE GOES TO SCHOOL

'Papa! Papa!'

The door banged open and George leapt down. He sprinted across the platform and hurled himself into Charles's arms. Charles hugged him while keeping an eye on the carriage door for his first sight of Nellie. He was magnetised despite himself. The nursemaid Marie emerged next, a youthful manservant came after, and last of all a stout housekeeper passing out luggage. What an entourage.

Then there was her. She stood in the doorway of the carriage and something happened that made Charles shrink from witnessing it. A cry went up, a stranger shouted:

'It's Madame Melba! Good show!' She was a star, a person of glamour and note, even here among the soot and cinders of Victoria Station.

A policeman took Nellie by the elbow, guiding her along the platform. 'Make way, please. That's enough, now,' the bobby said in his mild, nursery-like English way as the crowd pushed and shoved.

Nellie, looking palely beautiful in her Paris fashions, directed the policeman towards Charles, George and Montagu.

'Let's go,' said Montagu, seeing a chance to deliver a rebuff. 'Now!'

But Charles was mesmerised, snake-charmed. She came up to him and held out her hand.

'Hello, Charles, how are you?' she asked.

'Well enough. Have a good crossing?'

'Like a mill-pond.'

'Good.'

'Here's Georgie, then. He's been so excited.'

'Yes. Indeed. Say goodbye to your mother, George.'

'Oh, it's not goodbye,' murmured Nellie.

They were islanded, just the three of them, behind a luggage barrow, while a red-faced Montagu tried to catch their words, and the crowd of well-wishers, now joined by officials from Covent Garden, were held back by the bobby.

Nellie bent down to speak to George. This was the moment she dreaded.

'George, you're to go with your father, now.'

'Yes, Mama, I know.'

301

'He will take you to a school, darling.'

'School?' wondered George.

'Christ, haven't you told him?' said Charles through clenched teeth.

'There will be lots of other boys,' murmured Nellie into George's ear. 'You'll have such fun. You'll sleep in your own special bed and there'll be all sorts of games.'

George smiled delightedly, he could imagine no greater pleasure, and it was just as Nellie feared. He would go off like a lamb to the slaughter.

'Hooray, Papa! School!'

'Hurry up,' said Charles.

She knelt, her hand clutching George's. She could not bear the look of delight on his face.

'Charlie,' she stood, 'we can't do it, we mustn't. It's simply abominable.'

'Priory Grange has a superb reputation. You're making a scene. It's too late.'

'It's an English prep school, therefore bleak and cruel on principle.'

'Oh, shut up, he's listening, you madwoman,' snapped Charles.

George was not the only one. Members of the crowd strained forward. Montagu pushed past the policeman, exasperated beyond endurance.

Charles scooped George up and held him strongly.

Nellie fought back tears. They were snatching George from her, it had come to that, but she would not give them the pleasure of witnessing her grief.

'It's not as if you're losing him,' said Montagu, standing pugnaciously close, his legs apart, shielding Charles and George from her. 'You'll see him at weekends and between term, you know . . . When you're in this country,' he added.

'Let me kiss him,' she begged Charles.

'Watch it, now!' warned Montagu.

They kissed.

'I'll see you soon, I promise,' said Nellie.

Her last sight of George: a pale, apprehensive little face,

GEORGE GOES TO SCHOOL

peering over his father's shoulder. Then her well-wishers surged around.

'Gentlemen,' said Nellie, turning to face them with a smile.

She retained her self-control until the very moment of entering her hotel room, where a scene of disarray met her eyes. Piles of clothes were everywhere as her servants unpacked her portmanteaux. Everyone was chattering. Hotel butlers, footmen and maids milled about. She could hardly get in, there was so much bustle and organisation. She was struck by the transience of the life she was launched upon, its penalties and losses. To progress through the simplest intimacies of the day now seemed to require half a dozen paid helpers. How had it happened that she, the meaning of it all, had become an annoyance, an interruption in lesser people's lives? A footman, how dare he, voiced a muttered complaint about her. A miniature of George, commissioned in Paris, was flipped to the floor by a parlourmaid's carelessness, and lay face-down on the carpet. Nellie picked it up, only to be met by the sight of George's precious toy horse, spilling from a bag where it had been packed by mistake.

A sob rose in her, which she could barely suppress.

'Out, all of you!' she commanded.

'Madame?'

'That will do. Out!'

She stood with her hands on her hips. The hotel maids and porters went immediately, closing the doors behind them. Her personal servants sent her beseeching looks.

'Yes, you too!'

When they were gone, Nellie threw herself across her bed and wept.

For the first time since gaining success, her achievements mocked her. There was only an emptiness, a yearning to be filled.

22

Secret Love

La Traviata began at Covent Garden.

Each night, as Violetta, Nellie lived through the agony and the beauty of the story. An impossible love, a passionate sacrifice. The music possessed her, as it possessed the audience. Hushed, tearful, adoring, the houses were full to the doors as Madame Melba brought the role to perfection. Violetta died in the arms of her lover. The curtain calls were tumultuous.

But afterwards, when the flowers had been brought to her, and the cards and the callers to her dressing room had been despatched into the night, she was still alone.

She had been waiting for days for a sign, a message. Each night as she readied herself for bed her prayers resolved themselves to a simple cry from the heart:

'Philippe, where are you?'

On the third night of *La Traviata* Nellie entered her dressing room after the performance and knew at once the full measure of happiness. Her dresser was gone. The room was filled with orchids, among which burned small candles. All was as it once had been.

A movement of light and shade occurred in the mirrors, and Philippe stepped into the room. It was as she'd dreamed it might be. There was no doubt or hesitation or shyness: immediately they embraced.

He began to kiss her. 'My dear Madame,' he murmured, making a most gentle endearment of the simple words.

Voices came from the corridor. 'The door,' Nellie said.

There was a knock, and he sprang away from her, his eyes alight.

She hardly knew how, but within minutes they were gone from the theatre. She found herself seated in an enclosed carriage, being whisked around Hyde Park. Now it was as though there'd been no interruption to the embrace. Nor any end to it forseeable. They did not speak for what seemed like hours, except that Nellie sighed, and Philippe murmured ardently, and they kissed and touched, as the carriage-horse clattered along. The softness, the surrender were all. When lamplight showed through chinks of the blinds they were able to see each other briefly. *I am in love*, Nellie told herself, gazing at the object of her admiration and desire.

'Madame, I would like . . .'

'Yes?'

'To ask you . . . to propose . . .'

Anything, Nellie felt herself responding.

'That you join me for supper.'

It was long past midnight but the restaurant waited open.

Nellie pulled her cloak around her and hurried inside. The *maitre d'*, discreetly avoiding her eye, bowed low. Lights glimmered under doors as Philippe took her elbow and they swiftly mounted a stairway to a private room. Discretion was all. Everything had been arranged ahead, of course. Supper things were laid out in readiness. It would be like this now, she knew; the entire process of their knowing each other, from this night on, would follow a path of planned inevitability. She accepted that. She was grateful too that the young man with her was so practised, so confident. It removed her from feeling any responsibility.

The *maitre d'* retreated from the room, closing the doors behind him.

Philippe's hands trembled as he removed her cloak. His fingers were long and sensitive, his skin very white from his weeks of being shut away.

'We are together at last,' he said.

'How is it possible?' asked Nellie, as she touched his cheek.

'The world is ours,' he murmured.

'Your father . . .'

'Ssh . . . dear Nellie.'

It was so good, so delightful, to hear him using her name for the first time.

She used his, while her heart leapt: 'Philippe, oh, my dear, my dear Philippe.'

They kissed fiercely, the words burning between them.

'Darling . . .'

But abruptly she was nervous of waiters bursting in. To reassure her he strode to the door, and twisted the key in the lock. His eyes were so alive now, so light and glancing in their need. He had the grace of a wild creature adept at civilisation. She welcomed him back into her arms. They sank to a couch, and after more delightful kisses turned from their discoveries, and began to drink champagne and eat the supper.

A pattern was established during these short weeks of the Covent Garden season. Philippe watched from his box, sometimes with Lady de Grey at his elbow, as *La Traviata* gave way to *Lakme*. In the '*Viens Mallika*' duet he felt he was the one being sung to: he applauded and desired her. Later she told him what he wished to hear, that she sang for his ears alone, though this was not true, for even in love she would not betray her art with anxiety or longing.

She could deny him nothing. When the critics praised a new quality in her voice, she laughed. 'You have put it there,' she said.

The kisses, the carriage–drives, the suppers continued. Late each night Nellie returned to the Savoy Hotel, while Philippe, sometimes in the dawn light, drove back to Sheen House, Richmond, where his father lived.

Lady de Grey watched them closely. She was bemused by

the progress of the affair. She was not surprised it had happened, for of course it had been going to happen for a long while, and she accepted the inevitability of it at last, though certainly not the political correctness. Her confusion was over the participants appearing content with what they had of each other. There was an aura of youthful innocence about the pair, as if Philippe thought of her as Juliette still (Nellie had confessed this fancy); as if she, shaken by her awful marriage, wanted to begin from the beginning as in a first betrothal. From all this Lady de Grey deduced that the lovers had not as yet taken their embraces to the bedroom. This was unusual. In her experience, what smouldered must flare, and pretty quickly too. Surely it was not from mere lack of opportunity.

The Duc d'Orléans had a long-standing invitation to visit Studley Royal, the de Greys' country estate, where Nellie was a regular guest. The men came for the sport, the ladies, and certain of the gentlemen too, to divert Lady Gladys from her hatred of all matters relating to the country. 'I am essentially urban,' she often boasted. 'I do not wish to trundle through rough country lanes, listening to the cuckoo.' Having Nellie and other artists down at Studley Royal lent a touch of pageantry and artifice to the evenings. Besides she liked her.

One particular weekend, Lady Gladys looked in her engagement diary and found that the Duc d'Orléans and Nellie were to be there at the same time. It had all been arranged months before.

The signs she had looked for were suddenly obvious.

At breakfast after the first night at Studley Royal, Lady de Grey no longer doubted. It was plain to her that during the night one of the pair had stolen stocking-footed along the dim brown upstairs corridor of the guest wing, and a door had closed, and opened, on a stage in the relationship. Whereas before, at supper parties and receptions, Nellie and the Duc had exhibited barely restrained passionate glances, now at breakfast they showed a studied ordinariness as they ate sausages, drank coffee, and each talked to someone else at the table.

MELBA

'The poor bewitched darlings,' Lady de Grey thought to herself. 'They'd been waiting for an opportunity.'

She thought: Nellie will be blind now, and for a long time to come, to the impossibility of her position. Philippe, to an extent, also. For while Lady de Grey knew him to be an adept amorist for his age, there was a tenderness and vulnerability about his lovemaking. Both had fallen rather heavily for each other. She felt a pang of envy.

There were unavoidable facts to be faced, however: his rank, his hopes, his father's wishes. Perhaps even the fate of France, finally. Lady de Grey had, above all, her class and elevated responsibilities to consider. She wondered what to do. The lovers would ignore sensible warnings for now. Philippe's duty would be thrust into the unimaginable future, that being, to new lovers, not far; just the stretch of time until their next meeting.

No, there was only one way, and that was to conspire in their favour. For a time, at least. Lady Gladys believed the fire raging between them would be controllable only if it was allowed to burn out.

She decided to offer help. They could come here to Studley Royal whenever they were able, and also have use of a house she kept in London.

The following week Lady de Grey went to Nellie and placed a key in her hand.

The metal was as cold as tears; the look in Lady de Grey's eyes distant and sad; Nellie could not look at her straight.

'Now you know everything about me,' she murmured.

'Be happy,' whispered Lady Gladys.

It was a small house around the corner from Lady de Grey's place in Bruton Street. Nellie went directly from the theatre and found a fire waiting in the sitting room. Upstairs was a bedroom warmed and ready. An old maidservant, described by Lady Gladys as 'practically deaf and blind', waited to attend every need.

Nellie sat on a couch and warmed her hands. One part of

SECRET LOVE

her mind was agitated and aghast at what was happening to her. When she thought of Melbourne and her family nothing made sense. Morally, she had gone beyond the comprehension of all she had been brought up to believe. They must never know. She must close her mind to their point of view. Love had a way of purifying itself. She had only to turn her mind to Philippe, and everything was sanctified.

There were nice things in the room, engraved vases and carved cigarette boxes, silken cushions and books by advanced authors. It was a love-nest. How surprising Lady Gladys was in all her departments, thought Nellie, resenting her a little for having this place at her disposal while displaying a slightly puzzling edge of disapproval towards her friendship with Philippe. 'Who is she to criticise?' Nellie wondered, understanding her own situation less and less as her passion deepened.

She was still sitting there, wearing her cloak, wondering about things, when Philippe entered the house. The maidservant ushered him in to the room, and then withdrew to her own quarters.

Philippe sank down beside Nellie and took her hand. She rested her head on his chest.

'Did anyone see you come?' Nellie asked.

'I have already farewelled my father and left for the country,' he said, with a smile. 'He is in good spirits.'

Their affair was conducted with extreme caution. If they had been discreet before, now they wished to be invisible, here in London at least. In the country it would be somewhat different for both of them. Lady de Grey had granted them use of a lodge in the grounds of Studley Royal, with its own private drive and nearby wood. They would go there as often as possible in the coming weeks.

London was different. Nellie was terrified of the Armstrongs finding out. She feared Charles's rage, Montagu's malice, and the loss of Lady Armstrong's affection and respect. She feared word of her indiscretions reaching not just her family at home, but all of Australia, where almost weekly her latest doings were reported in the press. Beyond everything, she feared that motive would be found for George to be taken from her.

Philippe, for his part, had returned to favour with his father. The Comte de Paris smiled on this son who had proved himself in adversity. 'He is pale after eight weeks' incarceration, he must build himself up,' said the Comte de Paris at frequent intervals, urging his son to go to the country as much as possible, to rest and strengthen himself for the struggle ahead. The Duc de Luyns, Colonel D'Aurelle, and Monsieur Eugene Benoit, knowing Philippe maintained his liaison with the singer, held their tongues lest they disturb the Comte's new-found, and certainly temporary, equanimity.

The warmth and silence that first night in Lady de Grey's house was exquisite.

Philippe untied Nellie's cloak. His fingers worked at the silk ribbons at the neck of her costume, which she still wore from the theatre.

'I have something for you,' he murmured, as they passionately kissed.

Philippe reached into a pocket and withdrew an object clenched in his fist.

'What is it?'

He unfolded his hand under Nellie's chin to reveal a tear-shaped piece of amber.

'A simple gift,' he said.

Nellie took the amber and held it to the light. It was not strikingly beautiful, yet instantly she loved it, for it seemed to hold in its rough outline the authentic expression of their love. It had a hole drilled through one end, and could be worn.

'It comes from the tribesmen of the Atlas Mountains,' said Philippe. 'It banishes tears. It has the power to prevent sadness.'

'It is a treasure.'

Nellie tilted her neck accommodatingly while Philippe threaded a piece of *moiré* ribbon taken from her costume. He smiled rather remotely, boyishly concentrating.

'You are very sweet, Philippe,' murmured Nellie.

They stared into each other's eyes as he tied the knot.

'Your fingers are trembling,' said Nellie, guiding his hands.

Then they went upstairs together.

SECRET LOVE

In the following weeks they met often in London, and stayed twice at the lodge at Studley Royal.

Incessantly they scribbled each other letters and love-notes. Philippe made Nellie promise to destroy what he sent her, but she couldn't bear to, keeping them in a small bundle tied with velvet ribbon, carrying them with her wherever she went.

The intimate circle Nellie created around herself at this time was so private, so intense, so beautifully proper in all ways (from her inner perspective) that the adulation she received night after night at the opera house seemed to belong to her love affair, falling like a blessing from heaven, neither to be questioned nor properly known, only to be accepted like sunshine, breathed like air. It enriched her secret and most intimate life. She was happy.

Then suddenly, irrationally, she wanted George to share in it. She wanted to bring him, an innocent boy, inside the circle of love she and Philippe had created. Once the thought occurred to her she couldn't get rid of it. It was dangerous but her love seemed to demand an offering. Also, why should he see only the Armstrong side of life all the time, she reasoned, with its horses, its small dinner parties (though she'd thought them splendid once), and its intemperate Anglo-Irishness? At Studley Royal there was a grandeur that a small boy could boast about at school for weeks on end.

Nellie told Philippe of her wish and he raised his eyebrows, but said nothing; only he felt the first small dent of irritation in their relationship: *It's the thing about women*, he thought, *they must have their cake and eat it*.

One weekend she saw her opportunity. There would be a large party at the de Greys'. She and Philippe were to stay in the main house this time, where there would be many other guests apart from the Duc to draw George's innocent gaze.

Lady de Grey herself thought it an excellent idea:

'Yes, he is such a sweet child, I should be delighted,' she said, though she too had a private opinion which ran: *The sooner Nellie makes her acquaintance with the realities of clandestine love the better. She must run the gamut, and then be amenable to reason.*

Thus it was arranged that George would travel across from his school by train, and be collected from the station by a coachman.

Nellie forgot how at the beginning certain practicalities had declared themselves to her. How a new, perhaps dangerous life had opened ahead, and in that life, she had decided, there was no place for a small growing boy . . .

Her self-deceptions became more complicated, her ideas for herself enlarged. She thought by bringing George under the wing of her love, she would appease her guilt-feelings and her suppressed uneasiness.

A few nights before the arrangement took effect something happened to give Nellie's nerves a jolt.

A great crowd jammed into the foyer after a performance, waiting for a glimpse of her. She descended a stairway, as she sometimes did, and paused a moment while the patrons cheered. There was a sea of heads, she could never separate one from the other, but this night for some reason she found herself looking into the eyes of someone she knew: Lady Armstrong.

Lady Armstrong smiled hesitantly. Reproachfully?

Nellie, to her shame, turned quickly away.

The next morning she went to Lady Armstrong's house early, drawn to seek forgiveness. A maid led her upstairs.

Lady Armstrong was in bed, reading the papers. The previous night had tired her somewhat. The maid announced her visitor:

'Mrs Nellie Armstrong, my Lady.'

When Nellie entered Lady Armstrong smiled generously.

'My dear . . . My dear Nellie.'

'I happened to be passing,' said Nellie uncertainly. They kissed. Lady Armstrong patted the bedcovers, and Nellie sat down. They had not seen each other for almost a year.

'Good Lord! A year? I don't believe time has passed so quickly.'

Nellie was agitated. 'I've wanted to come so many times, but I was afraid . . .'

'Afraid, no, whatever for?'

'The difficulties with Charles . . . So much time has passed . . . You must have thought me very rude last night for seeming to ignore you. It was just . . .'

'All those people! I was no-one special.'

'Rumours abound in my profession . . .'

'Of what sort? I cannot imagine . . .'

'They say I am hard, ruthless, ambitious.'

Nellie shot a look at Lady Armstrong to test her reaction. Rumours about perfectionism were not her worry, but she would die if there was any hint of moral suspicion. She knew deep down such fearful disquiet, such churning guilt.

'You are doing something very difficult, very grand . . . I will never stop loving you, Nellie.'

'Never?'

'Never . . . Now, listen. Have you read this morning's papers? You were glorious last night, and I was there to witness it. How glad I am I had the chance . . . Tell me, what do you think of George? Isn't he growing!'

'I am seeing him this weekend, in the country. He is joining me at Studley Royal.'

'Oh, good.'

'Charles never writes,' Nellie said in a sudden outburst. 'He says I've ruined his life, and I have, I know, I'm sorry . . .'

Nellie dabbed at a tear, feeling real emotion mixed with something more calculating. Something she hated in herself. There was this straining after Lady Armstrong's approval. How she needed it! And yet, how little deserving of it she was, she knew.

She had come here to hide things, she realised, not to make them clearer.

'Blame the stars,' said Lady Armstrong. 'I won't take sides.' Meaning, *Any more than I need to as Charles's mother*, Nellie hoped, not wanting Lady Armstrong to go too far in her direction.

'Charles lives for his horses I know.'

'There is that,' nodded Lady Armstrong. 'He is in Ireland at present, for the fishing.'

Then they chatted for a while about the world of theatre and Covent Garden, which Lady Armstrong loved. The great danger passed and it was all right between them: everything on the surface. They parted as friends, promising to see each other much more regularly; perhaps an outing with George? Nellie promised to try.

She left the house happily enough, but soon a feeling of dread returned. Covering things over, pretending to worry about matters just a little to the side of her true worry . . . hiding her secret love. It was a feeling she hated. What would Lady Armstrong say if she ever learned the truth? Nellie shuddered, and longed for the oblivion of her lover's arms.

23

Eat, or be Eaten

Winter came early that year, blackening the woods at Studley Royal with driving rain and giving the soft landscape of the adjoining farms a forlorn, bedraggled appearance. From the conservatory window Nellie looked out at a wide, wind-tossed view. Branches lay crashed on the ground from a great wind the previous night. Cattle stood about in the sodden fields, their rumps to the weather. Shafts of cold sunlight and rapid, disintegrating rainbows alternated with blank sweeps of rain. Inside, the steam pipes under the conservatory floor rumbled and hissed.

Nellie wiped condensation from the glass and peered down the drive, awaiting the appearance of the pony trap that had been sent to fetch George from the station. She had promised to meet him herself, but bad weather and Philippe's persuasion had kept her away.

Philippe stood behind her, smoking near the doorway, observing her nervousness, her agitation. She was very tense. He wanted her to be calm and would happily surrender his midnight visit to her room for the sake of it.

'I shall not come tonight.'

'No . . . Do you mind? I should hate it most awfully if you minded, my darling . . .'

'I am not a beast . . . There is always tomorrow,' smiled Philippe.

'Yes, yes, tomorrow night, in London,' promised Nellie. She turned to the window again.

'Are you sure he must meet me?' wondered Philippe.

'Oh, I want him to,' said Nellie. 'He won't understand what you are, only who you are.'

'That was not true of me, so you say. I sensed a conspiracy behind every rustle of skirts in my father's house.'

'You were not an English boy.'

'I was raised in England, your son was raised in France.'

'Well, he's no longer French,' said Nellie wistfully.

She continued staring out the window.

'I never thought I'd hate England,' said Nellie over her shoulder, 'but there is a moment when I hate it. The onset of winter, so harsh and unforgiving . . . I wish we were somewhere else, anywhere else . . . my darling.'

'We could go to Australia, where everything is upside down,' mused Philippe.

'Go, as who?' Nellie laughed disbelievingly. She thought of her father, her family. Impossible.

Philippe put an arm around her, feeling a slight resistance. She was nervous because of the boy, he understood that. She was determined that he and George should become friends. It did not seem a very safe idea to Philippe but he was willing to try. He hated small boys as a rule, seeing in them only what he had grown away from, quite successfully. But he wanted to shake her from the mood she was in, and would agree to anything to achieve it.

'Go to Australia together, but as who?' Nellie repeated, leaning into his embrace, attempting to match his whimsy, indeed actually daring to wonder how it would be possible.

'I as the explorer?' suggested Philippe charmingly. 'You as the singer, entertaining your people? We could meet by the bushfire . . . campfire,' he corrected himself.

'How I love you,' Nellie kissed him passionately, then remembering George, broke quickly away.

'My son will be here soon,' she said.

EAT, OR BE EATEN

There was no reason, she repeatedly argued to herself, why a boy of nine should be suspicious. None whatsoever. There were all sorts of people George was likely to meet at Studley Royal, dukes, counts and so forth . . . and if a harder rumour ever did leak out, reaching Charles, why then, Charles would only laugh, and say, 'She's got a crowd of titles at her heels. George is always meeting them. They mean nothing.'

'Here he comes!'

A covered trap appeared, then disappeared, as it wound up the drive.

'I shall be in the library, studying the collection,' bowed Philippe.

Nellie ran through the house but when she reached the front hall she stopped and composed herself. Where was the mirror? She seemed to have loose strands of hair everywhere! She heard the carriage wheels grind to a halt.

A footman shouldered the door open against a gust of wind.

She stood waiting. George did not see her yet. His back was half-turned as he climbed down, as the coachman handed him his bag. He had grown taller. His soft complexion was wind-reddened from the drive, and from playing outdoor games at his school. She was fearful of greeting a stranger. They had been apart for many weeks. George handed the coachman a coin with a practised air, the man tugged his cap. What a fine-looking boy he was, composed and independent, already accustomed to going from place to place without adult company. He turned and saw her.

'Darling!' Nellie greeted him, hugging him tight. He gave her a quick kiss.

'Whose house is this?' George wondered, breaking from Nellie's embrace.

'Lord de Grey's, I told you,' she said.

'Oh, yes.'

She tidied his hair before they went in.

'You've grown so.'

'Have I?' The wind almost blew them inside. 'Will there be shooting?'

'In this weather? Oh, darling!' She need have no worries.

MELBA

He was already off in his own self-absorbed schoolboy world.

Later, after George had been shown his room, and had already become lost down one of the many corridors, he was ushered into the library.

'Oh, there you are, darling, I was just telling the Duke about you!'

'The Duke,' repeated George. 'Yes, I remember.'

Philippe was in the act of replacing a book on a shelf. George studied him. He was not as broad-shouldered as George had expected, nor as grizzled, nor nearly as old. Nevertheless he knew which duke he was.

'How can you,' frowned Nellie.

'You were in prison, sir,' said George.

'I was.'

'How are you?'

'I am very well,' replied Philippe, amused at the directness of the boy. He addressed George in French, asking how he enjoyed his school, but George made no reply, merely crossed to a glass case containing old manuscripts.

'Is this real gold?' he asked Nellie, studying the illuminated lettering. 'We have some at school, from before the time of Henry the Eighth.'

'Answer the Duc d'Orléans, George. How is your school?'

'They call me "Froggy",' shrugged George.

'How horrid,' said Nellie, covering her mouth with her hand.

'If I'm not back by four tomorrow, Mr Wentleford will cane me.'

George seemed rather proud of this fact.

'Barbaric,' frowned Nellie. 'What does your father say?'

'He says I am not a baby any more.'

Philippe studied another volume, then decisively snapped it shut.

'If you will excuse me, Madame Melba,' he bowed slightly, preparing to leave the room.

'Of course, Your Grace,' said Nellie.

'Perhaps we shall meet again, before you go,' Philippe shook George's hand.

'Very well,' said George.

When the door closed, Nellie said: 'George, you must not be so coldly polite.'

'It's how we are taught at school.'

'Yes, I see. You are the perfect little English gentleman, of course, but you must answer when spoken to.'

'Mr Wentleford says I am not to speak French.'

'George,' Nellie took a deep breath. 'I shall take you back to school tomorrow. Would you like that?'

'Yes, Mama,' said George, not caring either way. He was curious about something, however.

'Why,' he asked, 'do you pretend the Duke is a stranger when he was your friend in Paris?'

'I don't know what you mean. He was in prison then.'

'Oh, well,' said George, changing the subject. 'The footman said he would show me the gunroom before tea. May I?'

'Yes, but tell me what you mean about the Duke.'

'When Monsieur Benoit came, I used to hear you talking. He was your great friend because he was unhappy in gaol.'

'I see,' said Nellie with studied casualness. 'Tell me, George. Did you ever mention his name to your father?'

'No, never, Mama,' said George, avoiding her eye.

He thrust a hand in a pocket and walked to the door, holding it open for his mother to pass through. He was every inch the little man. For too long she had been blind to the growing up he'd done. Charles had said he was no longer a baby, and it was true. Nellie regretted bringing him to Studley Royal.

The next day they found themselves on a damp, slow, bumpy cross-county train. Nellie clutched a gaudy umbrella and was a splendid example of the day's fashions. But that wasn't the reason she attracted so many stares: she was Madame Melba, of Covent Garden . . . known everywhere.

Nellie whispered confidingly to George: 'It's getting quite silly.'

George noticed that while Nellie pretended to hate people's stares, she rather liked them too. It had been the same at Studley Royal, where people had made a great fuss of her, trying to persuade her to sing, which of course she had, after a time. George had been allowed to stay up late. He'd been so proud of her. 'Spellbinding' was the word everyone used, yet strangely, of all the titled people there, the only one who didn't come up afterwards and kiss her hand was the Duke of Orléans.

Nellie's magic worked its effect on the school population of Priory Grange, too.

By the time she and George reached a door marked 'HEADMASTER, J.K. WENTLEFORD, M.A.' they were trailed by about twenty boys of all sizes. George tried to pretend that Nellie had nothing to do with him. Mr Wentleford opened the door of his study and drew a sharp breath of surprise. An exhausted-looking, youngish, sharp-faced man, he recognised her though they had never met.

'Why, Madame Melba, what an honour,' he proffered a damp handshake.

He spoke with a tortured, artificial accent. There was a spot of egg on his waistcoat. The air around him smelt sweetly of sherry.

'Our parents usually make appointments, but you are an exception, Madame,' he said, to excuse his surprise.

'Hmm.'

'Please be seated.' He took her elbow and guided her to a chair.

Nellie wasted little time on the pleasantries. She had hated the school on sight; the downtrodden gardens, the sour pathways where boys loitered, knuckling each other on the shoulders; inside, the uneven dusty floorboards, the distempered walls, the pervasive smell of boiled cabbage.

Nellie eyed a rack of canes.

'Here we are, Mr Wentleford, it is twenty minutes past the hour of four, and you have not made a single move to cane my boy.'

'Madame?' Wentleford went pale.

'Are you a hypocrite, sir? One rule for the boys and another for the parents?'

'Well, I never . . .' Wentleford looked sideways at George,

EAT, OR BE EATEN

as if to say *Later, my boy, later*.

'Sir,' said Nellie, 'your school is no better than the worst sorts of school in Australia. All brutality and sneering.'

'Madame Melba,' Wentleford drew breath, 'I would not expect you to discern educational quality from its colonial imitation, why should you. However, the very best people send their boys to me. From here they go on to Eton, Harrow, and Winchester.'

'Not many, I'll warrant,' said Nellie.

The headmaster's shallow respect for Nellie's fame was overtaken by the thought that she was merely a woman of the stage. A 'singer'. He could afford his contempt.

George blinked, looking from one to the other.

'Mr Wentleford,' said Nellie, 'the very best people could buy and sell a person like you without blinking.'

'Armstrong, leave the room.'

'Yes, George, it would be best if you waited outside.'

George opened the door and dislodged a group of boys trying to peer through the keyhole.

'Hello, Froggy,' they said.

Alone with Nellie, Mr Wentleford almost hissed: 'The school was chosen by the father and uncle. Shame on you for belittling the boy's family, one of the very best.'

'You belittle my country in front of my son, you condescend towards his mother, but I must hold my tongue? You tire my patience, Mr Wentleford. You are just a common little scholar.'

'Oh, my gawd,' said Mr Wentleford, hand to brow.

'Yes, common,' pounced Nellie. 'I just caught a vowel.'

'We're not all of us continental-trained to disguise our origins,' said Wentleford, a little pathetically.

Nellie fumed, but made no reply. There was a sudden truce between them. Both felt slightly ill from the rush of vituperation.

'A couple of points for you to remember, and then I must catch my train,' said Nellie.

'What are they, ever?'

'George must not be bullied by you, or I will see to it that your school's name is ruined among people of quality.'

'Well, I never!'

'He will speak French whenever he wishes.'

'I will give it some thought.'

'And he shall never, never I say, be caned for returning late on a Sunday. He is a mere child, with a penchant for loitering, and I won't have him treated so.'

'We have our rules.'

'And I have my power to break you, Mr Wentleford,' answered Nellie.

The train carried her back to London. Darkness fell over the fields, rain lashed the windows. What had she done? Said? What was happening to her? She seemed to be forcing disintegration upon herself, creating a crisis over George at Studley Royal, drawing his attention most reprehensibly to Philippe, and then at Priory Grange making an enemy of a pathetic provincial headmaster who, even if he obeyed her instructions, which he would not, she knew, could still make life hell for George.

Nellie was not accustomed to examining her inner thoughts and motives, moodiness being intolerable among the Mitchells; yet now her thoughts ran away with her. Perhaps what she wanted was for George to make his life with her again. Perhaps her idea, which she could hardly admit to herself, had been to test out George and Philippe in each other's company for a special reason. Perhaps what she was looking for at the end of all the uncertainty was . . .

Was . . . She could hardly even glimpse what she meant . . . marriage?

The train entered a tunnel with a noisy gulp of sound, and the thought was swallowed up. Tonight she would be reunited with Philippe, that was all, that was all.

The thunderbolt struck. In George's weekly letter to Charles, who was still away trout fishing in Ireland, Philippe, Duc d'Orléans was mentioned. Light flashed into the dark recesses of Charles's mind, and the whole situation sprang clearly from between the lines.

EAT, OR BE EATEN

'Good Christ,' said Charles, reading the letter. 'What a fool I've been.'

'What is it?' asked Montagu, reaching out a hand. Charles passed the letter over.

Montagu whistled.

That was two days ago.

Slowly, swirlingly, a pretty, feathery object drifted on the surface of the water. It spun around delicately, catching the light. Then it disappeared in an eruption of water. A fish jumped clear with a hook in its mouth.

Charles flexed his rod with unemotional concentration and started bringing it in. Montagu followed him along the bank, muttering advice and urging Charles's every movement.

'Easy, easy Charlie my boy.'

'Christ, give me room, Monty.'

'All right, don't bite my head off.'

Montagu stepped back.

Charles then gave a virtuoso fishing display.

The fight, the line drawing in, the angle of the net, the capture. All were perfect.

Charles knelt beside the fish, removed the fly from its mouth, and looked up at his brother.

'Still time for another try?'

Montagu ran his tongue around the inside of this mouth. He was thirsty.

'Let 'em live,' he said with uncharacteristic generosity. 'Unless you want to feed the whole village.'

Charles killed the fish, gutted it, and rinsed it out in the water.

There was a flurry of fish around the entrails, a few seconds of savage feeding.

'Bloody cannibals,' said Charles.

'That's the way of the world,' said Montagu. 'Eat. Or be eaten.'

It was hours later, and Charles was morose from alcohol. Montagu watched him lurch around the billiard table. They'd

MELBA

kept pace with each other through pre-dinner whiskies, wine with the meal, and now port. It was the same every night. Monty's capacity was greater than Charles's, his hand steadier.

The game was snooker. Charles chalked his cue in an irritated, befuddled manner. His thoughts were on Nellie. He lined up a shot, but mis-cued . . . Nellie . . . Nellie and her supposed lover; what was to be done about them? How they rubbed their filth in a man's face.

Charles's thoughts were all-suffusing, acrid and smoky. He drank to focus his anguish but it only seemed to dim decision making.

Nothing was proven yet. All was suspicion. Montagu exulted in suspicion, and drew lurid pictures for Charles's mind to fix upon.

'Your shot,' said Charles thickly.

While Montagu took his shot, Charles slurred his way through a speech he'd been making, more or less, about this time at night for the past few days:

'Unpleasant. Off-handed. Very sure of herself. Conceited. And spoilt. Used to throw things at me. Uncivilised.'

Montagu had heard it all before, but enough was never enough.

'A brutal woman,' Montagu soothingly contributed, after driving a ball perfectly into a corner pocket, 'from a stunted, brutal place.'

Charles raised his head appreciatively. Sometimes Montagu understood everything.

'Her bloody father's the one, Monty, she takes his attitudes and applies 'em to the world. Never got along with him myself. Never liked him, really. Filled me full of mumbo-jumbo for a while, fair dealing, four-square David Mitchell . . . you know the sort of guff, Monty.'

'I do, I do. Disliked the man myself. Hated his great messy beard. Thought he was a jumped-up patriarch, the type who makes his pile in the colonies and rubs it in the face of the homefolk. Crammed with seething ambition. Greedy for his daughter's achievement, though he made a play of denying it.'

'A hard man, a bloody hard daughter.'

EAT, OR BE EATEN

'Happens with women,' said Montagu. 'Only way they can forge ahead, really. Take their rule book from Daddy . . .'

It was after midnight now. Montagu made another shot, driving his cue forward with a smart crack that sent two balls rocketing into pockets, while a third, more slowly, rolled forward and dropped in neatly.

Charles mis-cued again.

'Can't do a bloody thing tonight.' He lurched against the table.

'You'll feel better tomorrow,' Montagu promised. 'After we've had our talk with my lawyer in Dublin.'

Charles leaned his head agaitnt the door-jamb, his eyes closed, while Montagu blew out the lamps. After a minute Montagu took his elbow and guided him off to bed.

Charles's head thudded in the night. 'Wish I'd never met her, never gone to that bloody God-forsaken country . . . Wish I wouldn't drink so . . . What do I need, what do I need . . . Never thought I'd want to put my arms around her again . . . I said no, *I* said no . . . Could have her now . . . Makes me sick, mustn't think of him, the other . . . She's mad if it's true, something wrong with her, what they've done to her, done to herself . . . overstrained? Wish I knew . . . Older woman, mere boy, ardent and randy, capable of having woman of beauty, mere snap of fingers and she falls . . . Nellie, I knew you so warm, so willing . . . I walked away, left you at the window, in the rain . . . walked into the streets of Brussels, but came back, night, the crowds, all those people longing, thrilled, all of them, hundreds wanting you, thousands, and you so beautiful, alone on the stage, your arms outstretched and the music . . . It was all that you wanted . . . Didn't matter to me, then . . .'

Did the torture of desire mean he still loved her?

In the harsh light of morning only one thought: *make her pay*. Dublin, the lawyers, everything.

His name was Mr Whittaker, a sharp-eyed attorney with the reputation of a terrier in the divorce courts.

Charles, with much embarrassment and throat-clearing,

told Whittaker what he knew, which had seemed like a lot in his fevered night thoughts, but now, before a stranger, sounded dismally slim and supposititous.

'Let me attempt a summary,' said Mr Whittaker in his strong, reedy voice. 'The woman, your wife, Mrs Armstrong, now going about as "Madame Melba", has been seen in the company of a young man, one Philippe, Duke of Orléans.'

Montagu nodded vigorously.

'However,' continued Whittaker, 'this Frenchman is not the only man she's been seen with, as it were, since the time — in Brussels was it? — when you declined to share her travelling life, Mr Charles.'

'"As it were" is right, Whittaker, she's been blameless till now . . .' (Montagu again.) 'My brother would be taking no interest otherwise.'

Whittaker shot at him:

'How can we tell? I mean, you have only the word of an innocent boy that they were under the same roof together. So, I gather, were many another.'

'Yes, but whose roof,' said Montagu. 'Gladys de Grey's . . . my God, the woman has a reputation.'

'Let us be factual, please. The Duke has also been seen at the theatre, at the stage door, sending flowers to her hotel, and so forth. Common pastimes among theatrical enthusiasts, hardly indictable by law.'

'Well, they are hard at it,' grunted Montagu. 'Hard at another common pastime.' (Charles coloured deeply.)

'I have little doubt, little doubt,' murmured Whittaker, 'that their game is carnal indulgence, Mr Montagu, a game as old as Eden. However, if you wish to pin them down in the courts . . .'

'We do,' said Charles quietly.

'Make 'em wriggle,' laughed Montagu.

'Then,' continued Mr Whittaker, 'they must be given a little more time.'

'Time! My brother's no whoremaster, Whittaker.'

'That's enough,' murmured Charles.

Whittaker raised a hand in a cautionary gesture.

'We must wait till they come more into the open,' he said.

EAT, OR BE EATEN

'They'll get around in public soon enough. I know the course of illicit love, and it never did like to run smooth. They'll want people to admire them as a couple, for this is vanity, all vanity. Then you'll have them plain. Witnesses. Letters written in heat. Sordid material of all kinds . . . Bide your time, and then we shall put our man on their trail. Madame Melba is going to Europe shortly, am I correct?'

'Within the month.'

'Very well. We shall make a study of her there, through the services of our excellent contacts in the European capitals. Most discreet, most assiduous, but rather costly, I am afraid.'

'Money is no object,' said Montagu (who would supply it).

Charles glanced at his brother gratefully.

'Thank you both,' said Whittaker, bringing the discussion to an end.

'The woman is an adventuress, Whittaker,' whispered Montagu hoarsely, while Charles stood at the door, and waited for another of Montagu's rants to end. 'The Duke, though merely a boy, is, I hear, a capable sensualist. The European aristocracy has a craze for singers, and the ladies oblige, married or not. They must be made to pay. These Dukes of nothing-at-all make sport with gentlemen like my brother.'

'Indeed. Indeed, Mr Montagu,' said Mr Whittaker. 'When it finally comes into the courts it will be something to see. Humiliation applied with a scalpel, technically exact, and without pity. That is what is wanted. A much better thing than crude revenge. It is the purpose of the law.'

Outside in the street, Charles gripped Montagu's elbow.

'Say what you like, Monty,' he said, 'but remember one thing: my wife is no mere "singer". It cheapens the whole business to say so.'

'Sorry Charlie. I'll remember,' Montagu promised.

'She's a great artist.'

'Great, wonderful, and all that. Yes indeed,' said Montagu.

'Has her own rules . . . must be made to see that she can't break our rules, that's all.'

Charles then walked on ahead, until they found a pub.

'Damn this thirst I have,' he said, his hand on the door.

24

We have our Proof

Nellie's European tour began, and within a day or so of her departure Philippe slipped quietly away from England. He went with his father's blessing, choosing his initial destinations as he pleased. In a fortnight's time he was expected in Vienna, where social duty required him to mingle with Austro-Hungarian royalty, but until then he was without his usual companions. Colonel D'Aurelle had gone boar hunting in Romania. Eugene Benoit was in France, visiting his parents in Aix-en-Provence. They would meet up with their young prince in Vienna.

Philippe went straight to the Hotel Splendide, Brussels, taking a large suite as befitting one of his rank. He was well-known there, his family name revered. Many days passed in the pursuit of pleasure and duty. In the afternoons he called on ambassadors, and attended diplomatic receptions. Discreetly, an audience was arranged with the foreign minister. He dined with the King. At night he went to the opera.

In another wing of the same hotel, the beautiful young Madame Melba and her entourage, which included the singers Jean and Edouard de Reszke, created much excitement among the staff. Madame Melba's demands for perfection, which were beginning to be identified with her name, were never a trouble. No request was too much, no service too menial to render her. She was such a delight to have under the roof. In the mornings, maids and footmen would pause in their work, listening to the beautiful, peerless, perfectly fragile notes of her daily practising. Afterwards, she made it her habit to proceed downstairs, where she liked to sit for a while with Jean de Reszke and drink tea with a slice of lemon. It was assumed by many that the handsome, fortyish Jean de Reszke was her lover. He was so considerate, enchanting, gallant.

Until mid-morning Philippe stayed in bed, enjoying the emptiness of the early day. He turned the pages of a large travel book, his eyes lingering on engravings of elephant hunters, of forest canopies sheltering pygmy bowmen, of pith-helmeted gorilla hunters sighting their rifles. On a map his finger traced the course of the river Niger. He meant to go to those places when he could: Colonel D'Aurelle had been wanting to take him this year, but his father's illness, and other things, had intervened . . . Now, as Philippe pushed back the bedcovers, his gaze fell on the amber teardrop with its black *moiré* ribbon, lying where it had fallen, during the early hours of the morning, in a crease of the sheets. With a smile he picked it up, and then called his valet to prepare his bath, and make ready for his shave.

A short while later, with a newspaper under his arm, Philippe entered the dining salon and saw Nellie sitting with her friend the tenor.

He went over to their table.

'We seem to bump into each other everywhere,' said Nellie, with a quick glance at the imperturbable Jean de Reszke.

'A happy chance, Madame,' Philippe bowed. 'Last night I heard you sing. I was absolutely enchanted.'

'Oh, come now. Monsieur de Reszke had a much better night, didn't you, Jean . . . You must sit with us, and flatter him too.'

'She is too kind,' said the tenor, with a wave of his elegant hand.

Philippe sat, and ordered coffee.

MELBA

'For once I will have some too' said Nellie. She called the waiter back. *'Cafe, s'il vous plaît, M'sieur.'*

'Certainement, Madame Melba.'

'I feel so at home in Brussels, everyone knows me. It's where things began for me, I wish I could stay on,' prattled Nellie. 'But such a busy life we lead. Soon we must go to Berlin. After that, the Czar is sending a special train to take me to St Petersburg.'

'A happy chance, Madame. I too am travelling to St Petersburg,' said Philippe.

'How delightful!'

Jean de Reszke folded his napkin, and made ready to leave the table. Nellie delayed him.

'Isn't it nice, Jean, he will hear you there in *Lohengrin*, *Faust*, and *Romeo et Juliette*.'

'Eclipsed, as always, by Madame Melba,' said the gallant de Reszke. He bowed his excuses, and went.

Nellie and Philippe's eyes met and their hands touched briefly on the tabletop. Philippe was holding the amber talisman, which had been left in his bed.

'You are making me blush,' said Nellie with quiet intensity.

The hotel staff watched them from a distance, respectful, worshipful, adoring.

It was nice to linger. All of Nellie's tensions of the past weeks in England were gone. Foreign people seemed never to pry, and disapprove, the way the English did . . . She was a delight to Philippe, she had him enthralled; he could not bear to spend time away from her side; here in a public place he leant across the table and whispered that he loved her, adored her, desired her every minute of the day.

'Ssh!'

'It is true,' he finished intensely.

She laughed aloud, in her public manner, deflecting any thought in the minds of watchers that secrets were held between them.

One watcher had no such illusion, though.

In the foyer of the hotel a man in a checked cape sat idling away the morning. Each time the door of the dining salon

WE HAVE OUR PROOF

pushed open, he glanced quickly through. Most gratified he was to note that Madame Melba and the Duc d'Orléans were sitting together: he recognised a tête-à-tête when he saw one.

He waited a minute, toying with a newspaper, then went swiftly upstairs. A luggage trolley came rumbling down a long corridor; one glance was enough to establish that the Duc's luggage was being forwarded to Berlin . . . The man smiled to himself. If the luggage was to go from Berlin to Russia, why then, he would have exceptional tidings for his employer.

Outside the Duc's suite he detained a maid, spoke idly for a few minutes attempting to charm the poor girl, then having no luck, swiftly offered her a great deal of money if she would only allow him into the Duc's chambers. The maid raised her broom indignantly, and drove the man away. He merely laughed at her outrage.

Later, with embarrassed devotion, the maid reported the matter to the Duc, who gave her a gold coin for her trouble. He made no mention of the incident to Nellie. There were several possibilities, he thought, to explain the man's snooping. He might have been a French political agent. Yet the man's interest in bedroom arrangements suggested another line of enquiry that angered Philippe suddenly: he could be working for the Duc de Luyns, preparing a case against him to use with his father. If so, Philippe would show de Luyns who had the greater mettle in his blood. How dare he . . .

There was a third possibility that alarmed Philippe in a different way. It was that Madame Melba's husband had put private detectives on his trail. He thought it unlikely, especially as they were no longer in England, but there was no telling what a man would do in the circumstances.

Berlin, the eastbound terminus, midnight.

Jean and Edouard de Reszke emerged from a cloud of steam and walked the length of the St Petersburg–Moscow Express, taking their exercise before departure. At the end of the platform they turned and walked back again. Ahead, a dozen or more people crowded around a carriage door. They cheered, then burst into a distinctly German choral item, and draped a tribute of flowers around the neck of Madame Melba.

She sang a few phrases in response to the greeting, but the roar and bustle of the station drowned her voice.

The de Reszke brothers stood about for a few minutes more, rising on their toes and uncramping their travel-weary limbs. Edouard examined the construction of the Czar's special carriage. Jean watched people's faces. The whole story of Europe was here on the eastbound platform, the poverty, the riches, the disparate races. Suddenly in the crowd Jean glimpsed a familiar face. It was the Duc d'Orléans, wearing a hat pulled down over his eyes, and a large muffler. He came idling through the press of people like someone with no special destination in mind. When he saw Nellie, he drew back, and made his way to a forward carriage without revealing himself to her.

An announcement was made: the train would depart in three minutes.

Without saying anything to Edouard about who he'd seen, Jean took his brother's elbow and they made their way back to their carriage.

Jean had known from the very beginning about Nellie's affair with the young Duc. He'd guessed it all in Paris. There had been no need for anyone to tell him anything, or show him anything, it had all been in Nellie's eyes, in her nervous high-strung expectancy and distracted mannerisms.

Whistles blew, the body of the train jolted. Departure was imminent. Steam drifted through the chilly air. Berliner officialdom marched along the platform in resplendent uniform, warning people back from the train.

In the corridors, suddenly, there was a typical stillness. People hung from windows, stood in doors. The German choir would not let Nellie go. It was that minute of suspended motion in the rhythm of rail travel, and a certain man, last seen in a checked cape, now dressed in a dark suitcoat, and wearing an important hat, took advantage of it. He made his way down the corridor of the Czar's special carriage and shouldered open the door of Madame Melba's luxurious stateroom. He wore in his lapel a fair imitation of the badge of the German Railway

WE HAVE OUR PROOF

Police. He looked quickly around, noting the luxurious appointments made available to Melba by the Czar. He wasted no time as he flicked open a valise, plunged his hand into its contents and withdrew an embroidered handkerchief and a lace-fringed garter. Very nice, he thought, these will show her style. He stuffed them in his pocket. Then he felt deeper, and found what he had come for: a bundle of letters and love-notes. Most exceptional good luck: careless woman . . . not as adept at the game as she might be? He left the stateroom as swiftly as he came, unobserved, he thought: except suddenly, from the far end of the corridor, he found himself being stared at by Jean de Reszke.

The train began to move.

Jean gave a shout; but the intruder strode off in the other direction, knowing he was safe, ducking past Madame Melba in the doorway, leaping to the platform on the run and brushing aside the confounded German singers as the train glided away.

The man looked back, and laughed to see Jean de Reszke's angry fists waving at him impotently.

Now a rhythm was established that would last a night and a day. The train rushed eastwards through the cold and dark, heading for the Polish border. Snow began to fall, enclosing the serpentine, fire-breathing express in a timeless eddy of flakes.

Inside it was warm, lamplit, comforting. In his sleeping compartment Philippe sat scribbling a note which he gave to his valet, who carried it down the length of the train, where it was passed to Madame Melba's maid. After receiving Nellie's reply, Philippe went to the dining car and ate a good dinner. The wine was an excellent Burgundy. He thought about his father at this hour, dining in the chilly hall of Sheen House. The Comte de Paris would be imagining his son entrained for Vienna. What a shock when he learned otherwise, as the agent of the Duc de Luyns, if that's who the man in Brussels had been, would soon make it his business to reveal. Philippe had a moment of remorse, but rapidly forgave himself. His father,

God knew, had been young once. Nothing could drag him from Nellie's side now.

He drank his wine and thought warmly of the long night to come.

'This is madness,' said Nellie.

'Yes, a wonderful madness,' murmured Philippe, burying his lips in her loosened hair.

It was past midnight, their secret hour, the time of all their most passionate whispered conferences and fevered lovemaking. Their hour, as they liked to think of it, when the rest of the world turned its face to the wall, and slept.

Eventually there was a great calm between them. They sat together at the window, and Nellie leant back in her lover's arms. The shades were drawn. Soft gaslight illuminated them.

'Everywhere I go, there you are. Will that always be true?' she asked.

'Always, always,' Philippe romantically asserted, tracing his fingers on her lips.

But she wanted to go beyond this tonight, to speak of other things. She was emboldened. Something about the risk he had taken in throwing aside his plans for Vienna, travelling east instead of south, ignoring his father's wishes for her sake, made her feel he was more securely hers than she had ever thought before. She twisted around in order to look into his eyes.

He smiled at her, dissolving her intentions, making her shy, really, and she merely leaned her head on his chest. How curious, she felt younger with Philippe than she ever had with Charles.

After a while Philippe raised the blinds and peered out into the night. There was nothing to be seen except occasionally a flash of lamplight from a lonely cottage window.

'Emptiness, such loneliness and desolation,' he mused.

'Just like Australia . . .'

'Tell me . . .'

'There is nothing out there, you think, nothing at all . . .'

'How sad.'

'No . . . Thinking of it now . . . I am homesick.'

WE HAVE OUR PROOF

'Tell me.'

He liked her to talk about Australia. Anywhere he had never been fascinated him. He loved to have what he could not have, loved to savour and sample in his epicurean way. She did not think this was his attitude to her, of course, to women in general: she never doubted him in that direction. But in other ways, regarding other things. He collected books, paintings, masks, ornate knives, and fragments of ancient pottery. Nothing ever lasted in his enthusiasm or totally possessed him, except the will for travel, for change.

'Silences you could only dream about,' she said. 'Nights full of stars. But when morning comes! There are birds, countless beautiful birds all singing at once. Kookaburras, cockatoos, magpies.'

'The eucalyptus trees . . .'

'Yes. Every one different from the rest in shape and colour, not like Europe, where the forests are like armies standing at attention. More like . . . dreams. But dry, no rain. Or very little.'

'Deserts that bloom? A noisy silence? I should like to see this back-to-front sort of place.'

'Oh, I hope you shall, one day.'

She sought Philippe's closer attention again.

'If only you could meet my father,' she said. 'He is a wonderful man. When he decides a thing can be done, he does it. He's built a whole city out there from nothing. I wish I could show him the carriage the Czar of all the Russias sent for me.'

There was much more than mere boasting in this. There was nothing idle in Nellie's conversation tonight. In her mind, she was desperately trying to knit together her father's values with the honour accorded her by kings and princes; and thus, by connection, to validate her illicit love.

'What are you thinking?'

'Oh, of everything . . . nothing.' It was rather hopeless. The impossibility of it all made her sad. Her fingers traced the design of the monogrammed cushions, the coat of arms of the Czar. Tears filled her eyes, threatening to well over.

MELBA

How very lovely, thought Philippe as he studied the reflected gaslight glancing and filling those beautiful dark eyes. What a lovely effect. It roused his desire again.

He kissed her.

'Dear Philippe,' Nellie responded. Her thoughts ran on, began again. 'Tell me about your father.'

'He does not know how much I love him,' said Philippe, sitting up a little. 'He thinks because I am young, I am irresponsible.'

'Soon he'll want you back,' said Nellie.

Her statement caused Philippe to become guarded.

'What do you mean?'

She then used a word that had not been used in any connection between them till now.

'Marriage,' Nellie dared.

'Ah, marriage,' he repeated, hating the very syllables on his lips. Their affair had until now evaded the many implications of this word, its power to impose itself on his responsibilities, on her dreams, on the fears of both. Marriage: a word with too many meanings for these lovers, each pulling in opposite directions, holding no comfort for either.

Yet Nellie had spoken it, and so the conversation must proceed.

'Marriage,' responded Philippe, as lightly as he could make the word sound. 'I don't want to think of such things. No. I want to experience the world. That is enough for now.'

He took Nellie's face in his hands. She was very still. He did not know that his answer had frozen her blood. She dared not speak another word, all she could think was that his answer had given him away: he spoke like a member of a royal family, like an heir to a throne. He spoke as a young man sowing his wild oats, with Nellie a passing entrancement.

And yet she loved him more than ever.

In the Berlin cable office the private detective bit the stub of an indelible pencil and chose his wording carefully. He would have liked to use the lascivious English he sometimes put in his reports, but he must be succinct and confidential. He must

WE HAVE OUR PROOF

allude, conclusively. He thought of the padded bower supplied by the Czar, the heady reek of Madame's perfumes, the deep furs and the embroidered slippers he'd stepped over to reach her valise. He thought of the incriminating letters now safely stowed in his pocket, and the intimate articles proving he'd penetrated her closest privacy.

'THE SONGBIRD HAS NESTED, EGGS TAKEN,' he wrote.

He placed a pile of coins on the cable form and pushed it across to the clerk.

With a rattle of Morse keys, the cable sped across to Ireland.

At Sheen House, Richmond, nothing was known.

'Where is my son?' thundered the Comte de Paris.

'Sire, you must not agitate yourself,' counselled the Duc de Luyns.

'He is never where I need him, and I need him more than ever. There is such work to be done!'

In a large old-fashioned room with a cavernous fireplace and a bare flagstoned floor, the Comte de Paris paced up and down. A handsome, aristocratic man in his late fifties, he walked with the aid of a steel-tipped cane. He levelled the cane at his oldest and most trusted adviser.

'You said it was finished.'

'I said it meant nothing, was merely a dalliance,' said the Duc de Luyns. 'I am still not convinced otherwise . . .'

'You mince your words, my friend. He is a week overdue in Vienna, and we know nothing.'

'Well then, she has him at her heels.'

'In Russia.'

'Undoubtedly.'

The steel-tipped cane struck the floor.

'If once we achieve the throne we should be strong enough to maintain it. We must keep Catholics and Protestants united; we must win back the conservatives and above all keep the legitimists and Orléanists loyal. And he is in Russia, in bed with a woman.'

'The say she has the purest voice that ever sang.'

'My God. Music means little to Philippe, I know. It is the woman, the ankle and the pretty shoulder, the stocking and the bedsheet for him. It was always so, since his first indiscretion.'

'Please, these are angry words, your son is better than you say, we both know it.'

'If the Republic collapses we need a responsible ruler to end the chaos. A man of dignity and honour, not some *habitué* of the dressing rooms.'

'We have such a ruler in you.'

'I will not live much longer.'

'No, no.'

The Comte de Paris took a deep, difficult breath.

'I need to know. Is my son equal to the task that Destiny will soon thrust upon him, eh?'

The laboured sentence took its toll. The Comte de Paris leaned on his cane and breathed heavily.

'I shall depart for the Continent immediately. I shall bring him to order,' said the Duc de Luyns, bowing low.

'We have our proof,' announced Mr Whittaker as Charles and Montagu entered his office. 'Most excellent proof.'

'Bravo!' Montagu turned to his brother. 'What do you say, Charlie?'

'Show me,' said Charles, grimly extending a hand.

Whittaker handed across a bundle of documents. Charles untied the legal tape with trembling fingers. Montagu waited impatiently for his turn. There was a type-written report from Brussels, describing clandestine meetings in public between Madame Melba and the Duc d'Orléans. They had sat at a table together drinking coffee. They had used one Jean de Reszke, Czech-born singer of repute, as go-between: the pattern was that de Reszke escorted Melba to a public place, such as a hotel dining room, and there the singers waited for Orléans, a late riser, who 'would come prancing in, and sight Madame as if by chance'.

The detective had seen the pair touching hands, laughing

WE HAVE OUR PROOF

together, and engaging in quiet, intimate conversation.

'This is nothing at all,' grunted Charles. He passed the report over to Montagu.

'Pray continue,' said Whittaker. 'The cablegram . . .'

Charles read it with a sour expression. 'Songbird . . . Nest . . .' The words were abominably cheap. He turned another page and found, to his distaste, a handkerchief embroidered with an ornate 'M', and a garter of a kind he had never known Nellie to wear in her life before, the two items carefully flattened between sheets of tissue paper. This was really going too far, he thought. He was overcome by revulsion at the idea of doors being forced, possessions rifled. It was a most ungentlemanly violation of the other sex. It was unsporting. It was rape. It went against all his standards.

But when he reminded himself of who it was, and why, he tasted the poison he felt towards Nellie now, the hatred.

Next came a bundle of letters. Charles stared at them uncomprehendingly.

'Read the letters,' nodded Whittaker.

'I would rather not,' said Charles.

'Then I will, Charlie, show me,' urged Montagu, like a greedy schoolboy.

Charles withheld them from his brother's reach.

He went to the window, to the light. There he read words that washed over him like acid. Half the letters were in English, the others in French. What the French ones said he could not tell: those in English were plain enough.

Nellie did not discover the loss of her letters until she was installed in her hotel in St Petersburg. At first she was desolated, as if a whole part of her had been wrenched open and exposed to the dissection of strangers. Who among her staff was the betrayer? Why had she been so careless? Was the sheaf of intimate confessions merely lying, unread, in the dark of a railway yard somewhere? Or had the letters reached the Comte de Paris? Charles? She shook with impotent rage and remorse. She could say nothing to Philippe: she had promised to destroy them. Keeping the letters had been the only matter in which she had ever disobeyed her lover, or ever would.

For a whole day, now, she thought of nothing except the loss, while she went to official receptions, met the glittering and strangely beautiful people of Russian society, and rehearsed the magnificent performances planned for the Imperial Theatre, which were the talk of the capital.

Then on the evening of her first performance her worries and fears left her.

Shame, like a low cloud, lifted.

She was suddenly glad that the letters had gone because it was like a door opening from a stuffy closed-up room leaving her love exposed to the real weather of the world. Even here, in a city of spies and secret police, Philippe still came to her at night and was ardent, devoted, humbled by his feelings. He swore his love with helpless passion. His words on the train, when he had swerved so close to bleak acknowledgement of realities, were as if they had never been spoken . . . Let them come armed with evidence and shout it from the rooftops, thought Nellie: I am ready. She kept reminding herself that the very fact that Philippe was with her, here in St Petersburg, was a sign of what he intended for them both, even if he could not acknowledge it frankly yet, even to himself. Here they were, on the shore of a frozen sea, at the most northerly point of a bold journey together, and the city was a pivot, a turning point, from which they would return arm-in-arm to the civilisation they knew.

On the night of the first performance something astonishing happened.

It was the finale of *Romeo et Juliette*. The theatre was full. The Czar Alexander, the Czarina, and members of the Imperial Family sat in their box. Nellie and Jean de Reszke sang the duet 'Tis I, Romeo, thine own', and as the significant final notes came, she and Jean held each other's eye and their voices interwove in the air around them: they had never sung so perfectly together. *Now*, thought Nellie, the applause will come, it will rip through this resonating silence as it always

WE HAVE OUR PROOF

does, returning us to the moment.

But nothing happened. There was pure silence in the tiers and recesses of the Imperial Theatre. Utter silence. Just the crackle of a few programmes, and someone suppressing a cough.

Members of the audience turned and looked up at the royal box occupied by the Czar and Czarina. The Czar was leaning forward looking very spiritual, very preoccupied. Obviously there was a custom here that no-one should clap until the Czar.

One person could not bear this: Philippe.

In a box of his own, he glared down at the crowd. He had forgotten the Czar, the occasion, the place and the time. Only the glory of the woman he loved filled his thoughts as his hands came together and he clapped.

His applause alone echoed in the great theatre.

Nellie, as Juliette lying motionless in the arms of Jean de Reszke's Romeo, blinked and waited.

'My God,' Jean murmured.

'No,' Nellie whispered. The shock within the audience was implacable.

From the corner of her eye Nellie saw two burly footmen enter Philippe's box. They took him by the elbows and marched him away.

Only then, with methodical appreciation, did the Czar begin to clap.

Immediately the house was in uproar. There was wild excitement unleashed, fervent appreciation of the performance. The orchestra struck up, and Nellie and Jean were on their feet, stepping forward, bowing. Another strange custom showed itself: students tied together strings of handkerchiefs and lowered them over the balconies, swaying them frenziedly in time with the music. The roar subsided, the curtain calls began. Nellie could not think while this was happening.

Even when the performance was over the riotous appreciation continued. She was summoned to a great reception room and presented with a bracelet of diamonds and pearls by the Czar himself. She could not help thinking of

MELBA

Philippe, as she thanked him, and what his fate would be at the hands of this man of tyrannical power, whose eyes were remote and reverent.

When she stepped from the stage door the cold was breathtaking in its intensity. The moon shone, the streets were full of snow. As she walked towards her waiting sleigh crowds of students spread the path in front of her with scarlet rose petals, which looked black in the night. It was like a dream. The students waved programmes for signing, and she obliged as best as she could. As soon as she'd signed, someone would grab the pencil from her hand and bite it with savage ecstasy, distributing the pieces like relics among the others. They were mad. They were like young wolves in the snow. They frightened her a little.

Jean de Reszke hauled her into the sleigh and they were off, speeding across the snow with a tinkle of soft bells.

Nellie stared back at the crowd, getting her breath.

'What a country,' said Nellie.

'There goes your privacy,' said Jean, 'for as long as you live.'

Nellie stared down at the fur rug covering her lap. Was there a double meaning in his words, she wondered? Has he abandoned his magnificent discretion? Is he referring to Philippe?

'What do you mean?' she asked, trembling.

The real meaning of her question was, *What do you know?*

Jean leant forward and adjusted Nellie's wrap.

'Simply this,' he said pleasantly. 'Wherever you go, in whatever country or on whatever continent, in England, America, or in your own faraway country, you will have no secrets.'

'Then I will wear disguises,' said Nellie, holding part of the fur across her face.

'They will tear them off,' answered Jean. 'Anyway, they will be seeking a person who is not there at all, so the disguises will be pointless. They will want a phantom, not a breathing human being, my dear. You will be required to fill their dreams, not illustrate their weaknesses. It is the price of fame, I assure you.'

WE HAVE OUR PROOF

'Then I will give them something to think about,' said Nellie defiantly.

Jean then said: 'I suppose you know what will happen to your young enthusiast?'

'Tell me,' said Nellie breathlessly.

'Court etiquette requires that nobody should clap before the Czar. So. This forward young man will be told that St Petersburg and Holy Russia would be happy if he would take his leave. I should think, at this very moment, he is at the station, being put into a very comfortable stateroom on the Berlin-Vienna Express.'

Nellie looked into Jean's eyes with slow realisation.

'You *know*,' she said, feeling the utmost relief.

She leaned back and laughed, and Jean laughed with her.

She was so relieved to have her secret out in the open with someone.

The lamplight of their sleigh made quick, diamond-like reflections as it fanned out across the snow. The tinkle of the sleigh-bells was the very sound of Nellie's own happiness; it was so gentle, inviting, and continuously woven together that it seemed it would never end or be interrupted.

She took Jean's hand.

'I am so happy,' she said.

25

The Spinning Chorus

At George's school the evening ritual of passing out the mail was in progress.

'Holmes . . . Baxter . . . McArdle . . . Spence . . . Armstrong . . .' droned Mr Wentleford's voice. He passed a letter matter-of-factly to George. The postmark was London.

George waited for more. 'Nash . . . Endicott . . . Quincy . . . Well, well,' Mr Wentleford's pace altered. 'Armstrong again.' He held a large blue envelope up to the light, and waved it under his nose exaggeratedly.

'Attar of Roses . . . or is it Essence of Musk?'

The boys tittered as they always did when a letter came from George's mother.

Mr Wentleford made a show of reading the address. 'My goodness, it's from Holy Russia,' he said.

George grabbed the letter and sprinted off.

His private place for reading letters was down by the canal, at the bottom of the playing fields. A gravel pit was there, full of weeds and old buckets of tar: it seemed to suit his loneliness.

'I hope you are well,' wrote his father. 'There is a pony called Stitcher at your Uncle Montagu's place. You shall ride him when you please.'

'My dear, sweet, darling,' wrote his mother. 'I miss you

THE SPINNING CHORUS

dreadfully and wish you were by my side always. The snow is so very deep and we ride around in sleighs all the time, there is no other mode of transport. The river is solid ice. You would not believe the praise heaped on my head daily . . .'

There was lots more, but George was interrupted by a sharp tap on his shoulder. He turned around to see Holmes, McArdle and Spence leering at him.

'Are you ready . . . Froggy,' said McArdle, taking up a boxing stance, his feet positioned aggressively and his knuckles clenched. A great sadness welled up in George. He folded his letters and stuffed them securely in an inside pocket.

He went for McArdle as hard as he could, and might have got him down, except that Holmes and Spencer grabbed his arms, hurling him into a patch of thistles, where they thumped him as hard as they could. George held his elbows into his sides, and his forearms across his chest, and did nothing.

'Why don't you fight back, you rotten little cad,' they taunted.

'Jellyfish.'

'Mamma's boy.'

'Froggy.'

At the finish, McArdle bent down and punched him deliberately on the nose; McArdle was able to do this without causing nose-bleeds, but it always made George cry no matter how desperately he held back the tears.

Then he was alone in the gravel pit again, watching through a gap in the alder trees as a barge slid by in perfect silence.

When his tears were dry he trudged back to the school.

His only satisfaction was that the boys had been unable to take the letters from his inside pocket. The lump they made was like a strong heart he carried with him, a source of courage. The love between his parents had failed but strangely this did not isolate George. His love joined them now; it was the only thing. That night, with the moon shining through the window of the dormitory, he took the letters out and re-read them. His mother's he committed to memory before tearing it into small unreadable pieces. His father's he put in his bedside drawer.

Then he played with his lead-moulded cowboys and Indians

on the pillow, a sad, sleepless little boy passing the time.

Colonel Florian D'Aurelle knew no greater triumph than the moment when a bird of prey returned to him with a blooded beak.

In a forest clearing close to Vienna a falcon beat its way rapidly through the air. Uttering small, sharp cries, it circled the clearing several times, and then with astonishing speed whistled down to the wrist of the falconer.

'What was it today?' mused the Colonel, raising his voice a little so that Eugene Benoit, waiting near a stone wall, would hear. 'What have you killed, my beauty, a thrush? A songbird?' He slipped the hood over the bird, and stroked its trembling feathers.

He laughed harshly.

It was a long time since Benoit had seen D'Aurelle in such good spirits.

'You have located our friend?' Benoit called.

'Well, what do you think? Naturally!' replied D'Aurelle. 'He arrived from Budapest yesterday. I have spoken to him. She comes tonight.'

'You do not seem too concerned,' said Benoit. Usually Colonel D'Aurelle fretted savagely about Philippe and Madame Melba. 'What is your next move, then?'

'I? I have no part to play. I am merely a loyal servant, as you are, my boy.'

'There is a change in the situation, I can smell it,' said Benoit.

'Ah ha,' mocked D'Aurelle. 'You are too clever . . . Yes, the Duc de Luyns is expected at any moment, with orders for this foolishness to end forthwith. The Comte de Paris forgives all.'

'Philippe loves her, D'Aurelle.'

D'Aurelle laughed mockingly. 'Time cools all lusts, it is said. The woman is not even so very beautiful. I could not touch her myself. I have often said so. Now she is already filling out. In a year or two she will be as fat as your mother, Madame Benoit of Aix-en-Provence.'

'You sorely test me, D'Aurelle . . . Philippe loves her, I say.'

THE SPINNING CHORUS

'Of course. Yes, yes.'

D'Aurelle's chuckling tolerance was new also.

'What has Philippe said to you?' asked Benoit suspiciously. He was feeling a loss of influence over his friend the Duc. He cursed himself for holidaying with his parents at such a time.

'Nothing. But I am able to read his eyes.'

'You are wrong. He is absolutely devoted.'

'True. His adventure is not finished. Not yet, quite.'

D'Aurelle untethered his horse and swung into the saddle, the falcon still perched on his wrist. 'Coming up behind me, Monsieur?'

'I shall walk,' said Benoit.

'Please yourself.'

D'Aurelle rode alongside him through the sandy pinewoods.

'What else is love but an adventure, Colonel D'Aurelle?' mused Benoit as they went along.

'Pretty words,' said D'Aurelle.

'You are hard.'

'The woman has mesmerised our young friend. A difficult type, the worst possible choice. A true harlot would have been better; a whore would have no thoughts of marriage, like this one.'

'Marriage?' This was news to Benoit.

D'Aurelle noted Benoit's extreme surprise. He nodded.

'Philippe tells me as much. It concerns him gravely . . . I blame you, Monsieur. You were the one who put her in his way.'

'True,' muttered Benoit. He had not forseen such a crisis. Of course he should have remembered it was ever so with the English, that they took their pleasure, then tried to make it official.

'I've even heard it said that the voice is a freak,' continued D'Aurelle with a laugh. He was enjoying himself enormously. 'Too perfect to be human, a voice made by Jack Frost out of a silver mine.'

'You have listened to the wrong people, Colonel D'Aurelle.'

'True. I am no connoisseur. What would it cost to buy her off? She likes money. This is what I hear.'

'She is already rich. She is no common slut, D'Aurelle.'

'I think you are in love with her yourself, my boy,' mocked D'Aurelle as he spurred his horse into a canter.

Nellie and Philippe reached Vienna on different days, on different trains, from different directions. He came from Budapest, after meeting with D'Aurelle following his expulsion from Russia; she from St Petersburg in a fever of counting the endless miles and the slowly passing hours. Europe was a wasteland without him. She travelled alone, servantless, in anticipation of their time together. By secret arrangement their hotel rooms adjoined, and on that first night in Vienna they went to each other through a door to which only they held the key. A pale blue ceiling was edged with gold leaf. Cupids blowing trumpets were moulded in tiny, perfect detail all the way down the pillars of a great bed.

She drew the curtains while he turned the key in the lock. The long night was theirs. Doubt, hesitation and duty were dissolved as they entered each other's arms.

Philippe had given certain undertakings to D'Aurelle which he now proceeded to forget. In Budapest, in the company of that devoted, tough old steward, he'd gone drinking and riding. D'Aurelle, in typical fashion, had drawn him back to the stern prospect of his duty; had made him feel like a prince again in the tough old meaning of the word. And also, D'Aurelle had made sure that Philippe paid his diplomatic calls. These were not such a bind as Philippe had imagined. There'd been some exceptionally pretty young princesses in a palace overlooking the Danube, and he'd laughed and danced with them, gallantly expressing a fascination which surely confused the young women as they whirled under his guidance: they had of course heard of his affair with the singer, it thrilled them . . . But he forgot these young ladies now as he touched Nellie's fingertips with his own, studied the soft depth of her eyes, and begged to know if she loved him for an eternity.

'For ever, and beyond time,' she answered, in a trance of devotion.

Nellie had decided that all was lost to him. She would, if

THE SPINNING CHORUS

he asked, surrender career, reputation, decency, anything.

She waited, but he did not ask.

Therefore with much palpitation of her nerves she took a new step. *Juliette etait une affrontée*, she reminded herself. On their second day together, she proposed they take a box at the *Hofoper*, where singers of Nellie's acquaintance, including Blanche Marchesi, would be appearing in *The Flying Dutchman*. She had in mind a public declaration of her alliance with Philippe, a placing in peril of all she treasured, a declaration of ultimate value. Nothing less would satisfy her now. Her old teacher, Madame Marchesi, would be there in the theatre to hear Blanche. It would be the closest thing to revealing herself to a member of her own family; all of Europe would know; and whatever tied her to Charles would snap at last.

'Shall we go, then?'

She watched Philippe closely while he considered his response. Not a flicker of hesitation betrayed him.

'We shall go there tonight, my darling,' he said.

The rumour that Madame Melba was in Vienna, secluded with Louis Philippe Robert, Duc d'Orléans, had already reached artistic circles at the *Hofoper*. Backstage, there was much juicy talk about it. It was known that a box had been reserved in the Duc's name for the night's performance. Some of the younger singers were already nervous at the thought of the involuntary audition they would be making, should Melba come; the older singers weighed what it might mean to their careers, should Melba put her own at risk.

In her dressing room, Blanche Marchesi was being made ready for her minor solo role. She wore a fine wig, and her costume was all correct, but there was something wrong with her. She was too sharp-faced, too frozen.

'How am I, Mama?' she asked Madame Marchesi when her mother looked in at the last moment.

'You must stop *thinking*, my little Blanche. It is no time now to be analysing. You must go out there and perform. Remember how Nellie Armstrong used to wind her watch

MELBA

during rehearsal? Technical perfection whatever the inner perturbation. That is the secret of Melba.'

The reference to Nellie at such a time hurt Blanche, but nevertheless she smiled. 'Oh, yes, your pupil, Mama . . . You know of course that she is in Vienna at this very moment, with Louis Philippe Robert, her lover, walled-up in a grand hotel, making love day and night.'

'Of course I hear the stories,' replied Madame Marchesi. 'I do not believe them, however.'

In truth Madame Marchesi believed the rumours absolutely, and despaired for Nellie's future when the lovers' secret world started fragmenting, as surely it must.

'Kiss me, Mama, and wish me luck,' said Blanche, rather desperately.

'The Spinning Chorus' was in progress when Nellie and Philippe entered their box. As they took their seats they looked at each other in the light reflected from the stage. Philippe's manner was perfect, Nellie thought. It seemed to say, 'Here we are in public and caution be hanged.' It was her attitude exactly. He was such a courageous partner in the enterprise that she was convinced he had changed his mind about their making a life together. If not marriage then she would accept whatever was handed out. She told herself that, now. Let people say what they would say. How could it be otherwise between them? All else was impossible. She imagined a villa somewhere on the Italian Lakes, a place of solitude and beauty he often talked about . . . perhaps George would come in his holidays . . . and now she leant forward, determined to enjoy the performance.

During the progress of the act people began to notice them. From the stage Blanche Marchesi peered through a gap in the curtains. From the orchestra stalls a muck-raking journalist from the *Wiener Tageblatt* craned his neck and made a satisfactory observation. From a box on the opposite side of the theatre, the English Ambassador, a friend of the Armstrong family, had his attention discreetly drawn to the pair by his wife. A relay of nudging ran around the stalls.

Then it was time for the deepest plunge.

THE SPINNING CHORUS

Between acts, when people left their seats and showed themselves in the foyers, Nellie and Philippe emerged from their box and moved among the milling crowd. People of great rank bowed and smiled. Vienna, it seemed, graciously accepted the fiction offered. There was no earth-shattering crisis, and it was all right, Nellie thought, it was so good and proper that she felt no shame, only a glory in this love of hers.

'Shall we take a glass of champagne?' Philippe asked.

He was so confident, so strong. She found his power flowing over to her: it was the gift of royalty he granted, as surely as if he had raised her to a rank equal to his own.

But just as she put her wineglass to her lips her eyes met those of Madame Marchesi. She was there in the crowd compelling Nellie's attention. The heavy-lidded eyes spoke out their authority; the guidance and the truth that was in them . . . the stern, demanding love . . . The effect was just as if someone had shouted at her, loudly and harshly, among the pleasure-loving Viennese, and thrown a firework in her face.

And so the crisis Nellie thought was averted was upon her in a few hammering seconds of realisation: and she wavered.

The way her teacher looked at her made everything into a sham, told her that whatever she was chasing was a phantom, that in being true to herself tonight she was betraying a deeper part of herself. Marchesi's eyes told her that something much harder, more difficult than a social expression of passionate love was her lot in life.

She could not face the choice. It was too unfair.

'Take me away from here,' she whispered to Philippe, clutching his arm, feeling faint.

'Of course,' answered Philippe with impeccable courtesy.

They returned to their hotel, and through the night he offered her comfort, such sweet relief from torment, though he could not understand her, really. He thought she was complicating matters for herself. He thought: 'Artists!'

'What are we to do? What is meant for us?' she wondered repeatedly.

'Two angels are fighting for your soul,' Philippe observed in his polished fashion. 'The angel of art and the angel of love.

MELBA

Which is to have you, I wonder?'

'My darling, there would be no life without you,' she replied.

The next morning Nellie went to Madame Marchesi's hotel. The old teacher greeted her without pretence.

'Nellie, Nellie be careful,' she said immediately Nellie stepped through the door. 'The world is a narrow-minded place. If they keep you off the stage, that would be the greatest loss . . . There are many attractive men in the world, but only one "Melba" . . . Do you hope to marry him?'

Nellie spoke from the heart.

'He is so good to me,' she replied. 'So charming. He never says a harsh word. He makes me feel that everything is just beginning, even when I'm singing he frees me to do more than I've dreamt possible. He makes me feel loved, and that is everything to me.'

Madame Marchesi stared at Nellie and shook her head in wonderment.

'My child,' she said. 'My child.'

The doorknob rattled and Blanche burst in, clutching a newspaper.

She flourished the paper at Nellie. 'The *Wiener Tageblatt* is writing about you . . . and your friend.'

'The *Wiener Tageblatt* is a gossip-mongering scandal-sheet,' said Madame Marchesi.

'This time they need only print the truth,' replied Blanche bluntly.

'Blanche!' said her mother warningly.

'I am only saying what you dare not, Mama.'

Blanche almost spat her words at Nellie.

'He will never marry you. He will marry a young girl from the aristocracy. A princess of the blood. He is a Catholic, you are Church of England.'

'Presbyterian,' said Nellie, with ridiculous pride in the face of Blanche's onslaught.

'You are already married,' continued Blanche. 'You have a strong, unhappy man for a husband. But that is not good enough for you.'

THE SPINNING CHORUS

'He loves me,' said Nellie with simplicity.

'Of course he loves you!' snapped Blanche. 'It is the theme of a thousand forgotten operas.'

Now at last Madame Marchesi intervened with all her power.

'Blanche! You have gone too far!'

The three women were trembling, white-faced at the things being said.

Philippe clutched a copy of the *Wiener Tageblatt*. Nellie sat on a couch, in tears.

Philippe's words were gentle and reassuring.

'It is a simple report on the society page, that says we were sitting tête-à-tête in a box at the opera.'

'But the real meaning of it,' replied Nellie, 'is that we are sharing a bed together.' She had a bitter taste in her mouth.

'Is that not what we were saying, when we went to the opera last night?' pressed Philippe.

She had never heard him so realistic, so commanding.

'I don't know. No.'

'There is no escaping the road, once the turn is taken,' said Philippe.

She supposed his father talked this way, but he was right, of course. It was just that she wanted one thing, acted as though it were another, loved this young man smiling quizzically down at her, desired him so much, but believed the world knew nothing even as she trumpeted it from the rooftops. What a state she was in. If only he would throw himself to his knees and beg her to be his for ever, to live with him as his wife, companion, or merely as his friend. Then she would turn her back on all other imperatives.

Philippe tossed the *Wiener Tageblatt* into a corner of the room.

'What does Vienna matter? Tonight we leave on the train for Brussels, and the world will be ours again.'

'Dear sweet Philippe,' said Nellie. They kissed. Her tears flowed unceasingly. She held him with all her strength, and felt that as long as she clung to him, he would be there. But the moment she let go, what then?

Philippe thought: 'My appointment with the Duc de Luyns in the morning shall have to wait. He will be furious, but D'Aurelle will explain. I must not hurt her. She is slowly coming around to an understanding of our position. Our love has a little time to run.'

The story of Nellie's affair was now on everyone's lips in London.

Mr Whittaker, divorce lawyer of Dublin, quickly relinquished his role to a man of greater reputation, a Mr Jeffrys, of the Inns of Court.

'I want to file for divorce, and I want to cite the Duke of Orléans as co-respondent,' said Charles, banging Mr Jeffrys' desk with his fist.

'Think carefully about it, Mr Armstrong. Adultery. Are you certain?' asked Jeffrys. He was a man with diplomatic and aristocratic connections. He could see many implications which were obviously of no account to Charles Armstrong and his litigious brother Montagu.

'The whole world is certain,' answered Charles grimly. 'It's plastered across every scandal sheet from here to Botany Bay.'

'Well, then. We may have a promising case.'

'Promising!' snorted Montagu. 'It is solid gold and studded with diamonds, sir.'

'I shall study the papers,' said Jeffrys.

'She must hate me like poison to rub this business in my face,' muttered Charles.

'Send the boy in to me,' said Jeffrys.

George, waiting outside, was ushered into the room.

'So you are Master George,' said Jeffrys. 'Do you like your school?'

'Yes, sir.'

'Who do you take after, young man, your mother or your father?'

George did not know who he took after, or care. His love for both parents was equal and strong. He belonged to them.

'He's got a tin ear, haven't you, Georgie,' said Montagu.

THE SPINNING CHORUS

'I don't know, sir,' said George in embarrassment. He felt guilty even for being here, though he was not sure exactly what was happening; no-one had wanted to tell him. He just knew that if he had not been born, none of this dreadful, heavy, and obscure trouble would be affecting people.

George looked at his father and begged with his eyes for all their troubles to be ended. He knew that Charles wanted the same thing. But he would not help him.

Mr Jeffrys narrowed his gaze and thought: has there ever been a more unhappy boy on the face of this earth?

'Do you see much of her, my boy?' he gently asked.

'She writes to me all the time,' said George.

'In French!' exclaimed Montagu.

'Hmm. And what does she say, when she writes to you in French?'

'I can't say,' said George.

Two phrases repeated themselves to him: *I love you, I love you. I will come to you soon.*

Nellie would be coming to England next week, she had written the news in a letter. But if he told Mr Jeffrys that he would do something to stop it.

'Did she say she was coming to England?' asked Mr Jeffrys.

'With anyone?' asked Montagu.

George bit his lips and remained silent.

'That will do,' said Charles. 'Leave the boy alone.'

Charles's private humilation had been bad enough over the past year or so: the public shame he bore now was much worse.

It was necessary for an item to appear in the papers, in the divorce lists of the *Times*: Armstrong *v* Armstrong, citing the Duke of Orléans as co-respondent.

My God, what that did to a man!

Charles refused dinner invitations, scorned sociable rides and shooting parties. He could not look people in the eye. Women, especially, felt the strength of his venom. Finding themselves in the same room as Charles, it was as if they had no existence: or worse, as if he personally reviled them for being the wrong sex. His mother, even though she despaired of Nellie now (despaired of her morals and imperiled career, of the deceptions Nellie had woven about herself for longer than anyone realised), still thought Charles the greater worry. He was near-suicidal, she believed. Yet if she tried to speak to him he clammed-up.

The truth was that Charles needed a drug of stupendous power to rid him of his pain . . . a draught of exclusive love. On those rare occasions when he stopped thinking about Nellie and the wrong she was doing him, his thoughts took anchor on the idea of George. He pictured the two of them on some high mountain trail, plunging through snowdrifts with a string of pack-ponies following behind.

The English theatre-world affected 'not to know what Melba was doing'. Her indiscretion confirmed a view, held by some, that she was a naive colonial, unable to play by the rules of sophisticated society. Others thought the whole story delightfully romantic and operatic. The overriding point, however, was morality, public morality: a standard, not of behaviour, but of the secretiveness of behaviour. This was what had been violated. The measure of all such matters was to be found in the attitudes and dictates of a small, elderly woman at Windsor Castle, who tapped her slipper to music in a most melancholy and remote fashion.

At Covent Garden one day, Lady Gladys de Grey spoke with Augustus Harris.

'The Queen has commanded a performance of *Faust* at Windsor Castle,' said Harris.

Lady de Grey felt a dread apprehension on behalf of her friend; if only she had been at Nellie's side in Vienna, she thought, to advise and guide her through the perils of her position.

'Yes, Augustus? What did she say?'

'Her Majesty has requested Madame Albani for the role of Marguerite.'

'What did you say to that?'

'I said that Madame Albani was still a great singer. She will acquit herself beautifully, but she is ageing and no longer at

THE SPINNING CHORUS

her peak. I said that Madame Melba was the greatest Marguerite in the world.'

'And what did Her Majesty say then?'

'She said she would have Albani.'

26

Pawns in a Game

The Duc de Luyns returned to London and reported to the Comte de Paris. He spoke of Colonel D'Aurelle's favourable impression of Philippe's attitude. He had lost his head in St Petersburg, but that was the privilege of ardent youth. Now he was engaged in a sentimental farewell. That it was taking him back and forth across Europe once more was not to be misunderstood.

'Of this, D'Aurelle is certain,' said the Duc de Luyns.

'I would trust his assessment over any man's,' said the Comte de Paris.

'The woman has him a while longer,' the Duc de Luyns observed.

'I have nothing against her personally,' said the Comte de Paris, clutching his cane. 'I believe she is a great artist, and I think a person of noble character. Indeed, I would dearly like to meet her myself one day and listen to her sing . . . But my son must never see her again.'

'D'Aurelle is convinced . . .'

'So my son danced with the princesses . . .' The Comte de Paris allowed himself a smile.

'For many hours,' nodded the Duc de Luyns.

'Philippe is to marry Dorothea, daughter of the Archduke

Joseph of Austria, the Palatinate and Hungary.'

'The prettiest of them all,' bowed de Luyns.

'It is all arranged. This talk of divorce proceedings will be stopped.

'Yes. There are ways.'

'I am a dying man. I want an heir without blemish, and I want grandchildren for the royal house of France.'

'It will be so,' promised the Duc de Luyns.

On a return visit to Vienna for a secret meeting with Colonel D'Aurelle, Philippe was served a writ demanding his appearance in the English divorce courts.

'My father will stop this,' he said with confidence, handing the papers to D'Aurelle.

That night Philippe wrote the Comte de Paris a most confidential and passionate letter. It was full of anguish, expressing the difficulty of his position. Then he caught a train, and hurried back to Nellie.

'Listen to me, listen,' urged Philippe.

He grasped Nellie's chin in his hand and drew her around to face him. They were in a hotel on the seafront at Ostend. A wild storm blew rain onto the windows, and drove waves hard against the shingles. As soon as the storm abated, Nellie would depart for England.

'I am listening,' she said.

'No, you are not,' he smiled.

It was true. She felt as if she were outside in the storm, part of her at least, the part that Philippe would never have, must never have. She felt as if she had been turned inside out, and that something very precious, very private was being shouted from the rooftops. The irony was that she had caused it to be shouted, had brought it on by appearing at Philippe's side in public, in Vienna, and now, in desperate love and confusion, by never hiding her love wherever they went in these last weeks. It was all because she had wanted to force his hand . . . And had failed.

He does not love me as much as I love him. Yet what a tender soul he has, she thought. I must help him.

'People are pressing on me from all sides. They each want a little part of me. They're tearing me to pieces . . .'

'No . . .'

'What is left for us, dear Philippe? You never say, but something is over . . .'

'It is never over . . .'

'Oh, you are good . . .'

'You are very beautiful. I love you.'

'We thought the world was ours. Everything has finished.'

She held him desperately, helplessly.

Philippe slowly began to charm her out of her depression. He wiped her tears away. Even as he spoke his words, and they filled her heart and lulled her, she knew they were a death sentence to part of herself.

'No, no,' Philippe tenderly began. 'It is all right. Our love can never die. Wherever you are, for the rest of your life, I will be there in your heart. How can I tell you of the tender emotion I feel? I am so happy despite our sufferings now . . . My constant and faithful friend . . .'

'Oh, oh,' Nellie sighed.

'Listen to me, *listen*. I have a house on a lake, in the most beautiful place in the world . . .'

'Como . . . ' He had spoken of it often.

'Yes. Como. Come with me there. We'll go away,' he nodded. 'Together again, as always . . . It is like heaven. Even the storms, they are like poetry on the lake . . .'

'When?'

'Now. Tonight,' he said with great simplicity.

'I must see my son first. I am frightened for him.'

'Very well. I shall wait here.'

'You must promise.' She would have this at least from him: one iron-bound promise.

'I swear, on the honour of my family, that I shall be waiting here, on this very spot, when you return,' said Philippe.

That evening, when her boat sailed for Dover, Philippe stood on the sea wall. The worst of the storm had abated, but rain still came in gusts and a wind drove the whitecaps back on themselves. Nellie caught a glimpse of him from the deck, a small dark figure in the driving rain, his hands thrust deep in the pockets of his oilskin coat. Against the rain-darkened shore, his very pose exclaimed fidelity. He would be there on her return. It was the one certainty in her life.

She went first to London, to the Savoy Hotel, taking a deep breath as she sailed through the doors.

'This will be a test,' she thought, 'to see if I can hold my head up.'

Doormen and porters bowed her in.

'Madame Melba . . .'

'Madame . . .'

The manager approached: 'Madame Melba, how good to see you back in London.'

Professionalism: she recognised it and was grateful.

She raked her eyes around. She smiled. She would never avoid a direct stare, ever again, to the end of her days. Maids, waiters, and clerks all crowded out to pay homage. She climbed to the first landing of stairs, and then paused, glancing back at the raised faces. She felt for the first time something new in herself, something distilled from the storm of privacy . . . A directness, a challenge, a foil against rumour and gossip. It was beaten from sadness, this manner, this 'Melba manner', it was a shield for heartbreak, for introspective sorrow, for all that was private and deeply personal in her life.

Montagu was out of town when Charles found himself summoned to Mr Jeffrys' offices by special messenger. When he arrived, he was introduced to a tall, distinguished Frenchman, the Duc de Luyns. In great confidence he was shown a letter, signed by Louis Philippe Robert. The meaning of the letter, addressed to the Comte de Paris, was plain: Philippe was caught in the vice of gallantry. Honour would not allow him to abandon his mistress; she would have to abandon him. A few moments passed, while Charles assessed what was expected of him. Then to his considerable astonishment Lady Gladys de Grey stepped into the room.

The diplomat, the society woman and the wronged husband came to a swift and almost wordless understanding.

It was left to the lawyer to put the matter into words:

'You are now in an excellent positon, Mr Armstrong, to issue your wife with an ultimatum.'

That night, Lady de Grey came to see Nellie at her hotel. She was friendly enough as she removed her shawl, divested herself of her gloves in order to warm her hands at the fire, and talked brightly about various matters. Her topics were determinedly to one side of the main subject. She spoke about the *Traviata* being planned for Covent Garden in the coming weeks, how exciting it would be, how romantic. Nellie was to sing the role of Violetta at an unprecedented fee, and, as was becoming usual for such 'Melba nights', there was already a black-market trade in tickets.

'You are hardly a person any longer,' smiled Lady de Grey. 'You are becoming an institution.'

'I can tell you what that means,' smiled Nellie in return. 'The best of everything, wherever I go.'

'Well. What a lucky woman you are.'

'I believe so, Gladys, I give thanks every day for my good fortune.'

'Pray it continues,' said Lady de Grey. The air between the two women was brittle.

'I should add, however,' said Lady Gladys, coming to the point, 'that some of our patrons have determined to leave their boxes empty for the season.'

'Oh. For what reason, at all?'

'They cannot associate themselves with the merest breath of scandal. I must say, I think they are acting too hastily.'

'Do you, indeed?'

'*Traviata* is my favourite opera,' answered Lady Gladys. 'The most beautiful moment, and the most tragic of course, is when the elder Germont tells Violetta about his daughter, who is soon to be married, and that the joy of her coming marriage must not be shattered by scandal . . .'

There was a stony silence, then. Facing her friend across

PAWNS IN A GAME

the fireplace Nellie felt, simultaneously, a weakness in her knees and a rush of defiance.

'What are you trying to say?' she asked.

'There are things going on, my dear. One is, how shall I put it, a pawn in a game?'

'Well, I am hardly a person any longer,' said Nellie harshly.

'Yes, there are penalties,' said Lady Gladys, lighting a cigarette. 'Penalties for class, rank, and fame. We must murder ourselves by our own rules, that is the trouble.'

For a moment Nellie hated everything about Lady Gladys: her beautiful clothes, her every calculated gesture, the armour of her aristocratic intrigue. Wordlessly, each nuance of her manner declared that that which was possible in life was possible only by arrangement. It was how her own life was managed. 'Love would never strike her down,' thought Nellie, rather bitterly. 'She would select and dismiss her lovers by calculation. No matter what she says.'

'We apply certain standards to ourselves, and ask them of others,' continued Lady Gladys. 'My dear, sweet Nellie, I beg you to understand.'

'I love him. I go on loving him,' Nellie replied.

'Yes, I know that.'

'So what is it, Gladys? I am sick from apprehension. You must tell me. You must speak it out. Life is never as tragic as it appears on the stage, you know.' This was Nellie's defiance talking. 'What am I to do for the sake of you all?'

'For all our sakes,' corrected Lady Gladys, subtly including Nellie in the circle of superior people who determined the course of important events. She was clever in doing this. Like an inquisitor needing a victim's complicity in small and necessary ways, she played on Nellie's longing for established position.

'Yes, yes. Go on.'

'Decisions have been taken at the highest levels about the divorce case. It will not go ahead. Your husband has already agreed.'

'Oh, he would never do that without something in return. Come to the point, why don't you?'

MELBA

'There is a condition. You are to surrender your claim on Philippe.'

A coldness, a weakness flowed through Nellie's veins. It was out in the open now.

But really she had known what was expected of her ever since the dark night-ride into Russia, with snowflakes whirling against the train windows.

She would have only her singing after this.

'I am sorry to be so blunt,' said Lady Gladys, waiting for Nellie to speak.

'I thought we might live in Spain, you see,' said Nellie, almost at breaking point. 'Or somewhere . . . I had dreams . . . that he need never tell anyone about me.'

'My dear Nellie,' Lady Gladys smiled with superior knowledge. 'You are the last person in the world to hide away anywhere. Just imagine it! Locking up that voice . . .'

'Would that be necessary?'

'Not on the Continent, perhaps. But here, in England, we are ever-conscious of the epithet "royal". It is the Royal Opera House, no less. Your career is tilted on the balance already. The Queen has chosen Madame Albani over you for *Faust*. Something almost irrecoverable is beginning to happen.'

'You have always been the one shaping policy at Covent Garden, Lady Gladys,' said Nellie tartly.

'My power has its limits.'

'The Continent gave me my start.'

'Oh, yes, but I really do think it is England, always England, in your heart of hearts.'

This was true. It was emphasised by Lady de Grey never actually regarding her as an Australian. Nellie liked that, it made her feel truly part of an inner circle. But even so, Nellie felt a small drop of poison enter her attitude. She was to do this for England, was she? Very well, England had better not let her down then, ever.

'I need a little time,' said Nellie, 'to put certain things in order.'

Her thoughts raced. She must see her son . . . Philippe waited for her at Ostend . . . there was Como . . . and nothing else beyond those three imperatives.

'Yes, of course,' said Lady Gladys, feeling sadly triumphant. 'When I spoke of *La Traviata* a moment ago, I lacked the sensitivity to mention the fourth act, there must always be a fourth act before the curtain comes down.'

When Violetta dies for love, Nellie reminded herself.

'Gladys,' she said, 'I would very much like to be left alone, if you don't mind.'

Lady de Grey drew on her gloves, settled her cape around her shoulders, kissed Nellie's cold cheek, and departed.

After the meeting with the lawyers Charles had gone to his club and waited for Montagu to arrive. He was there now, close to midnight, filled with unaccustomed clarity of mind. For too long he had been a victim. He was only just coming to an understanding of the depth of his bewilderment, his wish to hit back, to inflict pain. He felt in control again, as he had not felt for many months. The proposed dropping of the divorce case had surprised him as a solution: it would not go nearly far enough to mend his pride, of course, but my God, he thought, he had frightened her, he had frightened a lot of people. They had come to him crawling on their knees.

Monty would hate it, of course, but withdrawal was part of attack. Charles would look people in the eye again, after this, for the short time that remained for him in this contemptible country of his birth.

And there would be the scorpion-sting in the tail he had in mind for her.

He sat facing a glass of whisky he had barely touched.

When Montagu arrived Charles told him the latest developments as succinctly as possible. Montagu's face fell.

'Give the fellow up?' said Montagu. 'She'll never agree. Dammit, you've made a mistake, Charlie.'

'I don't think so.'

'Good Christ, she's rich, free of restraint, in love, whatever the blasted word means . . . She'll dig her teeth into his back before she gives ground.'

'You don't know her, or what she wants.'

'What are you, the great authority? Don't make me laugh.'

'I learnt the hard way.'

'I wish you'd waited for me. I really do. You love jumping the gun, Charlie, always have . . . You never think . . . As with livestock, so with people . . .'

'Don't be a fool, Monty.'

'We had her cornered. Absolutely tamed . . . And you just opened the gate and let her go.'

'I say, you are the fool, then.'

'How could Jeffrys do it! I never did like the fellow, by the way, always thought he played a double game. And weak, yes, weak in the face of pressure . . . I think I know a little more about human nature than you . . .'

'Perhaps so, but not in this instance, Monty.'

'You're damned sure of yourself . . . Oh, I see.'

'See what?'

'You're in love with her still. Have been all along, and now this is your chance. Yes, what a fool I've been not to see it.'

Charles laughed at his brother.

'You're too close to me, always pushing me, pressuring me. You don't see what's in front of your eyes, Monty.'

'All right. What?'

'I hate her.'

Montagu hesitated. The force of Charles's words surprised him. 'And . . . ?'

'I've taken what she loves, bargained it right out of her . . . Broken its back on my knee.'

'If she accepts . . .' Montagu conceded, beginning to see what Charles might be saying.

'The Orléans family won't have her. Her mighty friends on this side have closed ranks. They won't have her. Lady de Grey is talking to her at this very moment. She won't have her. Not the way she wants.'

'Ha, ha. That bitch!'

'Don't be comical, Monty. We'll know everything in the morning.'

'And then?'

Charles stared hard at his brother, and reached for the whisky glass.

PAWNS IN A GAME

'America,' said Charles.

'That will solve nothing,' snorted Montagu. 'Might as well just bury your head in the sand.'

'First,' added Charles, 'I thought I might take a little trip down into the country.'

'Where, exactly?'

'Priory Grange.'

At this, understanding showed in Montagu's eyes. At last he understood everything, forgave everything.

'Why Charlie, you demon,' he chortled.

'Drink,' said Charles.

It was the next day. In the lowest form of Priory Grange school, at the bottom of his class, George Armstrong sat frowning over his Latin reader. The boys around him chanted their irregular verbs, and George's lips, from much practice, gave an impression of synchronisation with them. It was a desperate deception. His mind wandered: he went dreamily away to places where there was no Priory Grange, no Mr Wentleford. Sometimes he roved for almost an entire lesson, in a kayak among Eskimos in company with his father, the great Arctic explorer; or rode a frisky pony in the Bois de Boulogne, watched by his equally famous mother and her powerful friends. His father, sometimes a soldier, sometimes a sea-captain, took him places where they had nothing but adventures. His mother, always the famous person she was (there was no need to pretend about her), made him drunk with perfumes and promises.

A shadow fell over his desk.

'Armstrong!' A voice jolted him upright.

The boys had been silent for many seconds without George realising.

'Sir? I was following, sir, I was,' he began.

But it was not the Latin master who'd spoken, but Mr Wentleford, who marched down the aisle and grabbed George by the ear.

'You have a visitor, Armstrong. Take a look at her, lads,' he gestured towards the quadrangle windows. 'Make free. You may never see the likes again.'

He steered George towards the door.

As the boys rushed to the side of the room and stared out into the quadrangle, Mr Wentleford hissed:

'Five minutes, and no longer, you realise . . .'

In full view of his classmates, George ran to his mother, hardly believing the vision she presented.

'Georgie!' she greeted him, her voice echoing around the crumbling archways. There was no mother like her on earth, George believed, as he dashed into her arms and buried his face in the folds of her dress.

Take me away. Take me away, his inner voice pleaded.

'My dearest boy. Squeeze me. Squeeze me harder, oh you're so strong.'

'Mr Wentleford is watching,' said George, directing her behind a pillar.

'The man! Does he cane you? George, pay attention to me.'

George glimpsed Nellie's carriage waiting for her in the drive. He could see it was empty, except for the coachman, and wondered if that other, the Duc, was around somewhere. He could almost sense him, the way he had at Studley Royal, always in the next room, just around the corner, politely irritated at the presence of a small boy.

'Is he . . .'

'Who?'

'You know . . . here . . .'

'Lord, don't be silly, there's no such . . .'

'Yes there is, Mama,' said George with touching realism. How grown-up he was this year . . . 'The whole school knows about it. McAlister got the *Times*. His people sent it to him, and Mr Wentleford spoke to me about it too.'

'Such a small paragraph,' said Nellie.

'They said things,' said George.

'There won't be a divorce, Georgie . . . That's . . . that's what I've come to tell you.'

George blinked. 'Truly?'

'There will be another paragraph in the paper, denying everything.'

George believed this meant that his parents would live

together again. Nellie said nothing to make him think otherwise. Tears of relief and happiness streamed down his face. He kicked the flagstones with the toecaps of his shoes, to cover his pleasure and embarrassment.

'Don't do that,' scolded Nellie.

'Sorry, Mama.'

'Here is a present for you,' said Nellie, giving him the small exquisite yacht she had bought for him, which he cradled in his hands. He was so sad, so touching, so brave, and she spoke from the depths of her despair: 'You won't have to stay much longer at this horrible little school, Georgie. That's a promise. Your father will agree to take you away. He will do what I ask. He must.'

'Soon?'

'I will write to him today.'

George stared at the small yacht in his hands, hardly believing that any of this was true.

27

La Traviata

Nellie was reunited with Philippe at Ostend, and together they entrained for Italy. After a day and a night of exhausting travel they arrived at Lake Como.

Miraculously it was all as Philippe had promised. 'A dream of heaven,' declared Nellie, seeing the lake for the first time. The gardens and villas along the shores were entrancing: it was truly the most beautiful place imaginable.

'The world is ours, my darling, again and for always,' said Philippe, standing with his hand on her shoulder as they crossed to Bellagio.

'You speak such nonsense,' said Nellie, squeezing his hand.

'Let us make a pact, let us treat each moment together as a taste of eternity,' said Philippe. 'That way, we shall never part.'

She did not know how this could be done, but promised.

Their villa was set in a terraced garden tumbling down to the lake's edge. Fountains murmured continuously. Rhododendrons, azaleas, ferns and even lantana flourished in the sheltered climate. On the other shore, across a mile of hazy stillness, the slim *campanile* of a village church was visible, and then, heap upon heap, disappearing across the last of Italy into Switzerland, the Alps began their rise.

LA TRAVIATA

They had never had a time together like this. The nights were passionate and tender, the days dreamy with idleness. Their love was folded back on itself, it was everything. Nellie stored each intimacy away in memory. It seemed their pact might work, if only she could suspend the inevitable leavetaking and hold it framed, like a view of the lake, eternally perfect.

Too quickly, though, it was the fourth day. Nellie's dread, like a nightmare, recurred: she was a condemned person being granted her few last hours. She knew very well that Philippe felt differently: he must, being the one who had brought them here for the express purpose of saying goodbye. And yet she was unable to fault him on sentiment and attentiveness. There seemed no pity in his manner, and for this she was grateful. His passion burned equally with hers, as if in a contest.

A small landing stage jutted into the glassy water. From here, each morning, Philippe set off in a small skiff to enjoy the perfect weather. His oars dipped into the water, leaving a trail of swirling exclamations behind, while Nellie followed along the edge of the lake, walking a gravel path beneath elegant Stone pines and pencil-thin cypresses. She knew, if she called, her voice would reach him and draw him back: it had happened so on their first mornings, when an easy happiness had filled their hearts despite their knowledge of impending separation. Church bells clanged through the air from miles away. The bark of dogs on the other shore carried clearly. The knock of rowlocks could be heard as Phillipe leaned forward, took the weight of the oars, and hauled back strongly, making the bow of his light craft almost leap from the water.

Nellie watched the boat grow smaller and smaller as Philippe kept rowing. At any moment he would swing the craft around and come skimming back towards her. Four days together, surely there would be a fifth? She would torture herself, thus, even if they lingered here a thousand days more . . . She waited, and waited for him to turn, the water lapping the stones at her feet, making a weak echo of his presence on the lake. But he did not turn. Any impulse to call out went cold on her lips. This was mad, what was he thinking, was it to be now? She drew a sharp breath and shivered. No, it was not mad, she knew. It was the moment when she must take matters into her own hands. With crisp, dedicated strokes Philippe made himself smaller and smaller. She had the feeling of her existence being stitched down, settled for ever by each stroke of the oars. Very soon, Philippe was enfolded by the blue haze. He was a presence on the lake without any defining detail. She thought, 'I am to go now, find a sharp razor, and cut my wrists. It's what he's asking of me, it could not be worse, he does not know the pain.'

At her back, Nellie heard the crush of carriage-wheels on the drive. A visitor had arrived.

She willed herself to continue walking. No, she would not turn her head. She would stay here by the shore, she would become stone if necessary, until Philippe returned and warmed her in his arms.

But after a few minutes her courage got the better of her. If this was the moment indeed then she had better get on with it. She turned, taking the path towards the villa. When the upper terrace came into view she saw a man standing there dressed entirely in black. He raised a hand in greeting, but Nellie only dropped her eyes and kept coming.

It was the Duc de Luyns.

In the wide entrance hall of the villa she removed her hat and handed it to a serving maid. She tidied her hair, then took a slow, calming breath. The sound of her footsteps echoed across the tiles as she made her way into the reception room.

The Duc de Luyns advanced and kissed her hand. The light was at his back. He had deliberately placed himself to put her at a disadvantage.

'Madame Melba, please forgive the intrusion.'

'Please sit down,' said Nellie, swiftly positioning herself to put the light in her favour. They settled themselves in the window seats, overlooking the lake. Nellie could not bear to lose sight of Philippe.

'We have met briefly once before,' said the Duc, 'at the house of a mutual friend, Lady Gladys de Grey.'

'Dear Gladys, how is she?' said Nellie. 'I think you have seen

LA TRAVIATA

er more recently than I.' She held the man's gaze.

'Yes, that is true,' said the Duke urbanely. 'She has played er part and we are grateful.'

The Duke de Luyns cleared his throat and continued.

'The Comte de Paris is gravely ill. His last wish is to recall hilippe to his duty as a son of France. Philippe knows that uty, Madame.'

'Yes,' said Nellie, narrowing her eyes against the outside lare, and holding on to her sight of Philippe's small boat, as iny as a flyspeck in the haze. Oh, why did he stay there so till? Was it weakness, that fatal ally of charm? He should be ere at her side, ranting against the bonds of fate.

The Duc de Luyns suddenly touched Nellie's hand. It was s if he read her thoughts, so pertinent were his words.

'Madame, never doubt his courage, or what it costs him oday.'

At this, Nellie burst into tears.

'Madame, Madame,' the Duc offered a silk handkerchief.

'It is all right. I understand,' said Nellie, collecting herself.

They talked more freely, then.

The Duc had a speech prepared, which was entirely innecessary, but it helped her. 'Think of the glory of France,' vas part of what he said. 'The French people love your art, s they love the art of no other foreign singer. You have been . pupil of Delibes, Gounod, Massenet, Thomas. You are a laughter of France now yourself. And now your career Madame Melba is on the brink of ruin. There is a marriage rranged for Philippe.'

'Yes, I know.'

'Your husband has dropped the divorce.'

'Yes, I know.'

'You must end the affair.'

'It is ended,' said Nellie, surprising both of them by the clear inality of her words.

'Then my duty is done,' said the Duc de Luyns, with a gentle hrug.

'Wait, please.'

Nellie rang for her maid and ordered a valise to be hastily

packed. She turned back to the Duc:

'May I share your carriage, Your Grace.'

'Well, I . . .' He was rather surprised. He had expected a long drawn-out struggle.

'Now. Immediately. Save me,' asked Nellie.

'Madame, I am at your disposal. Come away as you please.'

Nellie stood for a moment looking out at the lake. Her heart gave a sudden leap, for she thought Philippe's boat made a quick movement towards the shore. But it was only an effect of the haze.

Ten minutes later, Nellie was gone from the villa. In the carriage, she gripped the arm of the older man. 'You are making me feel like Violetta in *La Traviata*,' she said, a dreadful lightness in her voice.

'Is it so very different?' replied the Frenchman. 'You are a woman of great honour and courage. You have renounced your lover for a greater good.'

Nellie made no reply, only hearing the music within her, faint and enticing, offering her her only hope of refuge from herself.

A pony trap set off from Priory Grange school loaded up with the meagre belongings of George Armstrong. The figure of Mr Wentleford waved from the forecourt. The sun shone brightly and the wind was fresh; a wonderful day for change and adventure.

'We're going on a trip,' said Charles.

'Where to?' asked George excitedly.

'America,' replied Charles.

'Hooray!' shouted George, though he wasn't really surprised. His mother had practically promised as much.

George was too happy to bother asking for further details. All the broken shapes of his world were fitting together again, that's all that mattered.

'We sail on the evening tide,' said Charles. 'From Plymouth. If we catch the train on time.'

Montague gave the pony a a sharp taste of the whip, and the pace increased.

LA TRAVIATA

Old Wentleford wasn't so bad, thought George, suddenly filled with generous emotion at seeing the last of the rotten little school. Holmes, Baxter, and McArdle weren't such bad chaps either. They couldn't help themselves, poor blighters. George believed himself to be the luckiest boy that ever lived. He enjoyed the freedom of the wind rushing past his ears and the lanes and hedgerows flashing past.

'Will Mama be there?'

'In America?' countered Charles. He needed time to think of an answer. 'Well, Georgie . . .'

'We can be pretty certain she will be. One day,' said Montagu over his shoulder.

'At the wharf, I mean.'

'Can't say,' said Charles, putting an arm around George's shoulders.

'I only wanted to say goodbye,' said George cheerfully enough. He trusted everything and everybody now.

'Well, you can write to her as soon as we're aboard,' said Charles. 'When they drop the pilot, he takes the mail bag ashore.'

'Does he?' said George. 'That will be fun, Papa.'

Como. The lake. The motionless water, the gardens, the villas and the terraced fields with their background of snow-capped mountains . . . Como . . . The idea of Philippe loving her through time. His courage and hers. The feeling of loss, of deprivation and denial. The way he floated suspended on the lake, never making a return move towards her. The impossibility of their positions held against the intimacy they knew. The pathos of her gratitude, the fact of his pity. The unreserved passion of all their nights together. Did he weep in the boat, leaning over the oars, keeping very still, his listening attuned for the sound of carriage-wheels? He might almost have heard her plea of 'Save me!' to the Duc de Luyns, it was so desperately wrenched from her.

And now the helpless longing she felt as her express rushed north, exploding through the darkened countryside of France. The shape of time always changing . . .

MELBA

She would try and hold something back from time, as they had sworn it together, for as long as she lived. She would try. Around her neck, attached to a piece of *moiré* ribbon, was the small piece of amber Philippe had given her.

It banishes tears. It has the power to prevent sadness.
It is a treasure.
Your fingers are trembling . . .

The train rushed through the night. What was the hurry, what was the urgency in everything?

With deliberate effort she thought about her son, levering her capacity for love towards him with all the strength she possessed. The idea of George, only of George, took on animation in her mind. Everything else was background, must stay that way for the sake of her sanity. She must never allow herself to picture, as she often had in the past, George and Philippe becoming friends as they grew older. Philippe would never grow older for her now. George would.

On her arrival in England she would go to Charles, demand an answer to the letter she had written about George's schooling, force a resolution in the life of the boy before it was too late. He was growing so fast, she would devote herself to watching every minute of his life, and give him what she could.

In the darkness of the villa, in the wide emptiness of his bed, Philippe thought back over the events of an exhausting day. His emotions were strained to the limit.

Out on the lake, he had been watching for the arrival of the Duc de Luyns with impatience. Then at last he had seen him standing on the balcony, the authority in his attitude unmistakable even from so far away. An arm had risen and fallen, giving a signal, issuing a command. The small and lonely figure of Nellie had disappeared from the shoreline. 'It is all over,' thought Philippe. He dropped a fishing line in the water. Whatever was being said in the villa between Nellie and his father's emissary was beyond him now.

For a while, he was at ease. The sun beat on the back of his neck. Fish nibbled his line. He looked forward to his marriage with the princess Maria Dorothea in much the same

LA TRAVIATA

way as an explorer, after great adventures in strange places, anticipates a return to the familiar country of his birth.

But then came a change. The wildness in his heart when eventually he rowed back to the shore was unexpected. He had seen the carriage race away, appear and reappear as it navigated the twists in the steep wooded drive above the villa; had smelt panic in the air, sensed changed plans, alarm, hysteria. How he hated hysteria! And besides, he had really believed there would be more time. Another day, another night. Especially another night, for Philippe had loved their bedding down together more than anything else. He even thought, in a panic of jealousy, that the serene handsome Duc de Luyns had snapped his fingers and got her from him, taken her back to his estate in France where Philippe could never follow.

He raced through room after room of the villa, flinging doors wide in his desperation to find her.

In London, a letter from Charles awaited her. Its wording made her uneasy.

'I agree wholeheartedly. What a good idea it would be to take George away from his school. I will start the arrangements at once.'

Nellie sent a messenger around to Lady Armstrong's house, but Charles was not there. Nor was he at Montagu's, nor in the country. She could not face Lady Armstrong in the state she was in, and ask the questions she wanted to ask. She had no rights, no hope, but still kept her pride.

'I am told he has gone to Ireland,' said one servant to another.

'Scotland, I think,' said a second.

'Isn't he in London, with his mother?' a third was reported as saying. It was a trail of confusion and deliberate lying.

'The woman has no right to ask,' thundered Montagu, raising his whip-hand, when at last Nellie's coachman tracked him down at his club, and handed him a beseeching note.

George, Georgie, oh Georgie, Nellie cried in realisation and fear.

MELBA

She rushed down to Priory Grange.

It was Mr Wentleford's greatest moment.

'Good grief, you are a little behind the times, Madame Melba.'

'What do you mean?'

'The boy is no longer a pupil here. He was taken away by his father and uncle more than a week ago. The day after your visit, as a matter of fact. I thought you knew. I let him go.'

'You . . . did . . . what?' she almost choked.

'A glass of water?'

'You are a pathetic, lying little weasel, Mr Wentleford,' spluttered Nellie. 'You are unfit to rule over anyone's life.'

'Dear me. It seems I have you.'

Nellie removed a glove, resolving to slap the man's face.

He drew back a little, lips tight.

'I shouldn't lose control, you know.'

Nellie hesitated. *Como*, she thought, her hand to her head. *Como has ruined me*.

'Take me to his room,' she demanded.

'His "room"?' he smiled. 'Of course.'

They climbed a bare, chilly stairway to a dormitory containing forty beds.

'It is like a prison,' she said.

'It is an English school,' said Mr Wentleford.

'I had no idea . . .'

'Seventh bed on the left,' said the headmaster.

Nellie went to George's bed. She ran her hand over the lumpy pillow. She lifted it up, and pulled back the bedspread.

'What on earth are you doing?' mused Mr Wentleford.

'Did they say where they were taking him?'

'If they had, I would tell you,' said Wentleford.

'I am sure,' replied Nellie.

She knelt at the bedside locker and opened it, looking for shreds of evidence.

She got down on the floor, and looked under the locker. The small sailing ship was there, its mast broken.

La Traviata opened, and it was wonderful. How she did it,

LA TRAVIATA

she did not know. The singing possessed her, elevated her: gave her strength. The critics wrote of her ease and her grace, as if it cost her nothing, as if Violetta's renunciation of Alfredo were something she had mastered in herself. As if . . .

There were flowers from Philippe, and a small card, *Adieu*.

The next day she gathered her courage together and went to visit Lady Armstrong.

She recounted her difficulties in locating Charles, and the terrible discovery she had made on visiting the school.

'If you had come to me first, I would have told you everything,' said Lady Armstrong, tenderly touching Nellie's arm.

'Everything?' wondered Nellie breathlessly. 'Tell me, tell me.'

'Everything I know,' Lady Armstrong corrected herself. 'Which is not much.'

'I am so ashamed, but there's no help,' said Nellie.

Lady Armstrong gestured Nellie to sit on the couch beside her, and shook her head. 'I am ashamed of my sons.'

'Please.'

'Charles has taken George to America. He did it to hurt you, to cause you pain. There is no forwarding address. Montagu aided and abetted him.'

Nellie felt numb. She saw herself stand and go to the window, where she wiped tears from her cheeks with two strokes of her fists.

'You know, my heart is absolutely dead. It only stirs when I'm singing,' she said. 'Then everything goes into the song. When I've finished there's nothing there again, it's as if I've emptied everything out.'

They were hopeless words. And yet her spirit contradicted the desperation.

Lady Armstrong looked at her wordlessly.

'That is all,' said Nellie, shaking her head.

PART THREE

The Twentieth Century

28

Legal Custody

The protective shell around her sadness was hard. It glittered.

Through the decade of the nineties and beyond, Nellie's habit of self-protection grew, keeping the eyes of the world constantly upon her yet shielding her from the deepest most percipient gaze. It was the 'Melba manner' serving its purpose. She worked. Her fame grew.

In the autumn season following her return to England without Philippe, to discover herself also without her son, she appeared in *Aïda*, *Lohengrin*, and in Verdi's *Otello* as Desdemona. The last after only four days' study of the role. Her travels stitched a pattern across the map of Europe and North America: Milan, Florence, Turin, Genoa, Lyons, Stockholm, Copenhagen, New York, Chicago, Philadelphia, Boston, Paris . . . The Metropolitan in New York became a second home to Covent Garden.

Travel and performance occupied every corner of her existence, and yet rumour and speculation found space to grow. At the close of her first New York season, in *Faust*, the audience went wild. The applause, the shouts, the stomping of feet were unceasing until Jean and Edouard de Reszke trundled a piano on to the stage and Nellie sang 'Home, Sweet Home' into a breathless silence. It was hardly ever remembered that she had a son, while she never forgot it. But it was often said she had a lover, a new one each tour; people asked which of the handsome de Reszke brothers was it now? This while there had only ever been one . . .

She bargained her own contracts according to the maxim of her father, David Mitchell: *Seek the advantage, and give the best*. She was a builder herself now.

The developing 'Melba manner' was recognised everywhere. It was a byword for rudeness to some, to others the mark of brilliant character; it was hardly ever seen for what it had been at the beginning, a shield for heartbreak, for introspective sorrow, for all that was private and deeply personal in her life. Restored to her opera houses and regime of constant travel, she guarded her privacy until it became a conundrum. That was the trouble. She lived in trains, in ships, in grand hotels. Her personal life was always there behind a bulkhead, a partition, a glass sliding door. An ear could be pressed close, to interpret the slightest rustle. In such proximity to the curious, it was believed she had no secrets at all. None that were unknowable, that is.

Guesswork, like an air-breathing plant, flourished on small nourishments. Fame, it was said, was her only goal; she would do anything to hold on to it, hated rivals, detested being paid less than any other performer. Greed (presumably) was visible at her late suppers, when, surrounded by a circle of champagne-drinkers at the Savoy or the St Regis, she confronted feasts, and had been seen to prod gleefully at a whole suckling pig, a slab of baked sturgeon, a bucket of strawberries. She photographed badly, she knew. And so photographers were driven to distraction by her demands to get things right. Had there ever been such vanity? Such perfectionism? She hated to be faulted. When critics lavished praise on her performances, when audiences jostled and pushed to fill theatres and halls, as they always did, as they would to the end of her life, it was never enough for her, she wanted more.

'Pride is seldom delicate; it will please itself with very mean advantages,' wrote the author of *Rasselas*. There was plenty of contempt in her manner, too. She was only human. She had earned the right to know this. And late at night, when finally she was alone, the reason was only too clear to her. Of all the jewels and priceless brooches that her great gifts had bought for her, the most precious had no monetary value; it was the smooth, tear-shaped piece of amber, ribbon-threaded, which she wore constantly wherever she travelled. Then there was the photograph of David Mitchell, and the small broken sailing ship she carried around, and would return to George one day. Last thing at night, when she prayed at her bedside, as she had taken to doing in recent years from loneliness and fear of the abyss, she asked God to watch over her absent father, her former lover, and her missing son.

There was never a mail delivery, an announcement of a telegram, or a knock on her door, when she failed to think, for the lightning-flick of a second, that it might be her son returning to her.

Almost ten years had passed since George was taken to America. She wrote to him scrupulously, in the care of Charles' lawyers at the beginning, and then to addresses in Texas and Oregon. He hardly ever replied. His letters were short, polite, misspelt. They rang of awkwardness and embarrassment, never flowering into the description and sentiment she craved. She felt Charles' influence in the stiffness, the withdrawal of emotion. Perhaps he dictated every word to the boy, it was possible. 'Look at this,' Charles' voice seemed to say through the crossings-out and inkblots: 'No bloody education. Like it? He's to be as different from you and your accursed values as it's possible to be.'

Near the turn of the century she undertook a concert tour deep into America, travelling in a specially appointed carriage, christened 'Melba' by the Pullman Company. Apart from her personal servants, comprising altogether a party of six, she took a chef, a waiter, a conductor, and a coloured porter. 'Say, Mrs Melba,' the porter greeted her, 'you don't remember me; but, you bet, I know you. A while back you travelled with me on train number 27,832, and I told you that I thought Mr Plançon was fine, but that I did not think there was much to your Marguerite. Yes, ma'am. But I take it all back now, for I saw you the other night in *Manon Lescaut*, and your singing beat the band. Yes, ma'am, you take it from me.'

There were people like this everywhere now, who were pleasant, who appreciated her, who were justification for the life she led, but who saw no barrier at all between her and themselves.

When she came closer to the West Coast, she scanned audiences for a sight of her son. How old would he be? What transformations had occurred to the questioning, boyish features? She wondered if he was artistic, enthusiastic, adventurous as she had been at his age; he would be twenty soon; or if he was like Charles, narrowed and narrowing through life. She hoped Charles would not be with him.

But neither of them came.

Charles' poisonous hatred in taking George she was unable to match. She could hardly remember the young man, Charles Nesbitt Armstrong, she had loved in Mackay, so many years ago, or what he had meant to her then. His kisses, which she had so desired, had soon enough betrayed themselves into lack of sympathy, refusal to communicate, irritation at the direction of their lives. His masculinity, in her eyes, was a shortcoming like his drinking, his bad temper, his silences. It had shaken her sanity and changed her character. In response, she could only display the unfaltering upward march of her career. He would see that, whenever he opened a newspaper. He would never escape it, no matter how long he hid away in the rangelands of Klamath Falls, Oregon.

The memory of the Duc she idolised. Any thought of his weakness or opportunism ('I know what you are thinking, Madame. That every young man must come to the theatre at a certain age, and seek out an *artiste* . . .') she purged from her memory. She was quite unable to compare him with other men; this ardent boy prince who would ever be secretly hers . . . there on the lake, suspended in time, whispering '*Adieu*'.

Full-blooded men, as intimate companions, she was not altogether sure about any more. The hurt was too deep. The stage door became a generalised phenomenon to her, and no-one penetrated through to her dressing room, as Louis Philippe Robert had done. She dined at great houses still, and circulated at country-house weekends with men of political power, personal wealth and, let it be said, advanced age. She learnt to 'josh' a great man, and leave him feeling pretty damned good about himself. Kitchener, Cecil Rhodes and Kipling were the types of power figure she idealised. There was something of her father in the empire builders. She had not seen her father for almost sixteen years.

The men she invited to her house, who shared her late hours in private suppers and gossipy intimacies, were playwrights, sculptors and painters with a connection to Australia, like hers. They shuddered when they talked about the continent they had left behind them, a dry, uncongenial place. Artists were pilloried there. In London, the men spoke in cultivated, Anglophile accents. Their small flats were intricately decorated with mementoes of the Greek Islands, of Napoli and Venezia. When Nellie shooed them from her house, at bedtime, they left making shrill, cheeky complaints. They disappeared from her mind completely, as if a light had been switched off.

She did not get along with other women, unless they were, like Lady de Grey, persons of elevated rank. She had loyal female secretaries and devoted hard-working household servants, and with them she often chatted freely. But they were underlings. When she called a halt to anything, it stopped. She needed it that way . . . She also began, from time to time, a passionate involvement in the careers of young female singers. She liked to have them go around with her. She liked to influence their fate. But if they had men-friends, got married and began families, she went cold. She reverted to the psychology of the overgrown schoolgirl. It was another defence against pain. She did nothing on a small scale.

Her sisters Annie and Belle were married now and had families. Dora was in her early twenties, still single. In time all her brothers and sisters made trips to visit her 'at home', sometimes at Nellie's expense. Like other wealthy Australians they were anxious to be accepted but never really fitted in, feeling like bulls in a china shop among the cultivated English.

They were amazed at the changes in their sister. They had heard about the Duc of Orléans from a hundred different sources, some of them undeniably truthful and accurate. Of course there had been many wide-eyed whispered speculations at Doonside, while David Mitchell went about like a sphinx. But whatever wounds Nellie had suffered were healed over, apparently. She hated to admit to scars of any sort. She awed them a little, too: there were no more critical intimacies of the kind they had shared when they were younger women. This new Nellie seemed to say, in her manner, her style of life, her interests and her entire bearing:

'It never happened. There was never any Duc.'

They were relieved to have the subject ditched.

It was something, really, to say they were staying with their famous sister, who had become, in a short time, the most famous Australian of all. Annie and her younger brother Ernie had been there when she sang *Manon Lescaut* for the first time in New York. They met Nordica, Calvé, the de Reszke brothers, and were introduced to the great Sarah Bernhardt, who was performing in *Adrienne Lecouvreur*. Their stories would mean a great deal when they got home. Nellie was talked about all the time in Australia now. The brighter her fame shone, however, the more attempts some people made, in the typical Australian way, to belittle, or worse, to bluntly disbelieve the extent of her achievements.

'When are you coming back?' her sisters asked.

'I'm having discussions with George Musgrove,' was all Nellie would say.

'Daddy will never travel again. It would mean everything to him to have you back home. Even just for a quick tour. To sing for him, in his own city. Think of it!'

'I know. I know. I think about it all the time. But it would be absolutely impossible to undertake unless it was brilliantly organised.'

'People wouldn't care. They'd bash the walls down to hear you.'

'I would care. He would care.'

They began to understand her better now.

LEGAL CUSTODY

At the time of his escape from England, Charles's thoughts had driven him to the brink of insanity. He resolved that Nellie must never see George again. Her influence would rot George's character, he told himself; he had been revolted by the way she dressed him, fondled him, pampered him, surrounded him with luxuries. It was no life for a boy, a real boy. She was a wrecker, selfish to the core, heedless of others, totally out for herself. Her real centre was the stage where she schemed and luxuriated. She was a monster-woman, his wife, 'Melba'. It wasn't just her affair with the Duc, the crowning humiliation: what a fool he'd been always. In the years following their arrival in England from Australia he'd kept hanging on in the hope that she'd change, that she'd keep her word, which she kept stretching, always claiming there was just one more goal ahead of her, always for a new reason: the London managers were too unsympathetic and must be shown, the Parisian teachers were geniuses and must be obeyed, the Continental stages were a challenge and must be won, the Covent Garden audiences were ignorant and would have to learn. The reasons were endless. Charles followed her career in the papers, a sour smile twisting his lips. The world was full of people who had not heard her yet, who must be given the chance. She had come shunting around America in a railway car, mopping up dollars in rickety opera houses built with speculators' gold. There was no end to any of it. If there was a way of getting off this planet and on to another then Madame Melba would be wanting that too. She'd go there in a gold-plated rocket. She would devour the praise of the universe if she could.

Fighting her in his mind had been a nightmare.

But with one blow he'd left her empty-hearted, her small-minded provincial Australian dreams of aristocracy all gone up in smoke. He would always have that satisfaction. The murder of the heart.

For six months he sent no forwarding address, only accepting mail through the office of his lawyer in Galveston. She tried hard to track him down, but not as hard as he thought she would. Maybe guilt stayed her hand. More likely it was the demands of career. They always came first. That was the point.

Charles' hatred began to cool in those first couple of years but he made one terrible mistake. He made George suffer. The boy had hardly eaten in the first year, had sickened and needed doctoring. George had been watchful, silent, moody. Frightened, perhaps?

But George was all right now. He'd gotten over it by growing up. They'd moved from Texas to Oregon and the life was better there. George had developed into a strong young man, good with horses, a crack shot. He had simple attitudes and an uncomplicated mind. He bore no grudges and had few ambitions.

One day Charles stood on the landing of their cabin and watched George approach on horseback. He made his usual hell-for-leather homecoming: crossed the wide white-water of the ford at a splashing canter, galloped through the cottonwoods on the bank, and emerged into the open to pelt across the mile of pasture-land between the river and the house.

The horse was shining black with sweat as George reined up where his father waited. He gabbled a greeting, slid from the saddle, and tossed the saddlebags to Charles. Then off he went to stable his pony, whistling cheerfully. For a time horses had been almost his entire life, Charles having made him into a fair sort of rider in his own stamp. They ran cattle here at the ranch but their real interest was a thoroughbred stallion named Nebo and a string of mares. When the time was right they would take them east.

Charles went into the house and upended the contents of the saddlebag on a low table. There were letters, packets of seeds, and a bottle of good whisky. He sorted through the mail. As usual, Nellie's handwriting on letters made him feel slightly threatened, slightly chilled. They were addressed to George and the postmark was New York. They had already been opened and read, then put back into the bundle as a way of telling Charles that his son had no secrets from him. Charles imagined George somewhere along the trail, sitting under a

LEGAL CUSTODY

tree, his lips moving as he deciphered Nellie's difficult, rapidly scrawled handwriting.

There was a letter from Texas in a long, fat, buff-coloured envelope. It made him nervous too.

Charles uncorked the whisky and poured himself a shot. He drank that down, then poured two more: another for himself, and one ready for George. They had settled habits together. It was a good life.

The ranch house living room was spacious and simply furnished with solid hand-hewn chairs and tables, broad couches draped with Indian blankets, and shelves of large leather-bound books, including complete editions of Dickens, Surtees, and Twain. There were also works on geology and natural history. A lot of living was done here during the long winters, when Charles concentrated on George's schooling, which had been badly interrupted by illnesses and moves. Charles had dreamed of a place like this as they had shifted themselves around in Texas, living in boarding houses, in rented ranch houses, or with friends whose generosity was unquestioning but provided no substitute for proper home life. Around the walls were hunting trophies showing Charles's sentimental affection for the wild west: a stuffed eagle on a stand, a buffalo skin pegged out. Yes, he liked the life all right. It was comfortable, quietly sociable, even moderately profitable. Charles was liked by the other ranchers in the valley. The women were charmed by his reserve, his good looks. But he made no intimate friendships despite the availability of certain willing ladies. His hair was steely-grey these days, and he cultivated a handsome moustache. No-one in Klamath Falls had ever heard him raise his voice in anger. People knew he was the estranged husband of Madame Melba, of course, but nothing was ever made of it. 'Kangaroo Charlie' had long since gone to pasture.

George came into the room and grabbed the mail order catalogue. He twisted it back until the spine cracked. Charles handed him his whisky.

'Thanks.' George sat in a chair and propped his legs up, just like his father.

MELBA

'Good luck,' said Charles, automatically raising his glass. He then began opening his mail. He wore reading glasses now.

George smacked his lips over the drink. It pleased his father to treat him as an equal in these matters, and he rather liked the stuff. He studied the gun illustrations for a while.

'It says here,' George jabbed a page with a finger, 'that the Holland and Holland hunting rifle can't be beat at the price they're offering.'

Charles wasn't listening. He just continued reading one letter in particular.

'Dad?'

'Eh?'

'You listening?'

'Pardon?'

'I said . . .'

Charles smiled rather humourlessly, and began folding the letter away. His hands trembled as he replaced it in the buff-coloured envelope.

'Something the matter?' George wondered.

'It's from my lawyers in Texas,' answered Charles at last. 'Your mother and I are finally divorced.' He wiped away a tear.

George had never seen his father cry. You thought you knew someone, then they cracked.

Embarrassed, George looked at his feet, at the wall, anywhere except at Charles, who now, confusingly, was laughing.

'It's been a long time,' said George conventionally.

'A decent interval,' nodded Charles. 'So many memories to bury. To burn. You couldn't imagine . . . Christ.'

'I guess not,' said George.

The idea of his parents as a married couple eluded him. He could hardly remember it, except underneath there had always been emotional tides pulling in both directions. He had felt them all right. Was that marriage?

'What difference does it make?' asked George. 'I mean, to me?'

'None really,' answered Charles. 'It just clears out a few legal cobwebs.'

LEGAL CUSTODY

'Like what?' George insisted.

Charles poured himself another drink. 'I don't know. Nothing much.'

'Dad, you're hedging.'

'Well, for one thing it gives me legal custody of you, Georgie.'

'I don't understand.'

'You're my responsibility till you're twenty-one. Here's the court order to prove it.' Charles handed him the buff-coloured envelope.

As from the said date, etc.

'What was I before?' George wondered. He shook his head in disbelief, studying the stiff document with its important seal. He felt resentful towards his father suddenly, and here was the focus of his resentment.

'You were loved and cared for,' said Charles. 'Always.'

George wouldn't be put off.

'Does this custody order mean that when you and Uncle Montagu took me away from that rotten little school it wasn't legal, you *kidnapped* me?'

'In a friendly sort of way,' admitted Charles.

'I don't know that I was ever told,' said George evenly.

'You weren't. You were just a baby, really.'

'That wasn't what you said then. I don't remember much, but I remember that one, Dad.'

'Take it easy, Georgie.'

'Holy cow. She must have hated you.'

Charles rolled his glass between the palms of his hands.

'She made a choice and stuck to it,' he said. 'So did I.'

George walked around the room for a while. Charles watched him and waited for him to speak.

'She wants to meet me in New York,' he said. 'She's sent rail tickets this time, sleeping car all the way, and tickets for the opera.'

'She lives in an artificial world, Georgie. You forget what it was like.'

'It seemed pretty good to me,' said George, choosing his words carefully. 'Some things I don't forget.'

He went to the window and looked out, his palms pressing

down on the rough-hewn window ledge. He loved it here but it wasn't enough. How could he ever tell that to his father? The last rays of the sun poured across the emptiness of the rangeland, illuminating the shining grass and shimmering poplars. It was so empty. He had an inexpressible longing to be among people.

'*Je suis Georges,*' he spoke softly. '*J'habite à Paris avec ma mère.*'

Charles grunted and cleared his throat.

'That's all I remember,' said George, turning to his father with sudden embarrassment. 'I'm not even sure what it means.'

'Don't ask me,' said Charles.

But George remembered the meaning very well. He had once gone around chanting the words to himself like a magic spell, reminding himself of his place in life. *I am George. I live in Paris with my mother.*

'George, let me make one thing very clear. Go to New York. I don't mind, don't consider my feelings. See her. Get it out of your system.'

'You mean it?'

'I do.'

'What if I went and never came back? What if she "kidnapped" me?' George taunted.

'She couldn't,' smiled Charles. 'Haven't I just told you? I have legal custody.'

It was typical of George that the rail tickets lay untouched on his dressing table for many weeks until it was too late to use them, that his letters from Nellie remained unanswered except for a brief acknowledgment that he was 'probably coming to New York for sure'. When the time came to make his decision he just couldn't seem to stir himself to go. He was shy at the thought of the crowds and terrified of what she would make of him. He had a good idea of the 'Melba manner', which he felt in her letters: the impatience, the imperiousness even when she pleaded and enticed him to join her. He was a hick, that was the trouble. How could he get that across to her? He studied himself in the mirror. Where would he get the polish needed to move about in her world? He had reached

LEGAL CUSTODY

an age of extreme self-consciousness about his appearance. He believed his face was too long, his eyes too close together, his work-roughened hands disproportionately large at the end of over-lanky arms. He was a good dancer, though, light on his feet and attentive to his partner as long as she wasn't important to him. The trouble was that exceptionally pretty women made him blush, they made him tongue-tied and when George thought of the theatre-world that was all he thought about: the pretty women.

In the end nature made the final decision. The snow was deep around the cabin by Christmas and when January came the ranch house was buried in drifts for weeks at a time. When they eventually made the trip to town for supplies the New York Melba season was almost over.

From the rail depot they collected the large bundle of newspapers that had built up over the weeks of isolation. George read that Nellie had sung the role of Brünnhilde in Wagner's *Siegfried* at the start of winter and that it had been some sort of mistake. A good number of the papers reported that she had been fine, all things considered, but others said she had taken on too much. There had been physical strain to her voice, a failure of sorts. That was clear, and if anyone hated failure it was her. 'Damned lucky I wasn't there,' thought George. 'She would have hated me to see her broken down.' He had a good appreciation of the work it took to develop into the best. 'Broken down' was an idea that made his blood run cold. He thought of horses . . .

The next thing he read was that she was planning a trip to Australia.

'Oh, well. That's that for a while,' thought George.

29

Progress by Rail

It was a bad time for Nellie. She had begun her New York season full of excitement and expectation. It wasn't just that she would be singing Brünnhilde after much careful preparation. It was George. She awaited his reappearance in her life with as much trembling and longing as she had once awaited her lover.

Then had come one of George's awkward blotchy letters. The touching grammatical confusion of 'probably' and 'for sure' expressed his character to her exactly. She itched to get him into her life and make something of him. And she really had expected him in New York, more than ever before.

But it was not to be.

She sang, she overreached herself, and she announced to the New York press 'never again'. She was finished with Brünnhilde. The German language had attacked her voice like sharpened wolves' teeth. 'It is beyond me! I have been a fool!' she said. A throat surgeon examined her and declared that she had come within a breath of irreparably damaging her vocal cords. As for George, she packed her sadness deep away like an item placed at the bottom of a travelling trunk: something that would not be needed *en voyage*.

She returned to London. Almost daily cables came from

PROGRESS BY RAIL

Australia imploring her to accept offers and assuring her of the greatest welcome ever accorded a homecoming Australian. Even her father had become involved, quite against his principle of never minding another's business. 'Father and all earnestly desire you may accept Williamson's offer,' came the message. How interesting. They were frightened she wouldn't come. As for her father, she loved him and longed to see him but resented his part a little because it showed there were still things he needed to learn about her after their long separation. Sixteen years! But after reflection she realised that he truly, passionately wanted to see her again too, that his old hurt over her going her own way was healed, that this was the meaning of his involvement. He urged her to accept the fourteen thousand pound offer from J.C. Williamson and she might have done so except a better one came from George Musgrove, for twenty thousand.

It was peculiar, she thought, as she went about cabling acceptance to Musgrove and making her travel arrangements. Money had less to do with it than her need to drive people to the upper limit of their regard. She had always had this need in different ways but the motive for it had changed over the years. At the beginning she had wanted people to recognise the special nature of her gift. Now she was aged forty. And while her voice was better than ever there was something about her outward person that was beginning to make people question her. Even make her question herself. She knew what it was: the beauty of her early thirties had given way rather too quickly to the middle-aged solidity called handsomeness. It was in the photographs more than in the mirror, but it was there. After the fiasco of Brünnhilde people were asking, 'Who is the next Melba?' She would prove them wrong, even though she hated more than ever to look at her own photographs except for one taken recently from a low angle that caught her with a look of unguarded nobility. It was a time of change: the new century, her forties, the return after sixteen years, the longing for George. The divorce. Especially the divorce.

She trembled when word of it became public but the papers made no fuss whatsoever. She waited for the inevitable clippings from Australia and was relieved to discover that only a small mention was made of it, even in the worst of the scandal sheets of Sydney and Melbourne.

Her relief had to do specifically with Australia and the way people thought about things there. It was a large country physically but consisted of a thinly spread rural population and a few small cities. As in a village, everybody knew everyone else's business beyond the range of plausibility. They would rather believe that a man had three legs, rode a satanical goat and kept a harem, even if he never did anything except drink cups of tea and rake his garden path in the open air. She had wanted to go back many times over the years. The divorce sent a message half-way round the world, 'My past is over, its raggedy ends are tied. Judge me by my voice, it's what I've always wanted . . .' Otherwise, too, the ghost of Charles might follow her into the dust and among the gum trees, blaming her for perfidy, and Louis Philippe Robert might appear at the campfire he once talked about, enticing her with his irrefusable love. She looked physically capable these days, bustling and energetic, as if nothing was too much for her. Let it be so! It was a way of keeping her inner emotions in order, packing them away, of proving that the inner self and the outer self matched. She sent a long cable to the Australian newspapers:

'It gives me very great pleasure to inform you that I have definitely arranged with Mr George Musgrove to pay a professional visit to Australia. I shall sail from England in August, and give a series of concerts in Melbourne, Sydney, Brisbane and Adelaide, during the months of September, October, and November. I believe that on many occasions rumours have been published of my going to sing in my native country, but they have never been authorised by me, as until now the difficulties apertaining to such a venture have proved insurmountable. Now that these difficulties have been removed, I cannot tell you how delighted I am in looking forward to a visit so full of potential pleasure to myself in the renewal of old friendships with the people among whom I was born and brought up; and if by the exercise of my art I am

PROGRESS BY RAIL

able to add some joy to the lives of my countrywomen and countrymen, my happiness will be complete.

Signed, Nellie Melba.'

So it was that she took the 'Melba manner' in her luggage when she set sail, but her voice, that third part of her, would be untouched by any brusque expedients.

She treasured a certain critic's opinion as she began her travels:

'One remembers Ben Jonson's phrase concerning "flight". Such a flight is Melba's, which seems to embrace the perfect feeling of attempting to ascend the heights, of attempting to descend to the depths, and all the way through of determining that there should be no sort of eccentricity, no sentiment of anything unconfirmed or not fully realised. She makes no unessential effects of sound, she never attempts to make of a song more than the song contains, but she insistently and most determinedly sacrifices every point in her absolute art towards the fulfilment of those great things of which she is so completely and utterly capable.'

There came another signal of her status. At Covent Garden just before she left, the King asked to speak to her.

'How will you travel in Australia?' he asked.

'By train though I dread the heat,' Nellie replied.

'Then you must use the state railway coach my brother used last year. He tells me it is even better than ours. I will order my governors to let you have it.'

'You overwhelm me with your kindness, Sire.'

She travelled a long way around, going across the Atlantic instead of by the Suez route, then by rail from New York to Vancouver, often thinking of George, embarking there for Brisbane on the *Miowera* which ploughed with faulty engines for weeks down the wide curve of the Pacific. She was alternately seasick and bored, and always impatient with captain and crew. No-one played deck-games like Madame Melba: she was the highest scorer at cricket and shuffleboard, quoits and darts. At night it was checkers and backgammon. There were books, but reading seemed a waste of time when there were activities instead. As the *Miowera* approached Brisbane there occurred a complete engine breakdown for two days. No Marconi transmitter on board then: across the waiting country rumours began to fly. Melba was lost at sea. The *Miowera* wrecked.

Then she was there. Brisbane. The city of her marriage, where beefy sunburnt crowds greeted her with casual friendliness. She spoke to clamouring pressmen through armloads of heavy-scented subtropical blooms: 'Here I spent many happy days before my dreams of a professional career had taken any definite shape . . .' The pressmen nodded and scribbled each word carefully into their notebooks. Everything she said, with only a few repetitions edited out, appeared in the morning editions. 'Oh, I do hope the people will like me in Australia. Everybody said I was never in such fine voice as this season in London, and I do hope it will be the same here. I have experienced many emotions, and I have enjoyed many successes, but I know that when I stand on the platform of the Melbourne Town Hall for my first concert I shall feel the greatest emotion of my whole life.'

She had not expected such thoroughness in the reporting. She would, she realised with relief, be able to tell her own story as she went along, and see it reliably printed in the papers. This was a marked contrast to America, where the motto was 'anything goes'.

'The Duke of York's own carriage has been promised me by the King himself,' she smiled.

This met a blank. 'The King,' she repeated, 'of England.'

'Well, Madame,' someone cleared a throat, 'we weren't game to tell you, you see. It's broken down. It's being shunted back to Sydney.'

'We're getting another one.'

'Never mind.'

'She'll be right.'

'Cheery-oh.'

She had forgotten the broadness of the accents, the flattened

PROGRESS BY RAIL

emotion in the voices. She loved it but would she ever quite like it? Australians in England, including Madame Melba herself, made extensive modifications to their vowels. Here there was no effort in the voices. The struggle went into other things. She had forgotten the furnace-blasting heat, the humidity of this northern city even in spring, so-called. It was like living in the mouth of an oven. The houses were made of wood and galvanised iron. Each had a backyard dunny, a sentry box. Reminders of Mackay met her at every street corner and railway cutting: swathes of lantana bush, choko vines climbing along fences, bougainvillea flowers, and the leafy banana trees. Here and there, bunches of sugar-cane struggled along. But it was all half-hearted, scratchy and incomplete. None of it was sedate, darkly rich and dreamlike as in tropical Hawaii or Fiji where the *Miowera* had made coaling stops. The Brisbane women looked scorched and defeated with fashions to match. Were all Australians like this now? Her own sisters? She would do battle over these people in the coming months, she told herself, not against them she hoped but within herself, in order to build her love for them. Great efforts were presently being made by George Musgrove and others to secure a special carriage from the railway yards in Woolloongabba and have it ready on time for her evening departure. Oh, she had forgotten that too: how nothing was too much trouble for these people.

Now it was the next day, after a night of jolting sleep, and for hours on end she sat at the window of her special carriage (just a sleeping car, but all to herself and her staff) watching the landscape wheel past. In the night they had left the steamy lowlands and climbed the Great Dividing Range, crossing the New South Wales border at Wallangarra. She had never been through these parts before, having used coastal steamers for her trips in the 'eighties before the rail. She experienced the dryness of the air, the sparseness of the vegetation, the tawny colours of the grass, the inviolate blue of the hills. They passed through granite country, the uplands of New England settled by Scots like her father.

A harsh wind constantly blew cinders from the engine back

along the carriages. She felt dulled in a most unpleasant fashion by the width and emptiness she witnessed. It was not as she remembered. It was nothing like the soft Lilydale country she had, for sixteen years, elected in her nostalgia as the true Australia. Or was it? Had she forgotten too much? Changed her allegiances? Been spoiled for the country of her birth? Hours passed without sight of another human being. Even the sheep that thrived here were sighted only occasionally. Half a day went by between small towns.

But when the towns came there was relief. Every man, woman and child appeared to wave her through. Bands played. Mayors and shire councillors made hurried, stumbling speeches. Tenterfield. Glen Innes. Armidale.

She had expected crowds. She had expected addresses of welcome. But this was something different.

'They love me, they love me,' she murmured to herself in amazement.

The line twisted down from New England into the Hunter Valley.

In a small town ahead of the train the sun shimmered and a crow flapped across iron rooftops, emphasising a loneliness that lay over everything like a spell. It was mid-afternoon. Faintly the voices of children rose and fell, reciting their multiplication tables under pepper trees in the schoolyard. At the railway station about a dozen people were gathered. There had been more earlier, but the rest had retired across the road to wait in the Railway Hotel. The train was late, very late, and expectation had evaporated. Those on the platform had been waiting so long that conversation was desultory; but there were no complaints; they were familiar with disappointment, their stoicism was a matter of routine. She would never get there and why should she? After the excitement of the morning, when they had risen, bathed and shaved, and dressed in their best clothes, they felt dull. It had now become almost impossible to believe that this really was Madame Melba coming, and that two amazing opposites would touch. But still they craned their necks and looked north from the edge of the

PROGRESS BY RAIL

platform, where the sun was almost white in its brilliance. Rails melted into the distance, disappearing as a blob of silvery black. An engine? Steam? Heat-haze made a mirage of constant suggestion. It was from out of there she would come, if she came.

A coatless sandy-haired man in his thirties leapt to the tracks and put his ear close to the rails. His name was Bill Carruthers, a journalist on the Melbourne *Argus* who had arrived from Sydney on the night mail to beat his rivals to the Melba story. He had breakfasted at the Railway Hotel, and already was accepted by the townspeople as one of their own. Among them he spoke as they did, hoped as they did, even though he would be gone within the hour as if he had never existed.

'Hear anythin', Bill?'

'Dunno . . .'

'It's hopless.'

'Wait . . .'

'He can hear it.'

'Can ya, Bill?'

'I think it's . . . Yeah . . .'

'She's really comin' now.'

'Yep.'

'Told you!'

'Hoo-ray!'

In his office the stationmaster donned his hat and coat. The town simpleton galloped across the road to bang on the hotel windows.

'Missus Melba! Missus Melba!'

A distant train-whistle blew.

Under the pepper trees twenty or so pupils cheered and went wild.

'That will be Madame Melba's train,' nodded the teacher, squaring his hat. The children clutched scrolls of welcome and bunches of wilting bush flowers and skipped up the dusty road towards the station.

An old lady hobbled as fast as she could, jabbing her stick in the dirt footpaths. A dog whizzed around a corner and trotted determinedly along.

MELBA

The train steamed slowly into the station. A vision materialised in the heat.

There she stood on the observation platform at the rear of her carriage, wearing a white dress and a wide pale creamy straw hat. She looked so cool, so composed as she raised an arm in greeting; she looked as if she had done no travelling at all. As if nothing was any trouble for her. Ever. As if she was not even mortal as other people were.

The train jolted to a stop and the Shire President mumbled a speech of welcome which no-one, including Madame Melba herself, could hear.

'How kind you are,' she responded.

A schoolgirl shyly stepped forward clutching a bush bouquet.

'How sweet,' said Melba.

'Three cheers for Madame Melba!' shouted the station master.

Everything happened so quickly. Bill Carruthers swung aboard, the whistle blew, and the engine strained.

'Give us a song, Nell,' slurred one of the drinkers from the pub. Nellie smiled and laughed. She blew a kiss. The train was already moving.

The drunk staggered back accusingly: 'That's all we get? A minute of yer bloody time?'

Bill Carruthers leaned from a window shaking hands. 'Good luck, Bill.'

'Give her a kiss from me, Bill.'

'See you later, Bill.'

The train shrank away from the platform and was soon drawn into the heat-haze again.

'Wouldn't even give us a bloody song,' belched the drunk.

They came into Newcastle; she walked among crowds on the platform; everything was larger, noisier, more riotous. People tried to touch her and take souvenirs of her clothing. It was a little frightening.

On their way again, Nellie fanned herself and drank a glass of iced water handed to her by her maid. The train picked up speed.

PROGRESS BY RAIL

'I've never seen the likes of it.' She was a practical cockney woman devoted to 'Madame'.

'I'm absolutely poleaxed,' said Nellie.

'You never show it.'

'Oh, don't I?' Nellie leaned back, exhaling.

'You never show it to them, I mean,' emphasised the maid. 'They think you're an angel, they do. Look at 'em now, Madame. They're out in them fields . . .'

'Paddocks, they're called here,' corrected Nellie.

'. . .Dozens of 'em.'

The two women pressed their faces to the window, which was closed against the soot blowing from the engine. Odd groups of people were everywhere now, farm people in sulkies, settlers beside the line, timber-getters on the edges of rainforests. All were waving, cheering.

'What have I done?' wondered Nellie.

'You've started something, that's the truth, Madame.'

The carriage was filled with floral tributes already withering. The maid struggled off, carrying excess bouquets through to the luggage van. Nellie sank even deeper into her seat. Her bare arms adhered to the sticky leather armrests, and at one small siding, where the train slowed for some reason, a small dark boy ran alongside, staring in at her, his face almost touching the glass.

What next? she wondered.

Her nerves, she thought, were in good order but she felt a certain tension. There would be days and weeks of invaded privacy ahead. She wanted to see her family so much, just to be with them, to recover something of the time she had sacrificed by going away. But would it happen? Had Musgrove over-organised her tour and raised everyone's expectations? No: whatever he'd done was at her insistence. The craving in the faces greeting her was almost otherworldly. What did they want? What thing extra? She had already volunteered her love; accepted their dry work-roughened hands into hers, stared with fellow-feeling into eyes that had never known glory. She had given, and would give so much more, but would it be enough? She hoped her feelings would not be over-tested. Her patience had a limit. They would have to be reminded of who she was. She had pretended not to mind the drunk who taunted her, but his words had cut, ridiculous as they were. *That all we get? A minute of yer bloody time?*

Adoration was such a delicate thing, it could soar or topple in a moment, and went beyond her gift into another dimension, having nothing to do with her music or the real nature of her personality. For years she had exulted in her fame. But this was different. This was Australia. It was a second coming. Even if she gave her very best it would be possible to disappoint these people, she thought.

'There's Mr Musgrove with a reporter in the passage, Madame.'

'What sort of reporter?'

'Young and cheeky if you ask me,' frowned the maid.

'Tidy me up,' said Nellie. And when the maid had helped her change, and made her hair neat, she asked her to show the men in.

'Madame Melba, please allow me to present to you Mr Bill Carruthers, of the Melbourne *Argus*,' said George Musgrove.

Nellie sat looking just as cool as she had on the observation platform.

'How do you do, Mr Carruthers,' she said.

'How do you do, Madame Melba,' said Carruthers.

'Bill Carruthers would like to talk to you, Nellie,' said Musgrove.

'I would love to talk. I'm weary of sitting here,' said Nellie. She eyed Carruthers. He was a handsome, openfaced young man. 'George Musgrove never comes and talks to me.'

'Madame,' chided Musgrove.

'No you don't, George,' she returned her gaze to the journalist. 'He never has a spare minute. How he organises me, Mr Carruthers. I have bestowed the title "my Bismarck" on him. Please sit down. You'll fall over with all this jolting about. My steamer was delayed coming in to Brisbane, the Duke of York's rail car lost its wheels, but no trouble, Mr Musgrove arranged everything and this carriage was waiting for me.'

'Only my duty . . .' Musgrove bowed himself out.

PROGRESS BY RAIL

As soon as Musgrove was gone, Bill Carruthers produced notebook.

'Now I see the kind of talk you had in mind, Mr Carruthers,' said Nellie.

'I'm a professional,' replied Carruthers. 'You're a pretty big prize.'

'The papers in Brisbane printed my every word.'

'What else was news that day?' wondered Carruthers.

'You are cheeky.'

'I like to shape and polish a little. I'm better than they are.'

'I hope you're not like the Americans,' warned Nellie. 'They put themselves above their subjects.'

'I do like the truth,' said Carruthers. 'If I can find it.'

'Then we should have no trouble with each other,' smiled Nellie.

'I guess you're right.'

'Don't pander to me, though.'

Carruthers couldn't seem to start the interview. There was nothing he could actually put on paper yet. Was Melba playing with him, merely passing the time? She turned and looked out the window. Long fingers of evening light stretched over the Hawkesbury River.

'Beautiful, isn't it,' she said.

'Indeed.'

'The Australian light is so harsh in the middle of the day. Things are blasted out of existence. But now it's all revealed. The small town where you got on . . .'

'Oh, you noticed me,' said Carruthers, surprised.

'The man who vilified me . . . Was he typical? I won't please anyone if that's what they want. All of me at all times. I'm a professional too, Mr Carruthers. I sing at my concerts and nowhere else. Unless I decide otherwise.'

'He was drunk. He was only a type. Not typical.'

'It is sixteen years since I was in Australia, Mr Carruthers.'

'Yes, indeed. Your life has been marked by many events since then.'

'Quite.' She gave him a sharp look. He was not writing anything down.

Carruthers took up his pencil. The interview had begun but Melba was taking the initiative.

'Well, now . . .' he said.

'I can't wait,' Nellie interrupted, 'to see Melbourne and all the old places I used to know . . .'

'Mackay?' asked Carruthers suddenly. He had meant to work round to this.

Nellie did not blink. She merely took her eyes from his and looked out the window again. Her manner seemed to say, 'False start.'

'Yes, wonderful countryside in these parts.'

The train jolted again. 'There's the train stopping. What's the matter?' wondered Carruthers.

'Picking up more reporters, I daresay, to cap your exclusive,' teased Nellie. 'I was in a train six weeks once . . .'

'In America? Where your son is?' Carruthers tried again.

'Where were we?' Nellie deflected him.

'The Duke of Orléans?' blurted Carruthers, going for broke.

He thought Nellie would order him from the carriage. She rose slightly from her seat. Her face darkened. But the moment passed. Then she said, very softly, 'I am grateful to you, Mr Carruthers, for revealing the level of curiosity about me in this country.'

'I'm sorry.'

'So you ought to be.'

'People want to know where you live,' Bill Carruthers swallowed. 'That sort of thing.'

'Well, it was Paris for many years. When I was not travelling, that is. But now it is a large house in Great Cumberland Place. I have it decorated in the French style of the Versailles period. Sometimes I go to the south of France. In summer I take a house on the Thames, at Marlow in Buckinghamshire.'

'Will you buy a house in Australia?'

'It is so far from anywhere,' replied Nellie, looking out the window. 'But my family is here. My father, my sisters, my brothers. Their homes are mine. Belle Patterson and Charlie Mitchell will be meeting me at Hornsby station, by the way.

PROGRESS BY RAIL

What time do we reach there?'

'An hour or so, I think.' It was quite dark outside the train now.

They talked on and on, and Carruthers filled many pages with notes.

'What are you paid per concert?'

'I never talk about money,' frowned Nellie.

'Can you name the Australian you are most anxious to meet on this visit?'

'My father. He is travelling up from Melbourne to meet me half way, at Albury.'

'What do you say to your critics, who say you sing with beauty, but no feeling?'

'They know nothing about beauty, or feeling,' replied Nellie. 'Nothing.'

Lights flashed against the windows.

'We're coming into Hornsby, I think,' said Carruthers.

'Oh, oh,' exclaimed Nellie, turning away from him to the window.

With that, the interview was over. Carruthers had run the gamut with Melba. He pocketed his notebook and stood at the door, waiting for a gesture of dismissal. There had never been an interview in his experience quite like it. He felt he knew her better, more roundedly, as a result of her evasions and exaggerations, her breathy dramatisations and sudden refusals to talk. But he did not know everything. She'd made him feel at one moment her most confidential friend, the next a hostile stranger, all with a degree of calculation that was quite breathtaking. He admired her, respected her. He would try and write the truth. But he knew it would not be the whole truth and never could be. Underneath, he felt an indefinable sadness. Something so private perhaps that she had never quite defined it properly for herself. Horrors, or mere regrets? The march of time, which had struck her with special force as it did many people in their middle age? She had painted a portrait of herself with great skill: it was up to him to frame it. That was the unspoken command she gave.

He smiled, watching her.

'Where are they?' Nellie was lost at the window, shading her eyes against the reflected inside light. 'Where are they, ever?'

Carruthers made a noise to remind her of his presence. But she had all but forgotten his existence. She banged the window-glass with her hand, calling, 'Belle! Charlie!' like an excited child. A crowd swirled alongside the carriage. Nellie wrenched the window open with force, and accretions of soot showered down.

Hands shot out. Sisterly arms folded around her neck. A brotherly hand was laid on her shoulder.

'Here I am at last!' announced Madame Melba.

As Belle and Charlie squeezed into her compartment her first question was:

'Any word of Daddy?'

30

Daddy

David Mitchell and John Lemmone were travelling north to Albury in a special carriage made available by the Railway Commissioners of Victoria. There were just the two of them in the plush, gaslit space. Tomorrow on the return run to Melbourne there would be three.

'How far now, John?' appealed Mitchell.

It was dark, they were tired, would they never arrive?

Lemmone peered out the window. 'I really think we're almost there, Mr Mitchell. Lights ahead. Must be Wodonga.'

'At last.'

Mitchell began a brief coughing spasm. Lemmone thumped him on the back, remembering what Annie had said at Spencer Street, as they left: 'Keep a close eye on him, John. He's like a small boy he's so excited. His pills are in the top left hand pocket.'

'You're managing, sir?' he asked.

'Don't fuss, Lemmone,' snapped Mitchell.

Lemmone drew back.

'Och, don't mind me, John,' said the old man, gesturing impatiently. The coughing had exhausted him. He wheezed, recovering, and dabbed his lips with a handkerchief. It was embarrassing to show weakness in front of another person.

MELBA

David Mitchell was in his mid seventies now, his hair peppery-white. The grip of his handshake was not as strong as he wished. Lately he'd been ill, this man who refused to admit the penalties of advancing age. Stubborn persistence had made him, and pray God he would overcome many more obstacles until he was called away to a greater home. Even pleurisy had been unable to keep him from making the trip to Albury to escort his daughter 'back to the colony of her birth'. Mitchell was proudly old fashioned, he would not adjust his thoughts to the idea of the recently-proclaimed Commonwealth. Victoria was still a colony to him and he was a notable citizen of it. His building business he had relinquished some years before, the depression of the nineties being the reason, not personal shortcomings of any sort. Other money-making ventures kept him going. There was the butter and cheese factory at Cave Hill, the ham-curing works, the limestone quarry, the brickworks, the farms, and the various company boards he sat on as a director. He spent his days going about checking on things, on people, all to increase quality and productivity. He made inventions; he was aiming at present for a fire-proof brick. At night he studied account books, as he always had, by the light of a much-polished oil lamp. It was clear now that his sons were not made in the same authentic stamp as himself. Even Frank, on whom he had once pinned all his hopes. They were colonials, born to take it easy, liking the trappings of wealth with scant thought for its moral foundations, buying nice things for themselves such as leather gun-cases, and sending their children to the best schools where they learnt to play sports but gained little else in preparation for life and success.

They'd all had music lessons, of course, the grandchildren, but none had persisted like his eldest daughter. There was a nice voice in one, a pleasant skill at the piano keys in another. But no fire anywhere to light up the horizon.

David Mitchell reflected on times past. He remembered with satisfaction the trouble he'd put in Nellie's way when she was younger. Isabella had always argued for her, and though he'd felt guilty about his attitude then, because Isabella had died,

DADDY

he was not sorry in the long term. He believed that Nellie would not have become the woman Isabella wanted her to become without his interference.

He knew how people spoke of him when he was outside their hearing: they said he was hard, even cruel. Well, people should look at what he had made.

John Lemmone understood. The flautist had given concerts with Nellie in the Old Country and had seen the world she moved in. Annie, Belle, and Dora understood, they were always travelling the high seas to stay with her. Ernie had gone for a look, and given a good account of life over there. Charlie, too, in his cynical deflating fashion, had helped convince David Mitchell that the time was right for her return, that all breath of old scandal had been laid to rest.

'Almost there,' said Lemmone.

'Aye.'

They crossed the Murray River into New South Wales. The bridge rumbled hollow under the train wheels. Swagmen's campfires glowed on the banks.

Lemmone held Mitchell steady while he looked out the window into the dark.

'There'll be crowds, they say.'

'Hundreds,' nodded Lemmone.

'Bands playing, addresses of welcome. I hope we're not late.'

'We're exactly on time,' Lemmone assured him.

'It's hard to believe,' said Mitchell. The lights of the station blazed up ahead. 'That all this . . .' he made a vague gesture, he could hardly grasp what was happening.

She was coming to them from another world, a different world. Though he would never admit it, that world of Nellie's now existed for David Mitchell in such detail that he hardly remembered banging his fists on desk-tops, burning with shame, trying to prevent it for her. Last thing at night he liked to take out the scrapbooks and leaf through. Sixteen years of astonishing fame . . .

Lemmone tapped him on the shoulder.

'Mr Mitchell. We're there.'

The train crept into Albury station and jerked to a stop. The mayor and stationmaster appeared at the window to greet the famous parent. But that was all. No crowds, no bands, only a few workmen on ladders erecting banners, and cleaners wielding long brooms.

'My daughter. Where is she?' muttered David Mitchell as they helped him down.

'It's all right, Mr Mitchell. Her train is delayed. She'll be here first thing in the morning.'

'Delayed, you say?'

There was a dinning in his ears. A rushing in the blood. He pitched forward.

The mayor and the stationmaster grabbed him.

'The excitement,' said John Lemmone calmly taking over.

'It's not that.'

'He needs a doctor.'

Lemmone spoke in a stern voice as they lowered him to a bench on the platform. 'Mr Mitchell, can you hear me?' The stationmaster blew his whistle and helpers came running.

'Fetch the doctor. Hurry!'

Mitchell's head was slumped on his chest. He was unconscious. The side of his face was pulled back in a ghastly grin.

Nellie's train clattered through the night. Blinds were drawn, lamps lit. The luxurious fittings of the Duke of York's railway carriage rattled and creaked: it had rosewood and cedar fittings under the windows, recessed brass screws, engraved mirrors, and a complete bedroom at one end. They had left Sydney after many delays and farewells and were now climbing through the Southern Tablelands. Albury was ahead somewhere at the end of the night. Nellie felt restored to herself after the contrary experiences of a very long day. She had her sister and brother with her, and her trusted brother-in-law Tom Patterson. They would see her home. It was all right, she was almost there. Only a few hundred miles to go. She would be with her father at first light.

She smiled to see Belle assessing the upholstery, smoothing it over with the flat of her hand and wondering if it was quite

DADDY

as good as it should be.

She watched as Charlie's eyes lingered on the whisky cabinet and cigar box.

'Not bad,' he smiled, as she caught his eye. 'You've done all right for yourself, old girl.'

'Isn't it wonderful?' laughed Nellie. 'King Edward meant me to have it from the start.'

'King Edward himself. Fancy that,' said Belle.

Charlie pulled a face as if to say, 'Not King Edward again.' Nellie and Belle had mentioned royalty by name at least a dozen times between them already. 'What do you think happened?' he asked. 'The republicans in the railway workshops pull a kingpin?' He leaned back in his slightly uncomfortable chair, chortling. 'What would it be like to be him, I wonder? A nuisance, I'd imagine.'

Nellie laughed politely.

'Please Charlie,' said Belle.

Tom Patterson crossed and uncrossed his legs, feeling slightly out of the family banter, which always had an edge to it when Charlie was involved.

Nellie's smile fell on him:

'What about a whisky, Tom? Help yourself.'

'Thanks Nellie. I will.'

'Count me in,' said Charlie. 'A loyal toast, anyone?'

Nellie swivelled on him with a glazed-over look that indicated her sense of humour had its limits.

Belle shot him a quick warning frown that meant: *Not here, not yet*. He had so little respect for people. She thought if anyone were to spoil this visit of Nellie's it would be Charlie.

'A small nip for the ladies?' wondered Tom.

'I've ordered tea,' said Nellie.

Belle stroked a tasselled bell pull, and prodded a cushion. 'It's just lovely,' she said.

'Anyone mind if I smoke?' asked Charlie.

'Not at all. Try one of these, Charlie,' said Nellie, gesturing at the cigar box on the side table. 'They're . . .'

'The King's?' Charlie finished the sentence. He would not be bowed. No-one laughed.

MELBA

He took one for himself and one for Tom.

George Musgrove knocked and entered.

'A very good evening,' he said.

'Join the party, George,' said Nellie. 'What time do we get there? Have you spoken to the conductor?'

'Nine at the earliest.'

'It was to be seven! Who's responsible for the delays, may I ask?'

Musgrove smiled indulgently. 'They're all of them blaming you, Madame Melba. Your popularity.'

'Oh, what nonsense.'

'Any word from Albury?' asked Belle.

'You father's train is due there any time now.'

'He so hates it when anyone's late,' frowned Nellie.

'He's a demon,' said Charlie, draining his whisky, 'for punctuality.'

'How I remember,' said Nellie.

'He'll have a good night's rest, anyway, that's something,' said Belle.

'And be up before dawn, standing on the platform, tapping his cane with impatience,' said Charlie.

Tom Patterson poured more whiskies.

'Your very good health,' said George Musgrove.

'Cheers.'

'Pleased with the way things are shaping, George?' Tom asked.

'I should say I am,' said Musgrove, beaming at Nellie. 'Latest news to hand: every ticket for the five Melbourne concerts has been sold.'

Charlie whistled and stared at his sister. He thought: multiply that by the other cities and what have you got? A bloody great fortune.

'There's good business to be done here,' nodded Nellie. 'Stop looking at me like that, Charlie Mitchell,' she added.

Charlie was just old enough to remember what it had been like before she went overseas: one long business of her getting her own way. That was the impression made on the younger members of the household. Well, he thought, good on her.

DADDY

This is what it led to. It's what she wanted and she's got it by the tail.

Nellie's maid emerged from the door at the end of the carriage balancing a tea tray.

'You're a treasure,' exclaimed Nellie in her best Anglo-Australian manner.

Charlie looked at Belle, silently mouthing his grand sister's polished vowels. He was unable to help himself.

Warningly, Belle put a finger to her lips.

Then the atmosphere settled down. Nellie held the floor. The women took their tea, the men cradled their whiskies. As the train rattled along she told them stories of other tours in other places. The magnitude of her professional life was epic. How she defied geography! She talked of railcars detached and forgotten, of waking one morning in a silent, snowy countryside. Of earthquakes, fires, and robberies. Of icebergs in the North Atlantic and of chestnuts roasting in the streets of Madrid at the first onset of winter. She spoke of her houses, of hotels, of ocean liners plying from one hemisphere to the other with the frequency of taxicabs. It was very unlike the life here.

Midnight came and went. Tom Patterson surreptitiously consulted his watch. George Musgrove stifled a yawn. Belle rubbed her eyes. Charlie was pleasantly aware of seeing double. It was clear that Nellie had outlasted them all.

Suddenly there she was, ushering them out. Kissing them goodnight. Standing framed in the doorway of her royal carriage.

They filed back to the ordinary part of the train and stumbled into the stiff leathery cold of their New South Wales Government Railways sleeping compartments.

Nellie climbed into her royal bed, pulling the heavy covers up around her. It had been rather an effort for her tonight. In the end, she had had to perform as she did with everyone: she hadn't quite been able to sink into the tides of family and drift with them, as she had hoped. A tiny premonition of disappointment nibbled at her. She had forgotten the rock-bottom cynicism of Australians like Charlie. She loved him, of course, but his particular brand of wit bordered on misanthropy and was rather wearing. Nothing ever impressed him enough. There were plenty like him in this country, she remembered. Everything was to be brought down to their own level, stamped on a bit, muddied, to make it real, and then after much scorn would come a begrudging acknowledgment: sudden flashes of absolute devotion would be allowed to show. But even then the recipient must show deep gratitude, or the whole cycle of disparagement would start all over again. It was a small country. A new country. Its belief in itself was intermittent, and a little dangerous.

All the tickets might be sold but Nellie would still have to give her utmost in order to make an impression.

She could even tell this from Belle, who was over-anxious to stress how natural and easy everything was about Nellie's return. But it wasn't natural, it wasn't easy, and so something was missing even there. They weren't able to recapture the frank easiness of their girlhood relations. It had been the same with Annie during their time together in America. Nellie blamed the others for being rather in awe of her, while her sisters thought it was her: she had become very grand. Fame had come between them although it left their love for each other intact. What a bind.

Oh, but she would find the family feeling she needed in the morning, in the meeting with her father.

She imagined it as she sought sleep. There he would be on the platform, clutching his hat in his fingers. It was an image from the latest of the photographs that had been sent to her over the years, each change in the man coming closer to the spirit he represented. Belle fretted that Nellie would be alarmed by the way he had aged, had changed: but she knew her father best, despite their long separation. His chin raised slightly, his weathered, fine head and bright eyes seeking her out. Causing her to stand a little straighter, a little more proudly than she might have otherwise . . . They would approach each other without overt demonstration of feeling. There would be a dry, rather diffident kiss . . . How she loved the magnetism of expectation that flowed from her father; from her idea of the man; there was a palpable impedance,

DADDY

as from like poles resisting.

She would slip her hand into his for a few moments, and know she was home. That would be all.

Sleep claimed her.

Immediately the train slid into Albury station Nellie sensed the difference. The waiting crowd seemed restrained, the band music muted, the approaching dignitaries wary in their manner. Nothing like the other places, where she had been mobbed. She swept her eyes around. The longed-for face was nowhere to be seen. A man appeared dressed in a black suit, clutching a black bag: a doctor. He seemed to want to speak to her, but first the mayor and the stationmaster had their stiff little recitations to make.

'Madame Melba, it is our great and enduring pleasure to welcome you to Albury and surrounding district . . .'

'May I add on behalf of the railway service . . .'

'Thank you so much. You are very kind. Where is my father?' she interrupted.

They looked at each other apprehensively. The man with the black bag stepped forward.

'I am Doctor Wood . . .'

'What is it? Where is he?'

'A stroke, I am afraid. He's resting in a house nearby.'

Just like that. Nellie swayed on her feet. She gripped the man in a panic-stricken gaze.

'Doctor Wood, you say. A stroke? What sort of cruelty is this?'

'Mild, minor,' the doctor essayed. 'Perhaps.'

Melba frightened him.

Belle and Charlie took her elbows, but they might as well have been strangers; really there was no help. Couldn't they see?

'Take me to him,' she commanded, while in her thoughts a black wave of depression took control. *What's the use of it all? What's the use of any of it now?*

Charlie noticed how in her grief she still made things happen around her.

MELBA

They had carried him across the road in the night, it was explained, to the the humble cottage of working people who had taken him in. It was close to the station and she could see him there before continuing her journey.

'Continue my journey? What are you suggesting . . .'

There was a picket fence, a short bricked pathway edged with struggling flowers. John Lemmone met them at the door.

'Nellie,' he greeted her with a kiss.

'John, what's the meaning of this?' she clung to him. They had last seen each other in London, at some grand occasion under chandeliers, while a string orchestra played. Now soot from the interstate railway junction peppered down on their heads, and they heard the distant bellow of cattle being unloaded at the saleyards.

'It was the excitement, that's all.'

'Let me in.' She stepped inside, followed by Doctor Wood, Charlie, Belle, Tom Patterson, George Musgrove, the mayor, and the stationmaster. Of all the things she had thought about, she had never considered the possibilty of death.

What a fool she had been. Death. Of course. There it was. Claiming all.

'Is she all right?' Belle whispered to Charlie.

'Don't know,' said Charlie.

Nellie had forgotten that they might have an equal claim to grief with her.

The lady of the house stood beside a doorway clutching an apron.

'He's inside,' she spoke with lowered eyes. There was peculiar shame mixed with stubborn pride in her manner. 'In there, Mrs Melba.'

David Mitchell lay stretched out on a bed with the covers drawn up to his chin. Nellie knelt at the bedside and took his hand.

'Daddy. Daddy?' she whispered. An image came to her from years ago, her father with his coat off, his sleeves rolled up, working alongside the men in the marble yard. He had seemed the same age to her even then, covered in marble dust, indefatigable.

DADDY

She willed him to react. Charlie and Tom crowded in with the doctor. The others waited in the narrow parlour while the woman served them tea.

For a minute there was nothing, and then, in the glistening slit beneath David Mitchell's eyelids a tear appeared and slid down his dry, weatherbeaten cheek.

'He knows me,' said Nellie.

The doctor leant over her shoulder. 'He does.'

'Daddy,' Nellie began to talk. 'Forgive me won't you. Please forgive me. There was never a time when I forgot you, ignored you, went against you. Not really. Not ever. Please understand why. Look at me, say it . . .' It was a rambling one-sided conversation that caused Belle and Charlie to glance at each other in wonder. 'I wanted to do my best for you, but you couldn't see it. Do you now? You must, you must.'

Tears flowed down Nellie's cheeks.

Belle thought: 'So this is the meaning of it all.'

Charlie thought: 'The old man might really have come up against it this time. He's had a good innings . . . Oh, but he's tough, he'll pull through if I know him. And if he doesn't, well, it's good that Nell is here. I wish she wouldn't carry on, though.'

Belle thought: 'It's breaking Nellie's heart. I hate to see it. Poor Father.'

Nellie continued with her quiet, tearful pleading.

Charlie thought, again: 'If this doesn't bring him back, nothing will.'

'He's squeezing my hand!' announced Nellie.

'Dear God,' breathed Belle.

'Yes,' Nellie was saying, 'Yes. Yes. You wanted to meet me here, and so you travelled from Melbourne when you were too ill for it.' She nodded frantically, finding the words for him. 'I know, darling. I should have stopped you, but how could I, ever? I won't leave you. I mean it.' She looked at Belle. 'The train can go on without me.' She turned back to Mitchell. 'I'll stay with you Daddy and nurse you till you're well . . .'

Belle shook her head firmly.

'He's trying to tell me something,' said Nellie. She bent her head very close to her father's, then shifted her gaze down to the old Scot's hand on the sheet. It scrabbled, making a gesture. Then it fell still again.

'*Go?* Is that what you want?' interpreted Nellie.

'Tens of thousands of people are waiting in Melbourne,' said Doctor Wood. 'He knows that.'

Nellie stood, still holding on to the slack hand.

'He wants me to carry on,' she said.

'Oh, Nell, it's only right that you should,' said Belle.

Nellie made space for Belle beside their father. Belle felt strangely reluctant to kneel there. It was almost as if she had no right; as if this shrinking old man in the bedsheets was the parent solely of the famous Melba. But she uttered a few seconds of fervent prayer: '*Lord watch over him and make him well . . .*' That was all she could give. She had no inner conflict to act out.

Charlie, surprising the others, leant over his father and kissed him on the cheek.

'He'll pull through, I haven't a doubt, old girl.'

'Thank you, Charlie. You're a brick,' said Nellie. They all felt released from a load. They smiled.

'Cup of tea, everyone?' whispered the woman whose house it was.

Nellie stood looking down at her father for a few moments longer. Although he was masked and bound as it were there was still a statement being made. *Prove it to me*, he seemed to say. *Don't just stand there. Don't beg for a blessing. Do it on you own. Do it without me as you have these sixteen years past. Prove you're the best, feel the greatness in yourself, as I have, lass. As anyone can if they only try.*

She understood him.

31

I am Chosen

Daylight. The train travelling through wide flat paddocks of early wheat, a massed shining green. Spring lambs at play. The softness, the longed-for familiarity of the Victorian landscape meaning little to her now. She had cried for an hour after leaving Albury, and then made her appearances at each of the small towns after the careful application of powder and rouge.

'I mustn't disappoint them.'

'You won't, Madame.'

'How do I look?'

'Splendid, Madame.'

It was different now that she had entered her native state. The adoration had a new quality . . . The crowds through Wangaratta, Euroa, Benalla, Seymour, all taking away a memory to last a lifetime of the woman whose longed-for arrival came and went with indelible brevity. Her offer: a smile of welcome, a few words drowned in cheering. For them, the meaning:

Melba came here, she chose us.

'I shall return one day and sing,' she heard herself promising in the bigger places.

MELBA

The meaning for her:
I am chosen.

Minutes later there was hardly a fact to cling to, barely a scrap of truth left fluttering in the wake of her carriage . . . The train puffing away into the last lonely distances towards Melbourne, and she more distanced, more untouchable, more unreachable. The beginnings of a legend.

She sat down with George Musgrove and together they worked on a written statement to be handed to the Melbourne press. She felt a need to take things carefully, to pace herself out. For a whole lot of reasons. A vision of change. A new idea of herself. Her father's illness . . . The strength of a new idea flowed to her while her father lay weakened at Albury.

At Seymour the rest of the family were waiting: Annie, Frank, Ernie, Dora. They swung aboard the train.

They crowded through into Nellie's carriage. Soberly they listened to the news of David Mitchell's illness. Emotion piled on emotion; reminders of change in all their faces, the inexorable penalties of time: a dulling of colour in the cheeks, the pinch of a habitual frown . . . quick reminiscence reproached in a glance. Dora, so pretty, a little reserved and withdrawn. Frank with business worries uppermost in his mind. Everyone changed.

'Frank, remember the time . . .'

'I was just a kid then, Nellie . . .'

Here he was, a youngish man still, but grey-faced with worry. He must be thinking: 'What if Dad dies, who is there with the gift to gather the threads, to make sense of things?' . . . This boy who had once carelessly dreamed in the marble yard.

They looked at Nellie and wondered about her.

She stared out at the wide treeless paddocks, the stone walls, the lonely pine windbreaks as sad as all time.

'Soon be there, old dear.'

'I wish he'd stayed at home.'

'No crying over spilt milk.'

'I tried to stop him, didn't I, John,' said Annie.

'Indeed you did.'

I AM CHOSEN

'There was no stopping him.'

'He's only down for the count,' Charlie reminded them, cheering them up. 'He's tough as old boots.'

There was less than an hour to go before Spencer Street. At rail crossings and sidings more and more people gathered. Flags and greenery decorated buildings. 'Welcome Home Nellie' fluttered a banner.

The familiarity was intense. Challenging. She would have to rise to match it, as she rose to match everything. Meet intimacy with intimacy on a great scale. To get through the next few hours she would have to take herself very seriously. If not, she would faint.

Frank gave an account of the crowds waiting since early morning at Spencer Street Station. They had pushed through them at first light when they caught the train up to Seymour. Thousands. Tens of thousands. Already people were saying it was the greatest public demonstration in the history of Melbourne.

'George,' Nellie instructed her manager: 'Read them the draft statement. I want to know what the family thinks.'

Musgrove cleared his throat:

'"I feel I would not be doing myself or the Melbourne public justice if I appeared while affected by the excitements of the rush by train from Brisbane to Melbourne, and the reunion with my dear father . . . and the members of my family after a separation of sixteen years."'

Musgrove waited a moment, then continued: '"This message is to ask the Melbourne public to allow me a few days' grace. It had been arranged that I would give my first concert in Melbourne on Wednesday the twenty-fourth . . ."'

'Read on, George.'

'"As events have shaped themselves, first the delay in the mail steamer reaching Australia; and secondly the tiring, if not exhausting experiences of train travelling; I feel that to hold the opening concert on the original date would be unjust to myself and my reputation. My most earnest desire is to keep faith with the public, yet here I ask them to allow me to change that date of the first concert from Wednesday the twenty-fourth to Saturday the twenty-seventh. In all other respects the dates fixed by my managers will be scrupulously observed by me."'

'Thank you, George,' said Nellie.

The train slid through the railway yards. People could be seen everywhere: sitting on rooftops, pressed to railings, pouring along sidestreets.

'My God,' said Charlie, his face pressed to the window. 'The world's gone mad.'

Lord Richard Nevill was there; the Mayor Sir Samuel Gillott; the Secretary for Defence and many other persons of eminence including representatives of all the churches. They were insignificant in the mass of others.

Nellie stepped lightly onto the platform and was met by a solid wall of cheering that melted and surrounded her. It was entirely human in its parts, but inhuman in effect.

'This is appalling,' thought Charlie. 'How will she ever escape it?'

'Wonderful . . . Wait till they hear me sing,' thought Nellie, making her way out to the streets of the city.

A few days later she gave her first concert in Melbourne:

She walked on the stage and applause found its whitest and most intense brilliant focus at last. She turned her head one way, then the other; she bowed, acknowledging the welcome. The smile on her face bore a trace of sadness. She wished her father were there, that was all. Then she was ready to begin, but the audience would not release her yet from its thunderous admiration.

It went on and on.

'Let me sing. Please. Now,' Nellie thought to herself, shedding all personal impressions. 'Let me sing at last.' She made a step forward, touching her fingers to her lips. *Please. You chose me. Let me show you why.*

It was no good. She could stop none of it.

Then in an uncontrollable gesture she spread out her arms. The people stood and roared.

I AM CHOSEN

Her second concert in Melbourne:

John Lemmone played the flute. Music, an intricate weave of burnished gold thread, commanded the silence. Nellie stood waiting as her accompanist led her in. It was the 'Mad Scene' from Thomas's *Hamlet*. As she gathered herself and sang she noticed a movement at the back of the hall: a man in a wheelchair being pushed down an aisle and positioned to listen. Her father.

She sang for him. For him alone.

Belle held his hand. He was much recovered although capable of little movement as yet. His eyes were bright and alert: they told everything.

But it wasn't just David Mitchell, long ago of Forfar, Scotland, who was so affected. Each member of the audience felt the same, as if they were being spoken to, reminded of their achievements, no matter how great or small they were. And if they had no achievements to boast of *this* was an achievement. This concert. Just being present would become the boast of a lifetime. This voice was a vindication, a proof. It was as if gold and wool, those staple products of Australia, had been taken away and hammered to a single thread, woven and flung out for this country's admiration. Avid crudity ruled their simple hearts, some said, and maybe it was true, but she meant more here than anywhere else, and that was something.

Realising this, she gave back what she had with redoubled vigour. The response she met with went on changing her.

And she thought that was all it would take to maintain the upward curve; personal effort and control in the interests of greater beauty and style. She thought, through all the intricate discipline of her art, that finally, whatever happened, she commanded the path ahead.

Doonside was a smaller house than she remembered. The rooms were no longer filled with running footsteps, laughter and tears. The room where her mother had died was dusty and stale. No-one used it now. David Mitchell slept downstairs, where it was more convenient. The proud rooftop tower seemed slightly ridiculous, though Nellie did not say so, colonial feelings being easy to wound. Having once denoted grandeur and tradition, the house in her eyes seemed more a gesture of defiance, of uneasy belonging, built at a time when it had been just possible to see, on a clear day, beyond the city and the bay, out to the wide shimmering otherness of the empty continent, against whose reality the Europeans had come to stay. Strangers lived in the streets round about, and Richmond was a less desirable address than other places across the river. The proximity of the brickyard and cement works was absurd. The windows, through which Nellie had first glimpsed the outside world, were dark and heavily curtained. Had they always been like this?

'Yes. Nothing has changed,' Annie assured her.

'You've grown used to palaces,' Belle laughed.

The sisters coloured slightly. The word 'palaces' touched on something in Nellie's past that none of them talked about or referred to: the Duc.

'Are you comfortable, Daddy?' Nellie turned to her father. They were sitting in the morning sun facing into the back garden, where years ago Mitchell had wandered in the evening light, listening to his wife sing 'Shells of the Ocean' while Nellie accompanied her on the piano.

'Aye,' he replied, his lips shaping the words with determination. 'Quite comfortable, lass.' He was recovering from his stroke with unequalled force of mind. The doctors were proud of him.

Nellie straightened the rug on his knees. Her sisters watched her. She had the ability to make the action seem absolutely essential to his recovery, though it was something either one of them might have done.

'There.'

'Thank you, lass.'

'I wish you weren't always dashing off somewhere,' said Belle.

'But it's my life, dears,' smiled Nellie.

In the afternoon she would be catching another train, and beginning her tour of the other Australian cities. The time in Melbourne had gone too quickly, with hardly any small private

I AM CHOSEN

moments like this one, which had taken a deal of organising. Even now, George Musgrove and John Lemmone would arrive at any minute to whisk her away. It was not how they had anticipated Nellie's visit to be; they should have realised.

'Don't you ever think of stopping? Even for a short time?' asked Annie.

'Yes, why don't you?' asked Belle.

'You mean "retire",' frowned Nellie.

'Well, you're past forty, and they say . . .' taunted Belle.

'Forty's not old,' said Nellie, almost snapping.

'I'm sorry,' said Belle. 'I just meant there were other things.' She meant family. Nellie pretended not to understand.

'There's George,' prompted Annie.

David Mitchell's eyes enlivened at the mention of this name. He adored his grandchildren, loved having them around him, always carried sweets in his pockets for them, and in their extreme youth they saw no shadow of the hardness, the unforgivingness, on which he had built his fortune. George was past that age now, but was still the eldest grandchild, and Mitchell had always placed special importance on the eldest in any family. Nellie waited for her father to ask about George. But he said nothing, in his Scottish fashion of reticence.

'He writes that he's well. I hope to see him in the coming year.'

'But you're always saying that,' said Annie.

'Am I? Then it must be true,' replied Nellie.

There followed an awkward silence, which was only broken by the ringing of the front doorbell. Musgrove and Lemmone had arrived to take her back to her other life. Her true life? Her only life?

Her sisters loved Nellie dearly, but wondered if they would ever be sure of understanding her again. Of course, they would never admit this to anyone else. Not even to each other, perhaps.

'I don't hold with Melba-mania,' said a loud voice in a public bar, a place frequented by newspapermen.

It was a week or two after the Melbourne concerts. Melba

429

was away, touring the other cities of the Commonwealth. In Sydney, at her third concert there, she had just established a world record for the sum earned on one night: £2,350 net. She made it look easy.

Too easy.

Bill Carruthers moved his head slightly in order to see the face of the speaker, then just as quickly turned away, hiding himself behind other drinkers. The speaker was John Norton, publisher of the *Truth*. His penetrating, sarcastic tones silenced the rest of the bar.

'The woman is overweight and over-greedy,' continued Norton. 'She's a lascivious tart. Madame Melba has an eye for the younger sort of man, the kind she can mould and use. Remember the Duke? Who's asked her about the Duke?' the speaker looked around the bar. 'Nobody. There is tripe being written about her in this country.'

'Too right, Mr Norton,' said a *Truth* man at Norton's elbow.

Carruthers looked down at his fingers gripping his glass. The knuckles whitened in an attempt at self-control.

'I say, young man!' chortled Norton. 'Carruthers!'

Bill Carruthers slowly turned his head. There was no escaping it. Norton, a man of Napoleonic build, raised himself on tiptoes and eyed his target. The voice climbed to a penetrating, carping pitch. He lifted his glass in mocking salute.

'I give you Bill Carruthers, boys. In ordinary times a journalist of the first water, but these ain't ordinary times, as Bill keeps telling us in his "Melba" pieces. Why, Bill's just reduced to jelly by the scrape of stockings on fat legs. Carruthers! Come around here and I'll buy you a drink.'

Bill Carruthers walked around to Norton's side of the bar.

'Give it to him, Bill,' whispered someone at Carruthers elbow. Another winked. But none of them had the courage to speak out against Norton.

'I buy my own drinks, Mr Norton,' said Carruthers, slapping a coin on the bar.

'That's not what I hear,' chortled Norton. 'I hear she pays, and well,' he cackled. 'I hear you *rode* from one end of New South Wales to the other in her train, drinking champagne

I AM CHOSEN

and kicking your heels up. Why don't you mention the gallons of grog she brought out for this travelling circus of hers?'

'Bullshit.'

'Well then,' said Norton, lowering his voice and speaking ominously: 'After this thousand-mile party, she had such a bottler of a hangover she cancelled her concerts as soon as she belly-flopped into her "beloved" Melbourne. Where she hadn't squatted for a mere sixteen years past, but no matter.'

'Not cancellation. Postponement,' said Carruthers tightly. 'For legitimate family reasons.'

Norton sucked his rum. 'Oh, I've read your stuff, Bill. Very nice it is, like a lavender bag in a bog. You're soft on the throat-peddler, it's as plain as the nose on your face. You're writing about a whore and you're writing like a cissy. What sort of a newsman are you if you can't uncover a bit of dirt?'

The voice, polished by drink, had a certain eloquent fascination. The bar was crowded with decent men who knew a lie when they heard one. Yet here they were grinning quietly to themselves. They would go home tonight and repeat the nonsense to their wives, shaking their heads in disbelief. Their wives would repeat it to others tomorrow, not so disbelievingly perhaps, and soon the head-shake of amusement would become the nod of received truth through all of Melbourne.

'You want the whole picture,' Norton was saying. 'Get out there and dig, talk to her family and friends. Talk to that old Jew, her father.'

'He's a Scot. I've been to the family, Mr Norton.'

Norton changed tack.

'You're a Labor man, are you not, Mr Carruthers?'

'I am.'

'Then what's your quibble? These Mitchells and Melbas with their brickworks and vineyards and their royal jewels are your natural enemies, mate. Make 'em dance on hot coals. See if their money and "artistic genius" can save them . . . Have a drink.'

Craving for liquor overcame Norton's desire to rant. He slurped another rum.

Bill Carruthers slipped from the bar.

MELBA

Through the worst heat of summer, over Christmas and the New year and into February, Nellie continued her mainland tour. The lushness of spring had vanished: all was brown and burnt. She had not remembered what a dry country it was, how creeks roaring with chocolate-brown foam in October were dusty dry water holes by January. Sheep and cattle stood about on spindly legs, or lay dead, bloated in the searing shade as she passed by on the various state railways. A dry, windy, scorched continent she found difficult to love as she said she did, when she was forced to look it in the face.

The family complained among themselves that the entire country was her family now. They had hardly had a free day together.

'Not really fair,' said Belle mildly.

'I understand it,' said Annie. 'I think.'

'Quite mad,' said Charlie.

She was about to leave them again, for England. There would be concerts in Tasmania and New Zealand, and then the enormously profitable Australasian tour would be done. She had exceeded George Musgrove's predictions and made a fortune. She filled the papers with promises of eternal devotion. Her desire to make a mark on the country beyond personal gain found dozens of focus-points outside her own person. She made an announcement to the papers: 'I have decided to appeal to a few of my friends in England and America, who happen to be blest with wealth and influence, and I have today despatched messages to about thirty people, most of whom live in London or New York, asking them to send me something for the drought-stricken Australians, whose terrible sufferings I myself have seen . . .'

A few days before sailing she went with her family to the beautiful countryside around Cave Hill, where the fingers of drought never seemed to reach. There was an ache of familiarity in each view of the old paddocks. The hills and gullies and creek flats were peopled with memories. The cattle-paths along the creekbanks had been trodden unchanged for a generation. The old gum tree near the house still soared to

I AM CHOSEN

he sky, and in early morning filled with cockatoos, rousing a cacophany of reminiscences. Here Isabella Mitchell had grieved before letting go; Aunt Lizzie had fussed; David Mitchell had paced the burgeoning rows of his grapevines; the boys had shot their guns at all small living creatures; and Nellie had been kissed by a stableboy, and had never forgotten.

Belle and Annie were busy preparing picnic things in the kitchen of the old farm house. Charlie lounged in a doorway clutching a newspaper.

'She must be off in the upper storey,' he commented, reading to his sisters the item 'Melba's Drought Appeal' from the *Argus*.

'Charlie, will you please stop questioning her, and accept her for what she is?' said Annie.

'Yes. But which of the many Melbas is she today?'

'Ours, you fool.'

They loaded his arms with boxes of sandwiches, cakes, and drinks to carry across to the picnic blankets.

'I mean . . .'

'We know what you mean, Charlie. We've heard it a thousand times.'

They thought it themselves too, but weren't free with their comments like Charlie.

'Get a move on, they're waiting.'

Nellie wore a cool white dress. David Mitchell was in shirtsleeves. They sat in deck chairs, contentedly chatting, under the shade of the old Linden that Mitchell had planted with his own hands, thirty years before. It was now a glossy monument to patience, a tower of coolness, with its wide smooth trunk and big-hearted leaves. Its roots went down and drank from under the stones of the creek. Nellie did most of the talking. Mitchell's characteristic taciturnity disguised speech difficulties remaining from the stroke. He boasted that he was entirely well now. There was a cricket match being played nearby, from which the nephews and nieces, grandchildren and cousins broke away whenever they could to come and stare at their fabulously famous relation.

Mitchell handed them sweets, but they were hardly aware of him today, whereas Nellie, adept at handling admiration, left each admirer with a memory.

A small niece presented her with a bunch of flowers. An even smaller, perfect little face, stamped in the image of long-ago dead Vere, peeped from behind the older one's skirts.

'Aunt Nellie, these aren't very beautiful but they're all we could find.'

'Oh, but they're very beautiful, my darlings.'

The little girls giggled and ran off. Shaping each word with care, David Mitchell said:

'You had your job to do. I see that now . . .'

'Everything is an effort, Daddy. But the rewards . . .'

'Aye, I know that. Few understand.'

Their hands touched. He was intensely curious about the money-making side of her career, but would never ask. It would be a breach of his principles. And so Nellie took the opportunity to tell him, mentioning yearly amounts, describing her favoured investments, listing the value of her various residential properties in London, Paris, and the South of France; the weekly rental of Pullman cars in America; the cost, per night, of a suite in the St Regis Hotel.

While she talked, David Mitchell shaded his eyes with his hat, pretending to watch the cricket match. Tom Patterson bowled to one of his sons, while a scattering of others lay in the bleached grass, panting like little pups, or else stood with legs apart waiting to take a catch.

'Well done!' Nellie interrupted herself, admiring a clean stroke played by young David Patterson.

David Mitchell's silence, when she had finished her account of her business affairs, told her he was well-pleased. The air buzzed with summery insects. The eucalyptus trees shimmered in the distance. Birds thrashed the leaves high in the Linden tree, then were still. It was a minute of dazed, dazzling fulfilment for Nellie; something only she and her father would ever understand; the apex of her life so far, in a fashion: incalculably precious, yet almost transparent in the wafer-thinness of its passing. Was this all? If so, how to make it last? What would speak for her, the way his building spoke for him . . . what family?

I AM CHOSEN

Her heart ached for George.

Today, the generations widened in a ripple before her eyes, but they were denied her, finally.

Father and daughter were lost in their thoughts for a while. Neither heard Charlie arrive with his armload of food till he lowered it to the blankets; neither noticed Annie and Belle with their baskets till they were there.

'Wake up Australia!'

'Oh,' Nellie shook herself back to the present. She helped spread the picnic things.

'See the lovely flowers the girls brought me. I shall press them and take them back to England. They shall remind me of home.'

'You said "home",' commented Belle, putting sprigs of parsley on a plate of boiled eggs. 'Meaning Australia?'

'Yes, why ever not?'

'You always call England "home".'

'It's been a dream, coming back. People have been been so nice to me . . .'

'I think rather more than "nice",' said Annie. 'The crowds have been positively alarming.'

'I've managed rather well, I think.'

'You can say that again,' said Belle.

'I suppose as soon as my back is turned they'll be after me with sharpened knives,' said Nellie lightly. 'Isn't that always the way?'

She did not believe her own words, however. She had been greeted 'like some northern comet flashing through Australia's silent heaven, bespattering it with brilliancy . . . ambassadress of that far romantic ideal world of art, of beauty'.

It was a declaration of love. She was happy.

'We hate to lose you, Nell,' said Annie, touching her hand. 'Must you go so soon?'

'It's been months,' said Nellie. 'Longer than I ever stay anywhere else.'

'It seems like days,' complained Belle.

'I'll come back year after year, from now on. I promise,' she said.

'Next time, bring my grandson,' said David Mitchell abruptly.

Nellie took his hand, and held his eyes. 'I promise,' she repeated.

32

Je Suis Georges

Later she told herself that she should not have trusted her own happiness.

She reminded herself that the whole country was like a small town, in which a whisper becomes a roar.

Bitterly, she remembered how she'd cautioned herself at the start of her tour, but then had forgotten. Who could blame her? She'd been hailed around the country as 'a living image of that ideal phantasm which lurks deep in our souls, and which represents our secret aspirations to all that is free, beautiful, and joyous in life.'

She must pay for that now.

It was like falling in love with someone, then finding the person was planning your murder. *Australia.* She spat the word in her mind. It ran like poison through her blood. For a time, she was unable to see reason.

Childishly, she wished she could undo certain actions: wished she had sailed straight for England after farewelling her family. Wished she had planned no Tasmanian tour, because crossing Bass Strait she'd become seasick as never before, and in the Launceston hotel where she lay with a stripped-raw throat, had taken a glass of the best champagne available. Then as she sipped, George Musgrove had ushered

437

in a small number of reporters to her sickroom, and there made the announcement that her Tasmanian concerts were forthwith cancelled, and that the Melba party would sail for New Zealand the next day.

Her agony had been over the cancellation. How she hated letting people down. But she believed they would understand. She believed they were good people, with understanding hearts.

So she had sailed on. She had sung in New Zealand. She had re-crossed the Pacific. She had gone through America again, singing here and there, thinking about George when she should have been steeling herself for a thunderclap. She had returned to England at last, amid reports of her Australian triumph.

Then the first cable. Then a flood of cables. And at last the very text itself of the most vituperative slander imaginable. Every word of it aimed at her.

She said to herself: 'My homecoming tour was a dream, a beautiful illusion. Now it's a nightmare. I shall make my home in England . . . Or in America. I shall never return.'

'Think,' her Anglo-Australian friends in London cautioned her. 'We know what it's like. But don't let the matter get out of proportion . . .'

'Remember your family.'

She only stared at them wildly. Another friend was Lady Gladys de Grey. She belonged with those who ruled the Empire but had never dirtied their feet with its dust. Nellie tried to explain to her what it was like but failed.

'You loved it, Nellie, don't go against your own feelings. Your letters were rhapsodic . . .'

'Ugh!'

'The truth can't be that you hate it now. The truth must lie between . . .'

'I have been betrayed,' said Nellie, dramatically.

Lady de Grey smiled to herself. There was something just a touch ridiculous about Nellie as she grew older. Lovingly excessive. How much larger than life she would have seemed then, in Australia, that remote antipodes of proper English

JE SUIS GEORGES

life, where they had greeted her as a 'fairy princess of legend', 'heroic comet' and whatnot. This attack was certainly larger than life too . . . ludicrous, naturally . . . but how interesting Nellie's reaction was; had she become so accustomed to living alone that her entire emotional life was now to be acted out in public? No children under the roof. No intimate family to check her, to take the pressure. That was the trouble.

'No-one can possibly believe it,' said Lady Gladys.

'You are a sophisticated woman. They are not sophisticated out there. They will believe it,' said Nellie.

In her anger and enforced shame, she piled everyone in Australia into the same mental tub, and pulled the plug. All because of John Norton.

She barely remembered hearing the name while she was there. Just once Bill Carruthers had spoken about him, warning her of the good and the bad, saying, at one of their many pleasant meetings at the Menzies Hotel, that John Norton was no more than a cockroach, a centipede, a fly on the window-glass.

She had forgotten him.

'Why?' was a word obscured by fury. She sought no reasons. She wished she had known that this viper, this envious sly slug, this bilious shameless hater John Norton had been in Tasmania at the same time she was there. She would have murdered him before the event.

Torturing herself with the waking nightmare, she saw the weathered, gullible faces of her fellow-countrymen reading to each other from Norton's *Truth*. Illiterates with their mouths open, dribbling amazement. The narrow-minded, the defeated, finding fuel for their ignorant prejudices. The self-righteous, waiting for someone else to throw the first stone. Norton.

Norton gloating over the words, congratulating himself that he had waited till she was on the high seas before printing anything.

Thousands upon thousands of words, with stressed capitals as false as gold paint on rotten wood:

MELBA

An Open Letter to Madame Melba concerning Her Champagne Capers, Breaches of Public Faith, outrages against Good Manners, and Insults to Australian Citizens ... From the day of your arrival in Australia you have scattered consternation in your wake ... flouted conventions, kicked up your heels at propriety ... Many a stage star has shot an erratic course before but none with such vicious vulgarity ... Your Melbourne concerts were postponed because 'Madame was indisposed'. You broke faith with the public a second time in Launceston Tasmania would not take you again at any price ... I am not going to dig up the squalid scandal of your married life or of your grass widowhood ... nor resuscitate the sordid story of your alleged intrigue with that French royal router the Duc of Orléans ... Your champagne capers in gay 'Paree', in the Rue de Revelry, in London at the Hotel Cecil, in 'Frisco, Sydney and Launceston, and not least at the Menzies Hotel in Melbourne lends colour to the suspicion ... The careers of great singers who have caressed the cup and drowned their songs in strong drink should cause you to look upon champagne with a shudder ... Your scandalous breaches of public faith and private propriety are no longer to be borne without protest. I invite you to vindicate yourself by civil or criminal process in a court of law.

The words defiled her. The rumour-monger was a cunning enemy. Denial was impossible. He knew she would have to return to Australia and spend a fortune, as well as time, arguing in the courts over each particular point. Saddest of all he knew, as she did, how certain things could not be denied. Intimacy, whether of memory or act, lost its hallowed self-justifications in the glare of day.

In the midst of her agony Nellie thought of George. She was glad he was still hidden away in Oregon.

But then:

'If he came to me now,' she determined, 'we'd make a new life together.'

JE SUIS GEORGES

However, she remembered that George and his father were great readers of the papers, and that old friends in Australia would be prompt in sending clippings from the *Truth*.

So she drove thoughts of George from her mind.

Her mental agitation whirled itself down into the concerts she gave. She began working again.

Relief crept into her days. Miraculously, she began to recover her nerve. The 'Melba manner' came to her aid with its zestful controlling power.

Not for nothing had she learned about the habits of the press. She exploited them. She made very sure that reporters were given full details of her continued triumphs. She knew that any references to Australia in the English papers were faithfully copied by the Australian wire services, so she filled her interviews with positive statements about the Australian tour. People back there would see that she wasn't the least bit fazed by Norton's attack, and be reminded too of what had actually happened.

Life in London was an example as well.

She was 'commanded' to Buckingham Palace by the King and Queen to sing for the French President; the next day, she gave a gala performance for the same notables at Covent Garden; two days later she threw an enormous party at her house in Great Cumberland Place. The guest list, printed in the Australian papers, would speak for itself: Prince Francis of Teck, the Duchess of Devonshire, the Duchess of Abercorn, the Duchess of Marlborough, Lord Sandwich, Mr Alfred de Rothschild, Lord Hardwicke, etc. She sang the Bach-Gounod 'Ave Maria' to the violin, harp, and organ accompaniment of Herr Kubelik, Miss Ada Sassoli, and Mr Landon Ronald.

'You've recovered your pride, I'm pleased to notice,' said Lady Gladys.

'It was never in danger,' Nellie raised her chin.

Her *La Bohème* that year was written about enthusiastically in the *Times*. She went to America again. She triumphed in Berlioz's *Damnation of Faust* and as she travelled around by train she studied for the the title role in Saint-Saëns' opera *Hélène*. Her engagements' calendar was filled for several years ahead: Monte Carlo, London, Paris, and America of course, to which she would return time after time. Once more it was as her family had said: she treated ocean liners as taxicabs, the world as her district, and took a train half-way across a continent in much the same spirit as a stroll around the block.

A letter from Bill Carruthers told her that Norton was incensed at her refusal to answer the attack. The man was splenetic-drunk day and night. Carruthers assured Nellie that no-one in Australia had taken the attack seriously, which was nice of him, though quite, quite untrue. For so-called well-meaning friends had already reported the more outrageous rumours circulating about her in Australia, stories grown from Norton's pages and threatening to take root in national legend: that she needed at least two bottles of champagne before she sang, that she would take a lover in her dressing room before a performance, that she had illegitimate children farmed out everywhere.

She readied herself for years of immersion in her career as she had in the past when emotional storms possessed her.

Then one Christmas in New York it all proved in vain. Her body ceased its resistance; she fell ill with pneumonia. She lay close to death in her suite at the Waldorf Astoria Hotel.

A blizzard blew through the darkened streets of New York, wild flurries of snow drove against the facade of the Waldorf Astoria. People battled along the pavements in fear of their lives. Heroically, the hotel doormen pushed and wrenched the great doors against the wind and cold.

In a blast that might have come from the Rockies a young westerner appeared, shaking snow from his shoulders like a bewildered bear. He wore a thick fur coat and a scarf under his hat, and carried a gift-wrapped parcel and a battered bunch of hothouse roses.

It was George Armstrong.

'Quite a night,' a major-domo greeted him.

'Sure is. Phew.'

George took his bearings. The atmosphere in the foyer was so different from the outside. A tall fir tree glittered with

JE SUIS GEORGES

electric candles. A merry seasonal atmosphere prevailed in the steam-heated air. George brushed snow from his shoulders and found himself descended-upon by staff who offered to take his coat, his parcel, his flowers; but he clung to them as if to his life.

'Madame Melba,' he muttered. 'Is she in?'

This caused a ripple of amusement around the place.

'Oh, she's in, all right.'

They picked George for a stage-door cowboy.

'I'm her son,' George explained.

This was different. The Manager appeared and took his elbow.

'Mr Armstrong? So pleased you're here. Come on up.'

George had no suspicion that his mother was ill until they passed the desk.

'How's the grand lady, Doc?' he heard a clerk ask of a man holding a black bag.

'It's no mere indisposition, I'm afraid. She won't be singing for a while.'

'At least she's alive, though.'

'Just,' said the doctor before anyone could nudge him about the son passing by.

George was shocked. His knees trembled. To think he might have missed her, missed her for ever . . .

Riding up in the elevator the manager told George about the illness. About cancelled concerts, exhaustion, the best doctors, the twenty-four hour care, and the fact that everyone in the hotel was praying for a speedy recovery. They loved her, you see.

Right up until the last minute George had been ready to turn back. Now his doubts and hesitations disappeared.

After making whispered introductions at the door of the suite the manager left him. A young nurse led George inside.

'She's not ready for you yet. It might be some hours.'

'That's okay.'

Wide-eyed, George looked around. His idea of a hotel room had narrowed in recent years to an iron bed, a basin, a dirty window. That's all he and his father had been able to afford in their travels. This luxury took him right back to his early childhood, to Brussels, Paris, London. He wanted to see those places again. He hoped she would live.

'Mr Armstrong?' A dumpy Englishwoman addressed him.

'Yep.'

'I am your mother's personal maid. You're not the least bit like her.'

'I can whistle, that's about all,' George smiled. 'But my cheeks are still frozen.'

'Would you like a glass of brandy?'

'I would, right enough.'

Returning with it, she said:

'We daren't tell her you're here. Not just yet.'

'Yes, I know. I understand,' said George.

'You'll bring her round,' beamed the maid.

He sank to a couch and made himself comfortable. The brandy burned him clean.

'Put your feet up,' said the maid, taking his empty glass.

'I rather think I will,' said George.

He was used to snoozing in unlikely places, and the heat made him drowsy, but he kept his eyes partly open because it was good to watch the pretty young nurses come and go. The things he noticed most here were what was missing from Klamath Falls. The things money could buy. Leisurely opportunity.

He thought: 'If she really wants me to, I'll hang about.'

Sometimes he heard faint cries, and once or twice a decent burst of cussing. That would be her, he thought complacently.

He wished he had come a long time ago.

In the next room Nellie's ribs ached, her head swam with confused impressions. Whenever she woke, the bedclothes ran with sweat. She hated being touched, moved, turned over by her nurses and attendants who seemed out to kill her, so sensitive was she in every part of her body; so inflamed, so molten in her nerve-ends. They bathed her, murmuring reassurance, but she railed against them.

There were other moments when she found herself cool and

becalmed, quite rational, and most beautifully pampered by
the skilled hands around her. Freshly-laundered sheets by a
miracle would be whisked onto the bed and pulled tight; her
forehead would be dabbed for relief by a gentle hand. Her
hair would be done, make-up applied. She would find her
maid at her bedside, sorting through the mountain of mail that
came hourly it seemed . . .

'Where is the mail? Any word from George?' wheezed
Nellie.

The maid met her eye. Then she ducked her head, and
looked towards the door of the room.

A figure stood there.

At first Nellie thought he was the boy bringing flowers, so
off-hand was he, propping up the doorjamb. The cheeky
confidence of these un-servile twentieth century Americans . . .
His winter-reddened features stared at her through the midst
of an enormous bunch of red roses.

'Put them . . .'

'Well, I'm . . .'

'It can't be . . .'

'I'm . . .'

'George?'

'Hi-ya.'

'My boy. My darling . . .'

He rested his gifts on the end of the bed and came around
to the side, where pale fingers reached out to touch him. He
took her hand. The maid retreated tearfully from the room.

'Is it really you?' said Nellie weakly. 'Come closer. Kiss me.'
She was glad that her hair was done, her face freshened; that
her people had made her ready so skilfully.

He kissed her forehead. The face that was famous
throughout the world was small and anxious in his sight.

'It's me all right,' said George with awkward confidence.
Je suis Georges. J'habite à Paris avec ma mère.'

'You've remembered everything,' said Nellie, squeezing his
hand with her depleted strength.

'That's what Dad said, but it's only the one thing,' George
confessed. 'Look, you're all right, aren't you?'

'Don't leave me,' she nodded.

With that, he was gone. What a fright. But only to fetch a chair.

'I won't leave you, Ma'am.'

'How quaint you are . . .'

'What?'

The fever left her feeling light-headed, clear-headed. She saw what he was: a simple, good-hearted youth. No wonder she had previously been unable to draw him away from Charles, despite her many letters. He was the sort of boy who hated to disturb the average. But what had done the trick this time, she wondered?

'Georgie, why . . .'

'Eh? Catch forty winks,' he told her.

No questions. Many thoughts rose in her, but she was too weak to give them expression. What did it matter, this was bliss. She sank back into her pillows and contemplated the wonder of his narrow face and full mouth, his rather untroubled eyes, his air of reliability. He was not a person to worry away at things, to hold them up for examination all the time. To think that she and Charles from their fire had produced a metal of such good medium lustre. She was glad.

A little later she drifted awake. And there he was, wrapped in a blanket, snoring in his chair with his stockinged feet casually resting across the end of her bed.

Later still, the room was flooded with light that hurt her briefly in the head. A ring of people including George stood around her bed wishing her a merry Christmas.

The doctor was there, pronouncing her fit to enjoy the day in moderation.

'Please,' she denied it. 'Christmas?'

More than a week, she realised, had been lost somewhere. And years gained, she thought, as George kissed her and unwrapped his present: a fur cap made from the skins of wild mink, trapped, skinned, prepared and sewn by George himself.

Later again: she wore it as they sipped champagne. George wore a party cap. The maid was slightly tipsy. The doctor entered playing a party whistle. The pretty young nurses, with

JE SUIS GEORGES

much giggling, sang a Christmas carol in conflicting keys. They would not be needed much longer. George watched them open-mouthed. *There's much to do with him*, observed Nellie, her energies beginning again.

'I'm ready for anything,' she declared.

'Two months at least,' warned the doctor, 'before you sing another note.'

'I know. I know.' In one of the lucid intervals of her illness she remembered striking arrangements off the calendar, from the map, releasing her hold on existence. As soon as she had her strength she would sail back to Europe. A dream of heaven: springtime in England with George.

In the evening she ate a supper of thinly sliced ham and steamed vegetables.

'George,' she ventured. 'Why now?'

He knew what she meant. It was the big question between them.

'I figured you needed cheering up. Christmas, and everything.'

It was an evasive answer, partly because he felt guilty about all the times he'd been expected but hadn't come. And he hated the thought of bringing his father into it, the kidnapper he loved, in any negative sort of way. He knitted his brows.

'There were lotsa times I might have come . . . Heck, I'm here, ain't I?'

'I assume you're talking this way to impress me,' said Nellie in parentheses.

'Another thing. Well, *the* thing, actually. Dad.'

'Charles. Yes?'

'He said I had to,' nodded George. 'Before, it was always up to me. But this time he kinda forced me onto the train.'

George was embarrassed. Hopeful.

'Please explain,' said Nellie seriously.

'Dad said that nobody deserved what they wrote about you. Not even you.'

'Not even me,' Nellie faintly repeated.

'He said that the guy, Norton, missed the point. You couldn't be all those things, he said, because what you cared about, number one, was being the best there was.'

'Good old Charlie, a backhander,' Nellie rallied.

George blinked. He was unravelling something. He was almost there.

'You couldn't do all that stuff and still be the best, is what Dad said.'

'I love you,' said Nellie, after a long time.

As each day passed she grew stronger. Mealtimes were like parties with George sitting on the bed coaxing Nellie to eat a little more and build up her strength.

'Take a little more champagne,' he urged.

'No, I mustn't.'

'Oh, be a devil will you, don't be such a schoolmarm.'

'Only one sip,' she conceded, charmed by his accent, his Americanisms: 'Because I am very ill, you must understand that, Georgie.'

'Oh, I do.'

She thought: he is as attentive as a lover. When he finds a wife, she will adore him.

As they talked, she acquired a clear picture of his life over the years. The cabin, the range lands, the men's world without women; she had often tortured herself with the idea of George imprisoned in space and time, of Charles pouring poison in his ear. But it hadn't been like that at all. He'd been a good father to the limit of his abilities. How surprising. Quite suddenly she felt something towards Charles; not love, of course, but it was as if now that all bonds had been cut they had a sort of marriage again, for they were equals in their aloneness, he without a woman, she without a man, and having this son between them. She had a fine sense of balance. Of course, she resolved a little grimly, there would be no sharing him out on account of the ten years' separation.

'George, stay with me . . .'

'What? I'm here, ain't I?' he grinned, pouring the last trickle of champagne into his glass.

'Yes. And polish up that dreadful cowboy talk,' she smiled.

'That's what Dad always says.'

JE SUIS GEORGES

'Does he? Good. You must obey your parents, then.'

He knew what she was after, she sensed, but he wasn't ready to commit himself. She would have to be careful not to overplay her hand. A few more days, perhaps, and then she might give him a surprise: a nice pigskin travelling wallet stuffed with first class steamer tickets for Cherbourg, and a wad of crisp new banknotes to spend as he wished. She was not above buying him.

'Georgie, you have a grandfather who's growing very old now, uncles and aunts, loads of cousins and they'd all be so proud to see you, a fine handsome young man . . .'

'I remember, I think.'

'Do you? Your grandfather?'

'Whiskers, shiny boots, a pewter watch chain, cigars. The story about Wee Sandy, who peed his name in the snow.'

'Good Lord,' said Nellie.

'No, I mean it was Dad who told me things about grandpa.'

'I know men tell stories when they're in their cups, but I thought my father was different,' said Nellie, amused.

'I don't remember anything much,' said George. 'Except . . . except . . .'

'Yes?'

'All those times we had in Paris.'

'We'll go there again . . .' said Nellie, taking an opportunity to lay the bait.

'You mean . . .'

'We'll go everywhere together,' Nellie suddenly was unable to restrain herself. 'George, shall we? As soon as I'm well?'

A nurse entered the room, the prettiest one. George followed her with his eyes.

'Bright lights. Pretty girls,' Nellie whispered.

'Out you go, Mr Armstrong,' ordered the nurse briskly.

In the night Nellie became feverish again, giving them all a fright. George was unable to sleep for worry, except towards morning he went out like a log. He had his own bedroom now, just along the corridor from Nellie's suite. He woke late, around eleven, hurriedly dressed, and went in to hear the latest from the nurses. It was good news. She was through it.

On opening his mother's door, he found her sitting up in bed answering her mail.

'They said you were a little peppier this morning.'

'I woke absolutely soaked in perspiration, but my head was clear as a bell.'

'That's good.'

'George,' she could hold back no longer, 'I will be fit to travel soon. I am sending for steamer tickets this morning. Will you come on the boat to England with me, and make me better?'

'Sure,' said George with simplicity.

'Oh, darling,' she stared at him, and clutched the bedcovers tightly. George shrugged and smiled, feeling a little awkward.

'Sure I will,' he repeated. 'It's up to me, and I want to. So I damn well will come on the boat to England with you.'

They kissed.

With that, all Nellie's papers slid to the floor and she stretched luxuriously, feeling energy flow through her weakened limbs.

'How long will you be able to stay? What will your father say?'

'I reckon he knows it's your turn,' said George.

Nellie knew then, with absolute certainty, that a new life, a new epoch in her life had begun. If she was lucky it would see her through. What fun they'd have together. She closed her eyes, unable to believe her happiness. She had something to work for now. A new beginning.

'You okay?' George wondered.

33

Jolly
Nice People

She was in her early forties when George came back, an age when she might perhaps have slowed down a little, given fewer concerts, selected the easy path, taken, in their abundance, the gifts of her gift. No chance of it.

Long ago in a lovers' pact she had made the world a private possession; that had failed except in memory and indeed was a phantom of sentiment compared with the practical life she now built around herself. She saw in others how time devoured hope with the roar of a hungry beast; in her it was otherwise, the penalties of time were infinitely deferred. Somehow secretly within herself she was still a young woman astounding the world with her prolific abilities. Having kept her voice for so long she disbelieved in its loss. The rocket was risen, it hung at the apogee for years. From there it was possible to make only one dip down, ever, and she did not allow herself to think about that. At forty-four, she knew people already defeated by the compromises and disappointments of middle life, who went about querulously complaining, who counted out their remaining years like misers and quailed at the trick played on them by the brevity of human life. She was unlike them. She wanted to see such people no longer. Their children would soon have them in bath chairs. She hardly understood them at all. She was managing George, a perplexing handful, at the time. Those others received no invitations to her houses, to her parties. Time was at her service, why not at other people's? They had only to try, she believed. Her voice went on possessing her, it possessed her audiences, pealing out undimmed, unblunted, over the heads of breathless admirers on three continents. Her art nourished her energies. When she thought about Larger Questions, the Ends and Outcomes of Philosophy, as she did when prompted by interviewers, then an image loomed in the back of her mind. It had been there at difficult seasons of her life, especially late at night in the bad hours when (immediately after Philippe, long before George) her resolution had wavered most uncharacteristically. She knew of a God who waited silently ahead of her, grizzly bearded, rather like an old Scottish Presbyterian, always expecting just a little more, demanding effort and perfection.

Sometimes, as if in a dream, she took from the secret drawer of a jewellery cabinet a small amber keepsake still threaded to its faded *moiré* ribbon. She spoke the name of her long-gone lover who was never seen at any of her performances; touched the cool resin to her cheek. It seemed so lax and dull now, whereas once it had crackled with electricity. She and Philippe had never crossed paths again, even when finding themselves in the same city at the same time. Wien, Bruxelles, Milano . . . Oh, it was a weary old keepsake, this love denied; it was so unliving.

Philippe and the Archduchess Maria Dorothea had no children.

She had George.

When she brought him to England from America they spent a dreamlike summer together. Nellie leased a thatched cottage in the Home Counties where the two of them began to know each other. On the wicket gate was a creamily painted nameplate: 'Coombe Cottage'. George whistled and practised his golf strokes in the garden, while Nellie watched from a rose-wreathed terrace, taking tea.

'If these walls could speak, George,' she called to him. His

JOLLY NICE PEOPLE

ball bounced up under her table.

'How come?' he looked around. She poured tea and detained him. 'Well, from here, if you look between the yew and alder, you will see the point where, according to tradition, King Henry watched impatiently for the hoisting of the flag that was to tell him that Anne Boleyn had been beheaded on the tower.'

'I'll be dog-gone.'

'George,' said Nellie warningly.

'"Cripes"?' he suggested.

'No.'

'"Fascinating", then.'

'Mmm. Better. A little *frisson* of Americanism is nice. But not too much.'

George was happy to oblige to the best of his abilities.

Nellie wrote to her old teacher, Madame Marchesi, in Paris: 'George is with me and sends his love. We revel in the garden here and enjoy ourselves to our hearts' content. Do please come and take a holiday with us. I shall arrange to sing *La Bohème* while you are here . . . The cottage is only forty minutes drive from London, and I have decided not to work so hard for the future and devote it to my beloved George, who is an angel . . .'

She bought his clothes from a Bond Street tailor, equipped him with premium-quality luggage, hired a splendid hunter from excellent stables, and cast her eye around for suitable young friends his own age. They went to garden parties and concerts. He listened to her sing, his chin cupped on his hands, his eyes shining. They hardly ever raked over the past because for both of them this was a recapitulation of the best that had been. At Covent Garden, George was fascinated by the backstage life. She often found him deep in conversation with the stage hands, or in quiet talk with one or other of the seamstresses. People liked him, he was unassuming, undemanding, not out for himself all the time, a good listener. He made friends easily; in fact, she had to face it, made them very well without her, for when Nellie returned to Coombe Cottage one day (she could not always be there) he was sitting with his boots up on the garden table, smoking a cheroot in the manner of his father, in the company of a sharp-looking young man. When George introduced him she was astonished: it was Jack Armstrong, George's cousin.

'Dad told me to look up all my relations. Well, I have,' said George disarmingly.

He and Jack then leapt on their horses and rode off to the Sheaftossers Arms in the village. Telling herself to be calm, Nellie waited hours for the sound of their return. They stumbled in long after dark, chortling and hiccoughing. She masked her annoyance with chilly politeness, but George was oblivious to the nuances of good manners, and Jack was drunk. The pattern was repeated whenever Jack visited. Nellie had reason to believe that on more than one of their outings they spent time with village girls. She resented Jack, who had the wildness of Charles in his youth without the easy charm.

'If there is to be much more of this,' thought Nellie darkly, 'I shall have to take George out to Australia and put him to work there.'

She talked around the problem with Lady de Grey. She hardly dared say that what she really wanted for George was a good marriage, children, a close family circle she could make her own. English, if at all possible.

'Have you thought of a tutor?' asked Gladys.

'Mmm . . . Why?' replied Nellie cautiously.

'To prepare him for Oxford, of course. I think Oxford rather than Cambridge, don't you?'

'Yes, Oxford,' breathed Nellie.

A new vision of George sprang into Nellie's imagination: an Oxford man, witty, charming, and casually in the know. Why hadn't she thought of it before? Gladys's easy assumption of the 'right thing' for George was such a help.

'He would be "the Yank at Oxford",' continued Gladys with a smile. 'Quite the success, I should think.'

When she told George he said, in his easy accepting way, 'Sure. Why not? Jack's preparing for Oxford too.'

This rather deflated Nellie. When the tutor came, however, clutching Latin primers and geometry texts under his arm, she

JOLLY NICE PEOPLE

noticed that George applied himself to his books rather well: his easygoing nature hid a capacity for learning, she supposed. The tutor encouraged her in this belief.

Even when he rode off with Jack he carried a book in his pocket. Nellie believed it was Euclid, but it was only a spelling guide. The tutor had begun from a point of despair.

'Mother,' George said one day, returning from one of these outings, the aim of which was to clear the cobwebs from the brain, 'I've met some jolly nice people . . .'

'Hmm?' frowned Nellie. 'Friends of Jack's?'

'Sort of. Their name is Otway.'

'Otway . . .' pondered Nellie. She had heard the name. They were certainly the right sort, from what she remembered: indeed, rather better than the right sort.

'Don't they own the Tufton art collection?' she asked.

'Something like that,' said George vaguely. The closest he had come to the Otways' house was the stableyard, where Colonel Otway had showed off his horses, while his daughter Ruby and her cousin Ayliffe watched.

Later he and Jack had chatted to the girls, who had then ridden off on their bicycles.

'The Otways' daughter,' George came to the point, 'Ruby, thinks you're rather smashing.'

'Ruby,' smiled Nellie. 'What a lovely name. Well, ask her for a visit, why don't you?'

'Could you do it, Mother?' asked George unabashedly. 'It might be better.'

'So it's a case of using the Melba advantages,' smiled Nellie.

'I guess it is,' said George.

'Oh, Georgie,' Nellie ruffled his hair and kissed him. 'You're sweet on someone.'

'I guess I am,' nodded George, in his simple uncomplicated way.

'Puppy fat' thought Nellie, on first setting eyes on Ruby Otway.

Then she revised her impression. A closer look showed wide serene features and a gentle complexion.

Her speaking voice was lovely.

455

MELBA

'Madame Melba,' she said, slightly overwhelmed, 'I think you are the absolute tops.'

'Thank you, Ruby,' said Nellie. She was little amazed. Ruby was hardly more than a schoolgirl. But then:

'*Merci de votre invitation, Madame . . . Heureux de faire votre connaissance.*'

Shy as she was in English, Ruby astonished Nellie by continuing with great confidence in French. She asked about the composers Nellie had met, the authors, the statesmen. In this foreign tongue Ruby was a more confident person. And it was nice. She had opinions, and they were good ones. It made an immediate bridge of communication while George looked on, benignly puzzled. Chatting away, Nellie and Ruby linked arms and walked through the cottage, out to the terrace, where a splendid tea table was laid ready. George followed. Holding Ruby's chair, he received a delightful glance of gratitude from both Nellie and Ruby for his natural good manners.

'*Merci, Georges . . .*'

The child was something of a prodigy, Nellie realised, turning her full attention back to her. At one point Ruby switched to German with a most engaging erudition.

It was only in English that she returned to her hesitant, blushing, schoolgirl self.

'How old are you, Ruby, dear?' asked Nellie.

'Seventeen,' Ruby replied.

'Gracious me.'

'It's Ruby who should be going up to Oxford,' said George frankly.

'Oh, one simply does what one can,' said Ruby blushingly.

'I'm a lunkhead with languages,' confessed George.

'"Lunkhead"?' smiled Ruby.

'One of George's Americanisms,' said Nellie.

'How nice, though,' said Ruby.

'I must say I never had any trouble with languages at all,' said Nellie, feeling a need to boost George's bloodline. 'Latin and French rolled off my tongue. Later I learnt Italian, all singers do, and German too, of course.' She began an aphorism

JOLLY NICE PEOPLE

from Goethe, in the original German. Ruby smiled anxiously when Nellie made a mistake.

She thought Madame Melba the most wonderful person she had ever met.

After the first visit, Ruby and her cousin Ayliffe cycled over to Coombe Cottage almost every day. George and Ruby sat on a blanket on the lawns, among his books.

Nellie watched them from an open window, while Ayliffe leafed through her scrapbooks.

'*Fuero, Fueris, Fuerit, Fuerimus* . . .' said Ruby.

'*Fuero, Fueris, Fuerit, Fueramus* . . .' repeated George.

'No, *Fuerimus*. You keep shifting from future perfect to pluperfect . . .'

'Do I?'

'It's all a bit much, isn't it, George,' said Ruby, dropping the book.

'Oh, I don't know. It would be worth it to get to Oxford.'

Ruby sucked a finger thoughtfully: 'But when she travels, won't she want you to go with her?'

'I guess she will. But she's rather caught up in the idea of the university.'

'Oh,' said Ruby. 'Nothing happens there. The scholar seeks, it's the artist who finds.'

She closed her eyes, and let the sun warm her face. Her ears strained, hoping to catch a sound of Melba at her singing exercises.

One day George took her by the shoulders and kissed her. The touch of her lips was like a trailed soft breeze; so tantalising. He kissed her again. She leaned away from him a little.

'Very nice, George,' she said in a small voice.

'I don't frighten you?'

'You? My dear George . . .'

It was a blissful, frustrating condition he found himself in. He wanted to advance their friendship as far as possible, yet at the same time wanted the summer never to end. He was in love. Ruby wanted to be with him all the time.

Invitations went back and forth.

MELBA

George went 'cubbing' with Colonel Otway and his friend Captain Monty Padgett.

Nellie held a garden party: the Otways came, and were very impressed to find Lady Gladys de Grey there.

A dinner was held at the Otways, where Nellie and George made differing impressions. After they'd gone, Ruby overheard her parents talking:

'I like George,' said Mrs Otway. 'Except I have great trouble telling whether these Americans are clever or not. I mean, everything is overlaid with a veneer of *bonhomie*. No English education, of course.'

'What about Oxford?' asked Colonel Otway.

'That's off, Ruby tells me, though his mother doesn't know it yet.'

'He's a good chap,' said the Colonel. 'They're a jolly nice pair, Melba and the boy.'

'One is born to a certain position, of course.'

'Hrrumph,' said Colonel Otway warningly, catching sight of Ruby emerging from the library in her nightgown, clutching a book.

'The Armstrongs are a fine old county family,' continued his wife in her loud voice. 'But I'm not really sure, my dear Jocelyn, if "Madame Melba" is absolutely and utterly the right sort.'

'Mother!' Ruby confronted her: 'I will have you know that Madame Melba is nothing less than the the greatest living voice in the world, a performer of genius, and a friend to some of the most supreme artists that have ever lived.'

'I would not deny it,' said Mrs Otway. Her daughter overwhelmed her sometimes.

'If George asks me to marry him, I shall,' announced Ruby. She ran up the stairs and disappeared.

'I would like a glass of brandy,' sighed the Colonel.

'I knew it would come to this. She's so headstrong,' said Mrs Otway.

'Ruby *will* have what she wants, m'dear.'

'Nor have you ever denied it to her.'

JOLLY NICE PEOPLE

'Mother,' said George to Nellie a few days later. 'About Oxford.'

'Yes?'

'Well, about Ruby, actually . . .'

'Yes. Yes?'

'What if, well, you know, what if I skipped Oxford altogether.'

'Oxford. Ruby. What are you trying to say, George?' smiled Nellie.

'Oh, nothing,' said George.

Nellie thought: 'I shan't push him.'

Nellie wrote to her sisters in Australia:

'My impression is that the world has become more youthful. We have a new century, a new king full of vitality and *bonhomie*, and I have a new life ahead of me. Nothing can spoil that for me this time . . .'

There followed a long dissertation about the lineal descent of the Otways.

Belle, on reading this letter, raised her eyebrows and said to Annie, 'What do you think of all that?'

'We've often said how nice it would be if she found someone to marry again. Well, she has. His name is George.'

'Where does that leave Ruby?' wondered Annie.

The summer over, people moved back to London. Nellie and George moved into Nellie's house at Great Cumberland Place, and society resumed the serious business of smoothing entries, opening doors, making connections. George joined one of the better clubs. Ruby began learning Italian, and was soon able to follow *libretti* with complete understanding. In Madame Melba's box at Covent Garden, on many nights of glorious entertainment, sat Captain Jocelyn Tufton Farrant Otway, of the Royal Berkshire regiment, his wife Eva May, a direct descendant of Edward III (1312–1377), their daughter Ruby, and Mr George Armstrong.

At the proper time an engagement was announced, and a splendid party held at 7 Park Lane, the Otways' London residence.

MELBA

In Klamath Falls, Oregon, Charles Armstrong opened a letter from his former wife, the first directly addressed to him in many years. 'There is to be a wedding in December . . .' it began.

It was clear to Charles from the way Nellie wrote that the entire business was the product of her spellbinding ways.

'Poor Ruby,' he said to himself, on his side of the world.

He replied tactfully, saying no, he would be unable to come to the wedding, he would be snowbound by then. Separately he wrote to George, sending his heartfelt best wishes, while privately he thought: 'If Miss Ruby Otway is as bright as they say she is, I give her six months, maybe a year, before she wants to be herself again.'

And he added to himself: 'Then we'll see what sort of stuff Georgie's made of.'

Nellie was disappointed about Oxford. But the marriage, detailed in an article in the *Times* of Wednesday, 19 December 1906, eclipsed all other hopes:

'A large congregation assembled yesterday afternoon in St George's Church, Hanover Square, to witness the marriage of Mr George Nesbitt Armstrong with Miss Ruby Otway, only daughter of Colonel and Mrs Jocelyn Otway of 7, Park Lane. The bridegroom is the son of Mr Charles Frederick Nesbitt Armstrong and of Mrs Armstrong, better known as Mme Melba, the famous singer, and grandson of the late Sir Andrew Armstrong. The church was decorated for the occasion with white flowers, arranged with tall Kentia palms, interspersed with foliage plants. The full choir of St George's took part in the service, and the rite was performed by the Rev David Anderson, the rector. The bride, who was given away by her father, was attended by nine bridesmaids: Miss Ayliffe Otway, her cousin, Miss Margaret Ryle, Miss Janet Mackay, Miss Julie Myers, Miss Ada Sassoli, Miss Valerie Churchill, Miss Georgina Appleton, Miss Fay Zarifi, and Miss Barbara Jones. Mr Jack Armstrong, cousin of the bridegroom, was best man. After the ceremony the wedding party reassembled at 7, Park Lane, where Mrs Otway held a reception, and later in the afternoon

JOLLY NICE PEOPLE

Mr and Mrs George Nesbitt Armstrong left for Highcliffe Castle, Christchurch, lent them for the honeymoon by Colonel the Hon. Edward Stuart Wortley.'

Thus was George inducted into the upper part of the English upper classes. Nellie's pride was complete. She sang the Bach-Gounod 'Ave Maria' at the reception, accompanied by Miss Ada Sassoli.

Ruby almost swooned.

Making a speech, George impressed everyone with his restrained politeness, his naturalness of expression. There were rough edges but they were expected from an American. More interesting, socially, was Madame Melba, who took great pains never to put a foot wrong. She settled £7,000 a year on the young couple, a veritable fortune.

Nellie thought: in a day or two the papers in Australia will contain cabled copies of the *Times* report. That will silence the scoffers. It was disappointing, of course, that no mention was made of George's Australian grandfather, but that was the way things were done here: they hated the idea of 'humble origins'. It was better not to emphasise them.

After their time at Highcliffe Castle the newlyweds left for America. Nellie followed them in a while: she had a $3,000 per-performance engagement to fill at the opening of Mr Oscar Hammerstein's Manhattan Opera House, which promised to be a great event in the musical history of New York. The Met, Hammerstein's rival, had for years regarded Melba as its own. But at the Met she was never quite allowed to be the *prima donna assoluta*. It rankled. In a fit of change to do with this, and with keeping herself sharp, confounding people's expectations, and for sentimental reasons too because she always liked a self-made man, she threw in her lot with the colourful Hammerstein, a theatre-builder, businessman, cigar millionaire.

'Mr Hammerstein is a genius,' announced Nellie.

The public was with her in their tens of thousands. The story of the 'opera war' with the Met was in all the American papers, every day. 'The crowd was so large at the Manhattan Opera

House last night, when Melba and Bonci sang in *Rigoletto*, wrote the New York *Times* early in the New Year, 'that it was necessary for Mr Hammerstein to telephone to Police Headquarters at 7 o'clock for a squad to control the mob of people in the lobby.'

'How splendidly exciting,' said Ruby. At the time of speaking they were crossing a railway bridge over the Mississippi River in total darkness and freezing cold.

Ruby, George realised, was resentful that she, Melba's daughter-in-law, was not there in New York as part of the great *diva*'s entourage.

Putting an arm around her, George reminded her of Nellie's promise that after the honeymoon they could go wherever they liked with her. 'So there'll be plenty more of it,' he grunted. They had their own money too. A good heap.

She shrank away from his words, from his touch.

'I think,' she insisted, 'there'll never be another moment in opera history quite like this one.'

'It's only singing,' said George peevishly.

'Only!'

He hated to be lectured on the subject of his mother, even by Ruby.

Especially by Ruby, after a while.

For the honeymoon continued, a long drawn-out business. Things had gone badly at Highcliffe Castle; they were worse in ships' cabins, and in the sleeping compartments of American trains. First class all the way of course but Ruby might as well have been going steerage. Ruby, precious desirable Ruby, George found, often had headaches and liked to sleep curled in a tight unapproachable ball. When George tried to unprise her, she was revolted by his eagerness.

'You've changed,' George accused her. 'Think of all the kissing we used to do.'

'Oh, I don't mind the kissing part,' said Ruby hurtfully. That was like a child's game to her: a goodnight kiss, a goodbye kiss.

There was no way around it. Ruby, who'd been just as anxious as he was to be married, had tied the knot for different reasons, apparently. Sensuous desire, bodily appetite, even

JOLLY NICE PEOPLE

quiet intimate pleasure had nothing to do with it.

'It's all so strange to me. I suppose I'll get used to it in time,' he said evasively. 'It's been a shock.'

'Didn't your mother tell you anything?'

'Mother doesn't have a coarse streak like you,' said Ruby, turning her head away.

'She must have done it at least once,' said George.

'Filth!' said Ruby, slapping him.

One day in Texas, in a fit of temper and frustration, George knocked her to the ground. There were no witnesses.

'I hate you!' screamed Ruby.

He pulled her hair, then drew back, trembling in astonishment at the depths of his rage.

They could not believe it of each other. They were like strangers. Charles saw it all but said nothing. The best teacher, in his experience, was time.

Time gave the marching orders to everyone. On their return to New York, to join Nellie, the young Mr and Mrs Armstrong found themselves hailed as celebrities. Separately, because they were hardly talking, they resolved to present a united front, and do their best. Nellie had taken an apartment for them in the Barcelona, at 59th Street and 7th Avenue. She was not there to greet them. While Ruby unpacked her bags, George drank two glasses of whisky to steady his battered nerves. They went to the St Regis Hotel, only to be told that Madame Melba was perpetually down at the Manhattan, from early morning until midnight. They caught a cab to the unfashionable part of town where Hammerstein had built his theatre.

Reporters mobbed them in the laneway outside the Manhattan.

'Which opera of your mother's do you like best?' George was asked.

'*La Bohème*,' he guessed.

'What about your mother?'

'She likes them all.'

Ruby smiled at the logic, and pointed out: 'Madame Melba does not sing in anything she does not like.' Staring at her, the reporters turned their attention back to George.

MELBA

'Play or sing yourself?'

'No.'

'Not even a polyphone,' intruded Ruby once more. She was the sort of wife who shaped her husband's opinions, it seemed.

'I play golf,' said George, trying to lighten the moment. 'I've brought all my clubs with me.'

'Will you please let us through, now?' asked Ruby.

They at last reached Nellie backstage. 'My darlings!' she cried, embracing them. 'My children . . . How was Texas?'

'Very nice.'

'Ruby?'

'Lovely, thank you.'

'Well, you must be tired,' said Nellie after a pause. She had expected a bit of fire, giggling, hand-holding. What else was love? She gestured around her at the busy scene-building and flat-painting. 'Isn't this all so exciting? We've had a wonderful season and now at last *La Bohème* is going ahead.'

She called Hammerstein over: 'Meet my darlings, Oscar.

'How are the lovebirds? Come to see your wonderful mother in action? Ready for the big night?'

Hammerstein chomped on a cigar and watched George and Ruby. When their faces turned away from Nellie their expressions changed. Hammerstein read the signs: thwarted passion, mistaken expectations, boredom, inequality, musical snobbery, suppressed rage, and even, in the case of George, youthful booziness.

'Those kids are in trouble,' he confided to Nellie.

'Nonsense, Oscar,' Nellie laughed.

It was the last night at the Manhattan. Ruby and George watched as Nellie sang '*Addio di Mimi*' from Act III of *La Bohème*. The stage was deep in artificial snow, Nellie's face expressive as she sang the tender aria of farewell, flickeringly beautiful in the pastel artificiality of the setting.

It took Ruby's breath away. Her hand stole into George's and she clutched it tight from an overwhelming emotion.

'So beautiful,' she whispered.

At the end the applause, the shouts, the cries of 'Melba! Melba! Melba!', the foot stamping and the masses of flowers

JOLLY NICE PEOPLE

borne up to the stage caused tears to run down Ruby's face.

When Hammerstein and Melba came on stage together there was redoubled thunder.

George stole a sideways look at Ruby. 'I love her,' he thought. 'She is only young. I will be very patient.'

Nellie's speech from the stage was one of the happiest she had ever made:

'I have never enjoyed any season in America so much as the one now closed. All through I have been in splendid health and spirit; I feel I have never sung better; I will never forget the kindness with which I have been received. I am proud to have been associated with Mr Hammerstein in the launching of his Manhattan Opera House. What courage Mr Hammerstein has shown and what wonders he has done. His pluck appealed to me from the first, and I leave as I came, his loyal friend and admirer.'

34

No Misunderstandings

'Those kids are in trouble.'

Back in England, Nellie mulled over Hammerstein's words. She thought them exaggerated, misdirected. George and Ruby were at odds, perhaps, but this was usual in young marriages. And they were of a new generation. Their problems were not overwhelming. It would be so easy for them, with Nellie's help, to avoid the mistakes she and Charles had made; they had plenty of money, for one thing; neither was eaten-up by the insatiable demands of a creative gift or by stubborn pride and resentment; neither had any trouble with the idea of a life moderately devoted to the pursuit of leisure and the arts. George would soon have a commission in the Royal Berkshires. He was often at his club. Ruby had her language classes. They were both devoted to Nellie. It was true that Ruby went to her room early when there were no guests. At times, sulkiness was in the air as thick as molasses. Each had faults that would need correcting in time, but were manifestly correctable. Ruby liked nothing better than to go to the opera, and was a superb conversationalist on intellectual matters. These were hardly failures in Nellie's eyes. George was proud of her when she showed what she knew. French, German, and Italian spoken with the flair of a seasoned diplomat. Literature and philosophy: why, she was like a brilliant little shark, the way she devoured each scrap of human knowledge. Their bedroom manners? These were very much their own concern. Nellie used her eyes, and Ruby's paleness, George's reticence she explained to herself as 'settling in'. Nothing more.

She resolved on a long sea voyage.

'To Australia,' she announced. 'Ruby darling, you will love my old father,'

'I'm sure I shall,' said Ruby brightly. 'I've heard so much about him.'

Ruby linked arms with George, thinking, 'With a third on our travels we won't be thrown so irredeemably upon each other.'

Marriage was tolerable for Ruby with Nellie close by.

In Nellie's mind there were other reasons for a visit to Australia apart from George and Ruby. She was still weak after her illness and needed sustained rest. She longed to see her father again. The Norton attack, while still making her flush with anger and shame every time she thought of it, had to be faced, had to be stared down. Her friend the journalist Bill Carruthers wrote again, saying it had all blown over: she thanked him, but privately doubted it. There were untold Australians who had heard *of* her, but had not *heard* her.

That was the point.

She renewed her longing to put people right, which was her oldest ambition; it was another version of how, at the beginning, the first beginning, she had longed to put the English right about a mere colonial.

And she needed something new all the time. She had to confess it. George had done the trick for a while, for those few blissful months at the cottage, before her joy had rotated to encompass Ruby as well. The triumph with Hammerstein had been splendid, but on their return, England seemed dull for once. There was a certain habitual smoothness about her position in England now. The social world of the upper upper-classes was all very well to conquer, but to live in it, as of habit, was not enough. She would confess this further aspect of it to no-one, but she had nothing left to conquer in England now, only needing to maintain her dominance at Covent Garden. She planned to go through to her twentieth, then to her twenty-fifth anniversary when she would be past her own half-century. That would be in 1913.

She trembled a little at the voracity of time.

A tropical night, the RMS *Oruba* moored off Colombo, the engines stopped, a moonlit silence, the merest breath of breeze across the water, and the only relief to be found on deck. At three in the morning Nellie, one figure among several dotted about, sat in a deck chair enjoying the silence, the otherworldliness, the quiet lap of water against the sides of the ship and the tantalising distant vision of the blurry tropical stars. People fanned themselves. They did not speak. The voyage had been wonderfully successful. With George and Ruby the 'Armstrong party' formed an inseparable trio at deck games, saloon parties, and celebration dinners at the Captain's table. Madame Melba was a great sport and joined in all activities. She invariably partnered herself with the younger Mrs Armstrong and the two played to win.

Now she heard the distinct sound of a small shrill scream followed by muffled weeping. It came, Nellie realised with horror, from the open window of George and Ruby's deckside cabin.

'Shut up, for Christ's sake,' George's voice muttered.

'*Never* call yourself a gentleman,' wept Ruby.

A shuddering groan. Silence. The skin prickled on the back of Nellie's neck. Was she the only one listening?

'I hate you,' came in a harsh whisper: echo and silence, two voices, almost in unison.

'I hate you.'

In the morning Nellie studied their white, drawn faces across the breakfast table. No explanations were given, none requested. The voyage continued.

The Melbourne *Argus* of 30 August 1907:

'Among the passengers from London on the RMS *Oruba*, which reached Fremantle this morning, were Madame Melba

NO MISUNDERSTANDINGS

nd her son and daughter-in-law, Mr George and Mrs
Armstrong. Madame Melba is travelling under the name of
Mrs Charles Armstrong.

'When press representatives approached Madame Melba she
expressed surprise at having been discovered, but said: "You
can tell the people of Australia that I made this trip purely
unprofessionally on account of ill-health. I must have rest. I
shall reside in Victoria at Ercildoune, near Ballarat, the
residence of the late Sir Samuel Wilson, where I shall stay from
September for six months".

'Will you sing here at all?'

'"No", said Madame Melba with emphasis; "I am to have
a thorough rest, and at the end of my vacation I must fulfil
a most important engagement in America. My European
engagements have been booked so far ahead that I shall not
be able to visit Australia professionally for three years yet. But,
oh, you don't know how I have longed to visit the dear old
place once more. We have had such awful weather in London.
The sun has not been visible for weeks."'

While Nellie spoke, the reporters glanced with shy curiosity
at George and Ruby.

'How do you like Australia, Mrs Armstrong?'

'It's far too early to say,' smiled Ruby. Her voice was like
a pretty icicle in the great heat of Fremantle.

'What do you do, Mr Armstrong?' George was asked.

'Do?' he repeated.

'My husband is a "gentleman",' answered Ruby, alluding
to George's seven thousand a year. The reporters wrote it
down. Dressed in creams and greys, the young couple showed
considerable *savoir-vivre*. Madame Melba, it appeared, was
intensely proud of them.

They were whisked away by motor car to lunch at
Government House.

Ruby had been rather looking forward to Australia.
Somehow, she thought, there she would be able to separate
herself from the constant presence of George: the shimmering
distances, the tang of eucalyptus in the air, the shaded
swimming holes and long sandy beaches of summer. She had

been told about these things by the few Australians she had met. By Nellie, especially. Closeness was what she hated in marriage.

But Fremantle and Perth astonished her. The geography was perverse. It was no place for people. She felt cast away on a sandy, salty wilderness. The heat clamped around her head like an iron band. At lunch the ham sweated, and a whole variety of foodstuffs tasted tinny.

After Fremantle they sailed through the frightening swell of the Great Australian Bight, and disembarked at Adelaide.

Here the reporters pressed in again. It was George's turn to be ironical.

'My wife? Oh, my wife likes nothing better than to ride with her legs astride the saddle and her hair flying free,' he said with a smile, to the correspondent from the Sydney *Bulletin*.

They caught the overnight train into Victoria. Even George was beginning to wonder where they were being taken. Australia. It was nothing like Texas or Oregon. The distances were American in scale, but after days of travel the places where they arrived were exactly like the ones they had left.

Dawn came, and Ruby faced again the emptiness, the featurelessness. The train rattled along. When they neared Ballarat it stopped and deposited them at a small, lonely siding. They drove to Ercildoune in a convoy of motor cars. The dust boiled up and drifted back into their eyes; grass was everywhere baked to a weedy straw, it neither shone nor waved like proper pasture; light revealed nothing, it merely hurt one's eyes; then there was the ever-present smell of dead animals, the sight of cattle bones and rotted sheep with crows perched on their swollen carcases.

Ercildoune, to Ruby's astonishment, was an oasis of green. A house in the baronial style, it had gardeners, shady English trees, ponds, and secluded walks. A petrol engine chugged in the distance, drawing water from a spring, while sprinklers sent arcs of water pattering against full rich foliage. There were maids, footmen, butlers and cooks, all employed ahead of time by Nellie in her passion for organisation.

It was not enough. Homesickness invaded Ruby.

NO MISUNDERSTANDINGS

She ordered the curtains drawn in her room, and breathed the slightly musty coolness. She tried to persuade herself that the feeling of being trapped, that had been growing within her ever since they left England, was all in her imagination.

Downstairs a stack of newspapers awaited them and Nellie was delighted to find that far from being attacked, the various articles about her gave a new sense of established position.

Ruby saw herself described as having 'the knack of liking the same things as her decided relative by marriage'.

'Is that the impression I give?' she wondered to herself. The long sea voyage and the progress across Australia had shown another side of Nellie to Ruby. She was a different person when there were no concerts to give. It was day after day of domestic arrangements, routines of dressing, eating, bantering with middle-aged males; an unvaried, unsubtle domination of everyone around. Ruby liked to sequester herself with a book, but whenever she did George and his mother took it as a personal affront.

On their second day at Ercildoune she found a shady corner of the verandah, where to satisfy a craving for England that was almost physical in its intensity she opened a novel by Thomas Hardy.

She had read two words when footsteps came towards her along the brown patterned tiles.

'They like you,' said George, placing the Sydney *Bulletin* in her hand. 'They think you're a pretty lively little *femme*.'

Ruby gave an irritated sigh. In private they had altogether stopped being polite to each other.

She read: 'Ruby is a short person of just nineteen years, with star-bright dark eyes, the loveliest of complexions, and a small, delicate, parrot-beaked nose. She rides astride when in the country, and lets her hair blow loose. But to hear her conversing in French and German (in a drawing-room where there were some foreigners who knew no English) is to believe that she has had unusual advantages. She seems to have read everything and been everywhere, and the overwhelming Melba hasn't even begun to whelm Colonel Jocelyn's one ewe lamb.'

Ruby hurled the magazine at George. 'I can see what your

mother has had to put up with, if they write in such a free and easy manner about people,' she said.

'It's our turn now,' frowned George.

He showed her another article where he was described as wearing corsets.

'Yes,' she laughed. 'I know what is meant. It's because your mother is always telling you to stand with your shoulders thrown back.'

At night before composing herself for sleep Nellie's ears strained for the sound of unusual noises. Muffled thud, book striking wall, slam of cupboard door? There was always something new.

At last it was time to meet the family, who arrived at Ercildoune in a convoy of motor cars.

Nellie waited at the top of the steps as her father climbed to greet her. The rest of them, brothers, sisters, in-laws, held back.

David Mitchell's devotion to Nellie was obvious, and it extended to George. The three put their arms around each other on the front steps. Ruby waited as tears filled Nellie's eyes. 'Lass, lass,' her father murmured. Ruby at last was introduced, but she felt absolutely excluded, as if, in the old man's eyes, she was something under glass. His hand clasping hers felt dry and work-roughened.

Nellie's brothers and sisters were about as different from the *prima donna* as could be imagined. They were unaffectedly homely and natural, whereas Nellie always made a point of normality.

'Well,' exclaimed Belle, holding George at arms' length. 'If you haven't grown into a fine handsome young man!'

Charlie swung his attention to Ruby: 'So you're the new acquisition . . .'

'Hardly that,' she almost grimaced.

'You think?' Charlie chortled.

Ruby could not quite place any of them. Their accents were drawlingly colonial, which by definition implied inferiority,

NO MISUNDERSTANDINGS

yet these Mitchells were at ease with the idea of property, money, travel.

Their deference to Ruby was what she expected, of course, yet it unsettled her because of a slightly truculent, barely detectable underlying message that seemed to say 'we're all equals here'.

They sat on the verandah drinking tea, watching as Nellie and David Mitchell walked arm in arm in the garden. Ruby had no trouble in placing David Mitchell: she saw immediately his class origins, his humble background.

'A type of old ghillie,' she would write in a letter to her mother. His world was so different from anything she knew that she could hardly believe him.

George, it appeared, was very comfortable with his relations, but they would never be hers. She found Tom Patterson and Harry Box the most sympathetic in the gathering. Perhaps they never quite fitted in either, being in-laws like her.

'I wonder what they're talking about,' said George, referring to Nellie and David Mitchell in the garden.

'Everything, George,' said Belle. 'All the things that have happened since her last visit.'

'He still seems very active,' observed Ruby.

'He's no ordinary mortal, Ruby,' said Charlie. 'Eighty years old next February, and he's just come down from a board meeting of the Monier Concrete Company.'

'Oh, really. Concrete,' said Ruby in a perfectly ordinary English way that nevertheless jarred.

Charlie cleared his throat. 'Can't keep up the pace myself, and I'm half his age.'

'None of us can,' said Annie. 'Except her.'

They all watched Nellie for a while as she and her father passed in and out of the trees, and quickly stepped under the moving arms of the water sprinklers.

'Do you like hunting, George?' said Charles.

'He adores it,' said Ruby.

'I do.'

'There's no shortage of sport around here,' said Tom

Patterson. 'Fishing, ducks, kangaroo shoots.'

'Oh, I thought you meant "hunts",' said Ruby in a disappointed tone.

'We shoot foxes,' said Tom.

'Heavens,' said Ruby, who had been brought up to believe that hunting was not killing.

'You'll find there's never a dull moment in Australia,' said Belle.

'Lovely,' said Ruby, with exquisite politeness.

Towards evening Nellie walked arm in arm with Charlie and Belle in the garden.

'Things must be strange for Ruby after the bright lights of London,' said Belle. 'Such a sharp young thing.'

Nellie considered her reply:

'The trip was rather a strain, but it's idyllic here for the two of them. They're so young. They have all the time in the world to get to know each other.'

'Of course,' said Belle.

Nellie spotted Ruby in another part of the garden.

'Excuse me. I must speak to her,' she said.

When she was out of earshot Charlie said to Belle: 'How long have George and Ruby been married?'

'Nine months.'

'Seems long enough to get to know a person, doesn't it?'

'Oh, Charlie,' answered Belle, arguing against her own thoughts. 'She's remembering *her* marriage, don't you see? You were too young to remember, but she had no time strictly to herself, no freedom, and she had so much to do. Now she wants others to have what she missed. I think George and Ruby are wonderfully lucky young people, constantly travelling, seeing the world, mixing with the most amazing assortment of people.'

'Hmm,' said Charlie.

In another part of the garden Nellie took Ruby by the hand and led her to a secluded seat.

'Ruby,' she said. 'I know how you must feel, a stranger in a strange land.'

NO MISUNDERSTANDINGS

'No, no, not at all,' said Ruby.

'My dear . . .' Nellie squeezed her hand. 'There is something the matter. What is it?'

'I am just a little homesick.'

'Is that all it is?'

Ruby turned her head aside.

'Of course.'

'Believe me,' said Nellie, 'if anything bothers you, you must say so. There must be no misunderstandings between us. None whatsoever, do you understand?'

'Yes. Yes, perfectly,' said Ruby.

'Well, that's all settled, then,' said Nellie with a half-smile.

Ruby was like someone whose decisions had been already taken, with whom all attempts at understanding were entirely superfluous.

35

Victory

The solitude of Ercildoune was soon broken by streams of visitors. People came daily from Melbourne: musical notables, old friends, diplomats, graziers, artists and politicians; a whole crowd Nellie had decided should share her 'quiet vacation'.

In a very short time she herself was motoring the ninety dusty miles to Melbourne to hear new young singers, to shop, to mingle, to lunch with the Governor-General, to humble herself with one crowd, to dominate over another, to establish herself at the Menzies Hotel, to catch her breath at Doonside and at her sisters' houses, to appear at the theatre as a member of the audience for a change, and to find every eye in the place turned upon her.

At first Ruby and George went with her. Then only George. Finally, even George found excuses to stay back at Ercildoune. He rather thought he would make a study of farm work. The shearing was about to start, and there was much to see.

'A farmer. Yes,' said Nellie.

'Not so fast, Mother,' laughed George.

'George,' said Ruby one day, after Nellie had disappeared in a cloud of dust, wrapped in her motoring veil like a solid ghost: 'Your mother has absolutely no idea of what to do with herself when she's not giving concerts. I see it quite clearly

VICTORY

now. She is really quite a superficial person.'

George stared at Ruby disbelievingly.

'What's that?'

'You heard me.'

'Why are you attacking her?'

'I am merely being realistic.'

'You could have fooled me.'

'It's what any intelligent person might notice,' said Ruby, a finger marking the place in her book. 'I have never actually seen your mother read anything, though the other day I heard her boasting to Lady Northcote about Hardy, only because she'd seen me reading him.'

'Come off it,' said George. 'She reads what she likes in just about any language she chooses.'

'She sings,' Ruby emphasised, 'in various languages, but I wouldn't say she speaks them terribly well. Certainly not grammatically, anyway.'

'Rubbish.'

'Lord, how would you know, of all people?'

'Attack me, but leave her out of it, all right?'

'I shall do as I please. You do,' said Ruby, fixing him with a cold eye.

'A man's differently made, I suppose,' said George uncomfortably.

'You are, certainly.'

'Oh, stop it, Rube.'

'Don't call me by that dreadful name.'

'You're always so damned serious about everything.'

With that, George reached over and snapped Ruby's book shut. Ruby pushed him away. Suddenly they were fighting, punching and hair-pulling like children. Ruby bit George on the upper arm, and he hit her in return, really hurting as his knuckles connected with the tenderness of her upper lip. Ruby knocked a tray of tea things to the tiles, the sound of smashed crockery bringing servants running out. But when they saw what was happening they withdrew into the house. It was pitiful the things that went on behind the scenes with these two.

MELBA

When Nellie arrived home in the middle of the night the bumps, the scrabbles, the scrapes, the whimpers and the screeches were still continuing. Held down, like something alive in a cooking pot, but struggling to get out.

In the morning, silence.

Nellie found Ruby on the verandah, reading a book in the early sunlight. George sat on the steps cleaning his Holland and Holland hunting rifle, a birthday present. They were sulkily silent with each other, and Nellie had a wild desire to send them to their rooms like the children they were.

'Possums,' said Nellie.

George and Ruby looked at her enquiringly.

'I suppose they were possums I heard last night,' she said.

Neither of them responded. Within, Nellie was coldly angry, but she smiled and kept her tone of voice light.

'Why is it always me?' she said suddenly. 'Why am I always the one to carry other people's burdens? I must keep my balance, while those around me falter and fall.'

George was embarrassed, but Ruby lifted her head to meet Nellie's eyes, grateful to have the attention removed from herself, as she thought: this was quite a statement from a woman who never spoke about her inner position.

George packed up his rifle, cleared his throat, appeared to remember important business, and disapppeared towards the stables.

'Is there any tea left in the pot?' Nellie asked.

'I shall pour, shall I?' said Ruby.

'Thank you.'

Nellie decided to try again, to go as far in Ruby's direction as possible.

'Men can be so ludicrous,' she said. 'You see, Ruby, I went through it all with George's father. I loved him very much, but he was a most exasperating man. A quick temper like George we have to face that, though I understand Charles has mellowed with time. Then just when I thought Charles understood exactly what it was I had to do, it turned out he didn't understand me at all. So I had to make him see my point of view. Men are like that. You will have to do the same thing with George, and I will do my best to support you.'

VICTORY

'Thank you,' said Ruby, wishing Nellie would go away.

Ruby felt free from her Australian imprisonment only when English people came. One day it was Lady Northcote and her husband's ADC, a Captain Parkhill. As usual, the visitors trailed Nellie around the garden while Nellie held forth about her plans:

'I would love to go to all the Australian country places, the little towns and outback settlements, and show them something they might only dream about otherwise. Because last time it was only the main cities, and tens of thousands couldn't come to hear me.'

'How very laudable,' said Lady Northcote.

An Australian couple, Mr and Mrs Chester Moran of Ballarat, followed in the wake of the two grand women.

'I've heard them say you'd like to find yourself a successor,' said Mr Moran.

'Believe me,' said Nellie, turning to smile at the man, 'if I found a "successor" I would gladly surrender to her. I would stop dashing around the world and put my feet up and live the life of Riley.'

'Spoken like the true Queen of Song,' laughed Chester Moran ingratiatingly.

'Your Madame Melba,' said Captain Parkhill in an aside to Ruby, 'certainly has the right touch with these Australians of hers.'

'Oh, yes,' said Ruby. 'As everyone says, the "Queen of Song".'

'After my outback tour,' Nellie loudly continued, 'I want to join forces with J.C. Williamson and bring out a grand opera company. Then I'll be satisfied.'

On hearing this, Ruby could not restrain herself:

'She will never be satisfied, Captain Parkhill. She's driven, you see. She might say she'd love to find a successor but it's not true. It's rather foolish really. There could be no-one like her and never will be.'

'Remarkable woman.'

'Oh, yes. Remarkable.'

'Gad, you adore her don't you,' said Captain Parkhill, admiringly.

MELBA

By February the summer heat at Ercildoune was at its height. A bronzed cloudless sky hung over the paddocks and the garden, and smoke from distant bushfires penetrated even the house, where windows were closed and curtains drawn to preserve the coolness of late night and early morning. The gardeners went on with their ceaseless watering but the vegetation drooped and the hectic bird life of the shrubbery fell silent as the heat swelled monstrously.

After midnight, when the earth breathed once more, Nellie lay awake listening to the night sounds that came to her, it seemed, not so much from the surrounding garden as from her childhood. So much time so fleetingly gone. Crickets in the grass, frogs in the ornamental pond, the shriek of a plover, the cough of a possum. At such moments, particularly after a strenuous day, she felt balanced between all the competing pressures and satisfactions of her life. As if, looking back, what she had achieved was as perfect as anticipation itself. George and Ruby would pull through, she was sure of it, and whatever the shortcomings between them Nellie would be the one to be strong, for everyone's sake; she had it in her. Perfection, she knew above all, came from effort and the quest, never from merely waiting for it like some lucky gift. George and Ruby had that to understand yet. What was true in art was also true in life. Ruby, with her sharp little mind, would see it eventually.

But then something happened to change everything. George and Ruby had another of their fights. The worst and most final.

It began in their bedroom and continued out onto the verandah. Under Nellie's window they scratched and pulled and struggled and thumped with hardly a word spoken. It was two in the morning. Lying rigid on her bed, Nellie closed her eyes and bunched her fists in horror. When the physical fighting stopped, the hoarse whispered talk began.

'You're such a damned snob about my mother,' said George. 'She's all right, you know. You used to think she was pretty red hot.'

'Your mother, George, gets everything her own way.'

VICTORY

George laughed in disbelief.

'Look at us, what she's done for us,' he said.

'Exactly.'

'I don't understand you.'

'George, don't be so stupid. When your father didn't do what he was told he was dropped by the wayside. Even your grandfather had to bend to your mother's will though he didn't approve. Do you really think George that if we don't toe the line we aren't going to be treated the same? Your mother's only real love is singing and always will be.'

'So what's your beef? You love her singing.'

'I've seen through it.'

'To what?'

'Those who don't fit in with her are simply cast off. Dumped, like your father. By singing, she keeps control. That's why she's back in Australia, not for our sakes, not for her precious vacation, but to get hold of everyone again. She's a dictator. I can't stand her.'

Nellie blocked her ears.

For many days after the incident Nellie went around in a state of shock. Events of the recent past presented themselves again in a different light. There was the image of Ruby listening entranced, on the night of the last concert before leaving London; Ruby in Naples, delightedly touching her arm to draw her attention to some small glimpse of antiquity; Ruby giving a discourse on Pompeiian frescoes in the ship's lounge; Ruby walking the decks with her, a sweet silent companion; Ruby delighted with Ercildoune, the lavish garden, the trout-breeding ponds, the good library, the overarching linden trees and dense young oaks. All this Nellie had bestowed on her. All of it now named as false. It was quite as if a lover had been found to be untrue.

Having had her say to Ruby, having gone as far as she could in the direction of appeasing the difficult young woman, Nellie was left with the realisation that none of her efforts mattered in the least. Her confidences, her private chats, her trouble in surrounding Ruby with people of her own class and background were all gone in vain. Ercildoune seen through Ruby's eyes was a mockery of Nellie's pretensions, the garden a poor relative of English gardens, Australian society a dessicated version of the one at home. Nellie herself was a member of the 'Bunyip Aristocracy', ridiculous phrase, a term of abuse employed by envious republicans and jaundiced socialists. Worst of all, she was now being faulted for her music, the very justification of her existence. There was no escape from Ruby's condemnation. Ruby had always adored her, the adoration was an indissoluble part of the marriage with George. Now she didn't love her, wouldn't, couldn't, and was utterly revealed for what she was: a dissatisfied, narrowly intelligent, emotionally underdeveloped child. What was to be done? What would happen to George? There would be no rest for her until George was happy.

Intolerable, these post-midnight visions in the February heat. They must be shuttered-over in her mind. She had the will. Yet with their own power they continued. Nellie reflected in agony on all she needed to find in herself in order to achieve the kind of life she wanted: the managing, the shaping, the arranging.

There was a distance to go yet.

With her father, Nellie went one day to look at land near the old family holdings at Cave Hill. She found acreage with a small cottage on top of a hill, offering sweeping panoramas to the blue ranges; it was the most beautiful Australian landscape imaginable, an image to comfort her dreams with its views of tree-fringed creeks, shimmering paddocks. While David Mitchell expressed doubts about the water supply and other practical matters, Nellie closed with the owners at a good price. There were several hundred extra acres of good farmland adjoining. This would be available for purchase at a later date, and Nellie took an option on it, saying nothing to anyone.

If things worked out she would build a larger house here, and call it 'Coombe Cottage'.

George and Ruby now slept in separate bedrooms. When he could, George absented himself from Ercildoune. He went kangaroo shooting in the Mallee district with his youthful uncles, went fishing at Warrnambool, and spent time visiting the Mitchell limestone quarry and cheese factory at Cave Hill, seeing how a good business was run. Sometimes he accompanied Nellie to the Melbourne Conservatorium, where she was making a great stir by listening to young singers. There, idling away an hour or two in his mother's company, George saw a pretty young womam named Evie Doyle who blushed when she met his eye. Nellie noticed and said nothing. Things were not over for George yet. There was always hope.

Ruby became a stranger to her mother-in-law, separating herself from the Melba party as much as possible. She went visiting at Government House, was seen to laugh only in the company of Old Etonians like Captain Parkhill, and while at Ercildoune stayed inside and wrote letters, read books. When she entered a room it was noticeable that conversations came to a dead stop. As soon as she left the murmur of voices began again.

Ruby and Nellie adopted a careful politeness with each other. There were not even undercurrents or emphases in what they said. This was because, on Nellie's side, whatever might happen next she was determined it would not happen in Australia. Ruby was pleased to oblige.

Nellie thought: 'She hates the way people speak, the way they dress, the climate, the distances, the sports, and everything else. When I seem "too English", as I do to many people out here, she smirks as if I have no right. When I act freely and breezily, as one can and must in this country, it seems I am "too, too Australian". This is the same Ruby I once had agog at Covent Garden. God help us.'

Nellie formulated a plan.

'I know it's hard for you,' she said to George one day, 'but you must try to mend your fences.'

'Tell it to her, Mother.'

'I want the childishness to end.'

'How?' grunted George. 'We don't even talk any more.'

'Be nice to each other in public, it is important to me.'

'Like I say, you tell her, Ma.'

'George,' said Nellie warningly, 'you are a good young man,

a true young man. You will go to her, and you will work something out. Or else my heart will be broken with shame, and I cannot let that happen again. Not in Australia.'

George stared at his mother. He owed her everything.

'All right,' he said.

There was one way to appease Ruby, and with simple courage George took it. He promised not to bother her with his attentions any more, his uneasy late-night taps on her door, his imploring desire, on condition that she was decent to him in front of other people.

Her gratitude, her relief, was total. With a barrier removed they found they were able to talk more freely with each other.

When Nellie decided to surrender to repeated requests, and present a series of concerts in Melbourne, Ruby's response was to give an amazed laugh.

'I am astounded,' she said, smiling knowingly the way any stranger might on hearing Madame Melba's latest plans.

'Careful,' said George.

'But don't you see? Your mother planned these concerts all along. Right from the start, before we left England.'

'Ease up, Ruby. She's not as underhand as all that, you know.'

Ruby laughed politely.

'Mother must live,' continued George. 'How do you think she pays for everything?'

'I have never met two people so obsessed with money. You hardly talk about anything else.'

'Christ, I've tried.'

'Please don't swear, George. This is not a barrack-room.'

'Your trouble is you've got no life in you. No independence.'

'That's what people say when they can't get their own way. Remember your promise.'

'I'm sorry,' George lowered his eyes.

Ruby felt sorry for him. Her voice softened.

'Our every move is dictated by her, our money comes from her purse, and where she goes, we go. Oh, George, Georgie, it wasn't like this at the start . . .'

VICTORY

'No,' said George, looking at Ruby with sudden hope. He didn't really know what she meant any more, but despite everything he still wanted to put his arms around her and be surprised by the soft unexpected surrender that had only ever happened in his imagination.

'But it's like it now,' continued Ruby.

George went cold. It maddened him the way she switched from softness to harshness in a second.

'What do you plan to do about it?' he said.

There was a long pause.

'I want to go home to England,' said Ruby. 'And when I get there, I never want to go anywhere else with her ever again.'

'Hell,' said George.

'I want a divorce,' said Ruby.

During Nellie's speech at the end of the last crowded concert of this unexpected 1907 season she searched the faces of the audience until she found the place where her family was sitting: her father, her sisters, her brothers and her son. It was so good that they were there, so solid and reassuring. But it was Ruby Otway's face that Nellie sought most keenly and Ruby's eyes that she held. She wanted to balance Ruby's thin contempt with something richer and more enduring. She would, whatever resulted, do that.

'Can you realise that this land is more than I can express, a great, powerful magnet to me?' she began. 'I am tied for years to engagements on the other side of the world, but through them all there is one object. You know how you look forward to something with a heart full of anticipation and longing. You know how you tick off every day and week, and don't mind plunging into your duties ever so deep, so that they may absorb all your thoughts, and then, when that task is over, you find, with a little compensating thrill of glee that it has absorbed a whole day. Well, Australia is always my objective. My old home is my dream country . . .'

'Will ye no come back again?' called a voice from the audience.

'So sure as I live,' answered Nellie, 'that magnet will draw me. It may be two years, it may be under that time, but I'm coming back to make a long comprehensive tour of all Australia, north and south.'

When the speech was finished the applause crashed around her and Ruby was forgotten, abolished, banished, extinguished just as surely as if Nellie had stamped on her and crushed her like a little spark.

The entire great audience in the Melbourne Town Hall including George and all the Mitchell family was on its feet, but Ruby remained seated. She intended no insult by this but was in a daze. Nellie's words had put her in her place. For months, in the privacy of her thoughts, she had seethed and condemned and hated as they shuttled between Ercildoune and Melbourne in the wake of the indomitable Melba. She had blamed without pity. But now she experienced the magnitude of her own failure: by marrying into Nellie's family she had hoped to possess something magnificently pure, something gloriously artistic worth a lifetime of proximity. How could she have believed it possible? It was greater than her, more vigorous, and cleverer too. And quite alien. In her high-minded way, Ruby habitually thought of herself as living in the service of art and beauty. But this was the sentimentality of the intellect: life had got the better of her. It defeated her. Melba defeated her.

A while later in the foyer, linked, as agreed, to George's arm, a limp and exhausted Ruby listened as Madame Melba spoke with a circle of reporters:

'What are your plans, when you return to Europe?'

'Truly, I should be singing in Paris in April for the grand opera season,' answered Nellie. 'Whether I shall be able to manage it is another matter, but on May sixth I go back to Convent Garden to take up the new role of Tosca. I have never been Tosca before, so, when the *Orontes* reaches Naples I must land myself and my motor, study the part thoroughly in its Italian setting, and drive overland to Paris. I shall be in London in May, and on the twenty-fourth, Empire Day, I feel so elated, I shall celebrate the twentieth anniversary of my life

VICTORY

at Convent Garden! Twenty years! And I have never missed a season! How shall I celebrate my birthday? Well, I think I shall give a popular concert in some big London hall to the poorer people of that great big city. I know their Majesties the King and Queen will be there too. They told me they would be. Say goodbye to everybody for me, won't you?'

The reporters cheered and parted their ranks to let her through. Out into the night she went, where a great crowd waited. It would be like this for years.

Epilogue

A cloud raced overhead. A small tree grew to a giant. Time surged like an emotion, folded back on itself. In 1908 George and Ruby were divorced. In 1913 George married Evie Doyle, and they were happy. Coombe Cottage, near Lilydale, became Nellie's home for the increasingly longer periods of time she spent in Australia. The house was enlarged and a pleasant garden laid out. Her twentieth, then her twenty-fifth anniversaries at Covent Garden came about, and then passed into legend.

In a darkening autumn of the war years, March 1916, David Mitchell died at the age of eighty-eight. Her name for him was inscribed on his tombstone: 'Daddy'.

She was made a DBE for her war work; George and Evie presented her with a granddaughter; and by the 1920s the young trees that Nellie had staked and tied at Coombe Cottage were part of a verdant Anglo-Australian garden, where Dame Nellie Melba entertained leaders of society, prominent musicians, artists, soldiers, landowners, governors and prime ministers.

She died in February, 1931.

Recordings exist of her voice, but they are dim fossils, shadowed outlines of the reality that was, which can only be guessed-at now.

Author's Note

I am grateful to Errol Sullivan, film producer, who commissioned this novel as the basis for his television series 'Melba'; to Rodney Fisher, who directed 'Melba' for television and whose extra research provided many new insights; to John Mitchell, for background on his great-grandfather David Mitchell; to Barry Waters, who gave encouragement and advice; and to Rhyll McMaster who gave practical criticism.

In addition to innumerable contemporary newspaper accounts, the following books about Melba were consulted during the writing: *Melba: A Biography*, by Agnes G. Murphy (New York, 1909), *Melodies and Memories*, by Nellie Melba (London, 1925), *Melba*, by John Hetherington (London, 1967), and *Nellie Melba, A Contemporary Review*, by William R. Moran (Westport, Connecticut, 1985). Other original material was studied at the Performing Arts Museum, Melbourne.

An early draft of Parts Two and Three was written in 1985 when I was Writer in Residence, Geelong College, Victoria. Assistance in manuscript preparation was kindly provided by the English Department, University College, Australian Defence Force Academy.